MW01233708

SLASH
OR
PASS
TYLOR PAIGE

Slash or Pass

Final Girls

Book One

Tylor Paige

Cover Design by Eve Graphic Designs

Edited by Zainab M. At Heart Full of Reads

This book is also Dedicated to Christina Hilyard. You were rooting for me then, and I like to think you're rooting for me now up in mermaid heaven. I miss you.

This book is rated R

Slash or Pass is a horror romance novel with topics that can be upsetting, uncomfortable, and for some, triggering. I encourage you to consider this list to know exactly what you are going to see while reading this book. This story features cults, religious trauma, purity culture, child neglect, child abuse, numerous discussion and threats of child SA, noncon, dubcon, murder, mass murder, mention of death by suicide, death by poison, torture, abuse through cult/religious actions, blood, blood play, knife play, stabbing, guns, gore, spitting, gaslighting, recreational drug use, noncon drug use, hallucinations through drug use, stalking, chasing, attacking, people in masks, police ignorance, mental health ignorance, callous mention of dementia, a FMC with a mental health disorder who chooses to be unmedicated, and lastly, dark magic lore created entirely by the author and not directly taken from any real-life religious or spiritual group.

The Soundtrack

Like music with your books? Here's the playlist I made to go with it. In no particular order:

https://spotify.link/SiTZezSlSCb

- Rountable Rival- Lindsey Stirling
- Afraid of Heights- Billy Talent
- Afraid of Heights (Reprise)- Billy Talent
- LIGHT SHOWER- Melanie Martinez
- Bulletproof Heart- My Chemical Romance
- Love & War- BAYBE
- Bite the Bullet- Vigil of War
- The Exit- Conan Gray
- The Jester- Badflower
- We're In Love- Badflower
- Teleport A & B- The Spill Canvas
- Dangerously In Love- Destiny's Child
- Captivate You- Marmozets
- Gods & Monsters- Lana Del Rey
- No Shame- 5 Seconds of Summer
- True Blue- Madonna
- Kiss Me, Kill Me- Mest
- Move Me- Badflower
- Johnny Wants to Fight- Badflower
- Stalker- Badflower
- She Knows- Badflower
- The Box- Ice Nine Kills
- Ex-Mørtis- Ice Nine Kills
- A Grave Mistake- Ice Nine Kills
- The Jig is Up- Ice Nine Kills
- Freak Flag- Ice Nine Kills
- Dinner For One- BAYBE
- Die Romantic- Aiden

- Tag, You're It- Melanie Martinez
- Kill All Your Friends- My Chemical Romance
- Bosnia- The Cranberries
- When You're Gone- The Cranberries
- Trinity- Paper Tongues
- Welcome To Mystery- Plain White T's
- Sarah Smiles- Panic! At The Disco
- Cemetery Drive- My Chemical Romance
- Sweetheart- Rebecca Black
- Freak- Doja Cat
- Not In The Same Way- 5 Seconds of Summer
- Domino- Vigil of War
- Demolition Lovers- My Chemical Romance
- Can't Help Falling In Love- Ice Nine Kills
- Raw Raw- K. Flay
- Save Yourself, I'll Hold Them Back- My Chemical Romance

- Tag, You're It- Melanie Martinez
- Kill All Your Friends- My Chemical Romance
- Bosnia- The Cranberries
- When You're Gone- The Cranberries
- Trinity- Paper Tongues
- Welcome To Mystery- Plain White T's
- Sarah Smiles- Panic! At The Disco
- Cemetery Drive- My Chemical Romance
- Sweetheart- Rebecca Black
- Freak- Doja Cat
- Not In The Same Way- 5 Seconds of Summer
- Domino- Vigil of War
- Demolition Lovers- My Chemical Romance
- Can't Help Falling In Love- Ice Nine Kills
- Raw Raw- K. Flay
- Save Yourself, I'll Hold Them Back- My Chemical Romance

The rules to surviving a slasher

Hey! So, first off, I hope you enjoy Slash or Pass. Please consider leaving an honest review wherever you do reviews when you're finished. If you do, tell us what rule was your favorite. I'm partial to Rule 71 myself...

Now, to cover some bases.

Spoiler alerts!

The cult in this book is absolutely, 100% made up. I purposely kept things vague, created a god from my head so that there would be no conversation about what religion it's supposed to be a nod to. It's not. In Mary Shelley's novel, *Frankenstein*, she keeps the science vague as well and if I took any inspiration for my made up cult/religion, it was from that. So please, when thinking back on the science or magic of the Reanimator, just know, its purely fantastical, and not a dig at any religion or spiritual practice.

Secondly, this book is *meant* to be fast paced, absurd, and well, a huge nod to slasher films. Not just with the Ghostface mask. That was purely for the Whorror Babies. No, I'm talking about it all. The classic, destined-to-be-offed friend group, the weird secondary plot that kind of just comes in and comes right back out, the quick kills and cheap thrills, and how we move fast to avoid thinking about how stuff doesn't make sense. (Why doesn't she just run the other way?) No, this was meant to be fun, spicy, and overall, a solid slasher story. Keep that in mind while reading, and I think you'll enjoy the book for what it is.

Rule 1 - Eisley
Follow the rules.

Ten years ago.

Don't talk to anyone.
Don't look back.
Just run.

"Eisley, we need to go. Get up!" Kansas pleaded and pulled me upright.

My bare feet slid in the thick mud of the forest. I was tired, but terrified. I had to listen to Kansas, my only remaining friend, and move.

"Run!"

I squeezed Kansas's hand tight and pushed onward. I couldn't see more than a foot in front of me in the pitch dark of the night. I was relying on him to see us through, despite him being just as beaten and abused as I had for so long. We were tired, our bodies and minds, but this was our one and only chance to escape. We had to keep moving.

"I'm scared," I said, as a bright clap of lightning lit up the sky. We'd been in the woods for ages, and with the moment of light, it didn't look like we'd gotten anywhere. "Kansas, where are we going?"

"Anywhere but there. Come on, Eisley, we're almost out." Despite his words, he was slowing down too. The strong wind continued to push us back. I tripped and fell, losing my grip. My hands scraped against a fallen log.

"Come on, Eisley, please. I can't leave you."

"Just go. Get somewhere safe."

"No!" He pulled off his suit jacket and tossed it aside. "Here. Take my shoes." He slid the loafers off his feet.

"I can't. You go, get help." My vision blurred.

"Eisley, get up. Please, don't leave me. I can't go alone."

I knew what he was thinking. We'd already lost Constantine; he couldn't lose me too.

His glasses were fogged up. I managed to sit upright, and as I always had, I pulled them off his nose and cleaned them as best as I could. While he was only eleven, like me, he always seemed older. Kansas was smart and cunning, and I trusted him with my life. Without him and Constantine, I'd be dead already. I had to get back up.

Kansas slid them back over his beautiful sea-green eyes and wiped his salty cheeks.

"Come on, we can do this. We've got to be close to the town. Someone will be there to help us. We just have to keep moving."

I stood on wobbly legs and tried to run again, only to drop a few feet later. A loud bang jolted us both. A gunshot.

He was coming.

"Kansas!" I cried out and reached for his hand again.

We ran as fast as we could. Another gunshot rang out, spurring us onward. The edge of the forest was right there, so close, but I couldn't go. I stopped dead in my tracks.

"Come on, we're close!" Kansas tugged on my arm.

"I want to go back."

"We can't!" True fear shone in Kansas's eyes. "Eisley, they'll—"

"What about Constantine?" I reached for the necklace I wore around my neck. A thin golden ring with a small diamond hung on it. "We shouldn't have left him.." Hot tears began to fall down my filthy cheeks. "We need to go back. He's waiting for us. We need to save him."

He squeezed my shoulders, forcing me to look at him.

"Constantine is dead. If we go back, the Minister will do the same to us. Come on." A loud whistle came from behind us, and we reacted. We stumbled down a hill and onto a road.

We kept running until we saw headlights. The car stopped and without glancing to see the driver, we dove in and screamed for them to go. The driver stomped on the pedal just as someone leapt out of the woods.

"That was a Father," I whispered to Kansas.

He put his arm around my shivering body and pulled me into him. "I saw. It's okay. None of them can get us anymore. We're safe. I won't let them get you."

"And what about Constantine?"

Our last moments before we fled the church flooded my vision. Whether I wanted to accept it or not, Kansas was right. Constantine was...

"We're going to make everyone involved pay for what they did to us," Kansas swore and curled his fingers around my tiny arm. While I wasn't sure how, I was confident that Kansas was right. One day we would.

Rule 2 - Eisley

Be weary of the shadows.

"What the hell is that?"

I turned away, spray bottle still in hand, and smiled at my best friend Emi. Emi Hajime and I connected right after the greenhouses opened last year and took me into her friend group right away. We'd been close ever since.

"It finally bloomed! Look at it! It's so pretty!" I squealed and grabbed her shoulder, pushing her toward my plot in the greenhouse.

"It's creepy." She dug her heels into the mat and shook her head. "I knew I shouldn't have requested the plot next to yours." She looked to her left where her garden was and tugged on her messy, ruby-red waves thoughtfully.

"I think your pumpkins give us a whole aesthetic." I waved over our two plots. Most everyone else was growing vegetables and sunflowers, but not Emi and me. I'd convinced her to grow a small pumpkin patch for October. "We've got spooky vibes for days. Your porch is going to look so cute."

"I can't have spooky vibes. I have a roommate, remember?

Soleil would kill me if I did anything but put these on our stoop and add gourds and daises next to them."

"You guys are so basic," I teased. "Next thing you're gonna say is you're headed to Starbucks for some Pumpkin Spice Lattes."

"Well..."

I gagged and clutched my chest. "That physically hurts. I can't even begin to imagine how bad those are for you."

"I actually stopped by to invite you." She shrugged her shoulders. "You weren't answering your phone, and I felt it safe to assume you were in the greenhouse." She looked around the large glass building.

"You were right to assume." I pointed back to my newest flower. "It's beautiful!"

"What does it do? Is it poisonous?"

"It's not edible, but it can be used for some stuff. Right now, it's just for the Halloween vibes."

She rolled her eyes. "It's October first. Calm down, you've still got a few weeks."

"Uh, I'm behind on stuff, thank you very much!" I gasped. "For a town named after the woman who wrote *Frankenstein*, Shelley Vale is painfully basic this year, and I need to start gothing it up before Christmas takes over."

"Speaking of stuff that will slowly kill you, are you coming or not?"

"For coffee? No thanks."

Emi stomped her foot. "They have tea too. Come on, we haven't seen you in, like, a week."

"Hard pass." I went back to misting my newest beauty. "I started these in June. Do you remember?" I sighed, admiring the black flower.

"I remember. You weren't sure it'd even bloom. What's it called again?"

"Tacca chantrieri is the scientific name, but it's most commonly known as the bat flower."

"Ugh, don't get all influencer on me. I hate it when you do that."

"What?" I laughed. "I was into this stuff long before I started my business."

"Take a day off, will you? We miss you."

"No, you don't." I eyed my friend suspiciously. "You want something. What is it?"

"Don't be mad." She put her hands up in innocence. "We all decided to sign up for the documentary."

My stomach dropped, and I blinked rapidly. "What? I thought we agreed—"

"I know. I told Soleil how you felt and I was on your side, but then Therese told us they upped the money and—"

"Of course they did!" I threw my hands up. "Because who would want to be in that? You really want to make money off of victims?"

We'd had this argument several times since May when Shelley Vale announced that a film crew was coming in the fall to shoot a documentary about what happened here ten years ago. The entire idea disgusted me, and my entire friend group participating in it downright hurt.

"All the victims are dead," Emi shot back.

Not true. Two escaped.

"Whatever. Do what you want." I dropped my mist bottle into my bag and untied my apron.

"Don't be like this." She sighed. "It's over. The crimes are all ten years old, and the Sinister Minister is dead. Along with all of his culty followers."

"You shouldn't make fun of them. They were victims, too."

"Sorry not sorry, but I don't consider any of the people

living inside that underground bunker church thing victims. You've seen the videos and books people wrote about him."

I put my hands up to cover my ears. "Yes, yes, and I don't want to hear about it again." I zipped my bag up and gave my newest flower one last look. "Look, go for it. Reenact the scenes, do interviews, whatever they want you to do, but I refuse to profit off of it."

"That's easy for you to say, Miss Half-a-million-followers!" she yelled after me as I stormed off.

I turned back to my friend. She was wonderfully kind and caring and supported me when I quit my boring day job last year to try my hand at streaming. This was the only thing we'd ever disagreed on, and it hurt. We stood in the parking lot, glaring at each other.

Emi threw up her hands.

"Soleil and I are barely making rent every month. Her dad cut her off and my parents stopped helping after I quit school last year."

A twinge of guilt seeped into my chest. I knew that.

"I get it. I'm sorry for making you feel shitty."

Emi hurried over to me and looped her arm through mine.

"Thank you. I knew you'd understand. I've been pulling double duty at the bait and tackle store for two months straight, but my paychecks still suck and I smell like fish."

"Aw, I think of it more as... earthy."

"So, are you coming then? Starbucks can't whip up fancy tea like you do, but I'm sure you can find something to drink."

I pointed my keys at my car. "Can't. Kansas is coming to visit this weekend. I need to get my place ready."

"Isn't he the one you used to date? The one in all those pictures in your living room?"

My face flamed and I looked away guiltily.

"Yes and no. Kind of. I mean, yes, that's him," I rushed

out. "It's a long story, but he's been away at school and I miss him and he's coming to visit so I need to go get ready."

"I see. Well, if you don't want him, is he single?" She wiggled her eyebrows and laughed.

A scowl slid onto my face for a split second.

No. Kansas was mine.

"He is, I think. But that doesn't matter because this weekend he's all mine." We reached our cars, then hugged each other. "Plus, you're with Micah."

"Yeah, but who wouldn't want two hot men fawning over them?" She nodded, and when I gave her a blank face, she rolled her eyes. "You have too many secrets. I demand you introduce us."

Oh, she had no idea how many secrets I kept.

"Fine. Maybe Saturday night. I want a little time with him alone first to catch up."

She gave me a knowing smirk and winked. "Sure. *Catch up* and then text me."

It was getting dark and I was ready to go home. I drove back to my two-story house I'd inherited from my foster mother. We'd grown close and when she passed away, I was left everything. I pulled into the driveway and parked. I reached for my seatbelt and then froze. Someone was sitting on my porch.

Rule 3 - Kansas

Be her friend.

Eisley's maroon, rust-covered, hatchback pulled into the driveway. She parked and stared at the porch. I stood and started down the steps.

A huge smile spread across her face and she threw open her car door. "Kansas! You're early!" She ran across her lawn and launched herself at me.

I wrapped my arms around her and spun her. "I wanted to surprise you."

"Well, it worked!" Her giggle made my mood soar.

I set her down, and she chastised me by smacking my chest. "You nearly made me pee myself."

"Wouldn't be the first time you've been that scared." I reached for her hips and pulled her back into my embrace. God, she was so beautiful. Time had only made her more desirable. I leaned down and tried to kiss her, but she turned her head and my lips touched her soft cheek. Both of us tried to pretend that the blunder didn't happen. I let her go and reached for the back of my neck, rubbing it awkwardly.

She forced a light chuckle and stepped back.

"I like the new glasses." She tapped her nose. "And the

septum piercing? Where is the man I waved goodbye to last year?"

I tapped the side of my glasses. They were large, with half wire, half thick black frame on top. "I'm an educated man now."

"I see that. And you've bulked up. You're huge!" She squeezed my forearms with a grin.

Pride swelled in my chest, and I flexed my pecs under my shirt. I'd specifically chosen a tighter-fitting one today to show off just how much work I'd done on myself. "There's a free gym on campus. It helps me blow off steam."

"Well, college is doing wonders for you. You look great, Kansas." A cold gust of October wind swept through the trees, and she shivered. "Why don't we go inside? I can give you a tour of the house. You haven't seen it since I redecorated."

"I can only imagine how spooky you've made it." I took her hand, and we walked back to her house.

The walls were brilliant maroon, and everything on the wall was black, creepy, or both.

"It looks like The Addams Family moved in," I teased her as she pointed out a few items.

"Good! That's the aesthetic I was going for."

"And the house is all paid off?" I paused near a picture on the wall. It was us at senior prom. We had worn black and red and looked every bit the gothic couple everyone thought we were. Only we knew the cold, hard truth of our relationship.

"I just pay taxes on it. My foster mom left clear instructions in the will about it when she died."

"That's great! I mean, not great about her dying," I amended. "But great for you!"

"Yeah, it sucked, but she was, like, ninety, so... You want to see my kitchen? That's where all the magic happens." She turned, and I followed quickly behind.

"Ninety?"

"Not literally, she was old though. If it's not too cold, I want to show you my garden," she added.

"It's getting kind of dark. We might have to wait for me to appreciate anything outside."

Eisley and I knew better than anyone that being outside in the dark was dangerous. You never knew what was out there.

Her eyes flicked nervously over me and nodded. "I forget how early the sun goes down in the fall. First thing in the morning I'll take you outside, we'll pluck some tea leaves, and prep them for drying. By the time you leave, I'll be sending you home with a jar!" She bounced on her feet as she continued through the house, finally leading me into the kitchen.

"Woah!" The room looked like a TV set.

"I know, right? I've put the most money in here. You know since it's my studio." She pointed to the ring light standing tall in front of the kitchen island.

"How did you find all this stuff?" I walked around the room, admiring all the black and green vintage appliances and decor.

"A lot of it was custom-made. Some of it, I did myself. I'm really proud of it."

"You should be. This is all impressive, Eisley. I'm proud of you."

"Thanks." She swept a tendril of her dark lazy curls behind her ear. "I know people don't really get it, but—"

"Who cares? I love your videos. And if it's paying for you to live your best spooky life, more power to you."

"You watch my videos?" Her chestnut-colored eyes lit up.

I nodded and then couldn't resist teasing her. "The 'suited for work' ones."

"Stop!" She laughed and came over to me to smack my

chest again. Her hand lingered on my pectoral. "They aren't that bad. Mostly a lot of talking."

"Just talking?" I raised my eyebrows skeptically. I had actually seen her NSFW videos, and they were a lot more risqué than just talking.

"Well, mostly. There are some where I show a little skin." Her cheeks flushed and she looked away. "But that's just a small part of it. You wouldn't believe how much people pay me just to chat."

"I can imagine, you've always been a great linguist."

She rolled her eyes and finally took her hand off my chest. She reached behind me for her tea kettle and went to the sink to fill it with water. She put it on the stove and turned the burner on.

"You watch *Witchful Drinking*? I'm hoping to be at a million followers soon."

"How could I not? I need to be up on all the hot new tea in the tea world. How would I know what was in season and what wasn't without your streaming channel?"

"Right? That means so much to me that you watch my stuff. I feel like we haven't really talked much since you've been away at school."

"I think we've both been pretty busy." I leaned on her island, and she walked to the other side and did the same, looking into my eyes.

"Well, now that I have you here all weekend, I want to catch up. What have you been up to?"

I snickered.

Oh, the stories I had for her.

"Not much. Just studying, working out, hanging with the new friends I've made."

"Friends?"

I lowered my gaze, and my glasses slid down the bridge of

my nose. I stared until she broke eye contact and looked away. We both knew what she was actually asking.

"I have been dating, a little." It was better to rip the bandage off now than to have a great weekend with her and then tell her.

She stood up straight, then turned her back and went to a cabinet, pulling out jars of various tea blends. "Oh, anyone serious?" Her voice was high-pitched and tight.

"Yes and no. I met someone when I first got to school. We dated a few months. The rest have been a lot more casual."

"What happened? Between you and her?" She spun around. Her eyes were large, and I could see the jealousy flaring behind them.

"I met someone else. I'd rather not talk about it." I put my hand on the back of my neck and looked to the ceiling. "It didn't end well. It was kind of messy."

"Oh. I'm sorry to hear that." She frowned, but her eyes didn't reflect what she was saying. It was always her eyes that spoke more than her lips. She wasn't sorry. She was glad. "I'm glad you're dating, though," she added. *Another lie.*

My expression darkened. "I thought we talked about this." I went over to her, pulling her against me. Desire coursed through my bones. "Just say the words, and I'm yours..."

There was so much more to it than that. I was already hers. We both knew that. I'd been hers since the day we'd been taken by the Family and tossed in a room together. We were so little, but I knew even then that I'd do anything for her.

"Have you seen my teapot collection?" she squeaked and pushed away from me. She went to two swinging doors and thrust them open.

"Holy shit," I muttered as I peered inside what once was a pantry to reveal a room lined floor to ceiling with teapots of all shapes, sizes, colors, and styles. "Where did you get these?"

"My private clients. I have a wish list they buy from. Or

sometimes they surprise me with rare ones. Come on, pick one and I'll tell you all about its history."

Just then, the whistle from her kettle blew, and we turned back to the kitchen.

"Another time." I smiled.

I didn't like asking about the gifts men gave her as much as she didn't like me fucking other women.

Rule 4 - Kansas

Play the long game.

"What tea have you tried?" Eisley peered into her cabinets.

My eyes traveled up her legs. She wore the same skimpy goth dresses and skirts she had in school. She looked way too sexy for a girl who didn't like to be touched. My cock grew hard the longer I stared at her perky ass. I wondered if she was wearing panties.

"The fruit ones mostly. I don't like anything bitter."

She turned back and rolled her eyes. "All right, I think I might have something you'll like."

"Do you have anything stronger?"

"You don't want tea?"

"Not really. Tea is more of a cafe date thing for me. I'd be a lot happier with a beer in my hand."

She scowled. "Fine. I don't have beer, but I can make you a cocktail. Ooh! I have a blueberry syrup I made myself. Do you like bourbon?"

I laughed at her quick shift and high level of enthusiasm. "Bourbon sounds good. Actually, can we order a pizza or something? I'm kind of starving."

"You're hungry?"

"You know, the whole broke college student thing. I'm rocking that." I gave her two thumbs up and laughed it off.

"Could have fooled me. You're twice the size you were when I last saw you." Her eyes drifted over my toned body.

"My little Eisley, if I didn't know better, I'd say you've been checking me out."

"Maybe..." She gave me a sly grin. There was a flush in her cheeks that made her look even sexier. "You're finally giving me something to admire."

I laughed. "Is that smack talk?"

Eisley slid along the island and then sprinted out of the room. I chased after her, laughing at the way she giggled excitedly as she raced through the house. I caught her as we rounded the opening into the living room and tossed us onto the couch. I dug my fingers into her sides and began to tickle her.

"Oh! Oh! Stop! Kansas!" She kicked and howled with laughter as I continued tickling her. I rolled so I was on top of her, and our cheeks were flushed. Her breasts were rising and falling as she tried to catch her breath. I stared deep into her powerful brown eyes. So deep, yet playful. And her lips...

I leaned down and tasted her. Our lips pressed together, and she was only hesitant a moment before her mouth parted.

My hands had a mind of their own. They slid down her hips and found the edge of her skirt. Wasting no time, I ran my finger up her panties. Soaking wet.

"Remember when we were younger?" I breathed into her ear. "When we'd play boyfriend and girlfriend? That we were like all the other kids. And you'd let me..."

I pushed her panties to the side and ran my hand over her smooth pussy. Eisley's eyes drifted closed and her muscles relaxed under me. I spread her pussy lips and kissed her again.

"Why don't we play some more? It doesn't have to be

real..." She turned her head, and I bent down, running my tongue from her collarbone up to her chin, finding her lips again. "You've missed me, haven't you, princess?"

I pushed my finger past her lips and swirled her wetness around. God, she was dripping.

"Ah..." she gasped. Her back arched, and I moved deeper, enjoying the way her body unraveled because of my fingers.

"Have you let anyone else touch you like this?"

When she didn't answer, I nipped her lobe and asked again, more demanding.

"No. And we shouldn't be doing this now, Kansas."

"Then stop me," I growled and pinched her clit. I took my time, getting her close and then drawing back, only to do it again.

She moaned and groaned against me, thrusting up and urging me to go deeper, slide a finger inside her, but I knew better. The moment I tried, she'd force me to stop.

My cock pressed against her thigh. I rubbed my thumb along her clit, moving faster and faster. Was she going to let me finish her this time?

She was squirming and whimpering so much I thought she'd allow herself to come, but right when she was about to go over the edge, she shoved me off of her and sat up.

"Kansas, we shouldn't be... we're not..." She brushed her hair back quickly and pulled her legs up to her chest. Her face was flushed, and I could only imagine the ache her body felt as she came back down.

I leaned over and brushed the thumb with her arousal on it over her lip. I slid my pointer finger into her mouth and shoved it as deep as I could. She sucked it for a moment and then blinked and pulled away. She leapt up and straightened her clothes.

"We can't. You know this. Not anymore."

"Not ever," I muttered, standing as well. I shifted my jeans and willed my cock to go down. The familiar deep ache in my balls returning with a vengeance.

"What does that mean?" She crossed her arms, making her tits look even better.

I looked toward the ceiling. She wasn't making this any easier for me.

"You know what it means. Tell me, are you still pretending that you don't want me as much as I want you?" I reached out, pinching her chin. With my other hand, I grabbed her hip and pulled her against me. My cock throbbed, sending my message home.

"It doesn't matter. You know that." She pushed me away and ran her hands through her hair again. "I should go get you that drink. Bourbon, right?" She didn't wait for me to answer and fled to the kitchen.

"Eisley!" I followed behind her. "I'm sorry. I thought we were—"

"Were what?" she snapped. Standing at the island, she slammed a tumbler down and poured dark amber liquor into it. She reached for a thinner bottle of purple liquid and added it to my drink. "We're not anything." She slid the drink over to me.

I reached for it and brought it to my lips. "You're angry with me."

She shook her head. "You don't get to come back and pretend like... like—" She stumbled over her words. "Like things are different. Nothing's changed." She fingered her necklace—a slim chain with a ring on it—as she swallowed and prepared the speech I'd heard a hundred times.

It wasn't fair. We'd escaped the Minister. Constantine didn't. And for that reason, we weren't allowed to be together. She couldn't be with anyone at all, not just me, knowing he died trying to save her. This was her eternal punishment for not going back. We could have saved him.

But for the first time, I had something to offer as a rebuttal to her reasonings. She said a lot of things with such passion and pain over the years. Her heart died that day, and she'd never allowed herself to move on.

We had escaped. Constantine didn't. She was right; but little did she know, there was one part of her story that wasn't true.

Rule 5 - Eisley

Be wary with who you trust.

Ten years ago.

"Kansas, I think I'm in trouble."

A single, dull bulb blinked above us, threatening to engulf us in darkness at any moment. I huddled closer to the eleven-year-old boy with the glasses to share warmth.

He pulled me in closer, and, teeth chattering, said, "Why do you say that?"

"Something happened." I shivered. "I told a Mother about it and she said the Minister would need to know. That's why we haven't gotten any food."

We stared at the large metal door that remained locked. We'd been trapped in here with no food and no information on why we were being punished or when it would end.

Kansas took in my words but said nothing. He knew as well as I did that once the Family decided something, they wouldn't go back on it. We wouldn't be eating until they decided our punishment was over.

It'd been five days.

"They'll come soon. I know it," he reassured me. We came here together years ago. We were raised with the Family, despite not knowing any of them. We shared all of what we could glean from them with each other. They weren't coming.

"Come on, we'll get some more water." He pulled me up with him. "And then we'll sleep. It saves energy."

My body wobbled as I dragged my bare, dirty feet across the cement floor. I held onto Kansas tightly, knowing I'd collapse to the ground if I didn't.

"It's okay, Eisley, we'll get through this. It's just another punishment. We've been through this." He reached the filthy sink, black with mildew, and twisted the old knobs. It squeaked and yellow water poured from it. Kansas picked up the green plastic cup we shared and filled it. We took turns drinking until our empty bellies were full. We'd grown accustomed to this, but it didn't make it any easier.

Then, we returned to the mattress. It had been here before we arrived. That and the sink were the only things in here. This had been our home for so long, and still, nothing had changed except our strength and will to keep fighting. Slowly, it was disappearing.

Had I been put in here alone, I would have broken years ago.

We were a foot away from the bed, when Kansas froze.

I looked up at him in confusion. His eyes were wide and his mouth had fallen open as he stared down at the floor.

"Eisley, you're bleeding."

I looked down. A long trail of red slid down my legs and dripped onto the cement. I dropped his hand quickly and hurried to the bathroom. I shut the old, metal door behind me and reached for the only towel we had. It was thin and ripped and covered in holes, but it was all we had. I shoved it between my legs and began to clean myself, but the blood kept coming.

I'd tried so hard to hide it. Ever since it started, I couldn't get it to stop. It hurt so much, and yet no one came to help me. I was being punished, but for what, I was still unsure.

Kansas pounded on the door.

"Eisley, are you okay? Where did you cut yourself? Do we need to see a Mother?"

Hot tears stung my cheeks as I continued to stop the bleeding coming from my privates, but nothing worked.

"No!" I shouted back.

This was why we were being punished. The Mother had said it was normal. How could it be though? There was so much of it!

I jerked my head up to the sound of a loud screeching in the other room. Someone had finally opened our door.

"Where is Eisley?" the Minister demanded.

My heart sped up and my stomach twisted. No! Out of all the family members that could have come through that door, the worst one was always the Minister.

"She's in the bathroom," Kansas said. "Leave her alone." Kansas, always the protector argued with him. "We need food."

"All in good time." The Minister spoke to him as if Kansas were a petulant child demanding candy. "I hear that Eisley has become a woman."

Something about the way he said that word sent chills down my spine. What did that mean? I was a girl. Eleven. I remembered because that was the one thing they'd let us celebrate. Birthdays were important here.

"You leave her alone," Kansas shouted. "Feed us!"

Loud, solitary steps echoed through the room as they came closer to where I was hiding, and then with a loud jerk, the bathroom door was thrust open.

I shrunk into myself as I stared up at him, my hands still stuffed between my legs, holding the blood-soaked towel.

The Minister grinned so wide, I wanted to cry again. His smile was terrifying. If he was giving you attention, that was never a good sign.

"There you are. Little Eisley isn't so little anymore, is she?"

I didn't respond. I had learned not to.

"Leave her alone," Kansas repeated from behind the tall, thin man in the black robes.

The Minister crouched down and reached for my chin. He gripped me tightly, forcing me to look at him. His piercing blue eyes, jet-black hair, and pale skin made for a startling creature. A monster.

"One of the Mothers informed me you have begun to bleed. Is that true?"

I gulped; my throat dry and scratchy.

He reached for the towel I was still clutching and raised it, showing both Kansas and me the blood that stained it.

I closed my eyes and hung my head in shame.

"She needs to see a Mother," Kansas said. "She's hurt."

"She's not hurt." The Minister chuckled and stood, letting me go. He shoved the towel into one of his deep pockets. "This is a good thing. A wonderful thing."

"How can it be good?"

I peered from behind the Minister to see Kansas shaking with rage.

"We're starving. You're punishing us because she's bleeding?"

The Minister returned to our room.

I hurried over to Kansas, throwing my arms around him. He held me close, protectively, as the Minister looked around the room. There wasn't much to see. Stone walls, stone floor, a sink, and a mattress.

"We have been busy, preparing."

"Preparing for what?" Kansas snapped.

"The ceremony, Kansas." The Minister was good at keeping his tone level. He put his hands behind his back and nodded. "We could not attend to you because we needed to focus on getting things ready. I had to buy new video recorders, clothing, and rings. Those things take time."

"We are going to die if you don't feed us." Kansas's resolve began to break. He was as weak and tired as I was. "Please, give us something to eat."

The Minster sighed deeply and nodded. "A Mother will come to attend to you. You will need to be bathed, fed, and dressed before we start the activities." He turned and grabbed the handle to lock us in, but he paused. He nodded to the corner of the room and then looked back at us.

"Wake up Constantine. We can't perform the ceremony if he's dead. We need all three of you."

Rule 6 - Eisley

Keep a weapon close.

"Eisley!"

I was jerked awake by Kansas shaking me wildly.

Tears made my cheeks itchy, and I sat up and rubbed them vigorously. I blinked, my eyes adjusting to the darkness of my bedroom. Kansas sat beside me, looking at me with concern, and I broke. I threw myself into his arms and sobbed.

"Are you all right? I came as soon as I realized what the sound was."

I sniffled and pulled myself up.

Kansas was in only his boxers. Even in the dark, I could see the outline of his toned muscles. But his chest... were those scars?

"Where are your glasses?" I asked, trying to divert the conversation.

"On the nightstand by my bed. Eisley, what were you dreaming about?"

I wiped my cheeks again. "Nothing. Just... old stuff. I don't want to talk about it. I'll be fine."

"Will you, really?"

No, I wouldn't be fine.

I stared at the thin red lines on his chest. They reminded me of... an autopsy cut.

"Kansas, your chest." I touched the scars, and he caught my wrist.

"Would you like me to stay with you tonight?" he asked, his expression darkening.

"Are you sure?" I lifted the blankets and patted the space beside me. I was too tired to fight it.

His eyes drifted down my face and to my body. I wore a skimpy, sheer black nightgown. All of my pajamas were like this. Flashes of our kisses, his hands, and his words on the couch ran through my mind, and I quickly pushed them away.

"You've missed me, haven't you, princess?"

"Eisley?"

My nightmare stirred again in my mind.

"I can't be alone."

Kansas slid under the covers and pulled me into his arms. I faced away from him, letting my back fall against his warm, hard body. I inhaled deeply, taking in the smell of his cologne and bourbon on his breath. After we'd fought, I went to bed early, and he sat downstairs and drank.

"You're still having these dreams?"

"Nightmares," I sighed. "Yeah. You don't?"

"I try to block out that time in our lives. We're more than that, you know that, right?"

I sniffled and moved closer to him. "I know."

He grew hard against my behind. My body tightened, and I shivered.

"Hush..." Kansas whispered in my ear. He kissed my lobe and nipped it gently. "Go to sleep. I'm not going anywhere."

I closed my eyes and relaxed against him, falling asleep in his arms.

I woke up the next morning with Kansas's hand cupping my breast. I shifted slightly and found him still stiff against my back.

"Mm... Good morning," he murmured, running his thumb across my nipple.

A delightful shiver ran down my body. The familiar ache roared between my legs. I forced myself to push him away gently. I sat up and covered myself with the blanket.

"Thank you for keeping me company last night. I don't usually have bad dreams like that."

"Why do I find that hard to believe?" He yawned and propped his head on his elbow. "If it means anything, I like sleeping next to you."

"Even if nothing happens?" I asked. Jealousy wafted over me, thinking about what he'd told me yesterday. That he'd started dating.

"I remain hopeful one day it will," he said matter-of-factly.

My nightmares from last night resurfaced. Constantine's face, bruised and bloodied, made me pull away from the adult Kansas in my bed. I reached for my necklace again and began to fondle the ring.

He sighed and rolled over, placing his hands under his head. His erection tented the blanket, but neither of us reacted to it. This wasn't new to either of us. We'd spent most of our teenage years in this awkward limbo of desire and doom. But, like all the other times, our need would pass and we'd move on, as if we weren't longing for more, knowing it would never happen.

"Kansas, what happened to your chest?" In the light of

day, I could see them more clearly now. Two scars formed a V and then slid down into one to his beltline.

"My tattoos?" He raised his arms, pointing to tattoos I'd already seen. I shook my head and pointed.

"No, the huge scars."

"Just a stupid hazing ritual. I was sewn up just fine." He traced the scar and then gave me a smile. "Looks pretty cool though, right? I haven't decided whether to cover them up or not yet."

My jaw dropped. "They should have been kicked out of school for that!" My mind raced as I imagined the scene. Kansas, lying on a table while a group of frat guys cut him as a joke. That wasn't a joke, that was sadistic.

"Eisley, stop worrying about me. I'm fine. This was so long ago. Let's talk about something else."

I huffed. "Okay, fine. The first time. Tell me about it." I wanted to know, had he thought of me when it happened?

"First time..." He looked between us, and then motioned to his erection, still standing tall. "You mean sex?"

I nodded.

"Her name was Harper. She was majoring in archeology. I met her at the university library, where she was working."

"Are you guys the same age? Did you date? How long did you wait?" I wanted to ask so much more, but I held back. I knew I had no right to know these things, yet I felt like I did in a way. Kansas wasn't Harper's.

He was mine.

"We were the same age," he responded. "We dated for about two months."

"How long did you date before you guys..." I didn't want to say it. Even Kansas touching someone else made me sick.

"Two weeks."

"Two weeks?" I tossed the blanket off and leapt out of bed.

He threw his hands up. “What was I supposed to do? Wait forever for something I know you’re not interested in?”

“I—I don’t know.” I huffed and began rummaging through my drawers for clothes. “I don’t want to talk about it anymore.”

“Are you mad at me?”

Yes.

“No.”

“Eisley,” he sighed. “Come on.”

“I told you I didn’t want to talk about it.” I spun around with a bundle of clothes. “Now, I have to shower and get ready for the day. Why don’t you do the same and then we can go do something?”

I rushed out of the room to take a shower. After I was done, Kansas traded places with me, while I quickly dressed and put my makeup on. By the time my hair was dry, he was stepping back into my room, showered, and dressed.

“Ready?” He gave me an awkward smile.

“Yes.” I couldn’t look at him yet. “Let’s go. I want to show you my garden.”

We went to my backyard, where I showed him the plants I used to make my tea.

“I grow almost everything I use on my channel.” I forced the fight we’d had earlier to the back of my mind and waved proudly at my plants.

“Almost?” He grinned.

“Well, I don’t make my own honey or milk. There’s a few other ingredients here or there I have to purchase, but if I can, I try to grow it.”

“I see that.” He nodded and gazed down the long garden. “This is all edible?”

“You can ingest it all, yes.”

He pushed his glasses up his nose and frowned at me. “What’s that mean?”

I laughed and poked his hard chest. "It means, if you want to steal from my garden, you best know your plants. You might end up eating something you shouldn't."

"Eisley." His expression darkened. "Are you hoarding..."

"It's fine. It's a comfort thing. It keeps the dark thoughts away."

"The idea of poisoning someone keeps the dark thoughts away?" He followed me back inside.

I put the tea kettle on the stove and turned the burner on. I turned back to him and grinned. "Exactly."

Rule 7- Kansas

Make nice with her friend group.

"I think it could be fun. A double creature feature, popcorn, and watching it under the stars? Come on." I pointed to the flyer taped to a store window.

Eisley frowned. We just couldn't find our footing. Last night, we fought, then she had her nightmares. She was still upset about my scars, and I was upset about her little poison garden she had in her backyard.

We were one passive aggressive comment away from exploding.

"Yeah, my friends texted me about it earlier, but I was enjoying our one-on-one time."

"Your friends are all gonna be there?" I perked up. "Now I really want to go. Come on, let me meet the gang."

"You won't like them." She scowled and reached for my hand, tugging me along and down the street.

"You think?"

"I know," she said firmly. "They are the exact type of people you hate."

"And what's that?" I smirked.

"Most of them have families that have been here for like a century or more."

I inhaled deeply.

"Oh, so their families knew about the Family. You don't want me to call them out."

"Kansas!" She hissed and looked around quickly. "See, this is a bad idea."

"If I promise to not say anything, can we go?" I pleaded. "I've been wanting to see the new *Glass Children* movie."

"Fine," she sighed. "But seriously, you can't say anything."

I pretended to zip my lips shut and we went back to her place to pack blankets and pillows.

"Everyone sits in the grass in front of our cars," she explained, then asked if I wanted dinner.

"I'll save myself for hot dogs and pretzels." I patted my stomach.

"I am kind of looking forward to the popcorn," she admitted.

"You?" I teased. "Miss 'everything homemade'?"

"You don't seem to have a problem devouring my food, Mr. Nine-buttermilk-biscuits-with-homemade-blueberry-jam. Nor do I get any complaints from people on my feed."

"Those biscuits are fire, for one." I reached for the plastic container where our breakfast leftovers were and pulled one out, popping a biscuit into my mouth. "And two, of course, no one on your channel is going to complain. You're fucking hot."

She laughed. "Are you driving then?"

I swallowed my food and reached for my keys. "Let's motor."

We left then, hopping into my car and taking off toward the drive in.

"What's got you so deep in thought?" I looked over from the driver's side.

Eisley was staring out the window, her eyes devoid of anything. "Nothing. I'm sorry, it's just weird. Who was after Harper?"

"Eisley, come on. Let's not do this." I tightened my grip on the steering wheel. It was interesting that she was more interested in a stupid ex than how I got the long scars on my chest. She was jealous.

"Why not? You came to visit me and then drop this on me. Why not discuss it in full?"

"Because you don't actually want to hear it."

"What's that supposed to mean?" She crossed her arms.

"It means, you only want to know who I've fucked so you can guilt-trip me. You promised you'd save yourself; I didn't."

We drove the rest of the way in tense silence. I turned into the drive-in and got in line with all the other cars to get our tickets and assigned parking spot. Once inside, I parked, and Eisley got out quickly.

"No friends?" I joined her, grabbing the bag she'd packed.

She smiled. "Nope. And that's fine with me."

"You're really that afraid I'll do something to embarrass you?" It was hard not to be offended by that. I sighed. "Whatever, look. I just want to have a good night with you, okay? The movie doesn't start for a half hour, so let's get our blankets spread out and grab some snacks."

We both looked toward the long line at concessions and then back at each other.

"I'll go get in line, join me when you're ready?" I offered.

She was looking around, seemingly distracted. "Sounds good. I'll be up there in a bit."

I turned to go when some guy who looked like he still wore his letterman's jacket was walking up.

"Hey pretty lady, what are you doing here?" He came over with his arms out. I walked back to Eisley, promptly throwing my arm over her shoulder. His arms dropped, along with his smile. "Who's this?"

"Eisley? I thought you weren't coming. You never text us back." A natural redhead wearing designer everything came up behind the guy. "Ooh, who's this?" She smiled at me.

"I was really busy today." Eisley cringed and stepped out of my hold. I cleared my throat, and she looked up at me.

"This is Kansas." She hesitated, almost as if she would give me a title, but held back. She grabbed the bag that held her blankets and began to pull them out. "Kansas, this is Soleil and Spencer."

Spencer. I knew that name, although I'd yet to see him in person. He was a Foxworth.

"What are you doing?" Spencer gave her a weird look. "Our cars are all over there. You need to come sit with us."

"Yeah, unless you're wanting alone time..." Soleil winked at me and giggled.

"We kind of were," Eisley mumbled.

The furious look on Spencer's face made me speak up. Did he have a thing for her? I slid my hand down and around her waist.

"Nah, let's join them. It sounds like fun." I spoke to Eisley but stared directly at Spencer.

Picking up our stuff, we followed her rich-looking friends across the yard and were directed to take an empty spot between Spencer and Soleil and another couple.

"This is Micah and Emi, and that's Therese and Rem." She pointed to the couples on their respective blankets. They waved and seemed a lot less threatened than Spencer had been in his welcome.

Emi, a pretty Asian woman with firetruck red hair and an oversized hoodie and sweats, came over to us. "We were just sending the guys to get snacks. You want to go with them, Kansas?"

Eisley looked at me expectantly.

I shrugged. "Sure. You still want popcorn with extra butter?"

"Yes, please!" She side-hugged me.

Feeling a little cocky, I took the closeness and leaned down, giving her a quick peck on the lips. She pulled away and blinked rapidly. A sly grin slid onto my face.

"You two are dating?" Spencer interrupted.

"Leave them alone, will you?" Soleil came to our defense. "Go get me some licorice."

Scowling, he stomped away. I looked around and the other guys were shaking their heads in confusion.

"Whatever, let's go." Rem, a large black guy with a well-groomed beard and friendly smile, motioned for us to follow, and Micah and I did.

"What's his problem?" I asked as we fell in line with each other.

"Who knows," Micah, a tan man with dark brown curls and arms so huge he could bench-press four of me, rolled his eyes. "Spence doesn't like new people."

"Sounds like he was jealous, more than anything."

"Ha!" Rem smacked me on the back. "Spencer thinks way too much about himself to be jealous of anyone. Don't worry about him, bro, we've got your back."

The three of us talked about movies, various sports games, and other surface-level bullshit while we waited and got our food. It wasn't until Micah asked what I did for a living, and I explained I was still in school for computer science did they both stop acting stiff and seemed genuinely interested in talking with me.

"My focus is cyber-security," I explained.

Rem nodded. "See, we need someone like you in this town. I just finished my degree in computer forensics. I fix everyone's computers after they've been attacked, and you come in and make sure they can't get hacked again."

"Then how will you stay in business?" Micah smirked. "Eventually you'll have fixed everyone's computers."

"Hey, at least I'm trying to forge my own path, rather than just taking over my dad's law firm."

"Don't act like your family didn't pay for that degree of yours."

The two went back and forth, and tried to draw me into their jokes, but I couldn't relate. I had to work for both my spot in school and the ability to afford it. They seemed like decent guys, but I still hated them for their family's wealth.

Wealth I deserved.

We made it back to the girls as the trailers were starting. I handed Eisley the giant bucket of popcorn and plopped down beside her.

"Thank you!"

I tried to get another kiss in, but she turned her head this time.

Micah put an old-school boombox in the middle of the blankets and turned the volume high, so we could all hear the movie.

Eisley let me put my arm around her, and soon, the group grew silent and we focused on the movie. This was the sixth movie in the *Glass Children* series, and it was like the first five that came before it, kids were creepy, they murdered unsuspecting adults, and it had plenty of jump scares. More than once, Eisley screamed and spilled popcorn all over us. It made me laugh every time.

"You know it's all fake," I teased. "That knife is far too small to do that amount of damage."

"How would you know?" She tossed a handful of popcorn at my face, and I opened my mouth to catch some.

Oh, darling. We didn't have enough time to dive into that.

We were an hour into the movie when the tension began to heighten. Three people had been murdered, and the rest were figuring out that the little blonde orphan children were the ones doing it.

Eisley's eyes, always so expressive, were terrified as she leaned forward, absorbing every minute. Right behind the main character was a pair of sharp blue eyes. Any moment now, we would get a jump scare. Right as the little Glass child leapt out of the darkness, someone crept up behind us and pressed a knife to Eisley's neck.

Eisley screamed, and I shoved the unknown assailant back. Everyone turned to see Spencer falling on his ass, clutching the large knife, and howling with laughter. Without another thought, I lurched forward and raised my fist. He tried to get back up, but I shoved him and threw myself against him. Getting him onto his back, I raised my fist again.

"You think that's fucking funny?" I shouted and swung my fist at his nose.

Rule 8 - Kansas
Remember important dates.

"Kansas, stop!"

Eisley's panicked voice burst through the autopilot my brain was on, but not enough to get me to pull back my fists and stop hitting Spencer.

He rolled me onto my back and got a few shots in, but I'd been working out and training for a year to fight and defend myself. This pretty boy had no chance against me.

Rem and Micah tried to pull us apart but quickly dropped us when someone reminded them that Spencer had a knife. I didn't fucking care. Let him stab me and see what happened.

"Berries & cherries," Micah groaned loudly. "Come on, guys, the cops are here. Spencer, put the knife away."

Spencer, suddenly finding new strength, shoved me off of him and stood, popping the knife back down and into his pocket. My glasses flew off when he pushed me, and I squinted in the dark, trying to find them. Someone handed them to me, and I shoved them on my face and stood. I looked to see who'd given them. Emi.

"What the hell, dude!" Spencer threw up his hands. "Are you some sort of psycho?"

"You had a fucking knife!"

"What seems to be the problem here?" Two officers approached us.

"He attacked me!" Spencer pointed to me.

"You a Foxworth?" the officer asked Spencer, who nodded eagerly.

I snickered. I knew more than anyone in this god forsaken town how important the Foxworths were here.

"He had a knife," I explained to the officer lamely. I knew I was fucked.

"I don't see a knife anywhere." The officer pretended to look around, but he wasn't concerned. "Now, why don't we scatter this little tussle before someone has to be cuffed and taken in?" He gave me a pointed look.

"Someone?" I laughed, but the officer didn't. To him, I was the criminal and not Spencer Foxworth.

"Is this the kind of man you want to be seen with?" Spencer turned his focus to Eisley. "This animal?"

"He's not an animal," she snapped, to my surprise.

"You're the one who put a knife to my girlfriend's throat," I added.

"Will you both stop!" Eisley threw up her hands. "I'm leaving." She stormed through the cars.

"Eisley, wait!" I glared at her so-called friends and took off in the direction she'd gone, but she had disappeared. I searched around the area until the police pulled up to me.

"Young man, I think it's best you get in your car and head on out. You're making people nervous."

"Me?" I pointed to my chest. "I wasn't the one with a weapon."

He ignored my comment and repeated his orders.

"Fine, whatever." Enraged, I got in my car and left. I gripped the wheel and drove slowly through the blocks, looking for Eisley. About a mile later, I saw her and slowed down. I rolled the window down and called to her.

"Eisley, what are you doing?"

"Go away!" She glared straight ahead and kept walking.

"Eisley, come on, get in the car."

"No." She took a deep breath and started to jog.

I drove right along with her. "You've got good cardio," I commented. "And stamina."

"Thanks. Go away."

"I'm going to follow you until you listen to me."

"I don't want to listen to you anymore. Go back to school. Go see Harper or whoever else you're sleeping with this week!"

I pressed on the brake, and my car jerked forward. I put it in park and got out of the car, storming over to her. She started to run when I strode over to her, but I caught her. I grabbed her shoulders and spun her around.

"What are you doing?" I demanded.

"I'm getting away from you!" Tears streamed down her face. "I don't know why you even came here this weekend. To rub it in my face that you're able to move on and live a normal life? Good for you, Kansas, but I can't do that."

"Why not? Eisley, nothing is stopping you from being happy except yourself. You can't keep living in the past."

"If we hadn't run—"

"Then we would have been forced to do that disgusting shit for him. We knew the risks and so did Constantine. That's why he stayed behind to give us a chance to escape. Eisley, he wanted you to live a normal life."

"With him." She shook her head. While I had moved to the final stages and accepted what happened that night, Eisley was forever stuck in denial. "Constantine wanted me to live a normal life with him. That's why I—"

"Sssh. You don't have to explain things. I know. I understand. I'm not upset about what happened at the ceremony. Eisley, this isn't healthy. You have to allow yourself to be happy."

"I am." She rubbed the tears off her cheeks.

"No, you're not. That's why I came this specific weekend."

She looked up at me curiously. "What do you mean?"

"Do you not remember the date?"

She blinked and then her deep brown eyes grew wide. "Oh my god. How could I forget?"

I gave her a tight smile. "Let's get back in the car and we can talk about it while I drive around, okay?"

Eisley licked her lips, and reluctantly, followed. I got back on the road again and drove aimlessly for a while, slow and steady.

"I should have remembered. Now I feel even worse." She put her head in her hands. "His birthday. God, I'm so stupid."

"You're not stupid. It's easy to forget."

"How old would he be now?"

"Twenty-two, I think." I pretended to not remember for sure, but I knew I was right. "He was a few months older than us."

"That's right." She nodded, and her eyes took on a distant look. "I remember. They served us cake."

Bitterness boiled in my belly. Birthdays were the only things celebrated in the Family. It was a disgusting show, and if we knew then what we knew now about why they did the parties, we wouldn't have been so eager to participate.

"I feel so shitty for forgetting." Eisley sighed.

"You shouldn't. It's called moving on."

"Sometimes I feel like I died just as much as he did that night."

Silence filled the car.

"Can we go to the memorial site?" she asked. "I know he's not really in there, but—"

"It's kind of dark. Can we go tomorrow? Why don't we go back to your place tonight and make a cake or something for him."

"A cake?"

I shrugged. "It's better than mourning him. Why not celebrate?"

"Okay, I kind of like that idea." She reached for my hand and squeezed. "I have a killer strawberry cake recipe. And I even make my own frosting."

I made an exaggerated moan. "Even better."

My phone buzzed in my pocket, but I ignored it. I knew who was texting this late, but he'd have to wait so I could tell him everything.

And he could thank me later.

Rule 9 - Eisley

Don't trust the police.

"First thing in the morning, we'll go out, grab some flowers, and head over to the memorial site," Kansas promised me as we walked hand in hand up my front porch steps and into the house.

"I like that idea."

I slid off my shoes at the door and padded to the kitchen. Baking always made me feel better, and Kansas knew that. I turned the oven on and then began pulling out bowls, pans, and my ingredients.

"You're fast," he chuckled.

I grinned. "My kitchen is my safe space. I can zone out and forget my problems while I'm here. I like to shut it all off and focus on the task at hand."

"I love that for you. I think it shows in your videos."

"Yeah?" I perked up. "You want to go live with me?"

He blinked. "What, like, right now?"

"Why not?" I shrugged. "Or are you camera shy?" I teased.

"I mean, I'm not, but..." He squirmed. "Won't your male viewership get jealous?"

"Maybe, but that just means I'll get a flood of messages, and messages cost them money." I grinned wickedly.

"You're evil," he laughed.

"Each message to send and receive is a dollar. I rack up a pretty penny some nights."

He shook his head. "I wish I was hot enough to do that. I could pay for school and not blink an eye."

"You're definitely hot enough." I raised an eyebrow as my eyes trailed down his body. "You just need some confidence." I turned to my fridge for the dairy and other various items. "If you took off your shirt, flexed, and put a book in your hand, Booktok would go crazy."

"Booktok?" He laughed.

"Yeah, those girlies love a hot guy who reads. Can you growl?"

"Growl?" He plucked a strawberry from my bowl the moment I set it down. "I might just keep eating ramen for a while. Now, how can I help?"

"Start some tea?"

He went to the stove and grabbed my teapot to fill it.

I finished the batter and poured it into three medium-sized circle pans and shoved them in the oven. I set the timer on the stove and began clearing the island to start working on the filling and frosting.

"What kind of tea do you want?" Kansas opened my cabinet filled with various jars of dried tea.

"I have a nice fall mix I made the other day. You want to try it?" I pointed to the jar I wanted him to bring down and he did as the whistle blew.

While I chopped strawberries to put in the filling, Kansas filled two tea infusers with my mix and poured us cups of hot water.

"Thanks!" I blew him a kiss, and he rolled his eyes.

"You really gotta stop doing that."

"Doing what?"

He sighed and looked directly at me from across the island. "Teasing me. You're so damn..." He sighed and slapped the counter. "I think I need some fresh air. I'll be back." He turned to leave the kitchen, and just then, a knock came from my front door.

"Can you get that?" I asked, raising my hands, covered in strawberry goop. He took off toward the door.

"Uh, Eisley..." Kansas's nervous tone made me wipe my hands off and go to the door. I turned the corner to the hall and paused. Through the frosted glass, I saw red and blue flashing lights.

Berries & Cherries, to quote Micah, the police were here.

I swallowed my nerves and went to the door, opening it quickly.

"Hello." I smiled at the officers from the drive-in.

"Eisley Doe?"

I frowned. "Yes." I hated my last name. I'd been given it after Kansas and I escaped, and they couldn't find my biological family. Changing it was on my list of things to do.

"We wanted to talk to your boyfriend. Is he here?" They peered around me.

"I'm here." Kansas stepped forward with a dark expression. "What is this about?"

"We're here about what happened at the drive-in this evening. Some patrons said there was a knife brandished."

"That wasn't him!" I blurted.

They looked from me to him skeptically.

"Let me guess," Kansas crossed his arms and replied dryly. "It's his word against mine?"

The one speaking nodded his head. "You've got it. What did you say your name was, son?"

"Kansas."

"Kansas what?"

"Kansas."

"All right, *Kansas*, I've never seen you around here. In Shelley Vale, everyone knows everyone. Strangers are treated as such." The officer tugged on his belt.

"Are you charging me with anything?" Kansas asked directly.

"Do you know who you're talking to, son?" the second officer barked. "Where did you come from?"

"He's just visiting from school." I crossed my arms and looked down at my sock feet. "He wasn't doing anything wrong."

"School?"

"Yeah, it's almost twelve hours away. Don't worry, I'm leaving in the morning."

"Oh, like some big-time school?" the officers mocked.

"I'm on a scholarship," Kansas growled.

"Oh, yeah, which one?" The officer laughed as if they knew one scholarship from the other.

"The Foxworth scholarship," Kansas revealed, hanging his head. I gasped. All laughter stopped in an instant.

"The Foxworth scholarship?" The officer reached for the baton on his hip. "Son, you realize you tried to fight with a Foxworth tonight? That boy can call his daddy and get your money pulled like that." He snapped his fingers.

"I'm fully aware," Kansas said dryly. "I told you I'm leaving in the morning. What more do you want?"

The officers shared a look and then nodded. "Next time you come for a visit, just be a little more mindful about who you speak to and how. The Foxworths run this town."

"Got it."

I thanked the officers and quickly shut the door.

"Kansas," I sighed. "I'm so sorry."

"Your boyfriend really doesn't like me." Kansas smirked as he stormed into the kitchen.

"What do you mean? Spencer? He's dating Soleil." I locked the front door and followed him back to the kitchen.

"Not by choice. The guy totally wants to fuck you."

My oven timer went off, and I reached for my oven mitts. "Stop. He's just protective of the people he cares about. He gets super jealous with Soleil too," I tried to say, but I wasn't entirely sure that was true. I'd never seen Spencer like that before tonight. It was weird.

"Sure." He grabbed his teacup, looked at it with disgust, and set it back down. He grabbed the bottle of bourbon from last night and popped it open, taking a long swig. "He'll get his. All those preppy, daddy's-money-will-take-care-of-everything motherfuckers." He stared at the bottle and then brought it to his lips, emptying it. He set it down sharply, and I jumped. He rolled his eyes. "They'll get theirs. I'm going to bed. I'll see you in the morning."

Rule 10 - Eisley

Don't reveal your hiding spot.

I finished making the cake in Constantine's honor alone and set it in my glass cake stand. When I dragged myself up the stairs, I paused at my guest room, where Kansas was. I heard nothing, and sadly, went to my room to sleep.

When I woke in the morning, I checked in on him. He was still fast asleep, and I presumed he'd be that way for a few more hours. He'd had a lot to drink.

I made more biscuits and then waited. At around noon, I heard the creak of the stairs as he came down.

"Hungry?" I hurried to usher him to the kitchen. "I made more biscuits. I can make eggs too if you want."

"No," he groaned. "Just the biscuits, please."

I pulled the jam out of the fridge and sliced a biscuit open, spreading the fruit on it quickly. He took it from me and popped it into his mouth.

"Thanks." He leaned over the counter and took another, spreading the jam himself. "I'm sorry I cut our night short."

"It's fine. That whole thing was so dumb. I want to focus on the good, and the good is that you're here."

"I promised the cops I'd take off today."

My heart sank. "Are you really going to? I thought I had you for one more day."

Kansas gave me a look over his glasses. "I'll stay for a bit, but I think it's in both of our best interests I take off. Don't want them to pull my scholarship and all."

"They wouldn't do that," I said, but I was unsure. "Spencer isn't always like that. The knife was just a stupid jump scare."

"Sure." He grabbed the water I had slid over to him and gulped it down. "I'll stay for the afternoon, but probably take off before it gets dark. What do you want to do?"

His mood was sour, and I suddenly felt silly for baking a cake for Constantine. I glanced at it and sighed.

"Well, if I have to condense your trip, I'd like to take you to see my bat flower."

"Bat flower?" He chuckled.

"It's so cool. Go shower and then we'll go."

When he came back downstairs, I was waiting by the front door eagerly.

"Do you have your leash?" he teased, patting the top of my head.

"If I do, does that mean I get a treat?" I bit my lower lip and put my hands behind my back, causing my chest to pop and his eyes to dip hungrily. He licked his lips.

"If you let me collar you, you'd get so many treats." He put his hand against the door, pinning me against it. My heart stuttered as he pressed me into me. "What do you say, are you a good girl?"

My jaw dropped as he cupped my sex.

"I love that you always wear skirts and dresses," he murmured, his head dipping down to kiss my collarbone. "Easy access." He rubbed over my underwear, and I moaned. Realizing what was happening, I pushed him away gently.

"Come on, I don't want to waste another minute."

The scowl on his face told me he didn't see it as a waste of time, but I wanted him to see my greatest accomplishment. I drove to the greenhouses and was surprised to find an empty parking lot.

"Usually Sundays are pretty poppin'," I explained as we started toward the line of glass buildings.

"Popping?" Kansas smirked. "I find that hard to believe."

"Hey! Not all of us are living a glamorous life halfway across the country."

He roared with laughter. "My life is not glamorous, but I love that you think that."

The greenhouse was locked, so I pulled my key out.

"If everyone has keys, then why is it locked?"

"To make sure animals don't get in." I opened the door and waved him in, following behind him. "Plus I think there are some rivalries between people in the other greenhouses. It was a whole thing a few months ago."

"Woah, it's uh... moist in here." He shuddered.

I snickered. "Well, yeah. What did you expect?"

He shook his head as he walked behind me. "I don't know, but I'm not a fan. I feel wet."

"You get used to it," I said as I took him to my plot. I stopped in front of my area and waved dramatically at the beautiful plant that had sprouted another flower in my absence. "Oh look, there's two now!"

"What is it?" Kansas bent over and looked at it with a mild look of disgust on his face.

"It's a bat flower. You know, because of how it looks."

"I guess. Is it poisonous?"

"Yes and no. I'll go with no." I swatted him away as he pretended to lean forward to take a bite of it. "I've been trying so hard to get one to grow and I finally did it."

"That's great, Eisley." Kansas stood. "I'm proud of you."

I threw my arms around him. "You are? Thank you!"

"Well, hello," a voice from behind us called out. Emi came toward us. "What's going on here?"

"I was just showing Kansas my bat flower. What are you up to?"

She pointed behind her. "Me and the girls are about to head to the set and I wanted to check on my pumpkins."

"Set?" Kansas asked, and my mood instantly fell.

Emi crossed her arms and nodded. "Yeah, we're all going to be extras in that documentary about the Sinister Minister. You know, that creepy cult guy that killed all those people ten years ago."

"I know who he is." Kansas's eyes darkened and his body stiffened beside me. I could feel the anger radiating from him.

"They still need people if you guys want to join us," Emi offered. "Spencer won't be there."

I reached for his hand and tugged on it, silently pleading for him not to say anything. He ignored me.

"No, I'm good. I'd rather not exploit the victims for my fifteen minutes."

She rolled her eyes. "You too? Well, I've got to go." She glanced at her pumpkins and then started off, leaving us alone. As soon as she was gone, Kansas spun around.

"Were you going to go?" he demanded.

"No! I told her that. It's disgusting." I put my hands up in innocence.

"Have they asked you to talk to them?" He started off toward the exit, and I followed him.

"No, have they asked you?" I shot back.

"I got a letter. I told them to go fuck themselves."

Kansas got a letter? Why hadn't I?

"What did it say?" I asked as I locked the greenhouse and we started toward my car.

"Just that they wanted to speak to me as they wanted victims to come forward. It's all bullshit."

I had so looked forward to this weekend with Kansas, and it felt like at every turn, it was disastrous. And now he was leaving. We drove back to my place quietly with him simmering beside me. I wanted to say something, anything, to quell the storm raging inside, but I didn't know what to say. We were going back up the steps when I saw something taped to my front door. A white envelope with my name on it.

While I didn't know the contents, I knew in my bones, it was from the same people who had contacted Kansas about the documentary.

They knew where I lived.

Rule 11 - Constantine

Know the layout.

Brush and dried twigs crunched under my boots as I trudged through the woods. It had been almost a decade, but I still knew the path well. I shifted my backpack and kept walking. I put my hood up to cover my face from the thin, long-reaching branches. I'd be covered in cuts and scratches if I wasn't careful.

What a pain that'd be.

The wind howled, creating a whistling sound as it moved through the dead trees. I came across a few indications that people had been through here. A filthy mattress, pop cans, snack wrappers, used condoms, and brown beer bottles. The stuff stupid teens brought with them when they were feeling brave and idiotic. I could almost hear them in my head.

"Let's go see the Sinister Minister's church!"

"I wonder if there's ghosts!"

"Who can last the longest inside?"

Over time, once the police were done with it, kids started using the church, the place I'd lived for the first twelve years of my life, as a make-out spot. As the original owner of the land was dead, no one could stop them from trespassing, so why not?

I was half a mile in when the large building took shape. From a distance, it was as I recalled when I saw it for the first time. It was a small church building with a large cross on its steeple. That was it. A church buried deep in the woods. Nothing... sinister.

What a fucking lie that was.

I kept moving. I had a goal in mind tonight. I wanted to see the damage ten years of reckless teenage drinking had done to the place and try to clean it up some. Just enough for me not to vomit every time I stepped inside.

It was my inheritance, after all.

I reached the double doors and pushed on them for half a second before freezing. Were those giggles? I listened harder, and sure enough, it was.

People were here.

Sliding my backpack off my shoulder, I unzipped it and pulled out my hunting knife and my mask. Quickly, I pulled the mask over my face and removed the knife from its sheath and held it up to the moonlight. I took pride in maintaining it, and it shone brightly.

I zipped my bag up, slid it back on my shoulders, and gently pushed on the door, rather than kick it down like I'd originally planned. The door creaked, but the voices were coming from down below in the basement. They were so loud, they didn't hear me open, close, and then lock the front door. I looked around and grinned. It was a miscreant's paradise. A good miscreant, anyways. Not the ones that used to occupy this place when I was here.

I explored the upstairs, admiring the graffiti on the once-pristine walls. Everything smelled like mildew and rat piss, which I almost thought was better than the lemon cleaner they used so much up here. That was how my dad and the rest of the Family got away with everything for so long. On the surface, everything was perfect. Deep red carpets vacuumed daily. Pews were polished weekly and hymnals were dusted as often.

The organ was expensive, as was the pulpit my dad stood at and spilled his bullshit out to the crowd. On days in which nosey people from Shelley Vale came to attend service, he'd change up his sermons to something more palatable. Loving thy neighbor was a common theme those Sundays.

Someone had spray-painted *CHOMO* on his pulpit. I pulled out my phone and snapped a picture of it. I almost wanted to frame it. The giggling grew louder, and I turned around. I had gotten so lost in the new look of this place, I had almost forgotten about the kids in the basement.

Carefully, I tiptoed toward the basement stairs. They were in the common room. If I went straight down, they'd see me. I tightened my grip around the knife and listened in.

"I can't believe I've never been down here," a boy said.

"The best time to go is in October," a girl said. "That's when it's the most haunted."

"You're so dumb," another girl said. "It's not haunted. Although it is giving that."

"It does serve," another guy said. I rolled my eyes. I stepped away from the stairs. I'd go the back way.

Despite there being no electricity anymore, the shattered glass-stained windows brought in the moonlight well enough for me to navigate through the mess of broken boards, twigs, and ripped-apart hymnals. I reached my dad's office and found more graffiti with disgusting, yet accurate words on the door, and inside on the walls.

His desk was beaten with a metal bat. It was broken into large chunks on the floor. Every crazy bible of his that had been left behind had been pulled apart and scattered. The carpets had been pulled up and it looked like small fires had been started in here, but I didn't have time to go through it all. I didn't fucking care. I wanted to push the bookcase aside and go through the door that led downstairs to... the studio.

When I shoved it aside, I was unsurprised to see people had discovered the not-so-secret door. There wasn't a door at all anymore, just a long, dark tunnel down. I pulled out my phone again and shone the flashlight down, half expecting to see something hiding in the dark. I crept down and paused at the base of the steps. I'd only been in this room once to film. It was the last time I'd spoken to her, during the ceremony. The memories flooded through me so fast, so hard, I had to lean against the wall.

"Eisley, you need to go. I'll be okay."

"But you won't! Constantine, I can't leave without you!"

"You see this?" I raised my necklace and grabbed the matching one around her neck. "It's going to keep me going. You run, and I'll catch up. I love you, Eisley."

"I love you too, Constantine."

I'd shoved her into Kansas and they ran. They flew up the very stairs I was stuck on and ran out, eventually making it through the woods and to safety.

I didn't.

I was left behind.

Mustering up the strength, I stepped down into my father's horror room and looked around. It was empty, other than the graffiti and blood on the wall. Blood I'd put there.

So much blood.

It was like my own little art project.

The laughter came again from the room just outside this one, and I gripped my knife tight.

It was time for another installation.

Rule 12 - Constantine

Don't leave any survivors.

"Did you guys hear that?"

The laughter stopped. I paused, having only nudged the door an inch over. Was my cover already blown?

"Fuck off, Sam. You're just trying to scare us. I can see it on Marnie's face. She's laughing."

"If I wanted to scare you, Joey, I'd pull a Spencer Foxworth. You know, run up behind you and pull out a knife, just when it gets to a good jump scare." Sam snickered.

"That wasn't cool," Marnie said. "Eisley is so nice. He shouldn't have done that to her."

Ah, yes. I'd heard about what that rich fuck had done. The cops had squashed that.

Joey snickered. "She's a whore. You know she's a cam girl, right? Shoving dildos up her ass for fat perverts on the internet. Who cares?"

I cared. I gripped my knife tighter and adjusted my mask. I'd make them care too.

"We don't slut shame," Sam said. "Right, Mike?"

"I do," Joey continued. "She's a slut and everyone knows it. Who cares if she gets her throat cut? I'd do it."

"You'd kill someone?" Mike asked.

While they were arguing, I opened the door wide enough for me to slide through. I stood on the other side, out of sight, and listened.

"I'd kill a slut, yeah. You know what we call prostitutes in the force?" Joey asked.

"You've done one ride along and now you're a 'we'?" Mike laughed. "You've got a ways to go before you're on the force."

"You don't know shit." Joey snarled. "They call them the 'less dead'. It means they don't give a shit how they die; they aren't looking into it."

"That's horrible," Marnie groaned. "Tell me that's not true."

"Oh, it's very true. They told me that last night when they were visiting her house. She's a less dead, so is her loser boyfriend."

"Fuck off, Joey." Marnie's voice cracked. "We shouldn't have come here."

"You're drunk," Sam added.

"I should fucking stab you," Mike said.

"Do it. Fucking do it, you coward." Joey laughed, and without missing a beat, I spun around the wall and lifted the knife in my hand.

"No, I'll do it."

The room became chaos.

Everybody began to scream as I swung my arm out, catching who I presumed was Joey.

He stared at his arm in horror as I slid the knife out and aimed for his chest. He let out a loud, terrified scream only once before I punctured the center of his chest and tossed him aside. The other three had fled.

Good.

I stormed down the halls, checking the rooms. Years ago, this had been our prison. Me, Kansas, and Eisley were in one room, and countless other children were separated into others.

Today, they had laughed about them. These stupid rich kids. They didn't give a shit about what their families did to us. Their kids were happy at home, safe, warm, and well-fed. These very ones.

They laughed and talked about Eisley as if she weren't a person. Less dead. It would be them, that was less dead, not her.

Kicking down every door, finally, I found Mike and one of the girls huddled together.

"Who are you?" the girl asked. Based on her voice, I knew it was Marnie. I didn't answer her, and instead straightened my back and slowly stalked over to them.

"Where's Joey?" Mike asked. "Why did you do that?"

"This isn't funny!" Marnie shook.

"This is a big joke, isn't it?" Mike nodded rapidly. "Because we made fun of Joey getting into the academy. Well, lesson learned, we're done." He raised his arms, and I raised mine.

Without another word, I plunged the knife into his shoulder, and then tugging it back out, I did it again and again. He dropped like a fly and then I turned to Marnie, who hadn't stopped screaming since the first stab. I lifted her by her hair. I ran the knife across her neck, shutting her up for good, and then tossed her down.

Three down; one to go. Sam.

I started to search upstairs, but then I heard a scream from the woods and darted out. She'd run, but I'd catch her.

I found her in less than ten minutes. I ran ahead of her and jumped out. Sam howled and fell backward.

"You fucking psycho!" she screamed, pointing at her fallen

phone. "I'm live right now, and they'll catch you, even with your mask."

I picked it up and put my fingers over the cameras. I raised it to my face. She was live, but no one was watching.

How sad.

I spun in a circle and saw a small puddle not too far from us. I tossed the phone and it sunk into the water. It was deeper than I had estimated. The grin slid off her face as I flexed my hand with the knife and turned my attention back to her. She began to scoot backward. I found it confusing until I looked down and saw bone protruding from her shin.

"Why are you smiling, you sick fuck?" she demanded.

"Because you've got a horse face and a broken leg. The best thing to do is put you down." Tired of this lazy cat-and-mouse game, I cleared my throat and stomped over to her, then I raised my knife. "Goodbye, Sam."

Rule 13 - Eisley

Keep your doors locked.

I stared at the letter the film crew had taped to my door. I'd read it to Kansas before he left and then read it again alone. Then again, with a bottle of wine.

Why hadn't they mailed it? It seemed so unprofessional. And creepy. Someone who knew about my traumatic childhood and wanted to use me to make money had been on my porch. Had they looked through my curtains? Checked out my backyard? Did they try the doorknob? The possibilities were endless, and I hated every dark thought.

I'd spent the afternoon in my bed drunk crying, eventually falling asleep. When I woke up, I was still holding the letter, but the bottle of wine was empty. Guilt swam in my stomach, knowing I hadn't taken my meds the entire time Kansas was here, and now, the alcohol?

Steeling my nerves, I went downstairs and to the kitchen to find something to put in my stomach. I'd deal with that later.

The first thing I saw was the birthday cake I'd made to celebrate Constantine, my dead friend. I couldn't even stomach looking at it or eat it, so I lifted it out of its glass case and tossed it in the trash without a single bite having been taken out of it.

I paced the house, allowing the alcohol to wear off. I was unsure of what exactly to do. I wanted to go to the police and demand the film crew leave me alone, but I knew exactly what they'd say:

The film crew was bringing in money for the town.

If I called the police, they'd want to see the letter and then they'd know my secret. They'd know that I was held captive by the Minister for almost five years before escaping. And once they knew, the whole town would too. I tossed the letter in the trash on top of the cake and grabbed my car keys. I couldn't be in this house right now. I drove around aimlessly, trying to clear my head, but nothing worked. I put the windows down and blasted Stevie Nicks, but I was still hopelessly miserable.

I should have taken my meds. The little alarm rang in my brain, telling me I was wrong for not doing so, but I ignored it. I hated the pills.

Somehow, I found myself outside of town, across the street from the woods where the Church lay rotting. I parked my car on the other side, away from the trees. I hadn't been back on that side since Kansas and I had pulled ourselves out. But there was some solace on the other side. A small wooden cross.

Constantine hadn't made it to the road, but Kansas thought it'd be good for us to have a representation of him somewhere so we could properly grieve. It helped.

When it was first erected, three years ago, I came here often. I made sure the area was kept tidy and the grass was cut. I would wash off gunk from birds or other animals and I'd always bring flowers. Sometimes I'd spend hours perusing flower shops for the perfect bouquet, despite knowing he'd never see them.

"You don't think he's in heaven looking down at them?" Kansas asked.

"I don't think there is a heaven." I shrugged. "Or a hell. I don't know, the idea that people are watching us from up above creeps me out. Same with the concept of god."

Kansas smirked. "You mean to tell me, we spent five years having god screamed at us and now you don't think he exists?"

"I don't. If he did, he wouldn't have let us stay there so long."

"So, I guess Constantine won't get to enjoy the flowers after all." Kansas frowned.

"I guess not. He's dead," I looked back toward the woods, where he most likely died. "That's where his story ends."

I shoved the brief memory out of my mind and returned to the present, where I stood in front of his memorial. The grass was overgrown and birds had taken it as their own. What was once a pretty, sleek black, now sat a sun-faded cross covered in white bird shit. I crouched down to clean it up some and drew back instantly. Sitting at the base of the cross was a pure white envelope, crisp and clean, with my name on it.

How did anyone know I was coming? How did anyone know what this cross even was?

Cautiously, I picked up the envelope. It was light, but something was definitely in it. I sat down on my ass and crossed my legs. With slightly shaky hands, I opened the envelope and pulled out its contents, unfolding the thick, formal-looking paper. As soon as I recognized the words, I let out a sharp gasp and dropped it. I scurried back and stood.

Who—How—

A scream came from the woods that chilled me to the core. Teenagers often used the Church as a place to get drunk, make out, and spook each other. I'd been here plenty of times and heard kids playing hide and seek, screaming and laughing like idiots. This one felt different. The same scream rang out again, and I turned and ran to my car. Maybe someone ran into a tree or fell and broke their leg. Either way, I wanted no part of it.

I started the car and then looked back at Constantine's marker. The document lay on top of the tall grass, almost as if it were begging me not to leave it there. With a sigh, I quickly opened my door, ran out, snatched the document back up, and flew back to my car. I only stopped once my car was parked safely in my driveway.

I sat for a moment, staring at the front door, searching for another unwelcome letter, but saw none, and relaxed. Then, I turned and took a deep breath, picking up the thick folded paper that I'd tossed on the passenger side while I drove. I opened it and reread it carefully. It was all there, including my shaky, childhood signature.

Someone had found my wedding license to Constantine.

Rule 14 - Eisley

Don't count anyone out.

"I don't want to go."

I clutched Constantine tight. Our hands shook as we squeezed them together on the filthy, worn mattress. I wasn't entirely sure if it was the cold, because we hadn't been fed in days, or because of how terrified we were of what was waiting for us on the other side.

"I don't either. We'll figure something out," he promised.

I turned my head, staring up into his bright blue eyes. Despite the years of torture, they remained vibrant and resilient. Constantine was a fighter, and he'd get us out of here.

"We better," Kansas, pacing the room, snapped at us. "Otherwise, one of us—"

"You can't think like that." Constantine rose, forcing me upright too, as he didn't let go of my hand. "We're all going to escape."

"How?" Kansas shouted. "We've been trapped in here since, since... I don't know how long! And now that she's..." Kansas's anger quelled when he flicked his gaze to me. He shook his head. "The Minister has already made up his mind, we're doing this.

And someone is going to..." His face crumpled. He turned around to face the wall as he sobbed.

He didn't need to finish his sentence. We all knew what he was going to say. Someone would die.

"I'm not going to let that happen," Constantine repeated. He'd been saying this since he woke up, but neither of us believed it. How could he save us? We were all the same. Weak, malnourished, and hurt. Over the years, they'd beaten us, deprived us of sunlight and fresh air, and forced us to listen to the Minister's sermons. We prayed to a god I never understood. If the Minister's god was the best one, then why did he require sacrifices?

"We need a plan," Constantine continued, ignoring Kansas's meltdown.

"You've been upstairs. How do we get up there without being seen?" I asked.

Constantine and Kansas were given special privileges as of late. Every week, they went upstairs with the Family and listened to the Minister speak. They hated it every time and always refused to tell me what he said.

"The Minister has a staircase in his office. It leads to one of the rooms down here," Constantine told us.

"What room?" Kansas wiped his nose and turned back to us.

"The room we're going to."

"You've been in there?" Kansas demanded.

"One time. There were some people from the town upstairs. He didn't want them to see me, so he made me go down the stairs and through the room. The door is covered by a bookcase. It's heavy."

"So what?" Kansas's eyes lit up. "If all three of us push, we can get it open, right?"

Constantine nodded. "I think so. And once we're upstairs, we just hold on to each other and run. Got it? Don't look back. As long as we stay together, we'll be fine."

Loud clicks came from the large iron door, and we froze. It creaked open and a Mother stood there.

"Come now. You need to be bathed and dressed."

"I don't want to go," I repeated in a shaky voice.

"It doesn't matter what you want." The Mother stormed over to me and snatched my hand from Constantine's. "The Minister has decided. The three of you will be bathed. The three of you will be dressed. And two will be married."

I woke up with a jolt on the couch.

The words she'd left unspoken screamed in my head.

And one will be murdered.

A frantic knock came from the front door.

My entire body was stiff from sleeping in my clothes. The knock came again, and I stood. The two papers meant for me fell to the floor. I picked them up and looked around for a quick place to stash them. The rapid knocking on the door made me worry they would just come right in if I didn't get to them quickly enough.

Folding them up, I shoved them in a book I had on the coffee table and went to the door. I opened it to find Therese on the other side.

"What's going on?" I asked. "Why are you here at seven in the morning?"

Her long brown hair was in a high, messy pony; her makeup was expertly done to highlight her hazel eyes, and she wore the tightest sundress, despite it being October, to highlight her massive chest.

"Sorry, did I wake you?" She cocked an eyebrow as she looked my wrinkled dress up and down with condescension. "I know you don't want to hear about it, but something huge has happened with the movie."

"The movie? I thought it was a documentary."

"Yes and no. There's some reenactments. They want to go for some award, I guess. I don't know." She pushed herself inside. "Have you seen the news? It's been circling on and off all morning."

"No, I don't have cable." I shut the door and followed her back into the house. It was far too early for this. "And since when do you wake up early enough to catch the news?"

"Hold on, I'll pull it up." She typed furiously on her phone, ignoring my comment. "With all your cam money, you should really get cable," she muttered.

"I'll pay for cable when you don't have your parents' credit card numbers memorized," I shot back.

She laughed it off and kept searching for whatever it was on her phone.

"They found a survivor," she said while continuing to stare at her screen. My blood chilled.

"What? No, there were no survivors. They found them all dead. The M—" I gulped and forced myself to slow down. "The Sinister Minister stabbed them all before turning the knife on himself." I recalled the articles and news reports. They'd confirmed it. All nine Mothers, all nine Fathers, and the Minister.

"Apparently, there was one who got away." Therese, ever the know-it-all, turned her phone and gave me the biggest shit-eating grin. "The Sinister Minister had a son."

My mind went blank as I stared at her screen. There, smiling, laughing, and clutching the necklace with his wedding ring on it, was a handsome man with black hair and blue eyes. He was talking to someone slightly off-screen and then turned to face the camera.

Constantine.

Rule 15 - Constantine

Always maintain your tools.

Sitting on the bed in my hotel room, I ran a rag covered in a salt and vinegar mix over my knife, cleaning away the blood from the teens I'd encountered earlier. After I'd left the woods, I went across the street and was pleasantly surprised to find my letter to Eisley missing. Considering only a handful of people on this god-forsaken sphere knew what that cross symbolized, and the state in which it'd been left, it was a safe bet that it was her who had picked up the white envelope.

I stood and returned to the bathroom sink, where I gave my knife another wash with dish soap I'd picked up on my way in, and then dried it with another towel before sheathing it and sliding it back into my backpack. Right along with my mask. Lying on the bed, I stretched out and put my hands behind my head.

Little Eisley was all grown up.

My cock throbbed as images flashed in my head of her in her little goth kitchen, brewing tea and talking emphatically about whatever cutesy little baking thing she made that day. She'd grown up to be so fucking beautiful. So sexy. And smart.

She knew what she had and used it to make money. I'd seen her bank account and the house she lived in. She was making a killing as a cam girl. A rather chaste cam girl. Which, was even more impressive.

When I'd first seen her pop up on my phone while doom-scrolling, it was a pleasant surprise. I'd always maintained that I'd come back for her, but to observe from a distance like this was... hot. I felt almost like a voyeur, watching the videos of her doing very innocent things while wearing clothes just on the edge of it. She was a minx, a tease, and the sexiest thing about her was that she was still a virgin.

I couldn't wait to change that.

Pulling out my phone, I clicked on the app that would take me to her channel. *Witchful Drinking*. It was a cute name. She hadn't streamed all weekend, but that was because she'd been busy. But she wasn't anymore.

I clicked on her name and a red circle around her profile picture came up. She was going live right this moment. I clicked on it. Thousands of people were watching her right along with me. Messages poured in through the chat. They moved so fast there was no way for anyone to even possibly keep up.

Eisley's so pretty.

I love your dress.

What tea are you drinking?

What is she doing?

You're hot.

Repeatedly, the comments kept coming, all along the same central themes. Either people were here to stare at her tits, or they genuinely wanted to hear about tea and the things she was interested in. I was a mix of both.

"Okay, witches." She grinned and leaned forward, her tits spilled out of the low-cut lacy dress she had on. "I think it's time to spill the tea. What do you think?" A flood of gifts appeared. I'd checked the prices of the diamonds, the crowns, the little hats, and other random items signifying real money. Eisley was making bank, even without the after-dark content.

"I had a friend over this weekend," she confessed. The blush in her cheeks as she nibbled on her lower lip caused a low groan to escape my throat.

You've got a boyfriend?

Boo

There's no way you're straight

Slut

Will it be on your site?

She read some comments aloud, laughed them off, and then kept going.

"He's not my boyfriend, guys, calm down. But I did have a fantastic weekend. I got to try out my newest tea blend with him. He also loved my blueberry jam. He ate almost the entire jar with my homemade biscuits. We also baked a cake."

She cocked an eyebrow and stared directly into the camera lens. A sly grin slid onto her full lips and she ran her pink tongue along her lower lip. My cock jumped to attention. Growing brave, I typed a comment.

I bet your cake tastes delicious.

. . .

She pulled back, eyed the comments, and kept talking.

"It was for a friend of ours. His birthday was this weekend, and we thought we'd celebrate by baking a cake in his honor." It was my birthday this weekend. She'd baked a cake for me? I sat up, now invested in this.

What was his name?

My comment sparked a flood of mimics. Eisley looked uncomfortable but finally answered.

"I'd like to respect his privacy."

Say his name.

I typed, and everyone did the same, which prompted her to put her hand on her hip and glare at the camera.

"Guys, this isn't cool. I've had a really emotionally draining weekend and I don't need this tonight. I'll try another live tomorrow." She leaned forward and started to shut the live off. I panicked. Groaning, I pushed the little tiara on the screen, sending her fifty dollars. That got her attention, and she paused.

Stay.

. . .

I typed. Not wanting to disappoint her paying customers, she put on a smile.

"Okay." She clapped and took a deep breath. "How about I do a little AMA, within reason. I can pick and choose what to answer, but since I got a gift, I'll let them go first." She squinted to look for my username. I stood up and, with one hand holding the phone, I grabbed my keys and backpack, sliding it over my shoulder.

"*Ministersmonster*, go ahead and ask three questions."

I left my hotel room and quickly typed as I walked to my car.

Who did you choose that night?

I hopped into my car and pulled out of the hotel parking lot. I was less than five miles from her place. I could make it by the third question. She was laughing and giggling and playing it off.

"I don't know what you're talking about. Maybe you can elaborate and I'll come back to you. Now, someone in the chat just asked what my favorite cake flavor is. I'm going to go with a homemade pineapple upside-down cake. Hmm, maybe that'll be the next cake I make for a video. Do you guys want my recipe?"

I took a turn and kept driving. When I paused at a red light, I pulled out my phone and typed my second question.

I'm ready for another answer since you didn't like my first question.

She huffed. "Fine, but I reserve the right to choose whether or not to answer it."

I rolled my eyes and typed.

What's up with the wedding ring you wear around your neck?

She read it, and her face went pale. She reached for the necklace, pulling the long chain from between her perfect breasts.

"How did you know..." Her voice trembled, and she sat back up.

The light turned green, and I floored it. I pulled into an abandoned parking lot a few blocks from her house, parked under a tree, and started walking. I only had a few minutes before the novelty of my gift wore off.

"Look, sometimes you guys are all too much. It feels like you, *Ministersmonster,* might want to talk in private, and that's fine, but you need to go through my website and not here."

One more question.

I typed quickly.

"No more questions," she snapped. "I'm sorry, this guy has really given me the creeps. I'm going to go, guys. I'll do a video soon." She shut the live stream off as I reached her backyard. I climbed over the fence and slowly made my way to the window that I knew was unlocked. With care, I slid it open and climbed inside, finding myself in her basement.

Pulling my phone, along with my mask from my backpack out, I went to her website and leaned against the wall. I clicked on the giant chat with me button. It said she was online. Would she pick up if I called?

I slid my mask on and steadied my breathing, and requested a video call. She did, and then for the first time in ten years, we were looking at each other.

"Ooh, a mask," she teased. "Ghostface? How original. I'm scared."

I nodded slowly. She should be.

"What exactly did you want, Monster?"

"You," I answered.

"Oh yeah?" She laughed and fell back onto what looked like her bed. "If you can find me, you can have me."

Oh, princess, don't make empty promises.

"Goodbye asshole."

She ended the video call a second later. I stared at the screen and then chose something that would truly scare her. I clicked off the web browser and went to my texts. I clicked on her name and typed.

I've already found you.

And I sent it.

Rule 16 - Constantine

Keep your mask on.

There was a long pause before her name reappeared on my screen.

Who is this?

I grinned.

Who do you want it to be?

And then my phone started ringing. I stared at it for a moment before picking it up.

"Hello." I kept my voice low to not be heard above,

although I knew she hadn't left her room. I would have heard the creaks of the floorboards.

"Who is this?" she demanded.

"Is that how you speak to your husband after all these years?"

Silence. And then, a whisper.

"Constantine?"

"I always knew you'd be pretty, beautiful even, but sexy? God damn, Eisley." I laughed dryly and began to pace her basement. Boxes of old clothes and gardening books sat all along the walls. "You're a fox."

"And you're a ghost, apparently."

I was still wearing my mask.

"Do you like it?"

Silence, and then again, a whisper. A confession.

"Yes. Although your username could be better."

"You don't like it?" My cock pulsed in my jeans. God, how I wanted to touch her. There was a long pause.

"I never thought you were a monster."

You would now.

I changed the topic. "A little birdie tells me your cherry is still intact. Is that true?"

"I—Yes. I just couldn't..."

"Without me?"

She sighed. "Without you."

"You saw the news," I said, not asking.

"I did. How?"

I ran my hand along my chest, feeling the long, thick scars under my shirt. "It's a long story, but, as it turns out, dear old Dad was right about some stuff."

"Constantine," she sighed.

"I've seen your website, Eisley. Do you strip for those men? Do you film yourself touching yourself for them?"

"Not even once."

"Why not?"

"They pay me enough just to talk to them."

Lies. I'd seen some of her more risqué ones. While she never showed nipples or her pussy, she sure moaned a lot while rolling around in lacy nightgowns.

"And if someone paid you more?"

"How much more?" she purred into the phone.

Oh, that minx.

"I'd love to watch you take a cock between your full lips," I confessed.

"Yeah? Which ones?"

My cock was now at full mast. The image of her sitting on a fake cock and working it like a real one made my heart palpitate.

"You're a tease," I chastised.

"What are you going to do about it?"

"I'm going to come up to your room and fuck you with my mask still on."

Her breathing hitched. "How do I know this isn't some sick joke?"

My heart tore at the crack in her voice. She'd waited for me, despite thinking I'd been dead for the last ten years. If she was being lied to about who I was, it'd crush her. Thankfully, it was me. The boy she'd spent five years in solitude with. The boy who protected her, held her when she cried, and eventually helped her escape.

I gulped and repeated the last words I'd said to her before I pushed her away, only to be brutally punished for it later.

"Don't talk to anyone. Don't look back. Run."

"Oh my god." She hung up.

She rushed down her stairs, and I thought for sure she was coming straight to the basement, but she didn't. There was clanging and rustling in the kitchen for a moment before she returned to her room.

This wasn't the first time I'd been here. I'd seen every inch of her house. I'd come and memorized where every room was for this very moment. I could tell exactly where she was.

I pressed my foot down on the first stair leading up but paused. Something didn't feel right. I paced for another fifteen minutes. Had I blown it? No, Eisley didn't trust the cops in this town. As she shouldn't. I was staring at the window I'd crawled through when my phone rang again.

"I-I don't believe it's you."

Ah, she'd gone down for more wine. Good.

"Why not?"

"Because the Constantine I knew wouldn't have abandoned me for ten years. And now you just show up? What's up with that?"

"What's your poison tonight?" I asked, reciting her catchphrase back to her.

"Wine, a very good wine. All of my very good bourbon is gone." She giggled. "Guess who drank it before you could get here?"

"Is that all he drank?" I snarled.

She sighed. "Yes, although now I wished I'd let him. I'm mad at you right now."

She must have slammed the bottle. Which meant the pill I'd slipped into the bottle on her counter when I was here earlier was in her system already.

"Apparently. Is this what you do when you're mad? Make drunk calls to your exes?"

"Are you my ex?" she asked. "Because last time I checked, we're both wearing our rings." At that, I started up the stairs, as quietly as I could manage. "Constantine, are you still in my house?" she purred into the phone as I walked right through her kitchen, past her living room, and up the stairs to her bedroom.

"What would you do if I was?" I growled.

"Mmmm… maybe I'd let you be the first… to watch me."

Like hell. I would not watch. I would participate. But, I'd shelve that idea for later.

I went to her room and stood in front of the door. The lights were off, and I could hear her speaking on the other side.

"I'm going to go now," I said, keeping my voice low.

"Why?"

"Because I've got an appointment."

I reached for the doorknob and turned it, letting the door swing slowly open. Eisley sat up quickly and stared at me in horror. I took a moment to soak in her beauty. She had changed out of her clothes and slipped into a black, lacy negligee with only panties to match. Her perfect tits shone right through. I stormed over to her and pushed her down onto her pillows, crawling over her.

She groaned as my hand slid from her hips up, grazing her breasts and collarbone and pausing at her neck. She was so beautiful.

"Constantine?" she asked me, but I didn't answer. Instead, I bent and inhaled deeply through the mask. She smelled divine. I'd spent so many years imagining this moment, and here it was.

"You're so fucking sexy," I murmured as my hands found her tits and caressed the budding nipple. "When was the last time you came?"

"Never." She gasped and put her hands around me.

"By choice?"

She nodded. Why was that so fucking hot?

"I'm going to help with that. You'll have no choice tonight."

"You think you can just force it?" She closed her eyes, and with great trepidation, I lifted my mask to my forehead, and began kissing down her body.

"I don't think anything," I said sharply, my hand returning to her neck. I dipped my other hand under the negligee and ran along the top of her panties. "Are you bare?" I slid under the thin fabric. Her pussy was smooth, and when I parted her labia, she was fucking dripping. I swirled my finger around in her arousal, and she groaned.

My cock pressed hard against her thigh as I kept working my fingers. Suddenly, I didn't want to come. My mission tonight was to watch her unravel on my fingers... and all over my tongue.

"Ah!" She bucked her hips, and I took that opportunity to let go of her neck and grab her hips. I shoved her panties down and ripped her thighs apart. Her hands went to my mask, but I glared at her. A low guttural growl came from my throat, and she dropped back down onto the pillow and released me. I adjusted the mask slightly lower, but kept it off my face so that I could eat her beautiful pussy as much as I wanted to.

I spread her lips apart and dove in, lapping at her beautiful body. She tasted as good as she looked. Her hands went to my head, and she shoved me deeper into her pussy. I gladly accepted the challenge of not breathing in pursuit of her coming. I sucked on her clit and slid a finger inside her. She instantly tightened, and I pulled back. I needed her to focus.

I ran my hands down her thighs, and she shivered as I continued lapping and sucking on her soaking pussy until finally, she tensed and let out a sharp cry. Her pussy pulsed against my lips and her orgasm gushed, making her even wetter than before.

Her face was a mask of pure surprise, bliss, and exhaustion. Her brown eyes rolled to the top of her head, and she promptly passed out. She wouldn't remember any of this tomorrow.

I kissed her plump upper lips before climbing off the bed to go.

Good girl.

Rule 17 - Eisley

Watch your drink.

I woke up severely hungover. Why did my head hurt so much? I could barely open my eyes without flinching. The dim light peeking through my dark curtains was killing me. What happened last night? I got out of bed on wobbly legs. I took a step and kicked a wine bottle. Did I drink? I scrunched my nose and went to the shower, trying hard to recall something, anything from the night before.

I'd been upset about the wedding license and the letter from the film crew. But after that... nothing. Carefully, I took off my necklace.

I considered the reality of my situation. I was a single woman living alone. With people trying to get me to react to... something. I needed to take extra precautions. I spent the morning looking up what kind of cameras worked best for home security.

Eventually, the headache began to disappear, and I started to feel like myself again. Albeit, still, I'd avoided my meds again. Did I really need them anymore? I felt mostly okay.

Around dinner, I messaged the group chat to see if

anyone wanted to go out, and I rode with Emi and Micah to the Shelley Vale tavern, a hole-in-the-wall bar.

"What have you been up to?" Therese asked me, dipping the last of her fries in ketchup.

I took a sip of my water. I was staying away from alcohol for a while.

"I went and bought a bunch of home security stuff."

"Why? Do you have a stalker now?" Soleil smirked. "I didn't realize you were that famous."

"Salty much?" Emi rolled her eyes at her. "It's probably smart, considering you're single, alone, and gorgeous."

I blushed.

"She's not single," Soleil objected. "I thought you had a boyfriend now. Kansas?"

"Yeah, what's going on there?" Spencer, her boyfriend, leaned forward.

"Nothing. We're just friends. I'm not seeing anyone."

"You know..." Therese grabbed another fry. "You could tell us if you were gay."

"Or Ace," Emi added.

"Or bi." Soleil, sitting directly beside me, slid her hand over my thigh.

"I'm not gay or ace." I shot my friends looks and pushed Soleil's hand away. "And if I were bi, you'd all be the first to know."

"Okay, but it's weird, right?" Therese looked around for support. "You're twenty-one and have never been with anyone. Like, even a date. It's weird, right?"

There were mumbles across the table.

"Maybe I haven't found anyone interesting enough." I sipped my water. "This town doesn't offer much."

The men around the table began to laugh and holler at my diss. I sat back, satisfied that they'd stop talking about me, when suddenly someone passed by the table, causing everyone to quiet down.

"Do you know who that is?" Therese hunched over the table.

"Who?" I looked around.

"That's the guy! The Sinister Minister's kid," she whisper-yelled.

"He's not really a kid." Soleil cocked an eyebrow. "He's hot as fuck."

"Thanks, babe." Spencer reached for his beer.

"What? Look at him." Soleil pointed to the man standing at the bar. "You can't tell me he's not hot." She looked at us for support. They all glanced his way and nodded eagerly. She nudged me. "What about you, Miss Picky? Is he interesting enough?"

I stiffened. My heart was beating so hard my chest hurt.

"I have to go to the bathroom." I shot up and out of my seat before anyone could argue. I stormed the opposite way of their pointing to the far back bathrooms, and shoved the door open.

I went to the sink and tossed cold water on my face while I tried to steady my breathing. He was here. Just outside the door at the bar, Constantine was alive and well.

Did he know I was here too?

The door swung open a moment later as if on cue.

"I'm in here!" I spun around to push the person out and froze.

There he was.

Constantine, all grown up, staring me down.

Jet-black hair shaved down at the sides but longer on top curved just enough for one strand to fall over his eyes. His jawline and nose were shaped beautifully, and his eyes were a piercing blue. Tattoos covered his arms, and a light, day-old stubble dusted his face. His muscles were large, highlighted by his tight black shirt and ripped jeans. Everything about him oozed bad boy, and something inside me told me he might just be.

I backed away toward the wall as he reached his hand back and locked the door.

"Hello, Eisley."

My heart sped right back up at hearing his voice for the first time in ten years.

"Constantine," I blinked rapidly, still in utter disbelief. "you're alive."

"I am. Did you wait for me?"

"Wait for you?" Suddenly, my shock and fear were gone, and all I felt was rage. I stormed over to him and shoved my hands into his hard chest. "What do you mean wait for you? I thought you were dead!"

"Did you though?" He grinned, but it wasn't funny. "I find it hard to believe you were sold on the idea."

"How could I not be?" Tears sprung to my eyes and I let them slide down my cheeks in hot, furious streaks. "The Minister said—"

"The Minister said a lot of things. Most of them were lies."

"Like father like son, huh?" I let out a scream of anguish and turned away from him. "I can't believe you've been alive this entire time and you didn't come for me. Ten years! Ten fucking years, Constantine!"

His hands squeezed my shoulders and spun me back around, forcing me to face him.

"You think I didn't want to come get you?" he said through gritted teeth. "Of course I did. It's not as simple as that. Our story is a lot deeper than what you realize Eisley. I had to wait for the right time to come back or I'd fuck everything up."

I closed my eyes and sobbed. I was mad, I was sad, and I was more than anything, confused.

Constantine's thumb ran over my cheeks, wiping the tears away. "Don't cry anymore. I'm here now, and I'm not going anywhere this time." How could I trust him? He'd been letting me live a lie for ten years. "You just have to trust me, princess."

Large, warm arms covered me, pulling me into him. I wanted to resist, to shove him away again, but... I didn't. I inhaled the smell of his cologne and slowly, my heart began to relax and I could breathe again.

"This can't be real. I don't understand how any of this is possible. I hate you."

"It is real, it is possible, and you don't hate me."

Constantine's hands began to roam down my back and rested on my ass. He squeezed.

"I do hate you." I repeated. "You let me think you were dead."

"I had to." His hands traveled to the front of my hips and began pulling my dress slowly up. He leaned down, and I felt his warm breath on my neck. "I needed to see how long you'd wait for me."

His hand dipped between my thighs, cupping my sex. "Did you, wife?"

"Did I what?" I gasped, as he began to massage me over my panties.

"Did you allow someone else to take what's rightfully mine?"

"What if I did?" My heart hammered as I tested him. I arched my back into him as Constantine slid under the thin fabric and teased my folds.

"You say you're angry at me, but your dripping pussy tells another story. Tell me Eisley, now who's lying to who?"

Rule 18 - Eisley

Don't get in the killer's car.

My mind screamed for me to push him away. This was a total stranger. But my body desperately begged for him to keep going. He wasn't… entirely strange. I knew him once, and I did love him then.

It wasn't until someone knocked, that I remembered we were in a public bathroom at a bar.

I shoved him away and straightened my dress.

"Occupied!"

"Yeah it is," Constantine tried to touch me again but I put my hands up.

"No, we can't do this here. We shouldn't be doing it at all." I glanced at my flushed reflection and scowled. What was happening?

I steeled myself and abandoned the bathroom, leaving Constantine behind. I returned to my table, where minutes later, a waitress came by with a beer for me.

"This is from the man at the bar." She pointed and all of us turned to see Constantine nodding at me.

"Do you know him?" Soleil asked.

"Uh—" I took the drink and sipped it while everyone stared at me in wonder.

"Maybe he's the one you've been looking for," Emi suggested. "Go thank him for the drink."

"Is that a good idea? The guy looks like a creep." Spencer shot her a dirty look.

My stomach, already tight with nerves, suddenly revolted completely. I stood back up, after just returning, and declared that I wanted to leave.

"See, I told you." Spencer snarled. "The loser isn't welcome. I'll take you home, Eisley." Spencer stood with me and reached for his keys.

"What? No!" Soleil pouted. "Come on, don't go. Look, let's just invite him over. Maybe he's not as scary as we think."

"No!" I shouted. "No. I just want to go home."

"I can take you."

I spun around to face Constantine, who had snuck up behind me.

"Do you even know her?" Spencer glared.

"We go way back." Constantine told the table and offered me his arm. "I'll get you home safe."

I felt like him and I had two definitions of the word. If safe to him was anything like our interaction in the bathroom, I was anything but. He put his arm around my waist possessively.

Therese cleared her throat. "Eisley, are you okay with this?"

I licked my lips. "Yeah, I'll have Constantine take me home. You guys have fun."

We turned and left before Spencer or anyone else could argue further about it. As much as I didn't want to be alone with Constantine, I also didn't want to stay and explain things to my friends.

"Let's go home, wife." Constantine whispered in my ear as

we headed toward the door. As soon as we stepped out of the bar I pulled away from him.

"Will you stop calling me that?" I demanded.

"Why not? You're still wearing your ring."

My eyes flicked to his chest and he pulled out his necklace with a small gold band on it. He still had his too.

"I can hardly call you my husband. Husbands don't up and leave for ten years without telling their wives."

"I didn't up and leave. If we're being technical, it was you, that left."

I opened and closed my mouth. I'd known him all of ten minutes and I was already pulling my hair out.

"That ceremony wasn't legally binding."

"If that's what you think then why are you still wearing that necklace if you don't want to be married to me?"

I looked around the parking lot. It was dark, but no one else was outside. The music from the bar was so loud it poured out, masking our argument to the patrons inside. Constantine reached for me and I jerked away.

"Don't touch me."

"Why not? I'm your husband, isn't that something I'm allowed to do?"

I blinked. Pure blind rage filled me as I stared at him. Who was this man? He wasn't the boy I'd left down in the basement of the Church. This man was demanding, snarky, and incredibly sexy. I hated how easily my body betrayed me in the bathroom and now. I was furious, but also insanely attracted to him. His touch had felt so good.

"My car is right there." He pointed. "Let's go."

"I'm not going anywhere with you." I crossed my arms.

Constantine stalked toward me. "Have you upheld your vows?" He repeated his question from before. The deep look in his blue eyes told me he was only interested in one part of it. Had I been faithful?

I swallowed, as my mind went to Kansas.

"I—Constantine, I thought you were dead."

"Answer the question."

"I may be your wife, but it's not the 60's anymore. I don't have to do a damn thing you tell me to."

A slow smile crept over Constantine's lips, and I wasn't sure if I was scared, or it made him even more attractive to me.

"Oh, you're going to regret that." With one fell swoop Constantine tossed me over his shoulder and began stalking toward the cars, stopping right in front of a muscle car that made my mouth fall open.

"That's yours?"

"You like it?" He grinned. "It's a 1972 Chevy Nova."

"Where did you even get something like this?" I asked, momentarily forgetting I was angry. I stepped up to the silver car with black hood chrome accents. It looked fresh off the lot.

"A lot of searching. I got into cars a year or so back. Get in." He opened the door for me, and I slid in. It smelled like new car.

"So what, you just show up right when the documentary crew comes around?" I asked, getting angry again. All this time, he'd been alive, and not once he thought to come find me. I'd been grieving over a much alive person.

"They invited me." He turned the key in his ignition and the car roared to life. He peeled out of the parking lot and we started onto the road.

"Oh?" Guilt washed over me, but only slightly. I understood not wanting to come back to Shelley Vale after getting out, but why didn't he come find me first? I would have spent my entire life in mourning.

"Yeah, paid for the trip out, the hotel, all that."

"When did you get here?"

"Just a few days ago."

"Where have you been this entire time?"

Constantine grew silent.

I turned my head and something in his expression chilled me.

"The next town over."

"What?"

"I know. I was aware you were still here, and what you were doing. I just couldn't come yet."

My mind went blank for just a moment, and then suddenly, an explosion of ten years flew through my brain of moments with just Kansas and I. Moments that Constantine could have been a part of, had he come to find me, and I lost it.

Without a second thought I unbuckled my seatbelt and opened the door. I lurched forward and Constantine swerved the car as he snatched me back inside.

"What the hell are you doing?" He yelled.

"You bastard!" I screamed. "This whole time you knew I was here and you did nothing! You let me mourn over you, when you could have walked right on over at any time. Fuck you!"

"You're not listening," he snarled.

"Oh, I'm listening." My stomach tightened as I began to put pieces together. "Did you know I was at the tavern?"

"I did."

I reached for the door again. "Let me out."

"Like hell! We're in the middle of the nowhere."

"Do you know where I live?" I demanded. "How long have you been watching me?"

I couldn't believe it. My entire life as I knew it had changed in just 24 hours. I'd spent half of my life grieving over a man who wasn't dead, but rather was stalking me.

Constantine turned and suddenly, we were at my house. I'd been so blindly mad, I hadn't realized he'd gotten me home safe, like he'd said. He parked and we stared each other down.

"I can't believe you. What made you ever think this was okay?" I demanded.

"It wasn't, but there was little I could do. If I came around while we were still in foster care, they might have sent us further away, maybe out of state. I couldn't come too close."

His words sunk in. He was right. The only reason I'd been allowed to see Kansas was because we escaped together. We'd been told we weren't allowed to see any members of the Family. If they'd discovered we were talking to Constantine, the Minister's son...

"Will you let me come inside and we can talk about it?" he asked.

I was still furious, but when he reached over the seat and gently squeezed my hand, I relented. We shared a look, and I wondered if he was remembering what had almost happened in the bathroom of the bar, and if his plan was to finish what he'd started. Did I want that?

"Yes."

Rule 19 - Constantine

Take your time.

"Do you want some tea?" Eisley asked the moment we stepped inside her house. It felt weird, using the front door.

"I'm not really a tea drinker."

She ignored me, going to the kitchen. "I need something to calm down."

I followed behind, and watched as she pulled out a mint green teapot with gold trim and a black bat on the side, and prepared it for boiling.

"What are the holes for?" I leaned over the stove and pointed.

"This is an assassin's teapot." She beamed.

"A what?"

"These two holes," she pointed. "Go to a different chamber. You can pour two different drinks into the teapot and serve one drink or both."

"And why do they call it an assassin's teapot?"

"Because one drink could be poison, and you'd never know because they were served from the same pot."

"This is pretty good. I can't even taste the poison." I teased.

"That's the point."

I studied her intensely. No picture or video could ever come close to seeing her in real-time. I'd waited so long for this very moment. She sipped her tea and glared across the island at me.

"So you knew where I lived. What else do you know about me?"

If she was mad now, I couldn't imagine how pissed she'd be if I revealed the truth.

I took a deep breath. "This isn't the way this was supposed to go."

"What do you mean?"

"When I went to the bar today, I was hoping you'd see me and be happy."

She laughed. "Ha! You're delusional."

"You're not happy to see me?"

"I mean, I am. But..." she looked down at the drink in her hands, and when her eyes returned to me, they glistened. "I wish you would have told me earlier."

Silence stretched between us.

"You saying it over and over won't change things." I went to her, pulling her into my arms. She was reluctant, but I wasn't giving up. I'd finally made my presence known, and I was claiming her as mine tonight. "It's best we move on and make up for the time we've lost."

"What do you mean by that?"

My cock twitched, but I forced myself to be patient.

"I could go back to my hotel and try again tomorrow," I

started. "Or I can sit and talk with you all night." I stared at her, waiting for her response. Slowly her eyes rose back to mine. Each second killed me with anticipation.

"I'd like that."

Eisley and I returned to her living room, this time with a bottle of red wine and two glasses. I sat and opened the bottle, while she turned on music and went around locking the doors. I had to choke back a snicker. She didn't have to worry about intruders tonight. I was already inside. She peeked out the window and shut the curtains quickly with a shudder.

"Everything all right?" I asked, relaxing on her couch.

"Yeah." She brushed her hair behind her ear. "I'm just a little paranoid. The other day, I got a creepy letter from that documentary crew taped to my door. No stamp or anything." She shuddered again. "Like, who does that?"

"Yeah, I've met some of the crew. They all are way too enthused about the whole thing." She joined me on the couch and pulled a leg up and shifted to face me. My eyes darted to where her dress had ridden up, revealing for a second, black panties.

She saw me looking and blushed, pulling the dress down. It was plain on her face that she was thinking about the bathroom. To her, it was the first time I'd ever touched her like that. But only I knew otherwise.

A flash of last night and how her sweet pussy tasted on my tongue flew through my mind. It was made even better knowing that she had no memory of it. She looked so beautiful when she came.

"To me, it feels so gross."

"What does?" I blinked, returning to the conversation.

"The documentary. It feels very exploiting. Normally, I'd say the money they earn should go to the victims, but everyone's dead." She shrugged. "So what good is this doing? It just feels like they are obsessing over something so vile, it should have all stayed buried."

"Did you tell this to your friends?" I asked. "I saw them all on the set the other day." I handed her the other glass of wine, and she simply stared down at it.

"I have, but they don't see it how I do. Emi needs the money and everyone else wants the fame."

"They don't seem like good friends."

"They are—" she started and then frowned. She took a deep gulp of her drink and then nodded. "Sometimes I don't think they are my friends. I was friends with Emi first, who introduced me to all of them. Soleil is a rich bitch, and Therese is a know-it-all. Gah! I can't stand her sometimes."

"Where do you fit in with them?" I watched her carefully, paying attention to her movements, what words she was saying, but most importantly, how she was saying them.

"I don't know. Honestly. We used to be super close, but then my channel blew up and I started making real money and it felt like they don't like it. I feel weird saying jealous, but it kind of feels that way."

"They should be jealous of you. You're smart, successful." I leaned forward and brushed the hair that had fallen over her face back. "And sexy."

She blinked rapidly and turned her head toward me. "I don't know what to say to that." Moving closer to her, I took the glass out of her hand and set it on her coffin-shaped glass coffee table.

"Eisley, I didn't come here to talk about your friends. I know, I should have visited you years ago, but I wasn't ready. But I am now."

She rolled her eyes, and a tiny smile fluttered on her lips. "Ready for what?"

I lowered my gaze to her breasts, spilling out of her top.

They were perfect. Slowly, I raised my gaze until my blue eyes met her gorgeous brown ones. I moved until our breath mixed into a warm, wine-scented haze.

"You," I growled and pressed my lips to hers. The kiss was hard and determined, and to my pleasant surprise, there was no hesitation in her response. Her lips parted, her tongue found mine, and she kissed me back.

"You've grown up so pretty," I murmured as I peppered kisses down her jawline until I reached her neck. She tilted it to allow me more room and began to gasp and squirm in my arms. I licked her skin and sucked on her neck, deciding then that I'd be leaving my mark tonight. My hands slid up and down her body, reveling in her soft skin. I pulled her onto my lap and she slowly ground her hips against my jeans. My cock was rock solid and demanding I take it out and show her what she'd been holding out for.

Eisley being my pretty little virgin was the hottest fucking thing in my mind. And I needed to hear it.

"How many men have you been with?" I demanded. She ignored me and continued to kiss me. I ran my hand over her chest, and when I found her tight nipple, I pinched it hard. "Tell me."

"Constantine," she sighed. "It doesn't matter."

Grabbing hold of her ass, I squeezed her cheeks and lifted her, quickly placing her on her back on the couch. I moved over her, pressing my entire body over hers.

"How many men have you let come inside you?" I asked, biting her lobe.

"None!" she gasped. My hands slid under her dress, up her flat stomach, and up to her chest. I yanked the bra down and began teasing her nipples.

"None? I find that hard to believe. You're too sexy to not have been with anyone." I pinched them, harder this time, again.

"It's true," she whispered. "I couldn't. Even though I thought you were dead, I couldn't be with anyone else when I'd promised myself to you. I'm still a virgin!" I released her nipple and sat up, grinning at her.

"Good. Let's rectify that."

Rule 20 - Constantine

It's okay to fuck the final girl if she's your wife.

I admired how she disregarded that I knew the layout of her upstairs without having been here before. Eisley was too drunk on wine and lust to care about how we got to her bed as long as it happened. I lifted her bridal-style and took her up the stairs and to her room.

She closed her eyes and stretched her arms over her head. The urge to pin them down and tie her wrists to her headboard was strong inside me. God, she'd look so fucking beautiful bound with no escape as I gave her orgasm after orgasm. I wanted to see her cry from how powerful the feeling was.

As I was admiring Eisley, I noticed the bedding. It was all black, which would serve well tonight. No need to stain anything. I pulled off my shirt and unbuttoned my jeans but left them on. My shoes were already off from originally entering her house, so I joined her on the bed.

My lips found hers again, and I lay on my side, kissing her and drifting my hands down her body. I raised her dress and slipped my hand under her panties, finding her like just the same as I had at the bar, bare and sopping wet. I spread her pussy and began running slow, laborious circles around her clit. She arched her back and gasped.

"You like that, princess?" I asked.

She nodded but only moaned in response.

"Words," I coaxed.

"I like it when you touch me there."

"Where?" I licked her from her collarbone to her jaw, finding my way back up to her mouth and shoving my tongue into it.

"There."

"Where?" I teased. Oh, how I loved teasing her.

"My—"

"Say it," I growled.

"My pussy. I like it when you touch my pussy."

"Good girl," I purred. My finger went down again and found her opening. Last night, she'd responded negatively, but tonight, I would not let her get scared and back down. Tonight, I would pop her fucking cherry. She stiffened when I began to push, and I pulled back. "Sssh," I whispered into her ear. "Don't be scared."

"I-I—"

I covered her lips again, kissing her until she relaxed. Removing my fingers from her pussy, I sat up and rolled on top of her, spreading her thighs apart.

"Let's relax you, shall we?" When she didn't move, I reached for her panties and began to tug them off, but she wasn't moving fast enough, and I wasn't enjoying this softness I had somehow developed while in her bed.

Sitting up, I pulled my pocketknife out of my back pocket and popped it open. I yanked up her dress and grabbed the fabric of her panties, slashing them off of her in two jerks of the knife against them. She let out a sharp cry, despite the blade not even touching her, and I pointed it at her.

"If you are going to be a little brat, you'll be punished like one."

Her mouth fell open in protest.

"What do you mean I'm a—"

I pulled her forward and ran my knife from her jaw down into her perfect breasts.

"You've got gorgeous tits, you know that?" I grabbed the fabric and began to pull down, taking her bra with it. Slowly, I unveiled her breasts and then shoved her back down, covering her body with mine. My lips went to her puckered nipple, and I swirled my tongue around it, all the while dragging the knife down her body until it reached her now exposed pussy.

"I can be a good guy and ease you into things." Slowly, I rotated the knife so the hilt was pressed against her folds. "Or, if you don't want to do what you're told..."

"Okay, I'll listen," she gasped.

"Good girl." I shut the knife and slid it back into my pocket. I planted a quick kiss on her lips and then lowered myself to devour her pussy for the second time.

Spreading her wide, I took in the stunning sight that was her. I ran my tongue down and up, lapping at her juices. She gasped and squirmed and pressed my face deeper into her dripping pussy, and I was happy to keep going. I wanted to use my fingers to fuck her, but upon a second attempt and her tensing again, I decided the first thing going inside her was my cock.

She gasped, moaned, and finally cried out and arched her back. Her pussy pulsed and gushed as her second orgasm ever rocked through her body. I stayed in place until she was done and then I brought her hands to my pants. Fumbling, she pulled on the zipper. Her hands shook as I gently coaxed her to help me.

"This is a two-person game, Eisley," I said as she leaned up, and I pulled the remains of her clothing off. She nodded and helped me out of my pants. My heart raced as I positioned myself on top of her.

"Do we need a condom?" she whispered.

A sudden jolt of anger rose in me.

"I'm your husband. I'm not using a fucking condom when I pop your cherry," I growled.

She blinked, and I quickly relaxed her again by planting kisses on her nipples, breasts, and mouth. I pushed her thighs apart with my own and raised myself up by my arms. My cock was dripping, having waited so long to feel what it was like inside her warm, wet pussy. I'd dreamed about it for years, and finally, we were here.

Gripping my cock, I directed myself between her swollen, puffy lips and to her entrance. Eisley clamped her eyes tight as I carefully began to push.

Her virginity, paired with how larger than average my cock was, made it more painful than I had expected, but I enjoyed it. I watched her face contort and flinch as I pushed my cock in one inch at a time. I felt the pressure of her pussy as the membrane tore away, and I got further inside. Tears streamed down her face, and I grinned.

"Ssshh..." I ran my hand over her wet cheeks. "You'll get used to it. The worst part's over," I assured her.

Once the base of my cock hit her lips, I stalled, and then slowly pulled back and thrust forward. I was slow in my thrusts, careful to watch her reaction to them.

She felt like fucking heaven, her pussy walls tight and screaming against my cock. I'd never fucked a virgin before. This was Eisley, the girl I'd been dreaming about for ten years, the first girl I'd jerked it to, the girl I thought of every time I fucked someone else, and now, we were finally together.

She was mine again.

Eventually, as I continued going slow and kissing her

breasts and lips, her painful expression subsided to an adorable look of surprise.

"You like my cock inside you, don't you, princess?" I asked. She was unsure at first but finally nodded. "Your cunt is very greedy. I'm going to make you come so hard and then I'm going to do the same, spilling myself inside of you."

Now that she'd stopped crying, I picked up the pace, ready to deliver on my word. I wasn't coming until she did. Eisley dug her nails into my back, pressing me deeper into her. I shifted my hips and rotated, coaxing her body to begin the process. She gasped and wrapped her legs around me, digging her heels into my ass. I pulled back and shoved myself deep inside her. She cried out sharply, and her pussy began to throb.

She gloriously unraveled, and I feverishly thrusted into her, spilling myself inside of her. I milked my cock into her pussy, then pulled out, satisfied that she had claimed every single drop. I dropped beside her and pulled her into my embrace. She curled up into me, and I heard a sniffle.

"I'm sorry I cried. Was I being a brat?" she asked.

I chuckled and ran my hand along her soft back. "No, you were perfect. You're such a good girl."

Rule 21 - Eisley

Pay attention to details.

The rhythmic sound of my shower running roused me. I yawned and then shot up, clutching my comforter to my bare chest. Did that happen last night? The shower turned off and I stared at the bathroom door from across the hall. A moment later, a hot tattooed man stepped out with a black towel around his waist.

He was dripping, but that made him even sexier. We had… It happened.

In the daylight, I could see the scars on his chest better. I'd felt them last night. Thick scars ran from his shoulders and down the front of him, down to his navel.

The same ones Kansas had. What were the odds of both men having that same scar?

Only these were older and more jagged. Like someone had done a rush job. Kansas's scars had been created by someone who knew what they were doing. It didn't detract from how attractive he was. The scars made him look tougher, hotter even.

I clenched my thighs and flinched at the soreness.

Constantine stalked across the room, looking so casual, so

comfortable, in my home. "You're awake. How do you feel?" He stepped over to me and leaned down for a gentle kiss.

I swallowed and blinked. "Confused, mostly. It still kind of hurts."

"It will. The more you do it, the better it will feel." He said so matter-of-factly, it sent my belly into a tizzy. He presumed we'd do it again? Did I even want to do it again?

Yes.

God yes, I wanted him again. I'd push through the pain.

"When did you get up?" I climbed out of bed, taking my blanket with me. Suddenly, I felt shy. This man had been... inside me. My cheeks flushed. Why was I so embarrassed?

"Oh wow, even with the black sheets, you can see it," he commented as he finished drying himself and slid on his clothes from last night. I looked back at the bed, and I was horrified to see several large pools of dried blood.

"Oh my god." I covered my face with a hand, the other still clutching the blanket.

"What? It's normal." Constantine strode over to me and put his arms around my body. He reached for my hand, pulling it away from my face. "That's what happens. Did you not...?" He stared at me curiously.

I rolled my eyes. "Of course, I knew that. I'm not a kid. Although I feel pretty childish right now. It's just all so weird."

"Why? Last night," he kissed me and pulled me tighter. "you had sex with your husband. What's weird about that?" He chuckled and tilted his head to pepper kisses along my neck.

"Constantine," I giggled. "I'm filthy."

"Fuck yeah you are," he murmured.

I gently pushed him away. "Not in a good way. I'm going to take my turn in the shower. Don't leave while I'm in there." I felt silly, but I wasn't ready to be alone yet. He stared at me intently and then nodded.

"Sure."

Taking the blanket to the bathroom like a petulant child, I dropped it to the floor and hurried to wash myself. I took my time, enjoying the hot water. I was careful when I went to wash between my legs. Flashes of last night returned, and I smiled. The pain was worth it.

When I turned off the shower and stepped out, I found the blanket gone. I wrapped a towel around my hair and another around my middle and walked back to my room. I was shocked to find my bed stripped down to the mattress.

As I was about to close the door to dress, Constantine came from downstairs.

"I got everything in the wash," he explained.

"Thanks, I'm going to change," I said and started to shut the door.

"What are you doing?" He smirked and stuck his hand in before I could shut it. "Do I not get to watch?"

"Well, I mean..."

No.

"Come on, you don't have to be shy around me, Eisley. You act like I haven't seen you at your worst. I'm not a stranger." His expression darkened. I relaxed my arm and allowed him inside. I went to my closet and pulled out a dress, then to my dresser and snagged my underwear, a bra, and a pair of black lace tights. I turned nervously to the bed, where Constantine lay with his hands behind his head, grinning at me.

I rolled my eyes and turned away. The most he would get was my behind.

"What are you doing today?" I asked him as we went down the stairs together. I took him to the kitchen, where I began a pot of tea.

"Hopefully you again, if I can."

I glared at him, and he laughed.

"You don't have a job?"

"I do," he said cryptically. "I make my own hours."

I wanted to ask more, but he didn't seem to want to discuss it further.

"I want to spend some time with you before I go and do a little work. Do you want to do something?"

I tried to think. "I have a scheduled live today, but after that, my day is free."

"Are you kicking me out now?" He cocked an eyebrow in amusement.

"No!" I blushed. "I just didn't think you'd want to... you want to join me on screen?" I grinned.

"Sure. Sounds like fun."

I watched him in utter awe. He was so aloof, so unlike the man in my bed last night. My stomach fluttered again as I thought about it. I liked both sides of him.

I went and got my materials from my extra fridge and various shelves and pushed play with Constantine standing beside me. My heart was beating rapidly as my followers began to log on. I'd never had a guest in my videos. How would my community take it?

I pressed my lips together tightly and waited. The comments began flooding in. Confusion, excitement, hearts, stars, and lots of gifting were going on. They liked him. Constantine snaked his arm around my waist and suddenly I felt more confident.

"Hi witches, I see we've got a lot of questions in the chat. That's great! So, before we dive into another project, I want to introduce you to..." I turned and smiled up at him. I wasn't sure how to introduce him.

He leaned across the counter to put his face right into the camera. "I'm Constantine, her husband."

My heart beat furiously. Husband? How would my following take that? Would showing my personal life cause them to stop supporting me and my income to tank? They wouldn't understand. I didn't understand. The entire wedding ceremony under the Minister's reign was nonsense! Right?

With his announcement, the comments and gifts began pouring in. Most were positive.

Instantly, I relaxed and reached for my vase. "Today, I'm going to teach Constantine how to make a spooky season wedding bouquet."

It was a blast working with him. He interacted with the viewers and cracked jokes with me. We laughed and flirted while we made an orange and black bouquet, showing and teaching my loyal fanbase how to do it themselves. A big gift came through, and I explained to Constantine they get one question.

"What's up," my smile faltered at the username and I gulped, as my stomach tightened. "*Ministerinthemaking*?"

Rule 22 - Eisley

Don't give out personal information.

What would be your perfect bouquet?

Relief rushed through me, and I brought my cheerful mask back to the surface. I tapped my chin and scrunched up my nose, pretending to think long and hard about it. I couldn't let them see how badly I'd been startled.

"So, as a rule, I don't keep fake flowers here, so I think I'll have to go to the store to do another video, but off the top of my head, clematis, some dyed roses, ooh, and delphinium." I nodded, picturing it in my head. "And I'd accent it with blue senecio and solidago. Those would be fake, of course, but a little bit is okay." I turned to Constantine. "What about you? Do you have flowers you like?"

He shrugged and shook his head. "Roses? I guess, I don't know. No, not really."

"Oh! Remind me to take you to go see my bat flower." I

turned to the camera. "I think we'll be taking a field trip soon. That will be my next scheduled live. Okay, we've got to go." I smiled back at Constantine, who waved at them. "See you later, witches." I blew a kiss to the camera and shut it off.

I spun around and relaxed against the island. "And that's how I do it. You were great," I complimented him.

"That was pretty fun," he admitted.

A chirp came from his pants and he pulled his phone out. He unlocked it and frowned. "I have to leave. Are you going to be okay?"

"Yeah, you don't have to stay. You've got your own life now. I don't control you."

Constantine reached for me. "Eisley, stop worrying. I'll be back. Here, take my number."

We exchanged contacts, and it relaxed my nerves. "See." He waved his phone as he walked to the door and slid his boots on. "I'm only a call away."

After he left, I finished my laundry and remade my bed. I stared at it for a long time, recalling the night before. I finally did it. I'd had sex. I'd had an orgasm. I now understood why people liked it so much. Sure, I'd let Kansas touch me, and we kissed a lot, but I'd never let it go this far before, and...

I wondered what he'd think about everything. Constantine being alive, the scars being the same, us having sex!

My mind was driving me nuts, and eventually, I grabbed my keys with the plan to go to the greenhouse. Some volunteers watered everyone's plants daily, as part of our membership, but it was my private sanctuary away from home, and I wanted to get out and stop obsessing over things. Just then Therese's car zipped into my driveway, and she and Emi leapt out.

"Oh my god, have you seen the news?" Emi cried out.

"No? Why?" My stomach dropped. Images of Constantine and his vintage car speeding down the road plummeted through my brain. I'd just gotten him back; had he been taken from me already?

"My cousin and her friends were just found murdered!" Therese had tears streaming down her face.

"What do you mean?" I asked as I directed them to my living room.

"My cousin, Sam. She's still—" She reached for my tissue box on my coffee table. "Was. She was a senior. She hadn't even graduated yet!"

I sighed and took the seat beside her on the couch. "Calm down, tell me everything."

Emi sniffled. Tears ran down her face, but she got words out better than the others. "They found them in the woods. Well, Sam. The rest were still back at the church."

"What church?"

"You know, the Sinister Minister's church." Emi shrugged. "I know you don't like talking about it, but everyone's been there at least once."

Therese nodded through her crying. "We've had so many ragers there. I made out with Rem for the first time in the basement."

I couldn't help the look of disgust on my face.

"They were murdered!" Therese wailed.

"How do you know?" I asked.

"They were stabbed," Emi said sharply, almost as if I should know this.

Therese dabbed her eyes with the tissue. "You really should get cable, sis."

I patted her thigh and she fell onto my shoulder and continued to sob.

"I'm sorry for your cousin," I said, rubbing her back. "Do they have a suspect?"

"Not yet." Emi shook her head. "My dad said they think it's someone excited about the documentary. You know, wants to give them more to talk about."

I had forgotten that Emi's dad was a police officer. He must have finally decided to try to repair their relationship if they were talking again. "What are they going to do about them, then?"

"They are going to talk to them all now. I think they'll catch him." Emi nodded as if saying it would make it true. Could it be true? Could one of the crew members have killed those teenagers to make for a more interesting story? The girls continued to sob in my living room, and I sat there, not sure how to respond.

My doorbell rang, and I hurried to get up and answer it, grateful for the reprieve. A delivery man with a stack of boxes greeted me on the other side and had me sign for all the cameras I'd bought just yesterday. I moved them into the house and gave the girls a grim smile.

"Well, I guess it's a good thing I bought these yesterday. Sounds like we all need to be a little safer right now if there's a killer on the loose."

"This isn't funny, Eisley!" Therese scolded.

"I wasn't being funny."

"She's right," Emi agreed. "We all need to be more careful. Do you have someone coming to set it up? Spencer did all of ours. I'll call him."

Spencer showed up, and Emi took Therese home.

"Thanks, Spencer." I patted his forearm as he began opening boxes and pulling out security cameras.

"Anytime, Eisley." He beamed. "You know I'm here for you, girl."

"Do you want anything for your work? I could toss you a hundred bucks or something," I offered.

"Nah, I don't want your money. Maybe some cupcakes though?" he asked hopefully.

I grinned. "You got it. I'll go get started now. By the time you're done, they'll be ready."

"Thanks, Eisley, you're the best." He leaned over and planted a kiss on my cheek entirely too close to my lips. I pulled away and hurried out of the room. What the hell was that?

In the kitchen, I put earbuds in and blasted Stevie Nicks, trying to drown out all the sirens going off in my head. Those teens getting murdered were something much more sinister than some random documentary exec trying to get more fame. I focused instead on my double chocolate fudge cupcakes that Spencer always raved about when I brought them to parties. I was frosting the last one when Spencer came into the kitchen looking slightly tired but smiling.

"Job's all done. I left the directions to download the apps and whatnot, but you're good to go. Are those mine?" He licked his lips and reached for a cupcake. Just then, my doorbell rang and we both turned.

"You have a camera for that now." He grinned. Everything about him lately was... uncomfortable, but I couldn't put my finger on why.

"I'll get the app tonight," I assured him as I went to the door and opened it. I blinked as a huge bouquet was thrust into my arms.

"Eisley?" the delivery man asked.

"That's me."

"Here ya go." He handed me an envelope and flew down my steps.

I took the flowers to the kitchen and once I could see them in better light, I froze. Delphiniums, dyed roses, solidago, clematis, senecio, all the things I'd listed this morning. How?

"Who are the flowers from? You got a boyfriend or something?" Spencer asked from behind me.

"I don't know." I opened the envelope, and my hands trembled as I read the note.

I'm cleaning up things for us, Eisley.
It's time to come home.

Rule 23 - Kansas

Put your education to good use.

I leaned against my wall, sitting on my bed, and typed on my tablet while I pressed the phone to my ear. It rang four times before I heard the click.

"Hello?" Eisley greeted me.

"Hey, it's me."

She let out a loud breath of relief. "Kansas, sorry. Things have been really weird here. It's just one thing after another."

"Yeah, I heard about the murders. Four teenagers, right?" I wasn't that interested, but I wanted to see if my skills were as good as I thought. I typed more, and a screen popped up. I scanned the small squares, each labeled with where the cameras were. Doorbell, backyard, front yard, and her kitchen. I squinted, saw something moving, and clicked on *kitchen*. And there she was, little Eisley, pacing and holding the phone to her ear.

"They were all stabbed. I guess it was pretty violent. One girl almost got away, but the guy ran after her."

"Have they made any arrests?"

She shook her head.

I grinned. She had no clue I was watching her.

"Not that I know of. I've been trying to stay updated. My friends text me when they hear stuff. One of the girls was Therese's cousin."

"Which one was that?" I asked, pretending not to remember.

"She's got brown hair and is dating Remington."

"Ah, I remember now. That's unfortunate. Is she doing okay?"

"I don't think they were super close, but she's scared that the killer may have targeted their group specifically."

"Why?" I fought back a smirk. She'd hear it in my voice. I'd looked them up before I called her. Those kids and their families all deserved whatever came to them. Their parents had no problem ruining other families' lives; why should we give two fucks?

"Three of them came from big families. You know the ones," she huffed. Using my thumb and forefinger, I pinched my screen and zoomed in to see her rolling her eyes. "They've got money, so just dropping their name gets them places."

"Like Spencer Foxworth."

"Like Spencer Foxworth." She nodded. "He's one of them, so is Soleil and Therese, and Rem, actually. Hmm..."

"Not your other friend? Emi?"

"Her dad's a police officer, but I think he's like the chief or something. He finally started talking to her again. It was a whole thing. But yeah, Therese is all paranoid that if they don't get the killer soon that she'll be next."

"Why would someone be picking off rich people? I mean, I'm all for eating the rich, but that's more along the lines of public figures. Not Shelley Vale donors."

"I know, right?" She chuckled. "I think it's absurd. Anyways, what's new with you? What are you up to today?"

"Just some studying," I replied, clicking on the other cameras and taking stills. This wasn't my first go-around with this brand of home security. With a few clicks, I turned off her cameras and put the stills in the live feed's place. Now, whenever she looked, all she'd see is an empty porch, yard, and kitchen. "I actually called to see if you got my flowers."

"Those were from you?" she gasped. "How did you—"

"I had a little help from your friend. I reached out to Emi online. She was able to give me exact details."

"They're beautiful. Thank you."

"They are kind of an apology gift. I hate how I left things when I visited."

"Oh?" She left the kitchen, allowing me to grab a photo of the empty room and slide it into place. That one would be trickier, as she was always in her kitchen, but I'd shut down her app or something later.

"Yeah, I was a jackass. I got drunk, pushed myself on you, told you about other people, and then yelled at you because you got a letter from that documentary crew. It was a shitshow."

She laughed. "I wouldn't say it was that bad."

"Well, I want to fix that. I'm cleaning up my act. I'm not going to drink as much, I'm going to focus on school and finish my degree, and then I'm coming back for you. I want to come home."

"Yeah?"

I wished she'd sprung for more cameras to line her house, but she'd only done the major rooms, and whoever set them up wasn't all that great at it. It was all so easy to tap into. I paused, planning my next words carefully. "And I don't plan on dating anymore."

"Kansas, I thought—"

"I only told you about Harper and the others to make you jealous and it worked. It was a dick move, and once I got home, I realized just how bad it was. I don't want to do that anymore. When I get back, I want to give us an honest go. What do you think?"

"Kansas," she sighed. "You know I can't answer that."

"So you'd rather be alone your entire life than be with me?"

"You're getting angry."

I took a deep breath. "Okay. I just thought that maybe you'd take the time and consider it for real this time. We're not kids anymore, Eisley. Eventually, we have to make a decision."

"It sounds like you already have," she said sharply.

"I haven't, but one day, I will. Plain and simple, right now, do you love me?"

"Yes," she whispered after a long pause.

"Then why is this so hard?"

"Because I love him too."

The doorbell rang, and the florist delivered the bouquet of a dozen long stemmed black roses I'd ordered this morning.

Rule 24 - Kansas
Trust your partner.

Ten years ago.

The thick iron door screeched open and light poured into the room.

"Constantine! You're back!" Eisley ran to him, throwing her thin arms around him.

His face lit up as he hugged her back. "I told you I would be."

A Mother came to the door and shoved them back into the room. "Dinner will be brought in soon." She slammed the door, locking the three of us inside once again.

"What's that?" I asked, standing and pointing to the bag over his shoulder. I remembered those. When I was in kindergarten, my mother, my *real* mother, had given me one to take to school. I'd filled it with pictures I'd colored and a paper plate they helped me cut into a mask.

How far away that seemed now. I couldn't even remember my real mother's face. Constantine rolled the bag off his shoulder and showed us.

"One of the Fathers gave me permission to bring it down here. I've got some things."

"Like what?" Eisley stood on her tiptoes and peered at it. He unzipped the bag and pulled out a thin gray blanket. It took up so much space that when he removed it from the bag, I thought that was all that was in it. He handed the blanket and then kept digging.

"I told them we were cold."

"Cold, hungry, bored, hurt," I complained. Eisley glared at me. Over the time we'd been here together, we'd made a rule to not complain, but seeing Constantine getting special privileges made my blood boil.

"Do you think we can all fit under it?" Her brown eyes lit up with hope.

I spread it out and walked to the mattress on the cement floor. I draped it over, and my heart burst with joy as it covered the entire mattress and pooled onto the floor on both sides.

"I've got some other stuff too," Constantine added. We turned back to him, and he began pulling out books. Books!

How to read was the only thing the Mothers and the Fathers taught us here. Which didn't serve us that well as we hardly had the opportunity to use our abilities once they considered us capable. Constantine pulled out two hardcovers and one coloring book and handed them to us.

"These are about plants. What's yours say?" Eisley asked me.

"The Minister's Manual." I struggled to sound out the words. I frowned. "What is this?"

He shrugged. "It was the only way they'd let me bring this other stuff back. They want us to read it."

I gave it back to Constantine. I could barely read the cover, I doubted I'd be able to read whatever was inside.

"Is that all that's in there?" Eisley asked.

"For now, but a Father said if we're good and memorize some of the books, he'll let me bring more stuff down."

"When can we go up there?" I asked.

The door flew open and the Mother from before returned with a milk gallon filled with water and a paper plate with peanut butter sandwiches. She placed them on the floor and pulled out three apples from her large dress pockets.

"The Minister has blessed you; I see." She eyed the books in our hands. "Congratulations."

Over the next few weeks, the three of us pored over the books. Eisley was fascinated by the plant books and spent as much of her time reading and memorizing all the fancy names for things. I took in Constantine's words and began focusing on the other book.

If we wanted to get out, we needed to show the Minister we were good. The next time I saw him, I would recite as much of his manual as I could. I didn't understand most of it, but I knew how to memorize.

One day, as I sat facing a corner, working on a page, Constantine returned from one of his upstairs trips. The door was shut instantly behind him, and he hurried to Eisley, who lay on the bed, staring blankly at the ceiling.

We were being punished again. Eisley had asked for more toilet paper, and one of the Fathers accused us of being wasteful. We hadn't been fed in three days.

"I have something," Constantine whispered. "They let me go outside."

I whirled around. "You went outside?"

Constantine nodded. "It's raining, and the Minister wanted to do a sermon in the rain."

His clothes were drenched, I realized.

"How long were you gone?" Time meant little to us here. And while I hadn't been outside in a long time, I knew that a simple rain couldn't have done that much damage.

Constantine's eyes darkened. "A while. It was thundering when they took me inside. The Fathers and the Minister are still out there."

"You said you have something?" Eisley interrupted. She sat up and eyed him with hope.

I hated how she looked at him every time he came back as if he had a magical key to get us out. Never once was his backpack filled with more than hopes and dreams that could never come true. Constantine dug into his pockets and pulled out fistfuls of yellow flowers. I squinted. I remembered those. They used to pop up in my yard at home.

"Dandelions," Eisley gasped.

"We can eat them." Constantine handed one fist to her and a second to me.

"Go slow," Eisley reminded me. It was another two days before they brought us anything. Thankfully, Constantine had stuffed his pockets with the yellow flowers. While it wasn't filling, I think it made us feel better.

I continued to sound out the long words and try to understand the manual, all while Constantine and Eisley huddled on the bed, so close they were touching, and read the plant books. Suddenly, I felt... angry. Why didn't she ever come and read with me? Why didn't Eisley ever ask me if I could get us out of here?

Sure, Constantine left and brought things back more often than I did, but I was doing what I'd been told, learning the book. Once I knew it all, I could convince them to set us free. Every day, I grew more and more upset over how close she and Constantine were, until finally, one day while Eisley was in the bathroom throwing up water from having drank too much in an attempt to feel full, he approached me.

"Why are you mad?" he asked me.

"You and Eisley are friends, and she doesn't like me," I confessed.

"She likes you." Constantine shook his head. "We're all friends."

"No, she doesn't." I stood and waved the floppy book in his face. "I've been reading and—"

Constantine put his hands on my shoulders, and I stopped talking. His blue eyes bore deep into mine. "I know. Don't tell her."

"But she's going to have to—"

"She won't have to. I'm not going to let that happen. Eisley loves us both. We can share her."

I wanted to believe him, but I knew the truth now. Eventually, the Minister would make her pick between us. That night, after Eisley was done throwing up, and we'd finally been fed, I went into the bathroom and began pulling each page out of the book and flushing it down the toilet. I didn't want her to know what the Minister had planned for us.

Like Eisley, I'd have to trust Constantine.

Rule 25 - Eisley

Don't exploit the victims.

That night, I dreamed about the two different bouquets resting on my kitchen counter. One, simple, pretty, and familiar. The other spectacular, breathtaking, but the note that accompanied it made it menacing. When I woke up the next day, I wanted to throw them out, but they both smelled so good, I couldn't bear to do it.

Emi showed up at my door before I had my first cup of tea. I invited her in, but she refused.

"The cops cleared everyone on the documentary crew of the murders, so everything's back on. I thought that maybe since you are friends *with* the son, you'd change your mind about going. They still need bodies."

"His name is Constantine," I corrected. "And no, I haven't changed my mind."

"He's gonna be there." She wiggled her eyebrows. "I saw the call sheet."

My stomach tightened. And reluctantly, I gave in.

"What time?"

Emi bounced with excitement and came inside. "I need to be there in half an hour. Can you get ready now?"

I wasn't happy about having to turn my kettle off, but I put leaves in a tea infuser and grabbed my titanium cup and headed out the door with her.

Emi drove us to the outskirts of town and to a forest I wasn't familiar with. Cars and large vans lined the road, and I saw people with shirts that said CREW on the back walking around with clipboards and other movie-looking stuff. The moment I stepped out of the car, I felt eyes on me and I wished I'd driven myself. Heat flooded my face as three crew members rushed over.

"Eisley, you came." One of them snatched my hand and shook it vigorously. "It's so nice to finally meet you. I wasn't sure if you got my letter. I'm Francis, one of the interns."

I stared at the young man with curly red hair and a splatter of pimples all over his face so thick I couldn't tell them from his freckles.

"That was you?" I pulled my hand away in disgust.

"Was that not okay?" He seemed genuinely confused.

Emi came over and wrapped her arm around my shoulder. "I brought another body. Does that mean I get the bonus?"

Another crew member nodded and marked something on her clipboard. "You got it. Actually, I think we'll give you a bit extra, for getting Eisley."

Emi started to scowl but then perked up. "Cool." She looked at me and shrugged. "I didn't realize your streaming channel was that famous."

I glanced around the small circle and glared. Francis coughed and reached for Emi's elbow.

"Why don't you go see Kaity in makeup? We can take care of this."

Emi gave me one last look, and I nodded for her to take off. She bounced away, happy as a clam that she'd been given a bonus to get me here.

"So..." Francis clapped his hands together and smiled.

"You read my letter, and you came. I should get you to Dave. He's the director. He's been dying to meet you."

"Dave?" I followed the group into the woods toward a large clearing in the center of their operations. "Are you filming here?" I asked.

Francis's smile stretched into a thin line. "Unfortunately. We were going to film in the actual forest where the Sinister Minister's church was. We got approval from the town and everything to go in and explore it, but then those teens getting murdered turned it into a crime scene and we can't get in."

"It was always a crime scene," I retorted.

His head jerked, and he shrunk into himself. "Of course, I'm so sorry. I should have realized... that was stupid of me, I'm so sorry."

"What's the problem?" A large, muscular arm slid around my waist and a cologne I had just recently become acquainted with in an intimate way wafted up to my nose. I clung closer to Constantine as he glared down at the pimple-faced intern.

"It was a slip of the tongue. I don't mean to make light of what you two—"

"We're not talking about this openly." Constantine shut him down. "Where were you taking her?"

"To go see Dave, sir. He'll want to be the one to interview her."

"I'll join you." Constantine squeezed me gently.

Francis took us over to a man who reminded me of Steve Jobs with his glasses and white hair. He lit up when he saw us. "We got both of you?"

"Maybe," I warned him. "I only came to see what exactly was going on."

Dave, the director, nodded. "Totally understandable. Well, today we're just doing some reenactments of the Sinister Minister's original abductions. When he would go to bus stops and find young, beautiful women and kidnap them. The ones that he'd end up calling the Mothers." His eyes lit up far too much for me to be comfortable.

"I know the story." I looked at the ground uncomfortably.

"Yes, I'm sure you do." He waved his arm toward a trailer. "Why don't we go inside and have a more private talk?"

I pulled myself from Constantine, but not too far, and together, we went inside the trailer. We were offered water and muffins, but we declined.

"Now yours and Constantine's roles are slightly different in this," Dave started once we sat down. "Firstly, we want to interview you. I have a list of questions, but also want to give you the opportunity to tell your truth."

"You want to exploit us," I clarified.

"Exploit?" The man laughed as if that were incredulous. "We are going to pay you."

"Neither of us needs your money." Constantine sighed lazily. He leaned back and crossed his legs and put his arm over my shoulder. "We want to know why you're really here."

"What do you mean?" Dave shook his head. "The Sinister Minister was one of the country's most monstrous cult leaders and child sex traffickers. People want to hear that story. His victims should be heard. You should be heard."

"Who else have you reached out to? Have you gotten permission from the other victim's families?" I asked quickly.

"How?" Dave laughed. "The only records we have are from the Sinister Minister himself, and they only have first names. All of his victims, except the final ones, were cremated by the Church. There's no way to find any family."

"How did you find me?" My eyes began to blur. "And Kansas? How did you find him?"

Dave laughed and patted his thighs. "Pure stroke of luck. I was digging through records Shelley Vale has and there was a police record about two children who emerged from the woods and told a fantastical story about a church and the Family. They were put into foster care, as they couldn't find their parents. It named you two."

"I've changed my mind. I want to go." I stood quickly, and Constantine joined me.

"I'll take you home," he said.

"Wait!" Dave threw up his hand. "Don't you want to know what else I found?"

I turned my head and glared. "What?"

"I found your parents."

Rule 26 - Eisley

Stay away from anyone making a film.

"What?" I froze. My biological parents? He found them?

"What do you want, piggy?" Constantine snarled.

"Piggy?" Dave stood up and put his hands on his hips.

"Yeah." Constantine pulled out his pocket knife and flicked it open. He pressed the tip to the director's chin. "You don't think I won't stick you like one for pulling this shit? If you got information to share, you better fucking share it."

"I'll tell you everything I know if you just sit down and answer some questions in front of the camera for me."

"You really want to make deals right now?" My husband slid the knife under his chin, pressing against his neck.

Dave smirked. "It's worth a shot. What do you say, Eisley?"

"How do I know you're not bluffing?"

"How about this, if you answer a question of mine, I'll answer one of yours, and then at the end, you can have the entire file I have on your family."

"Deal."

Constantine pulled the knife back and gave me a look that sent a ripple of stutters through my heart. "Are you sure?"

"I have to know."

He stepped aside and let me follow Dave out and over to hair and makeup. I saw Emi, Therese, and the others a distance away, listening to someone with a clipboard. They were covered in fake blood and had changed into neon colors, acid-washed jeans, and fanny packs.

"They're reenacting some of his first captives," the makeup artist explained. I had questions, but I was unsure of how much the crew knew about my history, and I didn't want to reveal any more to them.

"Did they get anyone to be the Minister?" another stylist came over and asked.

"No, not that I know of yet. They're still looking. They asked his son, but he said no."

I glared. Who in their right mind would think someone would agree to that? Constantine snickered, seeing my face, but said nothing. He simply stood like a bodyguard, an arm's length away, protecting me. Despite this being only the second time seeing him as an adult, the feelings of safety and home were still there, right at the forefront of my mind. He had been my protector then, and he was my protector now. An hour later, both of us were seated in a trailer that had been rearranged to do interviews.

"We had a deal," I reminded Dave.

"Yes." He tapped his tablet. "I've got it here. Are you ready?"

I glanced over at Constantine, who was watching me intently. I knew if I needed to stop, he'd defend me. "Let's go." Someone snapped the cut prop and they counted down.

"Tell us about the Minister, Eisley."

"He was tall, slim. Dark hair, blue eyes. Very blue eyes."

"We know what he looked like, but what was he like in person?"

"He was very intimidating. Everything he said was taken as the word of god himself. If he decided something, that was it."

"Did he make a lot of decisions?"

"He made all the decisions."

There was a pause, and he called cut. "Good, your eyes..." He gave me a thumbs-up that made my stomach roll. Did he think I was acting? I wiped my clammy palms on my dress. "Now, what would you like to know about your parents?"

"Their names," I blurted.

"Gael and Leah."

"Last name?" I rolled my eyes.

"Rosales. Congratulations, you're Hispanic."

My last name was Rosales. Eisley Rosales. I'd already assumed the Latino part, considering my skin tone and other physical tells, but the last name? I'd had no clue. They turned the cameras back on and we kept going.

"Were you ever told about what the Sinister Minister was doing in the room under his office?"

My eyes flicked to Constantine. That room was the last time I'd seen him before a few days ago. It was the room I thought he'd died in. "No. I didn't know the full details until after the news came out."

"So, you were never sexually abused by the Sinister Minister?"

I shook my head.

"But the other kids were?"

"I didn't know there were other kids," I answered. "I mean, I'd heard of others, but I never saw them."

"Jame Blackwood kidnapped over eighty-five children during his career and either sold them, abused them, or killed them all under the guise that he was just working his ministry. You never saw any of that?" Dave stared at me skeptically.

"I didn't say that. I said I didn't see the other kids."

"So, you were abused."

My stomach tightened, and I lowered my head to stare at my lap. "I was."

"Was it sexual in nature?"

"I don't think so," I answered honestly. "He never touched me. Nor did anyone, you know, like that."

"What other forms of abuse did he use?"

I steeled myself. This wasn't the first time I'd been forced to tell my story. Why was it so hard? "I want another answer."

"Go ahead."

"Where are they from?"

"You were kidnapped from Sherwood, Ohio. Your parents were born and raised there."

I took a sip of water and nodded. Shelley Vale, Michigan, was above Ohio. He hadn't had to travel too far to take me.

"I was starved a lot. That was their most common punishment other than being locked in the room. That was a given. Most of the time, I didn't bathe or change my clothes. I was only given new ones when I grew too much for them to fit."

"What did they feed you?"

"Sandwiches. Sometimes fruit. Apples were common. Boiled eggs or something warm like oatmeal, too, during the winter."

"How did you know it was winter down in the basement?"

"They'd tell us." I nodded solemnly. "We would get cold and shiver and then eventually they'd give us a blanket and warn us that it'd be taken come summer."

"You're saying *we* a lot. Was there someone else in the room?"

My eyes twitched, but I forced them not to look at Constantine and give it away.

"Sometimes. My turn. Do I have any siblings?"

"Unfortunately, no. You are the only child of the Rosales's."

I wasn't sure if I was happy or sad about that.

"Can you tell me anything about the children you shared a room with?" he asked.

"No," I replied firmly. "That's not my story to tell."

Dave was clearly irritated by my response, but that didn't deter him. We kept going for another hour, back and forth until finally, he said he was done for today.

"Do you have any more questions before I email this file to you?" he asked me.

"Where are my parents now?" I asked, my heart soaring with excitement. Could I finally get to meet the people I lost so long ago?

"In the Sherwood Cemetery. Matching plots. They died when you were nine."

Rule 27 - Constantine

Look for distractions.

"Fuck him!"

I followed behind Eisley as she stormed through the set, waving a check in the air. The girl who she drove in with hurried over. Her red hair had been covered with a plain black wig and she'd changed into a bright tracksuit. The reenactment actors were dressed similarly.

"Eisley, are you okay?" She reached for her friend.

"I'm fine," Eisley shot back. "I'm leaving. I knew this was a bad idea, Emi."

"What happened in there?" Emi looked at me and glared.

I almost laughed. Fuck her. I wasn't the asshole here.

"I-I don't want to talk about it."

"What's that?" Emi reached for the paper in Eisley's grip.

"I'm leaving." Eisley stepped back and looked at me for assistance. I slid my hand around her middle.

"I'll take her home."

Emi scowled. "I don't feel comfortable letting the son of a murderer take my friend home."

I blinked. "I don't feel comfortable letting my girl drive around with someone who laughs about the murders."

"I'll be fine. I've got to go." Eisley turned and together we went to my car and quickly sped off, away from the set.

"Do you wanna talk about it?" I asked.

"I can't fucking believe him." She shook her head and stared at her phone. "He led me on, thinking I was going to meet them one day, all the while he knew. All to get me to talk."

I stayed silent, letting her vent. Dave was a piggy. Piggies get stuck. "How much did he give you?"

She laughed dryly. "For my pain? Seven hundred and fifty dollars."

"It was probably all he had in his account."

"What a twisted fuck." She waved the check. "He thinks this is anything? I can make this in a few hours by flirting with some dudes online."

My face muscles twitched with irritation at the thought. I forced myself to focus on something else.

"What are you gonna do with it?"

"I don't know. Cash it now before he stops it. You have a pen?"

I pointed to the passenger's compartment and she quickly found what she was looking for and signed the check and began uploading it to the bank app on her phone. "Done. I should go shopping."

"When I get dumb money like that, I go get a tattoo," I joked.

"A tattoo?" She blinked. "I've always wanted one, but never had anyone to go with."

I grinned. "You want to go get one? You'd look fucking sexy with one."

She blushed and pushed her hair behind her ear. "You think?"

I bit down on my lip as my cock throbbed, just imagining her covered in ink. "Yeah, I know a guy around here. Let me call him." We paused for me to set up the appointment, and then an hour later we pulled into the shop and I introduced her to Boogie.

"Eisley, this is Boogie, he's done a bunch of my stuff." I explained. "Thanks for getting her in, bro."

Boogie stuck his hand out. "Nice to meet you. Me and Constantine went to school together. What are we doing for you today?"

Eisley pressed her lips together. We'd tossed out some ideas on the drive, but she didn't seem committed to anything. She looked up at me. "What do you think?"

"That's up to you, princess."

"Mmm, what if I did something like the one you have?"

My eyebrows rose. "Like what?"

She poked the space between my shoulder socket and chest. "That one."

"My moth?" I grinned. "That would be hot."

Boogie looked at me. "Let me see."

I lifted my t-shirt to show him the death's head moth tilted so its head pointed into my shoulder.

"Rad. I can totally do that. Same place?" he asked her.

"Yes, please."

Boogie took us to the back and let us sit while he prepped the stencil and his station.

"Good thing you wore a skirt today, instead of a dress," I teased.

She blinked and looked at the full-body mirror on the wall and frowned. "How is he going to..."

I stood and went behind her, my hands finding the bottom of her shirt. I began raising it slowly, my fingers grazing her soft skin as I went. I paused right at the edge of her bra and leaned in to whisper into her ear. "You're gonna have to show some skin, princess."

Her breathing hitched and her brown eyes flicked to mine

in the mirror. I pulled away as Boogie returned with the stencil in hand.

"Ready?"

Eisley nodded and returned to the chair. Slowly, she pulled off her shirt, revealing the black lacy bra she was wearing to be see-through. We could see her nipples through the fabric. Now that the cold had touched them, they were poking through. Eisley blushed.

"I have pasties," Boogie offered.

"Nah, let her squirm." I looked at Eisley and she didn't protest. She knew better.

Good girl.

Boogie slid down the strap that would cover the space he'd be working and pressed the stencil to her skin.

"I've never gotten a tattoo before," she admitted to him.

"I get to be your first!" He laughed and looked my way. I wasn't laughing back, and he quickly moved on. Once the stencil was placed, he finished prepping and then reached for his machine.

"Ready? You have to remain still."

Eisley took a deep breath and looked over at me. "Yep."

The machine buzzed to life, and he pressed it against her shoulder. She gasped but didn't wiggle or jerk away. I reached for her hand, and she squeezed.

"What's your favorite movie?" I asked.

"Spooky or not?"

"Either."

"*The Strangers*."

"And your non-spooky movie?" I raised an eyebrow.

"There is none." She grinned.

"Why do you like that movie so much?"

She relaxed as I stroked her hand with my thumb and closed her eyes. "The idea of a masked man coming in and tying me up, making me completely vulnerable to whatever he wants to do with me…" Her lips let out a small moan and then her eyes popped open. She looked over at Boogie, who was doing his best to ignore us.

"It's okay." I chuckled. "You can tell me all about your wildest fantasies. You like being tied up?"

"I don't know. That's all fictional. None of that ever happens in real life."

It could be.

"I think you underestimate a man's desire to please his woman." I reached up and ran my thumb over the tip of her nipple. "Like right now, I'd do anything to spread your thighs and eat your pussy while he works, right here, right now."

"Stop," she gasped.

"Why? You afraid he'll know how wet you're getting in his chair? I don't think he'd care." I ran my hand along the inside of her thigh. "You want to come, princess?"

Rule 28 - Constantine

Let the dog live.

"Will you fucking stop?" Boogie took his foot off the pedal and sat up.

We both turned our heads to see the tattoo artist scowling. "You're making her squirm."

"Well, I guess that answers that." I leaned back, satisfied that she was left flustered. It'd pay off later. I sat back and let my friend tattoo my wife in peace.

When Boogie had finished, she was hesitant to slip her shirt back on, afraid to irritate the sore skin.

"Here." I reached for the shirt and pulled out my knife. Quickly, I cut the sleeves and tore them off.

"Hey! Oh," she said as I shoved it over her head and helped her put her arm in the new larger hole. "Ah, it stings."

I chuckled. "It will for a few weeks."

We checked out, and I thanked Boogie by tipping him well.

"You want to get a drink or something?" I asked Eisley after we left.

"I could go for something." We went to the bar from the other night. This pathetic little town didn't have many options. We walked in with my hand around her waist and went straight to the bar, paying no attention to the booths behind us. We were handed our bottles when we both heard something that made us stop talking and listen.

"I can't believe it. I mean, I do, now. But, like, who would have guessed?" a female gasped.

"I could have. She's weird. No wonder she doesn't date anyone."

"Who wants to bet they knew each other in there?"

I recognized the last voice. It was her friend with the fake red hair. Emi. The look on Eisley's face told me she recognized all three women's voices.

"I should kick his ass," a man said. "He had no right to show his fucking face. It's probably triggering her PTSD or whatever."

"Or, hear me out," a woman said. "All the cameras were rolling when she threw a fit today. What if this is all some stunt? She's being over the top for the movie. You saw the check. She's getting paid."

"She is a cam girl," a man reminded the group.

"Not like that," the first man, the angry one, defended. "We need to do something about her and that guy."

"Just let them be. If she wants to be a little whore for the cameras, let her." A girl laughed and then everyone followed. For the next few minutes, they continued to drag Eisley. Eisley sat frozen with her hands in her lap, listening to every word.

"You want me to say something?" I asked softly.

"No, don't. I want to go." She slid off her stool, leaving the untouched beer at her spot.

I quickly tossed a few bills down and stood with her. I looked around for the table her friends sat at, but the booths had tall walls and they must have been on the other side. It wasn't busy, so it was easy to hear, despite not seeing them.

"Eisley?" We turned to see one of her friends, standing by the bar. "You guys leaving?"

"Yeah, see you around, Spencer." She kept her head down.

"Woah, is that a tattoo?" Spencer Foxworth, I realized, the one oozing money, stormed over and grabbed her shirt, peeling it away to reveal her shoulder. "When did you do this?" His expression was shocked and then angry. I shoved him back.

"I don't think she wants you touching her."

"Who the fuck are you?" He glared at me and then at Eisley. "Did he make you do this? You got a tattoo?"

"Why does it matter?"

"It matters because—" He stopped when the natural redhead came over.

"Eis? Oh, and you. What are you two doing here?" She put on a fake smile.

"We're leaving," Eisley snapped.

"Why? Come sit with us." The pretend friend grinned.

"This jackass branded her," Spencer snapped. "Look."

"A tattoo?" The girl raised an eyebrow. "Well, okay. Pop off, queen. We're going back to the table. Join us if you want." She looped her arm through Spencer's and pulled him away.

Eisley didn't speak the entire car ride home. She got out, thanked me, and went inside without so much as a goodbye or invite inside. I sat for a moment before pulling out and deciding my plans for the evening.

A quick search told me that Spencer Foxworth owned a house in a much more upscale part of town. No surprise there. I parked a few blocks away, grabbed my backpack from the back-seat, and walked over. He had no neighbors and the unlocked windows throughout his house told me just how confident he was about his life. I walked through the entire length of his home, and not a single window was locked, but his bedroom door was.

I found a large dog in his living room. I offered the St. Bernard a treat from the bowl in the kitchen I'd seen before I got to him, and he gladly cuddled up to me. While he chewed on his biscuit, I slid my mask on and took the knife from my bag. Together, we waited on the couch for Spencer to return home. Around midnight lights flashed in the windows and I hurried to find a dark spot to surprise him from. The front door opened, and he called for the dog.

"Rudy! I'm home!" The dog came running, vibrating the house as he did. Spencer shut the door. "Good dog. Did you miss me? You gotta go potty?"

The slur in his speech and the stumble in his walk made me question his sobriety. Did he drive home drunk? More reason to kill him tonight. I watched from my spot as Spencer stumbled to the back of the house, letting the dog outside. He closed the door behind him and returned to the living room, looking lost.

I gripped my knife and cracked my neck. He looked like he was a runner. He began flicking on lights. With no dog to give me away, I followed behind and, just for fun, I flipped them all back off. He was so drunk he didn't notice.

"Ugh, my phone is dead." He groaned as he started up the stairs, where the locked room was. I wondered what was in there for him to feel the need to keep private. Was he into hard-core shit? He seemed so vanilla.

He struggled with his keys, but finally managed to get it open, and then promptly turned and went the other way. I waited and then hurried into his room and froze.

What the fuck?

"Who the fuck are you?" I spun around and raised my knife. Spencer glared at me, and then his eyes flicked around the room in a panic. "Get the fuck out."

The balls on this motherfucker after what I just saw.

I cocked my head to the side and slowly shook my head. He eyed my knife and backed away.

"Is this a joke? Did Soleil send you to scare me? Where's the rest of your costume?"

I shook my head again and stepped forward. He turned and sprinted out of the room.

Knowing I'd catch him, I didn't bother running after. I'd save the cardio for later.

"Fuck!" he screamed from the kitchen. The dog began barking from outside as his owner was panicking inside. "Will you shut the fuck up?" he screamed at the dog.

Yells at dogs. Another red flag.

I slowly crept up behind him and raised my knife. With one quick motion, I plunged the knife into his back. It made a deliciously wet, slicing sound and he fell over. He screamed and spun around, swinging his fist.

I leaned away and swung again, sticking the knife deep into his shoulder. It came out easy, and he fell to the ground. He struggled to his feet, his arm now limp at his sides.

"Do you know who I am?" He began fumbling with the drawers, pulling them out and letting them fall to the floor. Knowing he wasn't getting away, I let him find a knife and point it at me. "Ha!" He grinned. "It's your turn to run, fucking Ghostface. You think just because your face is covered, you're safe? I know who you are." He'd fallen against the counter and was struggling for breath.

"You're one of her other guys, aren't you? You're fighting the wrong man," he cried as I came toward him to finish this. "I love her. We need to kill—"

"Constantine?" I asked. The image of what was in his bedroom sprang to my mind.

He nodded.

And I slid the knife against his throat.

Rule 29 - Eisley

Watch who sells you out first.

Badflower played in my ears as I pruned my garden in the greenhouse the next morning.

I was considering Emi's suggestion to use my money for a mini greenhouse at home. I glanced over at her plot where her pumpkins were thriving. I didn't want to see her right now. I didn't want to see any of my friends after hearing what they thought of me last night.

So what if I spoke to men on the internet for money? Slut-shaming was so over, and even then, I wasn't doing hardcore pornography. Not that I hadn't considered it. I'd been offered money to do so. There was one user specifically, *FarawayFox*, that had offered extravagant amounts of cash, but I hadn't.

What would Constantine think if I decided to?

My brain got lost in thoughts of him, naked, on top of me. Despite it only being two days ago, it felt like ages. The soreness was mostly gone. Would it feel even better now?

His voice in my head, growling the word *wife* sent a shiver of excitement through me, causing me to reach for my phone. I pulled it out to message him when I had missed calls from...

everyone. Not sure who to call first, I chose Therese, as she was the last to call.

"Hello?"

"Oh, my God. Eisley!" Therese screamed and then began to sob.

"What's wrong?" My gut tightened instantly. Was Emi hurt?

"Spencer's dead!"

What?

"You need to get over here. They're about to remove his body."

"From where?" I was already running out of the greenhouse and to my car.

"His house. Oh my god," she continued to sob.

"I'm coming. I'll be there soon." I hung up and floored the gas.

A twenty-minute drive took twelve. There were a dozen cars already lined on the side of the road, leading to Spencer's ridiculously large house, along with a mix of police cars. I parked behind Rem's truck and hurried to find the crew. Therese was wrapped in Rem's arms, Micah was standing still, watching the house, while Emi sat in the grass with an inconsolable Soleil, holding onto Rudy, Spencer's St. Bernard.

"What exactly happened? When?" I asked the men.

"No one knows much. Soleil found him in the kitchen. His throat was cut."

I covered my face with my hands. I couldn't hear that. I thought back to last night. I never could have imagined it'd be the last time I saw him. I'd been so hurt over what my friends had said about me, but now it all seemed so unimportant. Our friend was dead.

Police were draping the yard in yellow tape and shoving the growing crowd back. Shelley Vale was small, so I had no doubt the entire town knew about what had happened. I crossed my arms and watched the scene unfold. Spencer's name was on almost everything. The parks, the sports teams, every event our town had, the Foxworths were donors. This was bigger than those four teens in the woods.

Spencer's parents and siblings showed up. They looked more angry than grieving. They spoke to the police and tried to enter, but they refused to let them through. Mr. Foxworth then got on the phone, yelled at whoever was on the other line, and was eventually allowed inside.

"Why haven't the coroners gotten here?" I sniffled. I didn't want to see him like that, but it felt cruel for his body to still be stuck inside.

"Construction and a car accident." Emi stood, leaving Soleil for a moment. "My dad said it's pretty bad. They don't know when someone's going to come."

Micah swore. "This is so fucked up! First those kids, and now Spencer? It's a pattern!"

"Will you shut the fuck up?" Rem hissed. I was about to ask what exactly Micah was insinuating when a police officer came over to our group.

"Are you Eisley Doe?"

"Yes."

"I'd like to talk to you if that's okay?"

"Sure." I followed him down to where we were hidden from everyone's direct view. He pulled out a notebook.

"You were friends with the deceased?"

"Yeah, so was everyone else I was just standing with."

He nodded. "And did you have any relationship beyond friendship with Mr. Foxworth?"

"No? Why, did someone tell you that? Soleil is one of my best friends. I'd never."

"So, you were attracted to him. You just didn't want his girlfriend to know."

I opened and closed my mouth. What?

"I was never interested in Spencer Foxworth romantically."

"Because of his girlfriend."

"No!" I stepped away from the officer. "Because I wasn't interested period. What is your problem?"

"My problem, miss, is that I have a dead man from a very powerful family and you are getting defensive. If you don't want to talk here, why don't we go down to the station and chat?"

"I don't understand why I'm being singled out. I had nothing to do with Spencer's murder."

"You think he was murdered?" He cocked his head.

"He was stabbed!" I screamed.

"All right." He reached for his handcuffs. "We're gonna take you downtown to talk privately."

"I don't need fucking handcuffs. I'll drive myself." I stalked away.

"An officer is going to follow you!" he shouted after me.

I passed by my friends, who were as confused as I was. Rem and Micah were throwing questions at me, but the girls all sat huddled together, with Rudy, glaring daggers. Did Soleil and the others think I had anything to do with this? Why?

An officer followed behind me with his lights on, to the station. It was mortifying, but by the time I arrived, I was more pissed off than embarrassed. I sat in a room with a table and waited for them to come in.

"We've been told you are a sex worker. You've got your own website and large clientele." A different officer came in with a clipboard and opened his interview without even a hello.

"What I do online is not illegal."

"Not online, no. Although if you were offering your services offline, they would be."

"You are correct, and that has never happened."

"If there's feelings involved, naturally that line would be blurred."

"What are you talking about? What does this have to do with Spencer?"

"Have you ever been inside Mr. Foxworth's home?"

I nodded sarcastically. "Tons of times. As his friend."

"And as his friend, you're comfortable with his bedroom decor?"

"I've never been in his bedroom."

The officer raised his eyebrows. "I find that hard to believe." He pulled something from his clipboard and handed a photo to me.

"What is this?"

It seemed to be a... shrine. With my photos all over it. Flowers and other spooky things that you'd find in my house adorned the shelves, framing a dozen or more photos of me.

"This is Spencer Foxworth's bedroom. Now, tell us again about your relationship with the deceased."

Rule 30 - Eisley

Don't accuse anyone unless you have proof.

"I have no fucking clue what's going on. At all." I shoved the photo away from me.

"I do." Another officer came in, this one, a black woman. "I've just finished talking with his girlfriend. Did you know that Mr. Foxworth was one of your Johns?"

I shook my head. "No, he wasn't. That's absurd."

"Is it?" She was harsher than the other officers, who hadn't been nice either. "Because Soleil Walton gave us his account information and we were able to get into your website right from our phones to confirm. Not only is he a regular visitor, he's the biggest client you have. *FarawayFox*."

FarawayFox was Spencer? "Why? I don't understand."

"His girlfriend says he was obsessed with you. He was sending you gifts and money whenever you asked."

"I didn't know that," I told her honestly. "No one ever told me."

"I find that hard to believe that you spent so much time with the couple that you never caught on to his feelings for you, or his username."

I sat back, stunned. "Fox is a pretty common word for usernames," I said sharply. "But I mean, sure, he got a little handsy and weird sometimes. He'd offer to do things for me, but I never thought it was anything more than just friendship."

"Ms. Walton told us that they fought last night. He was mad that you had gotten a tattoo and wanted to cut you off. She told him he had to tell you the truth. Now, we're working on getting his phone turned back on, and the moment it's running, we're gonna see who he last spoke to before he died. Will your name be on his recent calls list?"

"No!" I bolted out of my chair. "I had nothing to do with his death. Now, unless you're arresting me, I want to leave. And if I am getting arrested, I want a fucking lawyer." They grew quiet and left a moment later. They returned twenty long minutes later and released me.

I stormed out of the station and sped home, furious. There were figures on my porch. I stormed up the stairs and swung my arm out into my yard at my friends.

"Fuck off, every single one of you. Get out of here."

Therese stepped toward me. "Eisley, we just want to explain. Soleil's just upset. You can't be mad at her."

"For accusing me of murdering my friend?"

"We know you didn't," Rem offered. "Therese is right. Soleil's just pissed and scared. Hell, we're all scared. I mean, it's weird, isn't it?"

"What is?" A million thoughts ran through my head. Weird that he was a client? Weird that his girlfriend knew about it. The fucking shrine he had of me in his bedroom? Micah came forward.

"That four teens from families with good names were stabbed and now Spencer? I mean, come on now. We're being targeted."

"We are?" I laughed and pointed to my chest. "I ain't shit.

I don't even have a last name, let alone one with status. Sounds like a *you* problem."

"Wow." Emi shook her head. "Since when did you become such a bitch?"

"Since I listened to my friends talk shit about me for ten minutes because of my past. Sorry if I don't feel bad you had a good childhood. Poor you."

"We should go." Therese tugged on Rem's sleeve and glared at me. "I hope whoever the killer is doesn't come for you next."

"It's probably her creepy boyfriend," Emi said, following the group down the stairs.

"Feel free to give the police more proof of that. You know, like Soleil did for me." I flipped them off as they left and then I went inside, slamming the door behind me. I fell back against it and then, only then, did I let myself cry for my friend's death. I crumpled to the floor and sobbed.

Spencer was gone. He was an asshole, but did he deserve to die?

I sobbed until my voice was hoarse and then I got up and went to my kitchen, where I reached for my bottle of rum. I drank straight from the bottle, and my vision grew more and more blurry with each swig. My phone began to vibrate in my pocket, and I pulled it out. It was a text from Therese.

Look, everyone's upset and angry. We all went home separately, but we'll try to talk like adults in a few days. Just give Soleil some space.

I text back.

> Fine by me. She knows where to find me when she's ready to apologize for accusing me of murdering her boyfriend.

A moment later, I received a call. I clicked on Therese's face.

"That's fucked up," she immediately said. "He was your friend too."

"She sure as hell doesn't seem to think so." I looked at the bottle on my counter. "I'm drunk. I need to go."

"I thought you weren't supposed to drink. You know..."

I hiccupped. I bit back the urge to tell her I'd stopped taking them. She'd only use it against me. "I'm fine without them."

"Well, we're having a party to honor Spencer after the funeral. I think Soleil said Friday afternoon for the service. Will you be there?" She asked.

"Am I welcome?"

"Of course. She held the phone away, mumbled something, and then returned to the call. "Of course. I know it's a little weird with the whole obsession thing, but we've talked to Soleil and his family, and they think you should be there."

"Can I bring someone?" My mind drifted to Constantine. I wanted him here with me right now.

"Sure, actually that'd probably look better. Yes, bring your tattooed boo, okay?" She was slipping back into the friend I knew and loved. She didn't believe I had anything to do with his death. We hung up, and still grieving, I swaggered to the living room with my bottle of rum. I pulled out my tablet and logged into my website and clicked on *FarawayFox*'s name.

I went through every message, looking for a hint that it was Spencer. We'd been chatting for over a year. He'd been my biggest client and my most eager one. He'd offered me the world, just to get naked, but each time I refused. I was grateful I hadn't done it.

The sun was going down, as was the alcohol left in my bottle. A knock sounded on my door. I wobbled to it and opened the door. Soleil, looking as drunk as I was, stood in front of me.

"I hate you, you know that, right?" she sputtered.

"I'm not loving you right now either."

She pushed herself inside and went to my couch, falling into it. "You're the only one I can mourn with. So come over so I can yell at you while I cry."

I closed the door softly and went to sit with her. Over the next hour, I did as told. I listened to her explain everything. How she found a picture of me on his dresser, and then caught him subscribing to my website. They later made a deal that if she could see everything, it was okay.

"What was up with the shrine?" I asked, after a few drinks.

"Oh I know, right? I tried to put my picture on it once and he nearly broke up with me. He wanted me to get you to do a threesome. I was going to try because you know, I loved the fucking bastard."

"If it means anything, I would have turned you down." I hugged her tightly, and we cried together.

"Yeah, because you've got that fucking hot as all-get-out new guy. I got wet just watching him drink his beer."

"Soleil!" I laughed through my tears.

"It's true. I imagined him the other night while blowing Spencer. Is his dick big?"

I blushed, and she kept going.

"Do you choke when you suck him off or is it like baby corn?" She giggled, which caused me to burst into laughter as well.

"I love drunk Eisley," she sighed. "It's been forever since we've done this. Are you not taking those meds anymore?"

I opened my mouth but a knock on my door interrupted our bonding tears, and I got up to answer. I opened the door, and a bouquet was thrust into my face.

"Eisley?"

I stepped back, thanked the man, and closed the door. I went back to the living room and sat the vase down. Another perfect bouquet. With the delphiniums and senecio. Suddenly, the air in the room changed. I glanced at Soleil and saw rage.

"You got flowers for *my* boyfriend dying?"

Rule 31 - Constantine

Learn how to be a good liar.

I pulled into her driveway, and she came out, dressed more modestly than usual. A black dress with sheer lace sleeves that went to her wrists and the neckline to her chin.

"You look good in black," Eisley said as I stepped out of my car and went around to open her door. "Is that a tailored suit?"

"It is. I brought it in case I needed it for the documentary."

"Well, good thing, I guess."

"How do you feel?" I asked her as we drove to Spencer's funeral.

"Like the mistress." She snickered.

"Soleil said it was okay, and his mom came over yesterday and asked me to come, but it still feels wrong."

"You had no idea it was him behind the screen."

"Yeah, but like, it was a lot of money. Money that he should have been using to get married and start a family with Soleil."

"Well, it's kind of a good thing he didn't know, don't you think?"

She glared at me. "That's not funny."

"I'm just saying. If he'd spent the money like you wished he had, Soleil would be a widow and a single mother."

"Yeah, I guess."

We pulled into the long line leading to the high school. Spencer's funeral would be so highly attended, they couldn't host it at the town's funeral home. He was a Foxworth, after all.

We were greeted by her friends, Micah and Rem. It took everything not to smirk at their suits. Despite them too coming from families as old and rich as Spencer's, their suits were off the rack and fit as so. My vanity was coming out, admiring my tailored clothes in one of the glass trophy cabinets as we walked to the auditorium.

"I just want to sit near the back," Eisley said, but that idea was squashed the moment we tried to sit and a middle-aged woman caught us.

"Eisley! Oh please, don't sit there. Sit with us." She scuttled to us and threw her arms around my wife. "I'm so glad you came."

"Hi, Mrs. Foxworth." Eisley patted the woman's back and eyed me nervously. "How are you holding up?"

"As best as I can dear." She sniffled and her shoulders seemed to cave in from heavy sorrow. She dabbed a handkerchief to her bloodshot eyes, and glanced my way. "And who is this?"

I pulled my hand from my pocket and offered it to her. "Constantine Blackwood."

She blinked rapidly and then squinted. She was looking for my father in my face. Unfortunately, she didn't have to search hard.

"You're the son." She gasped.

"I am."

"Welcome. Thank you for attending my son's service. How did you know Spencer?"

"I didn't. I'm here to support Eisley." I was surprised that she didn't want me gone. Did she know what I knew about her family? If she did, she wouldn't want me here.

"Oh? Are you friends?" She smiled nervously at Eisley and took my hand, shaking it firmly.

Eisley blushed and looked down at her stilettos. "Um—"

"She's my wife."

"Wife!" Mrs. Foxworth exclaimed and dropped my hand as if it were fire. She paled and pressed her hand to her chest. We were joined by Soleil, the natural redhead. She put her hand on Mrs. Foxworth's back.

"Is everything okay, Lorraine?"

"Eisley has a husband. Did you know this?" she asked Soleil. Her surprise shifted to anger at her almost daughter-in-law. Her tone almost accusatory.

Soleil blinked. "What? Who? Him?" Her head swiveled from Eisley and me. "When?" Her speech slurred and I could smell the alcohol on her. Her eyes drooped and she was slouching, despite trying to hide it.

I pulled my wife to me and stared Spencer's stupid rich bitch girlfriend down. "It was so long ago, I can't remember. Can you, sweetie?"

"I'd rather not talk about it today. We're here to honor Spencer. I'd like to pay my respects."

Lorraine sniffled and then burst into tears, startling all of us. She threw her arms around Eisley and then me. I stiffened but relented and pat her back.

"It means so much to us that despite having someone, you still cared about our son enough to talk to him for as long as you did. He needed you," Lorraine said this, while Soleil, his actual girlfriend, stood beside us, listening to every word.

"He had me," she said sharply.

"Yes, dear." Lorraine offered a tight smile that didn't match her eyes. "Of course. Which we are all glad. Since he couldn't have Eisley, he had you to take care of his physical needs."

Even I knew how catty that was. Spencer's mother gave a tight smile and strode away as if she hadn't tossed a fucking grenade. Soleil slowly turned her head back to us.

"You two are married?"

I grinned at Eisley and leaned in for a quick kiss. She wasn't comfortable with the attention, but she still reciprocated.

"We are. Given everything, we didn't find it completely necessary to share," I explained.

"What do you mean everything?" she snipped. "Are you talking about her little Onlysluts account? Or were you referring to the documentary where you just mysteriously showed up at?"

"Soleil," Eisley spoke up. "We are at the funeral for our friend. The man you loved. I know you're hurting right now, but this isn't an appropriate place to be like this. How much have you had to drink?" She leaned into her friend to whisper the last part.

"You think I'm drunk? At least I'm not crazy." The drunk woman shouted. "You need to leave. You weren't Spencer's little confidant like his mother claims. You were the other woman; he cheated on me with you for a year, and you shouldn't show your face here. It's disgusting."

Eisley put her hands over her ears and clamped her eyes closed. "I don't like that word."

"Why not? It's true. I know you're not taking your meds. You know, this makes sense." She waved a crooked finger between us. "You suddenly being married. Does he know?"

Know what?

Two men in suits came behind Soleil and reached for her

arms. They apologized profusely and urged her back. Eisley put her hands up.

"It's fine. We are all still grieving. If it's okay, I'm going to sit in the back and not be a bother."

They told us that we were invited to sit in the front with the family but Eisley politely declined, and we took seats in the back. Soleil was dragged up to the front, where Lorraine Foxworth glared at her every time she made a sound.

I zoned out during the sermons and speeches. I was genuinely surprised they held an open casket. I must not have done a messy enough job. After the family and friends paid their respects, we got in line to pay ours. We reached the body, and I stared down at it, wondering what he would have become if he'd been allowed to live.

A carbon copy of his daddy. A rich piece of shit that would use his money to abuse and hurt the community and cover up the crimes and other dark shit he was into.

I waited for Eisley to drag us away, and once we were off the stage, Lorraine found us and asked if we'd go to the cemetery.

"Only close friends and family are invited," she added when Eisley began to protest.

Eisley had cried on and off throughout the service and was now struggling to keep it together. I cleared my throat and spoke for her.

"With all due respect, Mrs. Foxworth, I'd like to take Eisley home. It's been a long day."

"Oh, of course!" Lorraine embraced me as if I were the son she'd lost. "Go, go! And thank you for what you did for our family. Spencer needed you two."

As I led my wife away, it took every muscle in my body not to laugh at his mother's words.

Lorraine Foxworth, you are welcome.

Rule 32- Constantine

Have tools of all sizes at your disposal.

"Thanks for getting me out of there. That was insane."

"Grief does weird things to people." I shrugged it off as I followed her into her house and kept fingering the item in my pocket that I'd grabbed from my glove compartment. Apparently, grief made me horny.

"I suppose. I just get tired of being Soleil's punching bag. If I knew it was Spencer I was talking to, I would have called it off. I don't need his money."

"Well, good thing, since it'll probably stop soon." We went to the kitchen, where she poured a glass of water for herself.

"I'm exhausted, and I didn't even do anything today." She chuckled lightly.

"You want to do something?" I clutched the item.

"I mean, it's only noon." She looked at the clock on her wall. "What do you have in mind?"

I reached for her shoulders. "I did something. And I don't know if it's going to upset you or not."

She looked at me with large, wet eyes. The beautiful

brown shade dove into my soul, begging me to be honest with her.

All in good time, princess.

"What?"

"I found your parents' house. I called the current owners, and they said we can visit if you'd like. It won't look like it did when you lived there, but maybe it would spark something in your memories."

"Constantine... How?"

I shrugged and dug my hands back into my pockets. "It's what I do."

"I don't understand."

"Real estate."

"Oh." She furrowed her brow in confusion and then beamed. "Well, yes, I'd like to do that. Wait, that's a few hours away. You sure you want to go today?"

"It's only two. Plus, I have something fun to keep your mind busy during the ride." I grinned wickedly, wrapping my fingers around the object in my pocket again. It bumped against the tiny bottle that went with it.

"That smile is making me nervous."

"It should." I pulled my hand out of my pocket and showed her the silver plug.

"Is that—"

"A butt plug? Yeah. I bought it just for you."

She took it turned it over. "What's it say?" She turned to see the flared base. It was a black heart with the words, *Good Girl*, written in cursive inside it. She blushed. "I don't know about..."

"What? Have you never done ass play?" I teased, knowing just how inexperienced she was. It was incredibly hot to get to teach her these things.

Eisley rolled her eyes. "No, I have not. And that wasn't exactly on my schedule for today."

"Neither was heading down to Ohio, but here we are. Come on." I took her hand and started to lead her to her bedroom. "Let's slip this inside you and we can go."

"Slip? I don't think it will just slip inside." Her nerves made her voice high-pitched as she followed me upstairs. In her bedroom, I shoved her head onto the bed, then yanked up her dress and smacked her ass.

"Constantine..." She yelped.

"Give it to me," I ordered. She handed it back, and I massaged the sting away. "Good girl," I purred, sliding her black panties down.

In the daylight, from behind, her pussy was gorgeous. My cock hardened instantly. Her pussy would be so tight from this angle. I ran my hand along her slit and up to her puckered hole. She tightened instantly.

"Constantine, I don't know."

"Ssshh..." I reached into my pocket and pulled out the small travel-sized bottle of lube. I let a few drops fall onto her tight little hole and began to massage it into her. "You just have to relax."

"I don't think that's possible."

"Oh, it is or else this won't be as fun for you."

"But it will for you?"

"Oh yeah." I pushed my finger inside her to the first knuckle. She gasped and arched her back, but I held her down and continued to use my words to relax her. "Come on, princess. Do this for me. Relax your ass and let me put this inside you."

"What does it do?"

"Stretch you. Get you used to the feeling."

"Of what?"

I ignored her question, as we both knew the answer.

It took everything in me to simply add more lube and work it past the tight ring of muscle.

She protested and tightened the entire way, but finally, it slid in and I could step back and admire the words on the flared base.

Good girl.

I pulled her panties back up and lowered her dress.

"Stand up," I ordered.

"This hurts," she winced.

"If you'll relax, it won't." She turned around, and I kissed her, letting my tongue slide inside her mouth. I reached down and moved under her dress, cupping her mound. "You remember how good it felt when I tongued you?"

She nodded.

"Then be a good girl, relax, and when I decide you've had enough, I'll take it out and make you feel good again. Okay?" I reached behind and squeezed her ass cheek.

"Okay."

"All right, let's clean up and then get on the road."

"I'm leaving the house like this?"

"Mmmhmmm." I reached for her chin, tilting her head and running my tongue along her jawline. "You're going to walk into that stranger's house, listen to them as they give you a tour of your childhood home, and make sure you don't let that plug fall out. It'll be our little secret." She shivered as my lips went to her ear. "Can you do that for me, *wife*?"

"Yes," she gasped.

I went to the bathroom to wash the lube off my hands and call the owners of the house to let them know we were coming today. Eisley took a few steps and looked stiff as a board, which amused me to no end.

"Are you ready?" I asked, finishing, and standing by the door.

"I guess, but are you taking it out and then putting it back in when we get there?"

"Why would we do that? You're gonna sit with it." She paled, waiting for me to relent, but it wasn't going to happen. If I was going to drive for two hours with a hard-on, she could sit with the plug in her snug little ass.

"Come on, princess."

Rule 33- Eisley

Walk normal.

"How does it feel?" Constantine gave me a sly look from his side of the car as he drove.

I swallowed and shifted uncomfortably. I was grateful that it was a cushioned seat.

"It's a little big for a beginner, don't you think?" Despite trying to relax and not focus on the plug lodged tightly in my ass, I couldn't.

"Sure, if you're a pussy. You took it like a champ."

My mind went back to the words written in the little heart base of my plug.

Good girl.

Constantine hit a bump, and I gasped. I felt every bit of it inside me.

"If you just let it, it'll start to feel good. Do you feel full?"

I nodded. That was exactly how I felt. *Full.*

"Good."

He tried to make small talk, but I couldn't focus, and before I knew it, we were parked in front of a large two-story house.

"Walk normal," he muttered as we started up the steps.

"What?"

"You look like you have something stuck up your ass."

"But I—"

"Eisley," he warned. I straightened myself and clenched, relaxed, and then clenched again, but to a lesser extent. I could do this. I took a few steps ahead of him and looked back. He nodded his approval, and my stomach fluttered. His brooding eyes melted me every time. "Good girl," he growled low in my ear as we reached the door and rang the doorbell.

A middle-aged black man with a receding hairline and square glasses came to the door and greeted us warmly. Constantine introduced himself.

"Thank you for indulging us, Stephen," he said to the man as we went inside the house.

"Of course. We didn't know the previous owners, but we're sorry to hear about your story. I was able to dig up photos from when it was originally listed for sale. When they took the pictures, all your parents' belongings were still here."

He took us to the kitchen, where he handed Constantine a folder. Constantine handed it to me, and I opened it cautiously. Would I remember any of this?

There was a full stack of photos. I took them and set the folder on the table. I looked around the kitchen. Everything was white with navy accents. In the photos, my parents had decorated in greens and reds.

"There was a definite apple theme." Stephen chuckled. "We kept the colors for about five years, but opted for a remodel after our kids left the house."

"Can we get a full tour of the house?" Constantine asked.

"Of course." Stephen smiled warmly and led us through the kitchen to a pantry, and slowly, we worked through the house. We stopped in every room so I could compare the photos to the current setup, and with each new room, my excitement began to deflate. I didn't remember any of this.

"How old were you when you were—" Stephen started but then stopped and cringed.

"I was five. I don't even remember what they looked like."

"I'm sorry to hear that," Stephen said again. We went upstairs, and I ran my hand along the wall. I wondered if my parents had hung photos all the way up.

"There's three bedrooms. When we did our first walk-through, there was a little girl's room and an office. This is the one. Yours, I imagine." Stephen opened a door and allowed us to go first. I stepped inside and froze as my gaze landed on the circular window at the other side of the room.

I closed my eyes, and suddenly, I could remember it all so vividly. My mom, with her long hair, standing on a chair, painting the ceiling.

"Starry night."

"Yes," Stephen said from behind me. "This entire room was painted to look like the painting. It was pretty cool. I wanted to keep it, but my daughter was obsessed with *The Princess and the Frog*, so we painted over it."

I stepped further inside, staring at everything. Despite the walls being shades of green, I remembered the blue and yellows. My blankets and desk and everything matched. I closed my eyes, and I could suddenly hear her singing as she painted and warned me not to touch the wet walls.

"Eisley, sweetie, don't touch the paint, or you'll ruin it."

"Okay, Momma."

A warm, large hand settled around my waist, and I turned into Constantine. "I remember," My voice cracked. "I remember her." Tears slid down my face. I'd been ripped from this warm, loving home, and taken to... that place.

"Shh, it's okay. That's good. What do you remember?"

I took a deep breath and looked toward the door. Stephen had disappeared, giving us some privacy.

"I remember her smiling and listening to Alicia Keys. She

liked to sing. She'd sing and paint, and she'd give me watercolors to paint pages while she worked." I shifted through the photos, finding the ones of my room, confirming the blue walls I remembered.

"And my bed was made of metal, and it was painted too." I nodded eagerly, the memories rushing to me. "I had so many stuffed animals, and most nights, they'd end up on the floor, but my dad would come and gather them up to help me sleep."

"You remember your dad?"

"A little. He had a mustache. It would tickle when he kissed my forehead. He was obsessed with the *Red Wings* and always smelled of beer. But I loved it. He was always wearing jerseys." It was all finally returning with gusto.

"They'd have barbecues, but I was the only kid, so I'd be allowed to hang out with them for a little bit, but then I'd be taken inside to watch movies on the couch while they hung out with all of their friends." We left the room and I took Constantine through the house, recognizing it now. We passed Stephen at the base of the stairs, and with his permission, we went to the backyard.

"Do you remember any of them?"

I shook my head. "Just blurs of faces. No names. But they were always fun. My parents were loved." I sighed, recalling goodnight kisses, burnt pancakes, and lots of laughter. I turned back to Stephen and offered my hand. "Thank you for allowing me to explore your home. It's lovely, the changes you've made."

He nodded. "I hope this helped."

"It did."

"The neighbors always spoke kindly of the Rosales when we first moved in," Stephen said as he led us to the front and out of his house.

"Rosales." Even though the truth about my origins had

been revealed a week ago, it still felt foreign on my tongue. "Sorry, it's just weird to hear."

"Is that not your last name?" Stephen frowned and eyed us warily.

"It is. I just didn't know until recently. Thank you," I said one last time, and together, Constantine and I went to the car.

"Thank you," I told Constantine, leaning against the car door.

"Of course. I'd do anything for you, Eisley." He put his arms around me and his hands slid down, cupping my ass and squeezing. I blinked, feeling the intense pressure of the plug still firmly planted inside me. It didn't hurt anymore. It felt... interesting. Constantine saw my face and a wicked grin spread over his lips.

He knew.

"Eisley Rosales." I smiled. "Weird to hear."

"Eisley Blackwood. We'll be getting that changed." He grabbed the necklace around my neck and yanked me forward. Pinching the ring between his fingers, he growled, "You're mine, in every sense of the word, wife."

Rule 34 - Eisley

Know who you're dealing with.

"Get in the car."

His growl vibrated against my neck as he whispered the command in my ear.

My pussy throbbed with sudden need, and I did as told. We sped off toward Shelley Vale.

"Spread your legs," Constantine ordered. I parted my thighs, and he inched his hand over, sliding under my dress. "You're so wet already." He chuckled, tracing his fingers over the front of my panties. "Is that because of me or because of the plug in your tight little asshole?"

"Both?" I squeaked out as he pressed his thumb against my clit.

"I knew you'd like it. You just needed to break out of your shell some more." He moved my underwear aside. Sliding a finger up my lips, he slid inside, and I gasped. "You walking around with that plug has me so fucking horny for you," he said, swirling his finger around my wetness. "I knew you'd wait for me."

I closed my eyes, and after taking a fortifying breath, said, "Constantine, I have a confession."

"I know."

"Know what?"

He slid two fingers into my hole, and I clenched. I was still not used to the feeling of something inside me, but the plug made it almost unbearable. Unbearably good.

"I know that you fooled around with Kansas," he said, pulling out and then pushing back in, slowly, almost tauntingly. "But you never came, did you? You saved that for me." When I nodded, he said, "Good girl, now come for me right now."

As if I'd been waiting for his permission, my body exploded. It pulsed as pleasure jolted my insides in waves. My asshole tightened and clenched around the plug, creating an even more intense sensation. I cried out, as Constantine continued to work his hand until I came down, and my body was too sensitive. I pushed him away, and he laughed, sliding his slick-coated fingers into his mouth.

"I love the way you taste."

The words sent a flurry of butterflies through my belly. He was incredible. When we were closer to home, I remembered what he'd said right before I orgasmed.

"You know about Kansas?" I shrunk into myself. Embarrassment, shame, and guilt flooded my system.

"I do."

"Are you mad at me?"

"You thought I was dead."

"Yeah, but I promised I'd wait for you."

"And you did."

"But I—" How could I tell him I loved Kansas as much as I loved him? There was a reason it all went down the way it did that night the Minister came for us. "Are you mad at me for leaving you behind and running away with Kansas?"

"I told you to go."

"I shouldn't have. I should have stayed and fought."

"You would have been killed."

"Like you were?" I shot back.

"Yeah, only—" He cut off, then amended, "I can't tell you everything that happened after you left. But let me just say that you had to leave. My dad would have made sure you never walked out those church doors. And no, I'm not mad at you for being with Kansas. I can't be. I remember the way you looked at him back when we were in the room. You loved him then too."

"I loved you just as much," I answered truthfully. "That's what made what the Minister said—"

"I know. It was horrible. But we're all safe and alive, and the ones that participated in our torture will be gotten tenfold."

I blinked. "What do you mean? They're all dead."

"The Family, sure. But who do you think was giving the Minister, my dad, the money to do what he did for so long?"

I'd never thought of that. Were there real people beyond computers paying to have the Minister film... us?

"You'd be surprised to know how dark Shelley Vale really is," he said cryptically and left it at that. When we returned to my house, it was barely evening.

"May I take this out now?" I pointed to my behind. Constantine rolled his eyes but led me upstairs and assisted me in removing the plug. It felt almost embarrassing, and I found that I preferred it going in, rather than coming out. I told him that, and he laughed.

"I told you. Just wait until it's a cock in there, and you're coming so hard you cry."

Was I ready for that? My ass was sore with the plug removed, I couldn't imagine something bigger.

"Have you spoken to him? Kansas?" I asked after I'd made a quick dinner for us. I had little of an appetite, after returning to town, where I remembered my friend was buried this afternoon. Constantine eyed me from the other side of the island. He reached for his beer.

"That feels like a layered question. What do you actually want to know?"

"You are so full of mysteries. You seem to have the answer to everything. You found my parents' place, you knew about me and Kansas. What else do you know?"

He took a long drink and set the bottle down hard. "I've spent a large amount of my adult life searching for answers to the things my dad did, and in that time, I have found out some more... unsavory things."

"Such as?"

"Why some children were picked."

My stomach dropped. While I'd only ever seen Kansas and Constantine, we knew there were others down there with us. Some were older, some younger, but all in the same situation. Trapped, starved, tortured, and inevitably abused and forced into child sexual slavery.

"Do you know why I was taken?" I asked.

"No. But I know why Kansas was. And so does he."

I couldn't breathe. "Why?"

"Did Kansas ever tell you he discovered his last name? That documentary crew aren't the only ones that can dig up old records."

I shook my head and frowned. Why hadn't Kansas told me? If he had found out his last name, he should have told me. What other secrets was he hiding since he left for school?

"What is it? His last name."

"Foxworth."

Rule 35 - Constantine

Always accept the party invite.

I stared intently at her, watching the blood drain from her face as her brown eyes grew wide.

"Foxworth as in... like a cousin?"

"As in a brother. Kansas and Spencer are half-brothers. Or, were." I snickered and returned to my plate of food.

"Stop," Eisley said. "They were brothers?"

"Good ol' Teddy Foxworth had a side piece. He got her pregnant only months after he did the same to his wife. Spencer and Kansas were only a few months apart from each other."

"So, what, you think Mr. Foxworth gave Kansas to the Minister?"

"More like sold. Kansas was visiting with his dad and was handed off like he was grabbing a dime bag from his dealer."

"And no one knew about a missing boy? How did his mom not say anything?"

"Because she went with him. She was one of the Mothers." The gasp and sudden silence undersold the weight of my words. Yes, Kansas's biological mother had been an active member and participant in my father's church. She allowed her son to be abused.

Eisley ran her hands through her hair. "I don't understand. How could a real mother do that? What was the point?" She stopped pacing and glared at me. "Which one was it?"

I shook my head. "I didn't recognize her from the pictures. She died at some point. And you know my dad, he'd just replace them."

"No, she had to have gone with Kansas to try to save him." She nodded, formulating a theory in her head. "That's the only thing that makes sense."

"Doesn't mean it's correct."

Her plump lips trembled. "Poor Kansas. His own family. And he knows?"

I nodded solemnly.

She reached for her phone. "I have to call him."

My facial muscles twitched. She dialed and held the phone to her ear, but it rang and rang. He never picked up. Eventually, she hung up and sighed.

"It's getting late." She picked up her plate and took it to the trash without eating anything.

"Is that your way of kicking me out?" I teased, finishing my dinner and standing.

"Would you be offended?" She smiled softly.

"Only somewhat," I teased. "A husband and wife typically share the same roof, however, I do have some work to do tonight, so I should probably get going." I wrapped my arms around her soft body. My cock hardened, and she stepped back, having felt it on her leg.

"I'm tired."

Of course, she'd say that. She'd already gotten off. Wanting desperately to ignore her, bend her over the island, and fuck her anyways, I forced myself to step away and take my leave. There'd be plenty of time for fun, and it'd be worth it if I continued to wait.

The next day, I was woken up by a knock on my hotel door. Groggy, I opened it to find one of the geeky kids from the documentary crew looking up at me with skittish eyes. "Hello, Constantine, sir?"

"Yeah?"

"We want to invite you back to filming. We'll pay you triple."

I laughed in his face. "Why would I do that?"

"Don't you wanna be famous?"

"Not even slightly. I did the interviews you asked. I'm done."

"Dave said he's cutting your hotel and travel off if you don't come back and walk through the Church for the cameras," the kid blurted.

Hmm, interesting.

"What exactly is he up to?" I pulled the kid into my room and shut the door quickly. The kid continued to shake but didn't leave. I went to my suitcase and pulled out a T-shirt and jeans, tugging them on.

"I'm not sure, sir." The kid was staring at the long scars on my chest. "He's been studying the Minister's books. He thinks that maybe some clue to unlocking everything is in the Church."

"You're speaking in circles," I snarled. "Tell me what you really want."

"He wants to know why you're not dead!"

I paused and then turned to the pimply teen.

"Tell him, I want to know the same thing about him." He flew to the door then and ran. I sat on my bed and inhaled. This was not the way to start my day. Grabbing my phone, I found an invite to a party being thrown in Spencer Foxworth's honor tonight.

The invite came from Soleil Walton. How did she get my email?

I read through the details, and it felt standard, just a mass e-vite. I was sure Eisley had gotten the same one. But did she know I had? Right then, she called.

"Good morning, beautiful," I muttered into the phone. I loved the way her breathing hitched every time she heard my voice after not having been around me for a bit. It was so innocent, and something about that innocence of hers drew me in. "What are you doing?"

"Just brewing my morning tea. I wanted to see if you'd come to a party with me tonight."

"What party?"

"At Therese's. I really hate going there, especially at night. But it's a party for Spencer, and I feel like if I don't go, then it will be weird."

"Why don't you like going there?"

She paused. "The woods are in her backyard."

"What woods?"

"The woods where the Church still is. About three quarters of a mile in. They like to go there all the time but I can't stand even looking at the trees. I don't want to go to the party alone. Please come with me."

"Your friends aren't really my scene." I knew I'd go anyways, but I wanted to make her sweat a little.

"I know, especially Soleil right now. She's a mess. But I'll owe you one if you come."

"Owe me one what?"

"I don't know, what do you want?"

The thought of my cock resting between her perfect lips as her tongue swirled around it magnificently flashed across my mind.

"I'll figure something out. Sure, I'm down. Should we bring anything?"

"Like what?"

"Beer, liquor, weed?"

She chuckled. "Oh, maybe something to drink. I think Micah will have you covered if you're wanting to get high."

"You're not?"

"I don't smoke."

"That's no fun," I teased.

"I didn't say I don't get high."

"Oh? I bet you'd be fun. I'd love to make you come while you're high."

"Oh, jeez. Okay, I've got to go before you get me—"

"Wet? I have a feeling that ship has sailed. Has it, princess?"

"Just be here around seven, okay?" She hung up before I could reply. I laid back on the bed and put my hands under my head. I turned and glanced at my trusty backpack, which I'd need tonight. Who knows, tonight at Soleil's house, I might convince her friends to explore a little in the woods that hugged her back yard. The woods leading to the Church.

Rule 36 - Constantine

Keep your backpack close at any given time.

"What's the backpack for?" Eisley pointed to my backseat as she climbed into my car.

"Work stuff."

"It's weird to picture you as a real estate agent. Your vibe doesn't fit."

I rolled my eyes. "My vibe? What do I look like I should do for work?"

She looked me up and down and then squinted. "You're giving motorcycle club."

I pulled out of her driveway. "Motorcycle club?"

"Or tattoo artist, or a mechanic by day and *Magic Mike* dancer at night."

I threw my head back. "*Magic Mike*? That's a compliment, right?"

"Have you seen a mirror? You're hot, Constantine. Like, ridiculously hot."

I snickered and turned the music up. Eisley directed me to another extravagant house away from the rest of the town.

"Her parents gave it to her last year. They moved and sold it to her for pennies," Eisley explained as we walked up.

"I'm seeing a pattern with your friends."

"Stop, they're nice."

"Spencer sure was generous."

"Okay, you cannot talk about that tonight. Please," she pleaded. Before I could answer, the door was thrust open and a body was being thrown against me.

"You guys came!" Soleil's high-pitched voice caused me to jolt. I didn't hug her back, and she pulled away to hug Eisley. "I was worried you wouldn't show."

"Of course we would," Eisley eyed her friend warily. I did too. Why did she hug me first?

"I know, but I said all that stuff about you being crazy and made a scene at the funeral." Soleil laughed, as if it was just another day in the life of a rich bitch.

Eisley flinched again and I recalled yesterday when she'd gotten visibly upset.

"I don't like that word."

I made a mental note to ask about it later. Soleil ushered us inside.

"Come on, you two, we've got pizza and a mini keg set up in the kitchen. Micah is working on a projector, and Therese bought a popcorn machine."

"What are we watching?" I asked, keeping my hand on Eisley's back. We followed Soleil through the spotless house into the large living room.

"I was trying for a *Hellraiser* Marathon, but Emi threw a fit." Micah snickered as he pulled down a large projector from the ceiling.

"It's disgusting." Emi stuck out her tongue.

"We're gonna just do *Nightmare on Elm Street* instead. Spencer liked Freddy Krueger," Therese said from the other side of the room. She was pouring popcorn kernels into the machine.

"Honestly, it's probably a better choice. I think we could

all use a good laugh tonight." Rem came into the room, holding a beer.

"Which is why I brought shrooms for everyone." Micah darted his tongue in and out. "You do shrooms, Constantine?"

"I have. It could be a fun time." There was no fucking way I'd be taking drugs with these stupid fucks.

"Hell yeah, you picked a good one, Eisley."

"A good *husband*," Soleil exaggerated the last word. "They're married, remember?" She hiccupped. "Sorry, I started early today." She tried to rest her head on my shoulder, but I stepped away in time.

The rest of the room rolled their eyes, but Eisley, ever the sweetheart, nodded in sympathy. "Totally understandable. It's only been a few days."

"Less than a week. Just last weekend, I had his dick in my mouth, and now, he's buried in the ground," Soleil whined.

"But I'm so glad you brought your man. Finally, we know why you've never dated that other guy. The hot one with the glasses. What was his name? Kansas." Soleil spun past us, landing on the couch. Her legs shot up, giving me a good view of her teal thong. Her pussy was barely covered, and for the first time in my life, I was a little nauseated by the sight of one.

"Soleil," Emi warned.

"Oh, come on, I'm just teasing. Pop off, queen." Soleil gestured to Eisley. She then rolled her eyes and nodded to the screen. "Can we turn the movie on and pass the drugs, please?"

"There's beer and food in the kitchen," Rem told us, and we went and grabbed red cups.

"We don't have to go crazy tonight. It's been a long time since I've done mushrooms," Eisley admitted.

"I'll follow your lead." I smiled.

We drank and refilled our cups and returned to the living

room. The movie was getting going, and Micah was hunched over the coffee table with a small scale and a plate full of dried mushrooms.

"Come get some, everyone," he muttered as he began weighing and separating them into small piles. Soleil went first, grabbing a handful and heading straight to the kitchen. Therese and Emi followed.

"They're going to grind them up," Rem explained. He took his share and tossed them into his mouth without a second thought. I cringed. Eating mushrooms like that was like eating twigs. Eisley went over and grabbed some.

"I think I'll go with the girls. You want to come?" She eyed me.

I grabbed my share and followed. Therese was working a mortar and pestle, grinding the drugs into something more manageable to consume.

"I'm putting mine in strawberry milk. Anyone want some?"

Everyone else opted to drink theirs with their alcohol. Slowly, we all took our turns, with my handful being last. By the time I got mine ground up, everyone had returned to the movie except for Eisley.

I emptied the mushrooms into my hand and waited for her back to be turned to drop them into her drink instead of mine.

"Ready?" I asked.

She turned back and eyed her drink. "Ugh, I hate this part. You have to drink the entire thing," she reminded me. I nodded, and we toasted. I watched her carefully, making sure she followed her own directions.

Take every drop, princess.

We rejoined the group, and somehow, I found myself sandwiched between Eisley and Soleil. I clung closer to my wife, but Soleil seemed hellbent on making sure some part of her body was touching me. My fingers twitched with the urge to shove her away, but I knew what everyone would say.

She's grieving.

The psilocybin began to kick in, and soon everyone was giggling and saying odd shit as they watched the movie. I laughed along with them, doing my best to mimic what the others were doing. I'd done them before. I knew how to act. Everything was fine until Soleil put her hand on my thigh and ran it up, grabbing my cock. I stood quickly and looked to Eisley, but she, like the others, was far too high to notice. I made the excuse that I forgot my phone in the car and took off outside, only to be followed by Soleil.

"Don't run!" She giggled. "Or was this your plan all along? To get me somewhere private?"

"This wasn't my plan at all," I grabbed my backpack from the back and slid it over my shoulders. "Soleil, I think you should go back inside with your friends."

She ran her hand under my shirt and up my chest when I turned around. "Mm, you're yummy. Much hotter than Spencer was. Did you know he wanted to call me Eisley in bed? And I let him."

"That's unfortunate." I shoved her away. "But not my problem."

"She's cheated on you!" she screamed. "If you really have been married this whole time. That other guy, with the glasses and bull nose ring. He was calling her his girlfriend, and they were all over each other. What do you say?" She reached out and shoved my shoulders. "An eye for an eye?"

"You're not high." I stared at her eyes. They were clear. Was she even drunk? She nodded and tried to kiss me. I jerked away.

"I'm not. I dumped my share in Eisley's drink. She's double-dosed. She probably doesn't even realize we're gone. What do you say?" She reached for my very flaccid cock again.

"My nickname was Nancy Reagan in high school." She leaned in and ran her tongue along my jaw. "Because I'm the throat goat."

Sliding under her arm, I removed my backpack and unzipped it quickly, pulling out my knife.

"What is that? Are you trying to make some sick joke? You realize my boyfriend just died, right?" She put her hand on her hip as if I were the offensive one.

"I do." I nodded, pulling out my trusty Ghostface mask as well. I slid it on and then twirled the knife between my fingers. "But I don't really like jokes." I stepped forward, and she bolted. I was expecting her to go back into the house, but she didn't. She went around it. I paused and went the other way. Would I catch her making a circle?

I was only a quarter of the way around when I saw her, sprinting right toward me. I stopped, held my knife out at my hip, and before she could stop herself, she plunged right into me. I covered her mouth in an instant, stopping her screams.

"You shouldn't touch what isn't yours." I pulled the knife out and plunged it again into her belly. "So, to answer your question..." I brought the knife to her chest, right between her tits, and sunk it deep into her skin, making sure she would not survive. "Thanks, but I'll pass."

Rule 37-Eisley

There's safety in numbers.

"Slash."

"Pass."

"Slash."

"Pass."

Therese and Micah went back and forth. My vision was blurry and I couldn't put thoughts together. I clutched my stomach as I rolled with laughter at... everything. I'd never been this high before in my life. I fell over and splayed myself on the couch. I stared up at the ceiling and watched the glitter that was falling from it wash over me in a gentle dusting. I sighed contentedly and closed my eyes.

"Can you turn that down? That scream was too loud!" Emi shouted over the movie. "It sounded like it was right here."

"That's the drugs, Emi," Rem reminded her.

"Slash."

"Pass."

The glitter suddenly was smothering me, and I used all the strength I had to roll off the couch to hide.

"Eisley, are you okay? You're really fucking tripping." Rem's voice seemed so far away.

"It's probably just been a while since she's had anything more than tea." Therese laughed.

"Should we help her?"

"Where's Soleil and Constantine?"

"I'm here." Large hands reached under my arms and lifted me up. "You all right, princess?"

"She's just having a really good trip. She's fine," Micah said. "I did buy some really good shit."

"She needs some water or something." The blur of Constantine left the room.

I stumbled to my feet and reached for the red blur I recognized as Emi's dyed hair. I pulled her up and we began to dance as Freddy Krueger gave terrible one-liners to teens before slashing him with his knife gloves. Emi and I giggled and danced, running into furniture. I pushed over a lamp, and in an instant, we were shrouded in complete blackness.

"What the—Is the power out?" Rem asked.

"Must be, fuck," Therese groaned. "I'm too fucked up to go down the stairs."

"Where's your phones? We should call for help." Emi giggled.

"My phone isn't working," Micah said. "Is yours?"

Everyone began pulling out their phones and uttering words of dismay as they tried to call out.

"Who are you?" Therese's voice was sharp and caused everyone in the room to stop and look.

Emi, still standing with me, dropped my hands, and I collapsed onto the floor. I struggled to lift my head, but when I did, I saw someone crouching near me. A figure dressed in black, wearing something blurry over his face. It was too dark for me to see much of anything.

"Get away from her!" Emi screamed. "We're all seeing this,

right?" Was I imagining them? I'd been hallucinating wildly for hours. I reached for the figure, and they grabbed my chin.

"Eisley! Stop!"

The figure let go of me and my head became deadweight, falling straight to the hardwood floor.

"He's got a knife!" Therese shouted.

"Hold up, dude, calm down," Micah yelled.

"What the fuck is going on?" I heard a single boot step and the world around me turned into chaos.

"No!" Therese screamed as something crashed to the floor, shattering loudly. Everyone began to scramble, shoes flew past me, pillows and popcorn spilled everywhere, and I was still deadweight. Despite the screaming and running, someone helped me get up.

"Get up, Eisley, I think the guy who killed Spencer and those kids is here," Emi rushed out in a panic.

"Whaa..." My muscles weren't working.

"He tried to stab Therese. Come on, we gotta go now!"

"Const..." My feet began to move, but I couldn't get my tongue to work. The gold glitter was continuing to fall from the ceiling, making me feel so, so heavy. Like the snow in the poppy fields in *The Wizard of Oz*.

"He's fighting him off, come on!" She lifted my arms over her shoulder and we began to move. We ran out the back.

"No!" I get out as Emi started leading us toward the woods.

"We have to go! Look!"

I turned to see the masked figure stalking out of the house, looking around for us. My eyes focused for only a moment, and I saw Ghostface from the *Scream* movies minus the robe, a hulking figure, and the large knife in his hand, stained.

I was frozen, and when my brain finally responded to the danger of the man in the mask, I found myself alone. Emi had ran. And then, so did I.

I could hear screams and shouts but they were too far away. I couldn't reach anyone with the speed my legs were allowing. But each time I turned my head and saw a shadow, it stirred something in my muddled mind.

Don't talk to anyone.

Don't look back.

Just run.

I jumped at everything. The trees were stepping in my way, the branches twisting and lifting out of the ground to catch my feet. Animals were leaping out in front of me, running away to go tell Ghostface where I was. I ran and tried to catch up to my friends until finally, the mushrooms contaminating my brain overtook and I fell to the wet, mushy ground and decided to let them absorb me, like the mud puddle in *The Neverending Story*. I was Artax now, a horse, destined to drown slowly, head last.

My eyes drifted open, and I stared up at the navy sky. The glitter had stopped falling, and instead was replaced by the most beautiful night sky I'd ever seen in my entire life. My legs and arms slowly seeped into the earth when suddenly I felt a sharp pain as my hair was yanked upward. My head lolled to the side, and then, I saw it. My savior from the fate of being returned to the earth.

Ghostface.

I screamed.

Or, I thought I did.

I wasn't entirely sure until something was shoved deep into my mouth, causing me to gag. My tongue tasted leather.

"Suck it," a growling voice demanded. I struggled to focus my vision, but I was still too high to do it. Everything was blurry. "Suck this knife like it was the best cock you've ever tasted, or I'll spin it around and make you take the sharp end between your lips."

Shivering, I tried to do as asked. I tightened my lips and

began to move back and forth. I licked the knife and tried to focus my brain as it was shoved deeper down my throat.

I gagged as Ghostface pulled it out and shoved it back in roughly. "Do you like it? Do you want more?"

I couldn't answer, my mouth and throat hurt too much. Ghostface took that as a protest, and he pushed the knife as deep as he could into my mouth. Tears slid down my cheeks against my will, and I gave up. I sank, and finally, he removed the knife from my mouth.

"Good girl. Let's go."

Rule 38 – Eisley

Don't go into abandoned churches.

A sharp sting on my face roused me back to life. I blinked, and the world around me spun. Where was I? It was dim and reeked of mildew.

"Hello, Eisley. Welcome back."

Welcome where? I turned my head from side to side. I was on something... somewhat soft... but... I bolted up and was instantly snapped back and began choking. Something was around my neck. My hands flew up to it and fear slid down my spine as I felt cold thick metal. I'd been collared.

"Please," I tried to focus my brain, but I was still so intensely high. "Let me go."

"I don't know. Watching you work your pretty little mouth around the base of my knife was pretty sexy. It's got me all riled up. What do you say, want to play a game?"

"A game?" The weight of the metal collar pushed my head back down. I stared up at the concrete ceiling, and... I recognized it. I tried to sit up again but was instantly pulled back down. "I don't want to be here."

"You don't miss this place?" Ghostface kneeled alongside

me on the floor. He ran his hand up my thigh, lifting my skirt. "It's been so long."

"Who are you?" I demanded. I closed my eyes and tried to pinpoint his voice. It was gruff, yet not. Scratchy but not.

"It doesn't matter. All that matters is how I make you feel." Suddenly, the knife reappeared, and he brought it to my chin. I shivered as he ran it down my body. It scraped along my collar and slid down the rest of me. He reached the buttons on my top and as he moved the knife, he unbuttoned my blouse, exposing my bra. "You shouldn't be wearing this," he muttered. Lifting the middle, he slid the knife under it and began cutting through it until it snapped into two pieces. I stared as intensely as I could at the mask, searching for eyes under the black fabric as he peeled away my bra, revealing my nipples to the cold room.

Ghostface teased my nipples, rousing them to a point.

"God, you're so pretty, Eisley."

"Please." I reached for his face, and he snatched my wrist, clenching it tightly. I gasped. Suddenly he let go of the knife on my belly and reached down, grabbing something that scrapped and clanged sharply.

Chains.

My wrists were shackled, and I was forced to fight against the restraints I knew I couldn't escape.

"Was it worth it?" he snarled.

"I don't know why you brought me here," I protested. I closed my eyes as he bent down, lifting the mask and ran his tongue along my breast, taking a nipple into his mouth. The sensation was incredible. Everything behind my eyelids seemed to pulse as he sucked and nibbled on me. This was wrong, but it felt so good.

"He'll come find me," I gasped as Ghostface slid his hand over the apex of my thighs. The intenseness coming from the drugs and his tongue, my legs relaxed and he pushed my panties aside, finding my slit.

"No one's looking for you," he said as the knife ran against my panties. He cut those free and ran his hand along my pussy. "You're all mine tonight."

"You can't," I moaned, but my insistence on him stopping was waning with each touch. Everywhere he trailed his fingers, my skin felt tingly.

"I can do whatever the fuck I want," he said and stood, slipping the mask back on fully. Dazed, my head fell back and I watched as he unzipped his black jacket, revealing a tight black undershirt. He unbuckled his pants and slid them down, along with his boxer briefs.

My body cried out with a sudden need, and confusion ran through me. I should be terrified, not longing for his cock. But this man in the mask, why had he taken me? He dropped to his knees and came to my head.

"It's time to show me what you can actually do with your plump mouth, Eisley." Yanking me up by my hair, he leaned over and the smooth head of his cock pressed against my lips. I looked up at him, and despite not knowing exactly who he was, I wanted to taste him. Cautiously, I opened my mouth and took him into me. My tongue explored lazily, and I closed my eyes. I was still seeing swirls of stars and the feeling of him in my mouth was made more intense with the mushrooms still in full swing.

Ghostface reached down and fondled my breasts while I sucked on him, causing me to moan and shiver with delight. I could taste drips of cum from his tip, and suddenly he pulled away. I blinked, as he moved onto the mattress and pushed himself between my legs. Still wearing the mask and his shirt, he pulled the shirt off, revealing spectacular abs. And... a tattoo... and scars. I recognized them, even through my high.

Constantine?

No, he... was it? My vision was just hazy enough to make out some details, but not all. Ghostface and Constantine's bodies were similar, and the tattoo, and the scar. That was unmistakable.

It *was* Constantine.

He'd taken me back to the Church, to finally consummate our marriage. I relaxed my thighs, settled into the fantasy, and let him lift my hips. Still in his mask, Ghostface positioned himself and pushed his cock into my wet and wanting pussy. I gasped at the sharp pain. It didn't hurt as much as it had the first time, but I was still getting used to the sensation.

"Ssh... princess, you're fine. Relax, and enjoy the way this feels."

I nodded, accepting that it was Constantine, and untensed my muscles. With my hands bound and unable to raise myself, this was all I could do. I closed my eyes and focused on the full feeling. He moved in and out. I wanted to be angry, scared, and upset about being forced to return to the Church, but I couldn't be. I felt too good.

The night wore on, and it began to feel like a montage of intense pleasure. I was so high, I began hallucinating again. I was seeing double; taking double, as Ghostface went from my pussy to my mouth, and back again, over and over. I longed for both. When he moved to one hole, my body cried out for the other to be filled. At times, it truly felt like he was everywhere.

I came so much, I cried. I was at Ghostface's mercy, unable to do anything but experience every ounce of pleasure he was determined to give me. I saw and heard stars as the mushrooms inside my system intensified every one of my senses, and finally, after what felt like an eternity in a hellish paradise, I closed my eyes and fell asleep.

Eventually, my eyes popped open, albeit painfully.

Constantine walked into the room, wearing just black jeans. *No mask.* He glanced at me, assumed I was sleeping, and then turned his head and grinned at someone I couldn't see.

"I told you her pussy was tight."

Rule 39 - Kansas

Stay close to your final girl at all times.

My phone rang loudly inside the relatively empty store. I fished it out of my pocket and saw Eisley's beautiful face on my screen. I hadn't heard from her in days. Since she'd called me about those teenagers deaths.

I put the phone to my ear and answered.

"Hello?"

"Kansas?" Eisley's voice came through the other side of the phone, desperate and small.

"Hey, are you okay?"

"No. I need you to come home."

"Home?" I let out an involuntary chuckle. "What are you talking about?"

"I— I just need you here." The frantic tone in her voice was sobering. I looked at the basket on my arm.

"All right, I've got a few things to do, and then I'll figure out a way back. It's a long drive. I won't get there until late."

She was crying softly into the phone.

I grabbed a candle off the shelf and placed it in my basket. "Eisley, what's going on? Are you safe?"

"Yeah, I mean, I think so. I'm at home, and I've been watching the cameras. Kansas, I'm scared."

"Of what?" I picked empty jars and a packet of charcoal. "Wait, is one of your Johns harassing you?"

"No, Spencer and Soleil. They're dead. They just found her body this morning."

"Fuck." I sighed and rubbed my mouth. "All right, I'll leave as soon as I can." I hung up and went to the counter, buying everything in my cart.

"What kind of Magick are you doing?" the cute clerk asked.

I flashed her a smile. "Little of this, little of that. Mostly stocking up on stuff I use pretty regularly."

"Just as long as you're not doing any love spells." She wagged her finger playfully at me as she took my card.

"I think I'm managing fine without them," I flirted back. "I'm actually heading to see my girl now."

"Well, she's lucky, I'm sure. Enjoy!" She handed me a brown paper bag and I left, promptly heading to the hotel, just outside of Shelley Vale. I looked at my phone. I'd have to wait hours before I could head over to her house, but I was glad she called.

Now, I had a reason to be here. I knocked on her door a little after midnight. She opened the door and threw her arms around me.

"Oh, thank god, you're here." I held her in my arms, inhaling the sweet smell of her shampoo. She was so beautiful.

"I told you I'd always come for you. Now, what exactly is going on?" I feigned ignorance. She took me inside and instantly went to brew tea. I looked around the kitchen. Dozens of jars were scattered all over the counters filled with various herbs and seasonings.

"What is going on here?" I picked up one jar that looked like pink sand.

She sighed, stepping away from the kettle she'd put on the stove. "I had to keep my mind busy, so I was refilling my witchy stuff. Powders, herbs, stuff for spells."

"Did you do any spells today?" I eyed candles off in the corner of the counter.

"Not today, but I think I might tomorrow. I'm kind of tired now. It's been an exhausting day."

I nodded, setting the pink sand down. "Spencer and Soleil." I turned to face her. Eisley's chin quivered and her eyes grew shiny in an instant. I opened my arms and she drifted to them, resting her head on my chest.

"Spencer first, then Soleil last night."

"Oh. Two separate incidents?"

"Yeah, but they were both stabbed. Just like those teens. Kansas, the police think Shelley Vale has a serial killer on their hands."

"Another one?" I smirked. "Man, they really fucking suck at investigating."

"What do you mean?"

"Well, if they're investigating things like they did ten years ago, this new guy will kill the entire fucking town before an arrest is made."

"Kansas," she sighed and pulled away. "Don't be like this. It's serious."

I shrugged. "Why? Because some rich kid's throat was slit? Sounds like a quick death to me. Much better than any of those kids the Minister took."

She shuddered. "Please don't talk about that."

"Why?" I demanded. "Because it's ugly?"

"Yes!" she yelled. She threw her hands up as the whistle blew on the kettle. "I called you because I'm scared for my life. Last night someone was chasing us and then Soleil was found dead. That could have been me!"

Not likely.

"You asked me to drive halfway across the country because some guy in a mask is killing rich snobs I don't care about? Rich snobs who hurt us?"

"You can't keep bringing up stuff we can't change. I want to move on, you need to too." She pulled the kettle off the heat.

"How can I move on when you won't let me go?" We stared at each other for a long moment. I pushed my glasses up my nose.

Her lips trembled, and her head fell. She reached for the necklace around her throat. "I have a confession to make."

Any confession from her should come with her on her knees. I licked my lips, holding the words back.

"Okay."

"Have you been following anything going on around here?" She clutched that necklace so tight her hands shook.

"No. Why would I?"

"Constantine..." She paused and looked up at me, waiting for my response.

"What about him?"

"When did you find out?"

I stared for a long moment, and finally, I dropped my head. "When I was at school. He came to see me."

"And you didn't tell me."

"He told me not to."

"Why?"

I lifted my shoulders. "No idea. He never said. He came to see you, I presume." I took a deep breath. I'd been dreading this day. I hated to disappoint her.

"He did. Why didn't you tell me about who your dad was?"

"Because what was the point? What did Constantine say to you?" I stepped to her and put my hands on her shoulders.

She looked up at me with large, shiny eyes. "Or is it, what he did to you?"

"It was stupid, I know. But I saw him, and my brain just—"

"You fucked him." I stepped away and a dry laugh escaped from my mouth. "You asked me to drive hours and hours to you, just so you could tell me you finally gave it up to my childhood best friend?"

"No!" She shook her head rapidly, and tears spilled down her face. "I asked you to come because he's been arrested. Kansas, they think he's the murderer."

Rule 40 - Kansas

Follow your final girl's lead, and you'll be rewarded.

"There's no fucking way. What evidence do they have for his arrest?"

I sipped my tea and stared across at Eisley, who was shivering and looking over her shoulder as if someone would burst in. I wasn't sure why though. According to her, the bad guy was already locked up.

"None that I know of." She shook her head. "It was kind of a mess, the whole night. We were having a party at Therese's, and we'd all done a little bit of mushrooms. Then someone broke in and we ran. I guess he managed to catch Soleil and..."

"What about you, where were you?"

Eisley looked down at her cup. "I don't know. I was too high. All I remember is stumbling out of the woods and Emi running over to me."

I knew her better than she knew herself. She was lying.

"When did they arrest Constantine?"

"Shortly after everyone was rounded up. Everyone looked like hell. Dirty, ripped clothing, scrapes, and bruises." She raised her arms and showed me purple spots on her arms. She had some around her neck too, but didn't mention them.

"He looked just like everyone else. We all went back inside and were laughing about how crazy the night was and then Micah went to grab something from his car and he started screaming. He found Soleil."

"And she was stabbed?"

She nodded. "Just like Spencer and the high schoolers. We called the police and told them everything. Everyone was hysterical and then someone let it slip about us doing the shrooms and the cops lost their shit. They wanted to know who supplied us, and when no one came forward, they took Constantine."

"They can't just take him." I shook my head. The cops in this fucking town were useless.

"I know that, but what can we do?" She sighed. "Kansas, he needs our help."

"And you brought me here... to get him out." I pushed my glasses up my nose.

She flinched. "Do you hate me?"

"For fucking him first? A little. For calling me to help him? Nah. I think we can both say we owe him one."

"First?"

Heat flooded my face as I realized what I'd implied. "Sorry. Let's just—I'm tired. I've been driving all day," I lied. "Let's go to bed, and in the morning, we'll go get him out." I finished my tea and grabbed my bag by the door, fleeing to the safety of the guest room.

The next morning, I slid downstairs, still slightly embarrassed, but determined to move on. Eisley sat on the couch, shaking her head.

"Well, he wasn't arrested for murder, but now they are holding him because they think it was him who supplied the mushrooms."

"Do they have any proof?"

"I'm not entirely sure. I called Emi and she was kind of shitty about it. I asked her why Micah didn't fess up, considering someone else is sitting in jail for possession, and she hung up on me."

I stood, trying to figure out how the fuck Shelley Vale even ran when the doorbell rang. I went to it, and something large and wet was thrust into my arms. A bouquet.

I took them back to the living room and set them down right next to an almost identical one. Eisley looked up and swore.

"Someone is fucking with me. See, this is why I wanted you here."

"Because they sent you flowers?"

She stood and started rummaging through the bouquet. "No, because it's the same exact bouquet. They sent one when Spencer died, and now another one for Soleil. It's like..."

"A gift?" I snickered.

"God, this is so fucked up," she groaned.

"Do you want me to toss them?"

"No." She stared at them and frowned. "They're pretty. It's fine. Let's just go."

"Where are we going?" I asked after we'd showered, eaten, and were walking out the door.

"There's nothing we can do right now until Constantine sees a judge, so I wanted to go check on my flowers at the greenhouse, and then hopefully by then, we'll be able to bail him out." She drove us over to the greenhouse, and as we were walking up to it, someone called to us. We turned to see a flash of cherry-red hair running toward us.

"Eisley! Wait!"

"What's going on? Is someone else hurt?" Eisley asked quickly.

"No. I have to talk to you." Emi caught her breath and

then the relaxed look on her face turned cold. "The board had a meeting last night and followed up this morning. We are officially asking you to return your key to the greenhouses and not come back."

Eisley's mouth fell open, and I reached for her shoulder.

"What? Why?"

Emi crossed her arms. Everything about her stance and tone told me it had been her decision alone, not a board's.

"They feel that since your husband," she side-eyed me and my arm around Eisley "is currently in jail for murder, you make everyone uncomfortable."

"He's not in jail for murder. He's in jail because your loser boyfriend won't fess up about who actually had the drugs." Eisley pulled away from me and stepped toward her friend.

"Say whatever you want, no one believes you," Emi spat. "It's bad enough you were sexting Spencer for the last year, and now Soleil is dead after she said something to your man about being off your meds. Don't think we aren't putting things together. We don't want you here." She shooed us with her hands. "Take your boyfriend or whatever and get the hell out of Shelley Vale."

"What are you doing, Emi?" Eisley's voice cracked. "I thought we were friends."

"I thought so too, Eis, but then my friends started dying and a lot of it starts with you. So hand over your key and find some other town to ruin."

Eisley fumbled with her keys and then tossed a key at her. "I want to grab my plants."

Emi shook her head. "The board says you can't go unescorted, and I don't have time to do that today. I'm heading to go help Therese find clothes for Soleil's funeral. Which, you're not invited to, you know, since your man probably killed her."

"He didn't!"

I reached for Eisley's hand and squeezed. "Come on, we'll figure it out."

"You move on so fast," Emi smirked. "Maybe that's why he was so angry. Maybe he's nuts too. If he killed Soleil, he probably killed Spencer too. Lose my number." She turned and stormed away.

Eisley collapsed, sobbing. I rubbed her back.

"It's fine. Ignore all that shit she said. She's just pissed because you know the truth about her boyfriend."

"You know what?" She threw her head up and glared at me. "I think you were right. They should get theirs. Every single one of them. They're bastards. All of them."

My stomach tightened and then soared with elation. Finally, she was understanding my feelings. "What do you want to do?" I asked.

She stared at the greenhouse, still locked tight. "We're coming back later for my fucking flowers, and then we'll go from there."

Rule 41 - Eisley

If it's locked, don't go inside.

Kansas and I spent the day going over the plan for getting my bat flower and catching him up on what I was comfortable telling him. Naturally, he had a lot of questions about us.

"Are you two together then?"

Before Therese's party, I would have told him yes. Despite loving Kansas, I would always love Constantine too. But now, seeing what I saw down in the basement, Constantine, laughing about having let someone use my body while I was too high to realize... I didn't know. I wanted to say a direct no. I wanted to hate him for what he did, but I'd never experienced something so intense, so pleasurable, so... hot. Not knowing just exactly who was under that Ghostface mask... Was I sick for low-key enjoying it a little?

Actually, I liked it a lot.

"I don't really want to put a label on it right now."

"Are you glad you waited, even though you thought he was dead?"

"I am," I told him. "Especially more so, now that I know you knew he wasn't."

Kansas apologized for pushing me all these years, but the words weren't genuine. Kansas had always been jealous of the closeness I had with Constantine, despite us being close as well. Now, he had a real person to be jealous of, and his feelings for me only seemed to have intensified.

The entire, day he'd been finding reasons to touch me. We sat on my couch together, holding hands. He would step up behind me and put his arms around my waist in a backward embrace. I loved the closeness, and I didn't feel guilty about it.

"Do you have a specific time you have to be back at school?" I asked as we got into my car to head over to the greenhouse.

He sighed. "I probably shouldn't have left at all. It's fine, I'll work it out with my professors."

"I'm sorry, Kansas. I shouldn't lean on you as much as I do."

He rested his hand on my thigh. "I like that you do. Once I've graduated, I'll be closer."

"Will you?" Hope swelled in my chest.

"Yeah, of course. I'll go wherever you want me." The words settled around us, but one unspoken word hung between us.

Constantine.

We parked under a shade of trees. I popped the trunk and pulled out the bolt cutters I'd bought earlier.

"I know it'll be obvious it was me, but I really don't care at this point." I rolled my eyes as I closed the trunk and started off toward the greenhouses. "Those are my fucking flowers."

Storming the entire way, I looked around only briefly before reaching the doors and putting the simple lock between the bolt cutters. Crunching them, the lock snapped, and I tossed it on the ground. Kansas followed behind at a more leisurely pace, his head tilted upward.

"What?"

"Nothing. We going in?"

I creaked the door open and peered inside, and then, I laughed. "I don't know why I'm scared, no one's ever here this late." I held the door for Kansas and shut it behind us. I waved him in and we walked to my space. It was pitch black, so I used my phone's flashlight, scanning the rows.

"I hate how moist it is in here. I'm already sweating," he complained. We reached my row and started down the aisle, and I raised my light to see my plants and my heart dropped.

No!

I sprinted to the end of the aisle and instantly burst into tears. I collapsed in front of my plot and sobbed.

"Who did this?" Kansas came up behind me, furious. I looked up and reached for the roots yanked from their home. Someone had not only pulled my plants up, but they'd sheared them into a hundred pieces. Black petals were scattered all over the ground, and not a single one was left untouched. Nothing was salvageable.

"Emi. I fucking know it was her." I glared over at her perfect pumpkins. I picked one up, tossed it as far as I could across the greenhouse, and erupted into sobs again. I'd poured so much love into those flowers, and she'd destroyed them just because I told her to make her boyfriend own up to his shit. She was beyond cruel.

Suddenly, warm arms slid around me and soft lips kissed my neck. I closed my eyes as a delicious shiver ran down my body. Kansas's hands moved up and under my shirt as he continued kissing me.

"Even crying, you're beautiful," he whispered. His fingers pushed under my bra and cupped my breasts. He pinched my nipples, and my clit throbbed with desire. My core began to ache as he pressed his hard cock against my backside. "Is it fucked up that even though I know you love him, I still want you?"

"I love you too," I gasped as a hand moved away from my chest and began creeping down my belly, reaching under my skirt.

"Do you? I always thought you loved him more, even in death."

"Why does it have to be one or the other?"

"What are you saying, Eisley?" He pushed my panties to the side and spread my pussy lips, diving into my wetness. "Are you saying you're going to let yourself feel good with me?"

That was a good question. For years, I'd only allowed myself a taste of what it could be with Kansas. I was so guilt-ridden about abandoning Constantine; I couldn't even consider enjoying another man. But I had.

Constantine had chosen that for me the other night. I hadn't even known the other man, but I had liked it. I nodded and pushed against Kansas.

"I want to feel good."

"Good." His hand slid up and clutched my neck. He squeezed, and I gasped, and then, in one quick motion, he grabbed my necklace and ripped it off me. At that exact same moment, he slid a finger inside me, as if staking his claim.

I gasped as he thrust it in and out. I tried to turn but he wouldn't let me. He pressed his cock harder into my back and continued fucking me with his finger.

"I want you," I gasped, shoving his hand away. Quickly, I reached for my panties and shoved them down to my ankles. "Please." I spun quickly and reached for his jeans. I pulled at his belt and he grinned wickedly.

"I love greedy Eisley, but if you remove my belt, I'll spank you with it."

I paused, unsure of how I felt about that. Would I like that?

"Good girl." Kansas pinched my chin. "Now turn back around."

I did so, and he pushed on my back.

"Bend over and spread your legs." Pushing my skirt up, he revealed my ass to the empty greenhouse. I heard the clink of him undoing his belt and the tell-tale sound of his zipper. He stepped back, and I tilted my head to see him pulling his shirt off. He put his hands on my hips, centering my focus again. I turned forward and closed my eyes. A moment later, the familiar feel of a soft cock head was pressed against my lips.

"I'm not using a condom," he growled. "You're going to feel every fucking inch of me, skin on skin." My stomach fluttered excitedly. Why was that so hot? I stood on my tip toes, and he aimed his cock further against my pussy, and slowly, began pushing inside me. I gasped as I was stretched with every inch. He dipped his fingers between my legs, finding my clit and swirling my arousal. I moaned as I was soon lost in the feeling of being so full.

It felt incredible. Here, with Kansas, knowing anyone could walk in at any time and catch us. He began to move, slow at first, and the more I responded with quick pants and loud moans, the faster he pounded, and as I was reaching my peak, he slowed, and my body cried.

"Not yet, princess," he purred and slowly continued fucking me. He tugged on my hair, and I moaned loudly. Then, his rhythm shifted, and he was pounding his cock into me harder, but slower, like a hammer. My body exploded into a million tiny, hot electric pieces.

Kansas kissed my neck and then picked up the pace, tugging on my hair so hard it stung, but in the most erotic of ways. I wanted him to pull harder as he fucked me. And then, he groaned and stiffened. His cock pulsed inside me as he found his release. He then scrambled to put his shirt back on and raise his pants, and I searched the floor for my underwear.

We intertwined our hands and walked toward the exit of the greenhouse. My arms were empty, but my body was full, and the euphoria I felt after coming made me temporarily not care about my flowers. Suddenly, the doors burst open from the outside.

"What a performance," Emi said, clapping, as she stepped into the greenhouse.

Rule 42 - Eisley

It's always the best friend.

"Were you watching us?"

Emi raised her phone and waved it. "Free porn, who doesn't like that?" She stepped further in and looked around, shaking her head. "There are cameras everywhere, you know that, right?"

I did now.

"Why did you destroy my bat flowers?" I demanded.

She blinked and tried to feign shock, but I knew my best friend. That was her lying face. "What do you mean?"

"You ripped them up from their roots and then shredded them!" Tears flooded my eyes again. "All because what? I wanted Micah to turn himself in?"

"Micah," she repeated his name, "is on his last leg with his dad. They can't know it was him who supplied us the other night because he'll stop paying for his car and school and everything else."

"But Constantine has to sit in jail for it."

"He's sitting in jail because he's a creep who probably did murder Spencer and Soleil. I mean, isn't it suspicious that people started dying as soon as he came into town?"

"Or someone who lives here is using it as a great diversion," Kansas suggested. We both turned to him as if remembering he was here.

"No one would do that," Emi insisted. "Everyone in Shelley Vale is good people."

"Good?" Kansas laughed. "Everyone here is basically pedophiles."

"What are you even talking about?" Emi rolled her eyes. "I'm calling the cops. I should have done it on the way, but I wanted to see your face when I called them. Now you can join your husband in jail." She smirked at us. "I'm sure he'll be so excited to hear about what happened to land you there." She began typing on her phone, and I jerked forward, slapping it out of her hand. It flew into the air and skidded along the dirt floor, landing underneath a flowerbed.

"You bitch," she snarled and dove for it. I dove with her, taking us to the ground. We rolled, and she reached for my hair, yanking it hard. I yelped and closed my fist, aiming for anything that was hers. I landed on her shoulder and pulled back to do it again.

She rolled onto me, and I shoved her off. She leaped to her feet and looked around for her phone. I saw it before her and quickly rolled under the elevated bed and snatched it.

"Give me that you crazy manic bitch!" she screamed.

I rolled again until I reached the other aisle and then stood, looking for something, anything, to fight back against her. I ran to the hoses, and found a bucket under them, already filled. Looking back at Emi, I made sure she saw me drop her phone into the water.

"Don't call me that."

She let out a guttural scream that was so loud, so shrill, I leapt back. Emi looked around and found a hand tiller. I began to back away, looking for the door. It was behind her. I'd have to get around to get out.

"You stupid, crazy slut," she screamed and jumped over the beds and ran toward me. I ducked in time as she swung the till. I screamed and ran, looking for something to defend myself with. "Everything was fine until you threw a fit about the documentary," she accused.

What? I paused, and she glared at me from the other aisle.

"Everyone just let you do your little thing. Drink your gross tea, practice your dumb witch spells, and show off your ass to weird guys on the internet, but then you had to get all high and mighty and everything went to shit." Emi dropped her arm and shook her head. "Spencer's dead now. So is Soleil. All because you couldn't just let us be happy."

"Emi." Baffled, I said, "I was a victim of the Minister. You know that." I pointed to my chest. "I sat in a basement room for five years of my childhood, praying that I'd survive another day, and you're complaining that I don't want to relive it?"

"It was ten years ago," she protested. "Who cares? They stopped my check, you know. The bonus I got for getting you to the set. And because you were upset, Spencer was looking at quitting too. Right before he died. And then of course Soleil bailed after. You're messing everything up!"

"Are you saying what I think you're saying?"

"What?" Her face fell, and I saw genuine confusion.

"Soleil and Spencer were killed right after they said they were dropping out of the documentary."

She blinked rapidly, and then her mouth fell open. "Do you think they're the ones doing it?"

"Well, it's not Constantine." I crossed my arms. This was all so childish! I was covered once again, in dirt and scrapes and bruises, and trying to figure out who was murdering everyone.

"If that's the case, then the next person to die is the last person to quit the project," she explained.

"And who is that?"

"You."

The air intensified, and my eyes shifted to the till still in her hand. I swallowed, and my stomach tightened.

"I need the money, Eisley. I don't have a golden spoon." She took a step forward. "And I can't shake my ass for a little cash."

I put my hands up and began backing away. "I get it. Emi, you don't have to hurt me." I glanced at the door, and then I remembered I wasn't alone. Where was Kansas? "Did you hurt Spencer and Soleil?"

She shook her head but didn't stop creeping closer. "No, but I think I get it now. That's the angle. It wasn't just a straight documentary about the Sinister Minister. They were always complaining about how boring the real story was." She nodded, her eyes taking on a faraway look. "It makes so much sense. Go to make a documentary, and everyone starts getting murdered. It's genius."

"Emi. Whatever is going on, you don't need to be involved."

She shook her head. "No, don't you see? I figured it out. Now I have two options. I could help, or I could blackmail them. Either way, I'm getting paid." She raised the till over her head, and finally, our eyes met. "Sorry, Eis, it's just business." She screamed and lunged. I turned and bolted to the door and then I heard a loud clink! And a large thud. I spun around, horrified. Kansas stood with a shovel, eyes wide, glasses falling off his nose, and looking as surprised as I was.

Emi lay on the ground, unconscious. I hurried to her.

"Emi, Emi, wake up." I shook her, but the only thing it produced was a trickle of blood out of her mouth.

"Eisley." Kansas's voice brought me out of the fog. I looked up at him and saw his grim expression. "I need you to get out of here."

Rule 43 - Kansas

There's always one that's a fighter.

"What?" Eisley stared at me from the ground. I nodded to the door.

"Come on, you need to go. I'll take care of this."

She stood slowly. "What does that mean?"

I held back the urge to roll my eyes. "It means, if you stay, you're going to be an accomplice. Get out of here, drive home. You came, discovered your flowers had been destroyed, and left." She was blinking rapidly. I reached for her chin and forced her to look at me. "Do you understand me, princess?"

She swallowed and nodded. I dropped her chin and motioned again to the door. "I'll see you back at home. Get some rest."

"Why?"

I smirked and stepped over the body. I pulled her into me and let my cock, roused already, rest on her hip. "Apparently, the idea of burying a body makes me incredibly horny. When I get home, I'm going to fuck you like I'm trying to wake the dead." I'd gotten a taste; I wasn't going to just let her slip away.

She turned and fled. I counted in my head to 237 and then I began to move. I went to the plastic cabinets in the back, looking for something that could help me torch the place. I opened the cabinets and found rows of chemicals. That would work. I pulled them out and began pouring everything around. *Fuck all of it.* Eisley's flowers had been destroyed in such a ruthless manner, no one deserved to have plants. I dumped all the bottles and reached into my pocket, pulling out my lighter. I leaned down and ignited one of the small pools of fertilizer. It lit up instantly.

I looked toward where we'd left Emi. Who knew she was a psycho-cunt? I started in her direction and froze when she wasn't there. She was alive?

Fuck.

She'd been wearing a white shirt, so she'd be easy to see in the moonlight, which, by the looks of the open door, would be where I'd find her.

Kind of fucked up that the bitch who was going to kill her friend was a runner. I stretched quickly and reached into my pocket, slipping the lighter back and exchanging it for my pocket knife. I flicked it open, cracked my neck, and started forward.

I'd find her.

The fire I'd started licked my shoes, and I glanced around. It was picking up. I needed to get out of here. I rushed out and looked around. There were a handful of other greenhouses, but then clear fields and the parking lot. She wasn't by her car, so I moved toward the buildings.

"Emi, I think we should talk," I called into the open air. I heard a loud rustle and turned in time to see a blur of bright red hair rushing into the last building. She was trapping herself. I was at the door in seconds, but then I hesitated. Was she trapping herself? Or me?

"Emi, I know you're in there. Why don't you tell me

exactly why you're running?" I called into the building. I popped my head in and something zoomed over it, hitting the grass behind me with a heavy thud. I looked back and saw it was a spade. Fuck. That could have done some damage. I pushed my glasses up my nose and stepped forward. Fuck it.

"You tried to kill me!" She screeched as I stepped into the greenhouse. I looked up at the corners.

"Where's the cameras?" I asked, ignoring her comment.

"This is the only one without them. Small town budget and all." She stepped out from behind a tall tomato plant.

"Why would you lead me to the greenhouse without cameras?" I eyed her cautiously.

A slow, haunting grin spread across her face.

"Because I lied to Eisley." Slowly, she pulled a knife from behind her. It was almost the same as the one in my hand. "Didn't I?"

My eyes darkened. "I don't know what you're talking about."

"It wasn't you I saw leaving the director's trailer, holding a check?" She began walking through the beds, and I matched her, keeping our distance the same. "Must have been someone else with glasses and a bull ring through their nose."

My nose twitched involuntarily and I rubbed the ring running through it. "Why are you doing this? Hurting someone isn't going to make you rich."

"Only if I get caught. My dad is an officer in Shelley Vale. Even if I was caught holding onto your dead body and saying I killed you outright, nothing would happen. Just like everyone else in this town, my crimes will be forgotten and forgiven."

"You know about your friends and their families?" I had to keep her talking until I could get close enough to disarm her.

Emi cackled. "Who doesn't know? Eisley, probably. She's got her own problems. You know, I was the only one who knew? She told me once when I saw her taking the pills and I kept that secret. And then when I found about her past, I didn't tell anyone then either. My dad spilled all the tea about her and everyone else. I keep everyone's secrets."

What was she talking about? "And you were still friends with them? After what you know?"

"My friends weren't the ones paying to keep you captive. Just their parents. With the Sinister Minister's church, the rich could indulge in their most evil fantasies from a safe distance. I heard that some of the kids came from the town itself. But I guess you'd be able to elaborate on that more, wouldn't you, Kansas Foxworth?"

My muscles tightened. She knew the truth.

"How many people did you tell that bullshit to?" I asked, trying to stay aloof.

"What bullshit? About you being Spencer's long-lost half-brother? Just his dad. You'd think he'd be able to come up with a bigger check to keep that hidden. He only gave me five grand. How much did he give the Sinister Minister to take you from Shelley Vale, and more importantly, why do you keep coming back?"

"I can't leave Eisley," I blurted.

"Why? She doesn't care about you. She's been all over the Sinister Minister's son since he showed up. It's almost like you don't even exist to her. Sounds just like your dad."

She found our abuse funny?

"I'm going to kill you, claim self-defense, and then threaten to reveal your identity to Shelley Vale. I'm going to get paid by everyone for my story."

"You must really need the money."

I was surprised she could still hear me talking. She seemed off in her own little world. She'd turned away from me completely and wasn't batting an eye at me creeping closer to her.

"Everyone has secrets, Kansas." The words halted me, and she spun around. It was a trap. I should have known. She lunged her arm forward, swinging the knife. I dodged it and smacked her hand. The knife flew out of her grasp and landed blade up in a bed off to the side. In a flash, both of us were scrambling to collect it, shoving the other aside. She scurried underneath me, and as I shoved her away, she fell forward and I heard the sickeningly sweet sound of the knife piercing her insides.

Emi stood up, slowly, with the knife embedded in the side of her belly. The white shirt was stained a deep red from the wound. Emi stared at me in shock. Her mouth fell open and blood poured from it as she collapsed to her knees.

She reached for the knife and then looked up at me for help. I shook my head. There was no helping her. If we removed the knife, she'd only die faster.

"I guess you're right, Emi." She fell face-first, her body relaxed and her last breaths were taken. I counted to 237 again, just to make sure she'd died, and then crouched down to pick her up and carry her body to the greenhouse that slowly went up in flames. "Everyone does have secrets."

Rule 44 - Kansas

Know your enemy.

Ten years ago.

"Constantine, I have to talk to you." I lifted the Minister's Bible and my eyes flickered with panic to the steel door. One of the Mothers had closed it, taking Eisley with her. Constantine glared at me from in front of the door. He had fought with the Mother to not let them take her but ultimately lost. We always lost.

"What?" he snapped. His chest was heaving and his fists bleeding from pounding on the door.

"Do you ever listen to the Minister's sermons?" I crept cautiously toward him. Constantine had anger problems. He exploded so easily and would fight whoever got in his path.

"No. I'm too busy trying to find food for us. I don't care what he has to say." He turned and pounded on the door again, causing a loud thump and echo but nothing else.

"Well, you should. Constantine, we have to get out soon. I think..." I gulped. My empty stomach tightened. "I think they are going to murder us."

Constantine blinked. "What?"

I handed him the floppy, worn bible. "It's all in here. It's hard to understand, but I think there's a reason he put us together. Me, you, and Eisley. It's all part of his plan."

He began flipping through the text, shaking his head. He walked over to the bed and flopped down.

"Where? Show me." He thrust the book at me. I joined him on the bed and flipped to the pages I'd found. I pointed.

"Right here. Two Sons and one Daughter of the Family will be brought forward to wed. In order to serve the Family, the unwanted Son will be given up to the Reanimator. Our Minister shall bleed the Son and spread his flesh, burning his insides, and asking the Reanimator to take his body and feed his ministry. With the unwanted Son's sacrifice, the Family will flourish, and the Reanimator's word shall be spread throughout the land." I stumbled on some words, as I wasn't used to reading aloud. It had taken me a long time to figure out what most words meant, but once I did, I knew we had to escape.

"What does this mean?" Constantine looked at me. "Who's the Reanimator?"

"I don't know." I shrugged my shoulders. "I can't remember. It's hard when my brain always feels fuzzy!" I slapped my hands against my head. Without food and clean water all the time, I couldn't think straight.

"I never thought he was talking to us," he muttered. "I was told to keep my head down."

"We need to ask. Ask to go up there," I said.

He paled. "I don't want to go up there. The Minister is not nice when I go up there, Kansas."

"We have to do something," I argued back, and then, a moment later, the door screeched open and Eisley was thrust back inside. As the Mother was pulling it closed, I called out to her, "Mother! Wait!"

She paused and glared at me. "What?"

"We would like to hear the sermons. Please, we need to understand who we are praying to every night." I never prayed unless forced to do it aloud, but she didn't need to know that.

She considered my request and then nodded. "Of course. I will speak to the Minister."

When the door was shut, I explained to Eisley that something was going to happen, but I left out most of the details. She was as confused and scared as the rest of us, I didn't need to make it worse. The Mother returned with the Minister, much to all of our surprise. He came inside and zeroed in on me.

"Kansas, Son. I hear you are interested in hearing my sermons."

I gulped and forced myself to stand still and not shy away from the cold, cruel man who had beaten, starved, spit, and yelled at me for the last five years.

"Yes, Minister." His lips curled upward into a grin so sinister I wanted to cry. My gaze flickered to my best friends. My companions. The only true family I knew in this hellhole. "I've been reading your book."

He nodded. "Well then, that's a great place to start. Tomorrow, I shall take you upstairs and we shall begin your lessons. In time, you will understand it all. Both of you." He stood straight up and nodded to Constantine. Constantine didn't look happy.

That night, we huddled together, with Eisley in the middle as always, and tried to piece together who the Reanimator was. We were woken up by a Mother coming in with fresh clothes for us. That was rare for us.

"If you are to truly become a student of the Minister, you must dress like one. You will be clean for him," she explained when we didn't jump to change. Reluctantly, we peeled off the thin, too-small, filthy clothes and put on the clean ones that fit nicely. Eisley stared longingly at us in our new clothes, but as she was not coming with us, she was not given a new dress. The one she wore now barely covered her bottom. It was a small child's dress, not one for an eleven year old.

Constantine reached for my hand and together we followed the Mother out of our room and up the stairs, through the pews and clean hallways that smelled of lemons. We were taken past the giant cross and pew and to a smaller room, an office.

The Minister came in behind us and ushered us to sit in the chairs in front of his massive desk. As I sat, my head swung back and forth, trying to take in everything. Bookcases lined every wall. Some with books, others with weird candles and rocks, and other knickknacks I didn't quite understand. I pushed my glasses up and squinted. I needed to remember everything I saw today.

"So..." The Minister went around and sat at his desk. He folded his hands and sat forward. "You've read the scripture."

In tandem, we nodded.

"You have questions." He nodded. "Where shall we start?" He leaned back and smirked. "Are you truly here to learn who the Reanimator is and how to serve our savior, or are you here to ask which one of you is going to *die*?"

Rule 45 - Eisley

Play innocent.

It wasn't until I was in my car, blocks away from the greenhouse, did I realize I was missing my necklace. Panic set in, and it took everything in me not to turn back around to retrieve it. I sat in the car with my hand pressed against my chest, where the ring had sat around my neck for the last ten years. How things had changed in such a short time.

Oh, Emi.

Tears came then as it hit me. Emi was dead. She'd tried to kill me, and in the fight, it was her that had lost her life. It had all happened so fast, I wasn't entirely sure I could fully understand. She'd been my best friend!

Kansas's grim expression drifted through the fog of Emi. I had to get out of here. He'd take care of it. He'd take care of me.

I put the car in reverse and made sure to drive slow through town and back home. I slid into my bed and stared at the ceiling. It felt wrong to be doing something as normal as sleeping, knowing that Emi was dead.

How was Kansas handling it? Thoughts of everything that

could go wrong, *more wrong*, ran through my head, and I couldn't sleep. I got up and tried to call him, but there was no answer. I paced my kitchen, trying to absorb everything. Constantine was in jail, Kansas was disposing of a body, and I... I was in love with both.

Out of the need to clear my head, I pulled out the ingredients for pumpkin rolls and began mindlessly making the batter for it. I pulled out the cake at seven in the morning, right as I got a text from Therese.

I know Emi was a bitch about it, but we convinced Micah to confess and get Constantine out of jail. He talked to his dad last night.

Another message came with an attachment of articles.

WTF is actually going on in this town?

GREENHOUSES UP IN FLAMES LAST NIGHT, POLICE SUSPECT ARSON.

I clicked on the article quickly and scanned it, my heart pounding furiously with every word. There wasn't much to the article, as the story was still developing. All they knew was that the fire department had been called, it was contained, and so far no injuries had been reported.

That was because there were no injuries to report, just a death.

Steeling myself, I texted back,

Omg! Does Emi know???

We're not talking but I'll text her.

Trying my best to keep my nerves in check, I turned my music on and Fleetwood Mac played loudly as I continued to make the frosting that would go inside the pumpkin roll. I'd made enough I could go around the neighborhood and pass them out to my neighbors like I had last year. They'd loved that.

Would they love me now?

Emi and Soleil's last conversations with me were so hateful and full of distaste for my choice of career. If my so-called best friends said that, what was everyone else saying?

I spent the morning baking loaf after loaf, and I continued to try Kansas's phone, but he didn't answer. Once I'd run out of ingredients and the last loaf had been pulled from my oven, I turned everything off and went to the couch to rest.

I was awoken by a knock on the door sometime later. Groggily, I sat up and blinked away the sleep. I went to the door and opened it, revealing Therese, with her wide, expressive eyes showing a glint of excitement.

"Did you hear?"

"Hear what?"

She pushed through me and sniffed the air. "Ugh, I love coming to your house. It always smells so good." She turned, and remembering her trail of thought, she perked up again. "Girl, the tea is spilling!"

I yawned. "I just woke up," I confessed.

Therese looked at me and nodded. "I can tell. How about you feed me whatever you spent all day making and I'll tell you about everything I found out today."

Dragging myself to the kitchen, I pulled out one of the finished rolls from the fridge and began to cut and plate it for her.

"Oh score! I love it when you make these. I love fall." She pulled the plate toward her and grabbed a fork from the drawer to dive into the dessert. "So, where do I even start?"

I shook my head. Beats me.

"So, first thing this morning, Micah went with his dad to the police station and confessed that Constantine wasn't the one who gave everyone the mushrooms. He made up a story about some weird stranger and the police bought it. Constantine was released an hour later."

Constantine was out of jail?

"When he gets out, some of the documentary crew are standing by the door, waiting. As soon as he steps outside, they start filming and acting like paparazzi. It's nuts. Constantine tries to ignore it, but they follow him through the parking lot."

I leaned forward on the island, enthralled by Therese's story.

"And at that point, he loses it. He turns and yells at the police waiting by a car, telling them that it's real convenient that the moment they come to town, people start getting murdered. How it tells a real good story. He asks how the cameras knew exactly where to be at any given moment, and then someone else says to them, 'Hey, weren't you at the fires this morning too?' and then the whole place got crazy."

"How do you know all of this?" I pushed my hair back.

"Oh, I was there. Me and Rem were waiting for Micah. We were gonna go pick up Emi and go to the movie set."

It was on the tip of my tongue to ask if she'd seen Emi, but it felt too suspicious.

"Needless to say, we didn't get to go today. They pulled those people in for questioning right then and there."

"What about Constantine?" I asked. She shrugged and took another bite.

"Said he wanted to get a shower in and was taking off. I assumed here. No?"

Why hadn't he stopped over?

"But that's not the biggest tea." She pointed her fork at

me. "I heard that the greenhouses had cameras, and the feed gets sent straight to the cloud on Emi's computer. As soon as they get ahold of Emi, they think they'll find who did the fires, and according to my sources, they think it's also the same person who killed Spencer and Soleil."

"Well, where's Emi then?" I felt like it was safe to ask now. It was genuine curiosity. A wicked grin spread onto Therese's face and she cocked an eyebrow.

"That's a good question. They seem to think she skipped town. Eisley, Emi might be the murderer."

Rule 46 - Eisley

Use the clues you're given.

"Can I take that loaf home? Rem loves your pumpkin stuff."

I was so taken aback by all the words spilling from Therese's mouth, I didn't know what to say. So, I packed up the loaf and sent her on her way.

"You really think Emi could have murdered them?" I swallowed, leading her to the door. I mean, Emi had tried to kill me. And she'd been going on and on about wanting more stories for the documentary. What if they'd been working together this whole time? Was I next?

"I don't know. Emi has been going through some stuff lately. You know, money-wise. Micah told us last night. She's been hiding something from him." She turned and leaned into me. "He told us that if he wasn't scared of her, he would have broken it off a few weeks ago. But now, he can't if she's killing people."

"You should be taking this more seriously," I chastised. "What's to say she doesn't come after you next?" I knew that would never happen, but she didn't.

"Because I'm not pissing her off. You are."

Well, she had a point.

"Look, we're all taking precautions. Whether it's Emi or someone else. Don't go anywhere alone, probably don't get high for a while, and stay in the daylight. Which is my cue, as it's getting late." She gave me a hug and left.

Realizing I still hadn't showered or changed since our fight in the greenhouse, I went upstairs and turned the hot water on in the bathroom.

Feeling restless even after the hot shower, I dressed and drove around, trying to recall if Constantine had told me which hotel he was staying at. At some point, I zoned out and was simply driving, and finally, I parked at the cross we'd used to mark Constantine's supposed death for so long. I got out and sat beside it, staring at the forest on the other side of the road. Buried deep inside those trees was the Church. I spent so long trying to run away from the prison, but now, I wanted to see it again.

I'd been in it. Just days ago. I was sure of it. With a collar around my neck and my wrists shackled. I'd been taken to the Church and...

My body shuddered at the memories. I hated myself for how much I'd enjoyed it. Why had it been so erotic? Was it the mask, being tied down, or was it simply the massive amounts of drugs in my system, making me believe those things?

I stood, brushing the dirt off my knees, and looked both ways before crossing the road. I had to see for myself what the Church had become.

I'd been walking into the dark woods for about ten minutes, so unsure of where I was going when I heard noise from behind me. I spun around and saw a figure in the shadows. I stiffened. It was a hulking man. Large, bulky... and wearing a Ghostface mask.

Fear jolted me forward. I turned and sprinted away, but my follower did the same. I heard his heavy footsteps thudding through the woods after me. Was it Constantine? I hadn't had the chance to talk to him about what had happened that night.

The last time I'd seen that mask... Soleil was found dead. What if Emi had an accomplice? Was it Micah? Or one of the documentary crew members?

I kept looking back and still, the man was gaining on me. Slowly but surely, every time I stumbled on a root or stopped to catch my breath, he was catching up. Fear propelled me forward. My brain seemed to be going into some sort of shock. Suddenly, I looked back and I didn't see a man in a mask. I saw the Minister.

It wasn't like the first time when Kansas had helped me keep going. I was on my own, and he was coming to retrieve me.

I came upon a small crest, but I hadn't noticed it before it was too late and I fell into the hole, face first. Instant pain shot up from my shin, and I screamed. It was involuntary, and as soon as I could manage it, I slammed my mouth shut. It was too late. I'd drawn the masked man and I was defenseless.

I rolled and tried to stand, but it felt like my bones were splintering inside my body. I looked to see if I'd visibly broken anything, but nothing was protruding. It meant I still had a chance. Just then, arms wrapped around my middle and lifted me. I tried to scream but he shoved two fingers deep down my throat.

I gagged and tried to kick, but Ghostface was stronger than me, and I couldn't fight. He threw me over his shoulder and squeezed my throbbing calf. He squeezed so hard my vision grew spotty.

"Let me go," I gasped, but he ignored me. His hands slid up my leg, moving up my dress to cup my ass. He squeezed and then spanked me. The sharp spank caused me to emit a small shriek.

As he strode further, memories assaulted me.

Me fighting as the Minister lifted me out of his car and hoisted me over his shoulder. Me kicking and screaming as he took me into the Church and right down the stairs, ignoring my pleas. And then finally, him opening the door and placing me onto the stained mattress.

"Welcome home, Eisley," he had said then, before closing the door.

I blacked out. When I opened my eyes, I found myself in the same position I was ten years ago. Same room. New mattress. Only this time, I was alone, and once again, had been shackled.

Rule 47 - Kansas

Some surprises are good.

Ten years ago.

"You really think any of that is true?" I asked Constantine after our first lesson with the Minister. We'd spent all day up in his office, learning about the Reanimator.

He blew air upward, his black hair flying up for a moment. "I don't know. He says it is, but it's weird. Why would a ghost want our organs?"

"And what happens if we don't do it?" I stood and paced the room. We could speak freely, as Eisley had been taken again. She'd been having a really bad bout of sickness, and they'd been trying to heal her with various drinks and herbs, but nothing seemed to work.

"According the Minister, the Family will die." We stared at each other, weighing his words. Were we willing to take that risk?

"I don't believe it. I know that's what he says, but it can't be true. Someone who makes him do bad things can't be good. We have to escape and get help."

Constantine's shoulders slumped and he fell back against the stone wall. "I don't know where to go. I've never been outside the Church."

I squinted. "I have. There's people called police. They protect us. I remember my mom saying that once."

"Police?" Constantine tried out the word. "What do they look like?"

"They have blue or black clothes. And funny hats." It was so hard to describe things from the outside world when it had been so long since I'd seen it.

"And they'll save us?" he asked, his blue eyes hopeful.

"I think so."

Constantine pulled his legs up and curled his arms around them.

"I don't want to do those things," he confessed. "To Eisley. The girl in the movie was crying. She said it hurt. The Minister said she liked it, and that it felt good, but I think he's lying!" Tears burst from his eyes and he buried his head in his knees.

The Minister had said it's what Mothers and Fathers did once they were married, but the boy and the girl looked our age, and they'd both been crying.

"I don't either."

Later that night, Eisley had been returned, along with food for us and two bigger books for Constantine and me.

"I don't want to read any more of it." He slid his book away from him. "It's disgusting."

"We need to know how to fight it."

"How can you fight a ghost?" he hissed. "I think you're right. The Minister has been lying to everyone."

"Constantine," I hesitated. He looked up at me. "You said you'd never been outside the Church before."

His face drained, and for the first time, he looked scared of... me.

"Is that true?" I asked.

He didn't say anything for a long time but eventually nodded. "Only just outside the building. I've always lived here."

"Alone? In this room?"

I recalled vaguely when I first was taken. Constantine was already here, and Eisley came later.

"No. I lived with the Mothers and Fathers. I was put in here the same day you came. I was the only other kid though."

"You were born here?" Pieces of the puzzle were coming together. Why he was allowed out sometimes when we weren't? How he seemed braver than Eisley and I. Could it be... "Constantine." I crawled over to him and leaned over to cup my hand around his ear. While the Family could not hear us on the other side of the door, I was suddenly scared. "Are your parents here?"

"I'm not allowed to tell you."

It was as if a large boom fell among us. My entire life, it felt like, was a lie. I scurried back, horrified. I stared at Constantine, taking in his features.

The Family was his family.

"I'm not like him." Constantine stood and tried to come toward me, but I moved fast and he stopped walking. "I swear."

"Him? Who? Which Father is it?" I demanded.

I scanned him up and down when he said nothing. Jet-black hair and blue eyes that were strong, but on another person, they were cold and scary. And then, it hit me.

He was the Minister's son. Constantine put up his hands.

"Please, don't be mad. I don't like him. He's mean to me too."

I shook my head. "How can I trust you?"

"I don't know. They hit me too. They don't feed me too. I'm not special."

"Then why were you allowed upstairs?" I demanded. "Why did you get to bring extra food down?"

"Those yellow flowers?" he yelled back. "Because no one saw me pick them! And being allowed upstairs is only because I don't know where to go if I try to run. He told me that."

"Who, your dad?"

"The Minister." Constantine's eyes darkened. "He doesn't love me."

"What about your mom? Which Mother is she?"

He shook his head. "None of them. She died."

"When?"

"I don't know. I don't remember her. I swear, Kansas, the Minister doesn't treat me special."

Eisley began to stir, and we turned. She sat up, groggy, and rubbed her eyes.

"What's wrong?" she asked.

Constantine and I shared a look. Both of us were still haunted by the movie his father had shown us. How could we possibly do that to Eisley? I didn't even like to see her frown, let alone sob like the other girl had been.

"Nothing. Go back to bed,." I said. She patted the bed.

"You guys too. I sleep better when you're here with me." Constantine and I shared another look and reluctantly joined her, sandwiching her between us. We covered ourselves with the blanket and closed our eyes, attempting to sleep. Our conversation wasn't over, but one thing had been decided, as we lay with her. We'd figure out a way to get us all out.

Rule 48 - Kansas

Take an acting class.

I stared at my computer with my brow furrowed. I was exhausted. I reached for my hotel coffee. It was bitter and cold, but at this point, it was the only thing keeping me stable. I couldn't sleep until my work was done.

Emi's body was probably already found, along with her phone and everything else on her person. I'd stopped by her car on the way from the fire and found it unlocked. There was a backpack inside with her laptop and some notebooks. I spent an hour trying to unlock the laptop before finding a page in one of the notebooks with her entire list of passwords.

I got into her laptop and was on my way to finding the camera footage when she received an email from a name I'd seen before. Clicking on it, I found a long thread of emails between her and Dave Hues, the director of the documentary.

Emi had contacted them first, almost a year ago, begging them to come to the town. She told them about the Minister, his crimes, and how it'd be a great documentary to film. She'd secured an acting role and a good-sized 'finder's fee' bonus before they'd even shown up. All of it was only mildly interesting until I saw the email with Eisley's name.

Dave wanted to know if Emi knew her. Emi then apparently made it her mission to befriend her and convince her to do the documentary. She'd been working with them the entire time. Eisley was too trusting. She saw only the good in people. She would have never suspected someone with a kind smile to be anything other than good.

Good fucking riddance.

After I deleted the camera feed, I was going to ditch this computer and leave it somewhere for it to be found. They could do what they wanted with the information given.

The videos were easy to find. I was surprised to see so many. I hadn't noticed any of the inside cameras, but there we were. Eisley and I, me pulling her dress up and shoving my cock deep into her pussy. My dick twitched as I watched her flushed face fall apart as she came. Fuck, she was beautiful. With great reluctance, I deleted the footage after watching it in full. There would be other opportunities to make home movies. Ones with fewer stakes.

I wiped the greenhouse cloud and stood, shoving all of her shit back in her backpack. I got in my car, driving straight to the police station. I put on my best concerned face and strode in, asking for someone who worked with computers.

"We're kind of swamped, kid." The female officer at the desk rolled her eyes.

"Well, it's not an emergency. But I think it may be important. There's been a string of murders around town, right?"

I had the officer's attention then. She stood and eyed me suspiciously. "Yes. Do you have any information that could help the ongoing investigations?"

I shrugged. "I might. I uh—" I'd rehearsed this in the car over and over on the way in. I lifted the backpack. "I do IT work, and my girlfriend's friend asked me to fix her laptop. There's some crazy stuff on here."

She snatched it from me. "Who is your girlfriend's friend?" She opened it and began sifting through it.

"Emi something. I don't know her last name. She's tall, thin, Asian, bright red-dyed hair."

The woman's head shot up and she visibly paled. Then, she stared at me again. "Sit down, I'm going to grab the sheriff."

I took a seat, and a moment later, three officers came. I was taken into a back room, where I explained that her computer hadn't been taking a charge.

"Everyone's always asking me to fix their shit, so I always bring my tools with me wherever I go. I popped her laptop open and was able to fix her problem easily, and then, I went to test it." The officers nodded, their eyes glazing over. It worked every time. Just toss out a bunch of tech lingo and people assumed I was telling the truth.

"And then what?" a tall, Asian man with a permanent scowl asked me. He was holding her laptop but hadn't bothered to open it.

"I was booting it up, making sure all of her programs were as they should be, and an email came through. It was from the director of that documentary they're filming. You know, about the Minister."

"The Sinister Minister."

"Yeah, sorry. I— I'm tired. I didn't get much sleep. I was trying to decide whether or not to come forward. Tossed and turned all night." It was a good half-truth. Make the lies more believable.

"What's in the emails?"

"She was the one that brought them here. She gave them details about the Foxworth family, and how rich they were. Soleil's name was in there too. Along with Eisley, my girlfriend. She purposely befriended her to get her to be a part of the documentary. She promised to give them a good story, and they were paying her for it. The emails that came after they got here were... bleak." I swallowed and looked down.

I was selling this shit. They were eating it up.

"What do you mean?" the female asked softly. She reached for my hand on the table. "Tell us what you know."

"They were giving vague threats about how she needed to give them a good story because so far it was pretty boring. And she said she'd deliver."

"Can you get into her computer still?" the man demanded.

"I can, but isn't that illegal? Emi doesn't know I'm here, obviously."

"We'll take care of that. Help us get in and then you can leave."

I nodded and directed him toward the notebook with the passwords. "Everything you'll need is in there." I put my hands up innocently. "I want no part of this. I just—She seems like she's involved in stuff that's beyond me."

They led me out and thanked me for the assistance in the investigation.

"Of course. I hope you figure out who's doing this." I said and left quickly. I drove back to the hotel, trying not to laugh. I would get some well-earned sleep, and Emi would take the blame from beyond the grave for everything. Win-win.

Rule 49 - Eisley

Speak up.

I closed my eyes and kept them shut. The familiar smell, sounds, and cold air were far too much for my senses to handle. I couldn't bear sight as well. The bed was new and came with sheets, a thick comforter, and a pillow. I hid under them, dragging my heavy, shackled, and injured leg up onto it.

I covered my head with the blanket and closed my eyes, pretending this wasn't happening. The screeching door opened, and I shrunk into myself. Memories of the Mothers and the Fathers coming in to beat us, taunt us, or toss us the bare amount of food to survive flashed in my mind, but when I heard nothing, I peeked my head out of the blanket.

The man that had stalked me through the woods and brought me here stared down at me. I eyed him. I recognized him completely, and yet, my mind wouldn't let me settle on it. It couldn't be. Constantine would never bring me back here. Not when he fought so hard to get me out.

"Why are you doing this?" I asked.

"Why were you running through the forest?" he asked. His voice wasn't... his own. It was scratchy and cold. Not the grumbly and sexy voice I'd heard before. Could I be wrong? Maybe it wasn't Constantine.

"I don't know," I answered honestly. "It felt right."

"To come back home?"

"This was never a home." I looked around the room, where so much time had been passed simply staring at the walls. "But I did want to come back."

"Why?"

I didn't want to tell him about the greenhouse. I couldn't. I shifted my leg and winced at the pain. His eyes trailed to it.

"Are you going to keep me here?" I asked.

He shook his head. "Just for tonight. I can't be worried about what trouble you're getting into while I'm working."

"Working?"

He nodded grimly.

"If I agree not to run, will you let me go?"

He shook his head.

"Come on, I'm hurt." I motioned to my leg. "I literally can't run."

He crouched and reached for me. "Just stay here, princess, and I'll be back in a few hours." He pulled a small bottle from his pocket and handed it to me. "Drink this."

I laughed and dropped it. "Nice try."

He gripped my injured calf and squeezed. "Drink it."

I cried out in pain as he continued to squeeze. I scrambled to grab the bottle and unscrew the cap. He squeezed until every drop of the liquid had passed through my lips. It had a faint taste of artificial blue raspberry flavor.

He dropped his grip on my leg and reached for my chin. "Good girl. Now, rest, and I'll come back later." He stood and went to the door. "Would you like the door open or closed?"

"Open, please," I whimpered and leaned back on the pillows. My leg was throbbing, and my head was dizzy. Whatever had been in that drink was strong. He nodded and walked out, leaving the door wide open. Turning and cuddling into the blanket, I looked out.

My vision grew blurry, but I could make his shape out as he walked around the room. There was a table, where he was organizing... cups? I could only see vague shapes and colors. He was pouring things and moving them.

I was having trouble holding my eyes open. I closed them and then I heard him talking.

I struggled to open my eyes, but I was too far drugged to do anything else. Sleep overtook me. During the night, I felt weight on the bed. Arms wrapped themselves around me and I snuggled into the body. It was hard, yet comforting. I inhaled deeply and I couldn't deny the familiar scent.

"Ssshhh..." Constantine whispered in my ear. "It's okay. I'm here. I'm not going anywhere." His hands drifted up and down my body. My legs fell apart reflexively. I wanted to be touched, to feel good, to feel... him. He chuckled. "You're a greedy princess."

Constantine ground his palm on my clit above my panties. I moaned and wiggled under his touch, whimpering with need.

"You can't speak, can you?" He chuckled. I tried. I tried desperately to form words, but my jaw was so heavy, I couldn't move the muscles. "I guess we'll never know what exactly you wanted." He lifted his hand.

"You're gonna have to be a little louder, princess. I can't help you if you don't tell me what you want."

Using all the strength I could muster, I reached for his hand and tugged him back between my legs. He trailed two fingers up my slit, still not moving my underwear aside. I raised my hips, and finally, he began to tug them down.

"Ah, I see now. You want me to play with your pussy. Are you wet, princess?"

"Mmhmm..."

"I'll be the judge of that." He pushed my panties to my knees and parted my thighs. He spread my lips and ran a finger up, circling my clit. "I guess you are. I love how wet you get so easily. You held out for so long, and now, you can't get enough." Constantine reached down and planted his lips on mine. His tongue parted my lips and snuck inside, twisting around my own. I groaned as his tongue matched what his fingers were doing below.

"You've got such a tight pussy. I can't wait to stretch you and fill you 'til you scream and plead for me to stop." He slid two fingers inside me and pushed deep. I gasped, and finally, the muscles in my face relaxed. My body exploded against his fingers. He pumped me until I came down and then he removed his fingers and slid them into my mouth.

"Taste how good I make you feel." Feeling uninhibited, I ran my tongue along his fingers and sucked. "Good girl," he growled. He fell back onto his pillow and pulled me into him. "Now go to sleep, and in the morning, when you wake up in your own bed, we'll talk about where your wedding ring went."

Rule 50 - Eisley

Don't argue with the killer.

I awoke in the morning in my own bed. The moment I realized it, I bolted up. I tried to stand but my legs buckled, and I crumpled to the ground. I cried out as pain shot up from my foot up my leg and to my ass. My hurt leg was wrapped with compression tape. I was so confused. Was this a nightmare or not?

Heavy steps came up the stairs and I froze. I closed my eyes and tried to remember the night before. I was upset about Emi and had gone for a drive. I had somehow made it to the cross that marked Constantine's supposed death, and then I'd walked into the woods. I gasped, as it came then. *Ghostface.* He'd stalked and kidnapped me and taken me to the Church. But… what then? Why couldn't I remember anything else?

"Good morning. I heard you wake up." Constantine came into the room, holding a tray. "You hungry?"

"I'm confused. How did I get here?" I suddenly felt filthy, and I went to itch my dry shoulder and stopped. I'd forgotten about my tattoo. "I need lotion."

He set the tray on my nightstand and went to the bathroom, returning with a small jar. "Here." He handed it and then put his hands under my arms and lifted me with ease as if I weighed nothing. He gently placed me back in bed. "You should probably lay off of your leg for a while."

"It was you then. In the mask, following me through the woods."

He didn't agree or disagree. "I don't understand why you were there in the first place. It's a crime scene."

I laughed. "Ha! I could say the same thing about you."

"I own it."

I shifted on the bed and winced as pain shot up my leg.

"It still hurts? I wrapped it up."

"A little," I lied. It hurt a lot. "Thanks, though."

"Sure, I found the tape in your bathroom cabinet."

My head shot up, and we shared a look. He'd snooped in my medicine cabinet? I waited for him to ask about the prescription for Lithium, but he didn't. Instead, he set the tray on my lap.

"It's not your cooking, but I managed to crack some eggs." He grinned.

My stomach fluttered at his sexy smile. His black hair fell over his right eye as he waited for me to pick up the fork and take a bite.

"It smells great." I wasn't starving, but I cut a piece of the fried egg and took a bite. I made a noise of surprise. It was good. "So, I have some questions," I said as I reached for the toast.

He snickered. "All right, I may choose to answer some."

"You own the Church?"

"Unfortunately. When my dad died, it went to next of kin, but I couldn't touch the property until I was an adult."

"What are you going to do with it now?"

"No idea. It's not a place I'd want to renovate and start a family in or anything."

"You want a family?" His smile wavered, and I thought I saw a hint of bashfulness in his cheeks.

"I don't know. Maybe. Not anytime soon. And definitely not here. I actually don't want you here either, for that matter. As soon as we can, you should consider selling this place."

"Why? I like it here." My house was a goth paradise. I'd spent so much time and energy decorating it, painting the walls, and making it feel like a real home.

"Yeah, but another body was found. Your friend, Emi?" My heart stopped for a moment, and I blinked rapidly. I'd all but forgotten about her.

"What?"

"I'm sorry. I probably shouldn't have woken you up so cheerfully. Emi was caught in a fire at the greenhouses. I was reading about it this morning. They think she started them as this ploy to drum up a more interesting story for the documentary crew."

"No, that's—" I blinked. "What about Soleil? And Spencer?"

"The article didn't say if they were connected or not, but that documentary is no good. And they're digging their heels in. They aren't cooperating with the police and said they were gonna finish their movie."

"How?" My mouth fell open in shock. "Half of their cast is dead."

"Money talks. Someone I'm sure will volunteer for a few minutes of fame."

"Poor Emi." Once I finished eating, Constantine took my tray and returned to rest on the bed beside me.

"Now, I have some questions."

"Wait, I'm not done with mine!" I said quickly. "Why is there a bed and blankets there?"

"The hotel threw my shit out while I was sitting in jail,

and I had nowhere to go. I went to the store and picked those things up so I could last a few days out here."

"What were you doing last night? On the table."

"What do you mean?" He shook his head.

"You were moving things and pouring things. I couldn't see. What were you doing?" He rolled over onto his back and laughed dryly.

"Oh. That. You're not the only one who's into witchy shit."

"Really?"

He turned his head and stared pointedly at me. "If I told you, you wouldn't believe me."

"Fine." I crossed my arms. "What questions do you have for me?"

"Where's your necklace?" He reached for my neck and tightened his hand around my throat in a way that was slightly scary, yet arousing. His gaze darkened as we stared at each other and then he let go. Flashes of two nights ago, in the greenhouse with Kansas, when he tore it off my neck as he fucked me from behind ran through my mind.

"Is it lost?" He raised an eyebrow.

"No."

"Did you take it off to shower?"

"No."

"Does someone else have it?" He said the last words through gritted teeth. I looked him dead in the eyes as I answered him.

"Yes."

"Do you think this is a game, wife?" he snarled.

"I don't know, husband. Do you?"

"What's that supposed to mean?" He stood, and I forced myself to my own feet, wobbling only slightly.

"That night with the mushrooms. I thought I was having sex with you, but there was someone else there. You let them touch me, knowing I couldn't tell the difference." His eyebrows jumped with surprise, and then he snickered.

"Yeah? And you liked it either way."

"That's not the point. Who was it? Who is your partner in crime?"

"What makes you so damn positive there was someone there? You were hallucinating."

"I know what I heard." We were at a stand-off, with me leaning against my bed, trying to stay standing. Constantine spun around and stormed out of the room. I rested back on the bed and when he returned, he yanked my legs up. Constantine wrapped something cool and thick around my bandaged ankle and tightened it. He dropped it, and I let out a sharp cry.

"I have to go do some stuff, and if you're going to be a tease and not tell me whose cock was inside you last, then you're going to stay here in this room until I return." He pulled out a thick cord from behind his back and quickly tied it to the leather band on my ankle.

"What?" I cried out, trying to kick him away.

"There's enough length for you to go to the bathroom. Have fun." He stormed out and I tried to follow him. I watched the cord grow tighter the farther from the bed I got until I reached the hall, made it to the bathroom, and saw he was right. I could sit down on the toilet and not another foot.

"Constantine!" I screamed. "You're a bastard." I snarled from my bedroom door. "What am I supposed to do all day?"

"I had bought you something fun for us both to play with, but now that I have someone's ass to find and kick for fucking my wife, why don't you just play with it yourself? Make a movie for me or something." He started down the stairs.

"What are you talking about?"

"There's a webcam that goes just to my phone. I think you can figure it out." The front door opened and slammed, and I returned to my room with a huff. I looked around for what he was talking about and sat the small ball camera at the end of my bed.

What gift was he talking about? I reached under the bed and pulled out a long silver-wrapped box. When I unwrapped it, I looked up at the camera as my face flushed with mortification.

"I can't—What are you expecting?" I asked aloud as I pulled out the dildo that looked extremely life-like. I knew exactly what he wanted. I stared hard at the camera, and I thought about his words. That the feed went right to his phone alone. The idea of him watching me pleasure myself was...

Could I do it?

Rule 51 - Constantine

Make sure everyone is punished.

I had to tug on my jeans and adjust before getting into my car and taking off, leaving Eisley to ponder her next move. She was a fucking brat.

And it made me so horny.

I sped away, glancing at the passenger's side seat, where my dad's scripture sat, weathered and worn. This was the only copy not in the hands of law enforcement. He'd buried it in the coffin meant to hold my dead mother's corpse. Instead, he disposed of her some other way and tossed a fuckton of gold bars, some legal papers, and this, inside and buried it for me to find after his death.

I parked and strode into the woods. To not be seen by police or anyone else trying to keep people out of the murder scene, I had to walk from the back, which was almost a full extra mile. Backpack on and knife and mask in my hand, just in case I came upon someone, I walked through the mangled forest until finally, I reached the Church. I gave one good look around and dipped inside.

Heading right downstairs, I found the lanterns lit already. I tightened my grip on my knife and stepped into the room. The figure turned, and I saw an all too familiar face. I dropped the knife and stormed over to him, snatching him up by the shirt.

"You think you're fucking funny?" I shoved Kansas against the stone wall.

"What?" A smile slid onto his face.

"You just couldn't wait to stick your cock in her, could you?"

"Oh, did she tell you?"

I reached for his throat and squeezed.

"I should stab you." I continued squeezing his throat until his face turned red and then I dropped him. He crumpled to the ground and began to cough frantically.

"It wouldn't do any good."

"No." I eyed the table on which I'd been working last night. All of my materials were still there with some new items added and shifted around. "But it'd make me feel better." I retrieved my knife and twirled it in my fingers before thrusting it into the wooden table. "Why are you here?"

"Where else am I supposed to go? You won't leave her fucking house."

"For good reason, apparently. I'm in jail for a few days and you sneak into her bed." I slammed my hands on the table and began examining all the items we'd gathered for the ritual.

He laughed and leaned against the wall, massaging his throat.

"We didn't fuck in her bed. We fucked in the greenhouse. Why do you think we had to burn it down? They caught us on camera."

"You can't be fucking serious."

"I took care of it."

"By killing her best friend?"

"By getting rid of several problems at once." He pushed

his glasses up his nose and twisted his septum piercing. "Now, are we doing this or what?" He nodded to the table.

"Yeah." I took a deep breath and reached for my backpack. "It's going to be stronger since we're here. Give me the details."

Kansas dipped into his jacket and pulled out a small wire notebook and tugged off a sheet. I scanned the list and looked at him.

"You found it. Great."

"This is all correct?"

"Every last name."

Foxworth
Du Pont
Palmer
Walton
Harris
Hajime

"I've met Mr. Hajime," Kansas said as I began writing their names down on individual papers. "He was Emi's dad."

"Yeah? He made sure that the police never investigated the Family while we were all down here struggling not to die," I snarled.

I wrote his name, along with the rest of his family, tore it out of my notebook, and folded it three times before tossing it in a cup. Then, I did the same for the others.

"Which one was which again?" Kansas leaned over me and asked.

"Du Pont made sure my dad had new kids whenever he wanted." I tore his name off the sheet. "That's Rem's dad."

"And Foxworth paid for us to stay locked in here, along with the cameras and shit."

"The Waltons, Soleil's parents, were up there with the Foxworths. Big donors. Whenever someone wanted to rally against my dad, they slid a check over to them."

"And which of her friends is Palmer?"

I squinted, trying to remember. "I think that's Micah. His dad was the distributor. He knew where all the sick fucks were and what they wanted." I checked the list and confirmed it.

"Who's left then? Harris. That's Therese, right?" I nodded and wrote her family's name.

"They helped clean the upstairs whenever people did manage to get through the doors to check on us."

I folded all of their names and put them into individual small cups. "Each and every one of these families had a direct hand in the sick shit my dad was doing down here and got away with it afterward. Well, not anymore." I pulled the knife from the table and raised my arm. "The stronger the binding agent, the more powerful the spell is."

Carefully, I slid the blade across my skin and began to bleed. Kansas quickly took the cups and began filling them.

"Is this enough?" He eyed the contents. There was just enough blood to cover the bottom.

"As long as the note is soaked in it, it is." I reached for my backpack and pulled out the bandages, quickly cleaning myself up.

"What do we say?" he asked me.

"Why am I still baby-spooning this shit to you?" I reached for a cup and shoved my fingers deep into it to make sure the paper was soaked. I looked around for the cooler I had brought down a few days ago and filled it with ice this morning. It would serve until I could put these in Eisley's freezer.

We set all six cups with the family's names on them, and together, we repeated the phrase.

"Stay there and freeze, as long as we please."

We stood back up and Kansas began wiping my blood off his hands.

"Now what?"

I laughed. "Now, we wait for the Reanimator to do his thing. It shouldn't take long."

"It never does."

Rule 52 - Constantine

Watch and learn.

Ten years ago.

My father pressed his hand firmly into my back, guiding me through the upstairs and to his office. "We're taking the back way as we have guests right now."

"Guests?" I looked up at him, fear striking down me. I'd been taught to fear guests. They were only here to make things worse.

"Yes, it's nothing to worry about, Constantine. Just some trouble in our little paradise. I shall see my flock through. Now, come, sit, I have brought you here for a reason."

"I don't want to watch any more movies," I said firmly, my fists clenching at my sides. They were disgusting and I couldn't bear to see the other boys and girls, the same size as me, be treated like that. I could never do that to Eisley like they wanted. I wouldn't.

"No, none of that today. Although I note your distaste. We will put a pin in that to discuss later. Tonight, once our guests leave, you will witness one of the Fathers giving us his greatest gifts tonight, and I think you will change your view on things afterward."

"A gift?"

My father grabbed a box from his office, along with a large book that looked so old it would crumble if I tried touching it, and took me back downstairs.

"What is this room?" I asked, stepping into it for the second time.

"All in good time, my son." He chuckled and led me into the common room. I recalled this room, as I'd spent most of my time in it before Kansas and Eisley came. It had been years since I'd been allowed to spend more than a few minutes here, but it looked the same. I looked around for the door in which my friends were. It wasn't too far away. If I had the strength and the keys, I could get them out and we could run so fast they wouldn't be able to catch us. But, I had neither of those things. They didn't feed us enough for us to be strong.

"Sit here, son." He sat a chair in the corner of the room. "Do not move from it. Your role tonight is to observe and nothing else. You will ruin the ritual if you do. Understand?"

I nodded and took my seat. Nothing happened for a long time, but eventually, he came down to announce that the guests were gone, and they could start the ritual.

Mothers and Fathers walked back and forth, gathering this or that, putting them on the large rectangle table.

One Mother slid a black velvet tablecloth over it, while another Mother put a smaller red velvet one over that one. Dozens of candles were brought into the room. The Fathers began to light them. I grew scared when they began setting them on the floor. Wouldn't this start a fire? My eyes flicked to the door across the room where Eisley and Kansas were. I wouldn't be able to save them if something happened.

My attention was instantly diverted when someone started humming. Slowly, other Mothers and Fathers began to join in until the entire room hummed a haunting tune. I began to count and found all nine Mothers and all nine Fathers in the room, holding tall black, red, and white, candles. Where had my father gone?

The Family hummed for some time, and then, they all stopped at the exact same time, sending chills of fear up my spine. The room split and my father returned, only now he wasn't wearing a suit like before. Now he was in a red robe.

The Minister.

"Today, we have collected the Family to honor the Reanimator and his blessings. To ensure our gracious God continues to bestow his gifts, a sacrifice must be made. Has the Family decided which shall give themselves to the Reanimator and to us?"

A Father stepped forward, his head high and his black candle firmly grasped his hand, despite the hot wax dripping onto his skin.

"I shall."

The Minister nodded his approval and took the candle from him, blowing it out.

"The Family thanks you for your sacrifice." He reached out and kissed the Father on the lips. "The Family will be rewarded greatly for you."

I didn't understand, but I continued to watch. The Father slid his robe off his shoulders to unveil complete and utter nakedness. I looked away quickly. He was helped onto the table and he stretched out. The Family circled him and began dripping their tall candles onto his bare body.

The Minister began to sing a hymn I was familiar with but couldn't remember word for word, as it was a different language. Soon, everyone joined in, creating a round. They sang as they continued to rain hot wax onto him.

The Minister shouted a name and a Mother blew out her candle and reached her hand out. I looked away instantly when I saw where her hand had gone and what she was doing with it. It was like the movies we'd been forced to watch. I closed my eyes and tried to pretend I was somewhere else.

Safe, back in the room with Kansas and Eisley.

Safe.

Back in the room.

With Kansas and Eisley.

I repeated the words and covered my ears with my hands as the Father began to make sounds. The Family began chanting louder to cover them. The Father suddenly cried out, and I knew what had happened. I understood why they were doing it and what would happen at the end. They were making him feel good, and then... I peeked my eyes open as the Mother stroking him stepped back and put her hand in her robe.

Then, they all put their hands in their robes and raised large knives over their heads and one by one, swung down, stabbing into his body.

He screamed, and the Minister quickly covered his mouth. Two Fathers held his arms and two Mothers held his legs as the rest continued to slice the knife into his naked body until he grew limp.

A Mother hurried to grab a large bucket from another table and they began to collect the blood flowing off the table. The Minister raised the old book from before and began reciting something in a language I didn't recognize.

They lifted the dead Father and continued to collect his blood. I put my knees to my chest and tried not to make any noise. Who knew what they'd do if they remembered I was here? When the blood stopped coming, they set him back on the table and then turned to the Minister.

I opened one eye and instantly shut it as I saw them peeling the skin off his chest and removing... pieces of him.

I was going to be sick.

Safe, back in the room with Kansas and Eisley.

Safe.

Back in the room.

With Kansas and Eisley.

All the while, they kept chanting, and then it stopped.

The Minister nodded his approval to his flock, who had set the dead Father's insides on the table in bowls, and dropped his robes. He, too, was nude. He went to the bucket and dipped his hands in. As if it were soap, he began rubbing it on his arms, face, and torso. He covered himself head to toe in the blood, all while continuing to speak in the unknown language. Once his entire body was red, he called to the others. They formed a line, and one by one, they stepped forward, and the Minister dipped his hands in the bucket and painted their faces.

They continued chanting until the Minister screamed and raised a knife. He swung it deep into his belly, and the room erupted into a panic.

I bit back my scream as I watched him stumble to a table. He slid the knife slowly out of his stomach and it clamored to the floor. A Mother ran to another bucket and dumped it over him. The blood ran off his body and everyone gasped. The Minister stood and opened his arms. The wound was gone. Everyone cried out in excitement, and the Minister told them to clean and put their clothes on.

"The Reanimator has accepted our offering and has gifted us again. Go forth and find a new Father." He grinned at his congregation, and then chuckled and pointed at me, shaking in the corner. "I have to go be one to my own son."

Snatching my hand, he pulled me up and dragged me through the rooms and back to his office up the secret staircase.

"What do you think, Constantine?" He grinned.

"I don't know," I answered honestly.

"In three months, we shall have a similar ceremony with

you, Kansas, and Eisley. Eisley will choose a husband, and the other shall be given to the Reanimator so that the pair can be blessed with his power. You need to make sure you are chosen."

I stood up and raised my fists to a man I'd seen almost die and come back to life. "I am not going to make her choose." How could I let that happen to Kansas? My best friend?

His eyes turned stormy and dark. He bent down and brought his face inches within mine. The smell of copper filled my nostrils, and I had to fight not to vomit.

"Either she chooses, and she chooses correctly, or I'll kill both of you and take your precious little Eisley for my next wife, you little shit."

Rule 53 - Eisley

Smile for the camera.

Testicles were attached to the flesh-colored dildo, along with a wand that I presumed was for me to handle it. As I poked under it, I found a button. The dildo roared to life and began feverishly thrusting upward.

I dropped it onto the bed with a small scream and watched it inch away from me. I snatched it back up and pushed the button furiously, watching it slow and speed up as I clicked. Interesting. Along with the toy, the box also had a handful of packets I originally thought were condoms but turned out to be lubrication.

I tugged on the leather bracelet around my ankle. The chain was shiny, but heavy and tied to the heater on the other side of the room. When did he have time for this? I ran my hands through my hair and fell back onto my pillows in a huff. I was losing time, and it was frustrating.

I pulled on the chain, but I knew it was futile. It was staying put and so was I. I tried to stand again, but the more I tried to walk, the worse it felt. I needed to let it heal, if only for a few hours. I fell back onto the bed and stared up at the ceiling, painted black with shiny bats stenciled across it.

Constantine wanted me to give my house up. For what? Where did he even live? And what about Kansas? I couldn't leave without telling him about Kansas and vice versa. I didn't want to pick one over the other. I couldn't.

I turned my head and stared at the small round ball attached to the foot of my bed. The small red light was taunting me. Constantine was taunting me.

I was still so new to sex, I'd look ridiculous. Sure, I'd watched videos to make sure my own content, while PG, was still just enough of a tease to get people to subscribe to my racier stuff. And my racy stuff wasn't even racy compared to many. Lingerie videos where everything was covered and I moaned a little?

This was... real porn. And he wanted it. From me.

I reached for the toy again and studied it with new intrigue. It wasn't obnoxious in length or girth, nor was it small. Perhaps I could enjoy it. Would it feel the same as it being attached to someone? My heart raced as I went back and forth and finally decided, if I was going to do this, I was going to do it right.

Being ever so careful, I made it to my dresser and grabbed my most flattering pajamas. A black, lacy negligee. For client videos, I wore pasties to cover my nipples, but for Constantine, *my husband*, I'd let them show through the sheer fabric.

Because of the chain, I couldn't put new underwear on, so I opted instead to slide my panties off and move them down the chain and go without. Considering how the toy moved, I would not need them.

My heart didn't slow the entire time I prepped for the camera. I had to consciously control my breathing. In and out. I could do this. It was for Constantine. He was the only one who was going to see this. Right?

I gulped. I had to trust he wasn't lying. Would he lie about this? If so, what else was he lying about? Constantine, my companion in the Church, wouldn't betray me like that. I may have met the adult version of him, but I knew who he was before. He was my protector then, and I knew in my heart, he was my protector now.

Before I climbed back into bed, I shut my door and spotted my smart hub in the corner of the room. I hadn't used it in forever. I didn't even know if it still worked. I was growing tired, and my leg was aching badly, but having music would relax me. I went to it, plugged it in, and it booted up. It lit bright blue and I spoke to it.

"Hub, put on a spicy playlist."

It flashed for a moment and then dinged. *"Putting on a spicy playlist."*

The room filled with Doja Cat. This would work. The beat from "*Freak*" gave me a surge of confidence, and I slid onto the bed and sat in the middle. I bounced slightly and shifted to make sure I wasn't putting any weight on my injured leg, and then I looked dead at the camera and smiled.

"Hey you." I waved playfully, then slid forward, reaching for the toy.

"I was given a gift from a very special man in my life. I won't say who, but let's just say..." I raised the toy to the camera and ran my hand down it. It was then that I realized I'd never touched a real cock like this before. "Let's just say it's not as impressive as the real thing, but considering the real thing isn't in my bed right now, it'll have to do."

Reaching for a lube packet, I tore it and eased the slippery liquid onto the toy, running my hands up and down it to get it lubricated. It felt like my own arousal, which relaxed me.

"It feels so real. I think I'm a little spoiled!" I giggled and bounced again like I'd seen other girls do. "I'm going to go slow, as to give you a good show," I said and fell back onto my pillow, bringing my knees up, and finally, with my heart beating out of my chest, I spread my legs, revealing my body to the camera.

I reached for the toy and brought it to my chest. I opened my eyes just enough to make eye contact with the camera. I slid the fake cock down my breasts, belly, and finally reached my lips.

I took a deep breath and slid my hand down to the handle, pressing the vibrate button. The machine hummed to life, and I gasped. It was so intense! I pulled it away instantly.

"Holy shit."

I blinked, absorbing the shock of how powerful it was. I ran my hands down my slit and found myself suddenly very wet. I bit my lower lip and smirked at the camera. "I don't want to come like that. I want to use every function this has."

I slid the cock down my wetness slowly. I paused at my opening. This was it. A deep ache came from my core, begging me to do it. Carefully, I pushed it inside me and felt the fullness.

I chose to manually work it, letting my body savor the feeling at its own gentle pace. I was still getting used to the interesting stretch that came from penetration. I raised my head and grinned at the camera.

"Why don't we see what it can really do?" I slid it out and pushed the button for thrusting. It whirred to life, and I pushed it back inside. In perfect rhythm, it was hitting something inside me that felt so incredible. It was so... deep.

I let my head fall back to the pillow, and I pushed it further inside, relishing in the feeling of being fucked by a fake cock. I closed my eyes and imagined Constantine over me, then Kansas, and then both.

I cried out as I came so hard my vision grew spotty. The cock kept pumping as my orgasm tightened around it, and it felt so incredible. When I came down, I removed it and turned it off. My body collapsed instantly, and I was so tired, so exhausted, I couldn't move. Then, I heard a ping come from my smart hub.

"New Message."

Sighing, I answered it. "Read off message."

"From Husband. Good Girl."

I felt the weight of the chain drop, and I lifted my leg to see that I'd been set free.

Rule 54 - Eisley

Anything can be a weapon if you know what you're doing.

Exhaustion over the powerful orgasm, paired with my throbbing leg, caused me to fall asleep. I woke up sometime later, still free, and my leg considerably less sore. I tested it first, and then finding it able to carry my weight again, I walked to my dresser and changed into clean underwear and a dress that wasn't see-through and covered my knees.

I glanced back at the bed, where the toy lay still. While it worked wonders, I decided I'd have a much more fun time with Constantine. Or Kansas. I wouldn't tell him that last part. Being with Kansas was the reason for being locked up in the first place.

As soon as my feet touched the base of the stairs, the energy felt off. I looked around, and seeing only dark, I began turning on lights.

"Constantine? Kansas? Are you here?" I called, but I was met with total silence. I sighed deeply at all the flowers in my living room and saw that the first one needed to be tossed. I grabbed it and started toward the kitchen, and when I flicked the light on, I gasped. My entire kitchen had been torn apart.

The cabinets were opened and the drawers were pulled out. Every jar of tea I had was on the counters, many were dumped. It was a disaster!

I set the dead bouquet down on the messy counter. Dried tea leaves and other herbs were scattered all over as if someone had been testing them. And then it hit me.

Someone knew what I had hidden.

Someone was looking for specific things.

I hurried to my pantry. A handful of my teapots were on the floor, some broken into pieces. Whoever did this was—was a monster! Tears spilled as carefully, I stepped around the broken pieces and crouched to see if whoever had been in my house had found my secret cabinet. They had. It was wide open, and all of the jars were gone.

Hemlock, pokeweed, parsnip, maidenhair fern, my juniper, Indian turnips, and all my meadow saffron. There were more jars I couldn't recall right away that I'd put in here. All things that were poisonous and I'd been saving for an emergency. All of it, gone.

But why?

Were they trying to hurt someone or were they sending me a message? Either way, the damage was done, and I sat in my pantry and cried.

Eventually, I mustered up the strength and returned to my broom. I cleaned up the floor and tried to salvage what I could from the counters. Whoever had come in knew what they were looking for. They did the rest of this simply to be cruel.

They wanted me to feel unsafe in my own home, but I'd be damned if I let them do that to me. Tossing the rag I was using to clean up the loose tea, I dove into a drawer and picked up my herb sheers and stormed out of the room. I had to search for my phone, but eventually found it resting in the living room, on its charger. So considerate, I smirked. While he had taken it from me, so I had no way to call for help,

Constantine made sure it was charged. I slid my gardening shoes on, grabbed my gardening bag, and went outside.

Thankfully, the asshole who trashed my kitchen hadn't touched my backyard. Crouching down, I opened my bag and grabbed gloves and my jars.

I had to be careful what I touched, but I trimmed a lot of my meadow saffron, along with some hemlock. That was the beauty of my garden. These plants looked like pretty flowers. No one had been the wiser the entire time I was growing them.

Not that I'd done anything but trim, dry, and store them. It was more of a security blanket. I knew it was absurd, but this was better than nothing.

Once all my jars were full, I put everything back in my bag and stood. I clicked my flashlight off and hurried back inside my house. While I hated it being true, I was now slightly frightened about who could be on the other side of the door. They'd scared me, but I had to get the fuck over it. I started toward the pantry, where my not-so-secret cupboard was, but paused, and turned back, opting to put them right with all my other dried teas. He may have taken some of it, some of me, but not all. I would always bounce back, and I wasn't hiding either.

Rule 55 - Kansas

Take your time when preparing your final kill.

My cock ached as it sat rock hard in my jeans, with me unable to do anything but watch the video of Eisley, pumping that fake cock into her wet pussy, repeatedly. A low groan rumbled up my throat, and Constantine kicked my boot.

"Will you knock that shit off?" He stalked over to the table and set his backpack on it with a heavy thump. I sighed and put his phone down.

"You don't understand." I stood and adjusted my raging hard-on. "I've been waiting fucking years to see her like this. My dick hasn't gone down since I finally was able to be inside her." He chuckled low and unzipped his bag.

"And you think mine hasn't? She's beautiful, isn't she?" He nodded to the phone I'd set down. "She came hard."

"She came harder with me."

"Oh yeah? I think next time I see her, I'll ask. You know, the reason I snapped her leg to that chain was because she refused to talk about you."

I rolled my eyes and stepped up to the table.

"That'll change." My eyes scanned the items Constantine

was pulling from his seemingly never-ending bag. "Be careful with all those jars."

"Why? It won't kill me."

"Gives you one hell of a rash though."

"Is she still crying?" he asked, setting a velvet tablecloth on the table.

"Let me check." I strode over to my tablet and clicked on her cameras. "No, she's cleaned it all up. Do you think we should tell her?"

I'd gone in to take all her jars full of poison for the ritual and had found someone had already been there. They'd destroyed probably over half of her teapot collection as well as made a mess of her kitchen. It wasn't until I got back to the Church, that I looked at her cameras and saw that it had been her friend Therese.

I wondered why. Did she know something we didn't?

"No. It would lead to more questions, and eventually she'd ask about the jars you took. Therese will have no idea what she's talking about. Just let it be."

He was right, but it still didn't feel good. Eisley should know her so-called friends were assholes. I kept watching the cameras. God, she was so beautiful when she was upset.

"It's bad enough I don't have the nine Mothers and Fathers, but fuck, could I get a hand from you?" he snapped.

"I don't know what I'm doing." I pulled my eyes from the cameras.

"You really fucking irritate me sometimes," he snarled. "So fucking smart but yet so fucking stupid." I sat the tablet down and shoved him.

"I'm not stupid, you asshole. I'm just lazy." I scooped up a giant bag of candles and began setting them all around the room. "Now shut the fuck up so I can count to 237."

Constantine cleared the table and spread the velvet tablecloths down and then made the altar. As we worked, we joked alongside each other, as if we were just regular men at average jobs, and not preparing a ritual sacrifice for a god that we still didn't fully understand.

"Be careful lighting those." He warned.

"What, afraid of fire, Frank?"

"I fucking hate you," he laughed. "Stop calling me that."

"If you're Frankenstein, that makes Eisley Frankenstein's bride. What does that make me?"

"Whatever you want to be, fuckface." With all the candles and Eisley's herbs that had to be set up just right, it took longer than we'd expected, but we both knew how important it was to get everything perfect.

"I have a question," I asked when we'd paused for a break. "What were the Minister's last words?" I looked around the room, trying to picture it all, ten years ago. I wished I'd been there to see the fucker die. Constantine looked up from his cigarette.

"He told me to save the books. That I'd need them when I got older, and as long as I paid tribute to the Reanimator, I'd be okay."

"And then what?" I took a drag of my cigarette.

"I stabbed the fucker." He pushed off the table and looked around the room. "It looks about done. Just make sure we have a few backup lighters and we'll be good to go."

I shuddered, as we stretched and walked down the hall, toward our respective rooms. "All those candles really freak me out."

"Now who's Frankenstein?"

I paused at my door. "You really think we're ready?"

"Not quite. A few more bodies should do it."

Rule 56 - Kansas

It doesn't have to make sense if it works.

Ten years ago.

"I saw it. He was bleeding and then he wasn't." Constantine pushed his finger into the page. "And this is why."

I glanced over at the bed. Eisley was sleeping. She'd been taken the night before and made to stand in one of the Mother's rooms as punishment. When she'd been returned to us, she could barely walk, and the back of her legs were bright red from being smacked every time she tried to sit. She was growing weaker, more tired, by the day. We had to get out of here.

Constantine cleared his throat and I returned to him. I looked down and read the text again.

Reanimation.

"So, you die and come back?"

"If you do it right. My— The Minister said it's easy to mess up. That's why he's the only one allowed to do it."

I read the text again, and again. I wasn't sure what to do about this information.

"I want to see it."

"What?"

"I want to see it," I said sharply. "It's impossible."

"It's not," Constantine argued back.

"It is, unless we try it ourselves." He was telling me that magick was real and I was just supposed to believe him? It could very well be the end of my life if I did and he was lying.

"If we mess up, we die," he whispered.

"There's mice all over here. Let's catch one and try to do it on him."

The next time we were taken to the Minister for lessons, we looked for rodents scurrying around. When I saw one, I excused myself to the bathroom and caught it. I stuffed it into my pants pocket, forever grateful that they were still giving us clean, fresh clothes to visit the Minister.

The mouse, while wiggly, stayed firm in my pocket the entire lecture. I petted it to soothe it some and made an effort not to wince when it nipped me. Constantine, seeing I had the mouse, looked for the other items we needed for the ritual. When we returned to our room, we emptied our pockets.

"What did you get?" I asked.

"Two candles and a lighter."

"I don't know how to use this." I took the red lighter from his hand and mimicked what I'd seen before.

"Let me try. You work on killing the mouse." I stared at the creature in my hand. I didn't want to kill him. What if he didn't come back?

"I don't have anything sharp." Realizing we had no way to kill the thing, we let it go and vowed to try again another day. Every day, we collected more items. In five days, we had nine candles, some dried plants, and a fork.

"I know what you're doing," the Minister said one day as we took our seats in front of his desk. "It's only natural curiosity." Constantine and I shared a nervous glance as he paced around us. "If you were reading the text properly, you'd see that if you do the ritual wrong, it can have dire consequences. Boys, I am disappointed in you for not coming to me about helping you." He paused behind his desk, putting his palms down and looking at us. "Would you like some assistance?"

We nodded. He left the room and returned with a box.

"Now, it will work to a lesser extent, as we are not sacrificing a member of the Family. However, consider this almost a party trick. Something to show others what the Reanimator, our true god, can do." He opened the box, revealing a live snake.

We fell back with sharp screams.

"It's fine, boys. Kansas, hold the box while Constantine and I set up the altar."

Once the altar was finished, the Minister told me to stand. He took the box from me and removed the snake.

"Now, we sing the hymns, boys. Use the book. Make sure every single word is correct."

The Minister took a small bottle off his desk and opened it, dousing his hand in the liquid. The snake responded to it, curling around his hand and wrist. Something came out of the snake, and I shuddered.

"To begin the ritual, the sacrifice must orgasm. Do you understand what that means?" I shook my head. The Minister chuckled. "When you tug on yourself until your body feels a really good feeling?"

I glanced at Constantine, whose cheeks were red like mine with shame. We understood that.

"Yes, that is an orgasm. The end bit. The sacrifice must do that before we kill it."

I couldn't look at the snake as it encircled the Minister's hand. Instead, I focused on the hymn, chanting it loudly with Constantine. After some time, the snake relaxed and was set down on the altar. I leapt back as The Minister abandoned him, but he assured us he wouldn't move.

"Now, while it only requires one piercing and three long slices along the torso, the Family likes for us all to participate during your ceremony. Whichever one will receive it," he paused and looked from Constantine to me. "It will be a lot more intensive."

"You mean, one of us will be—" Constantine's face paled. I recalled what he had told me about what happened, but it was nothing compared to seeing it.

"Will be the snake, yes." The Minister confirmed with such casualness it made me sick. "Now, let's see the Reanimator's powers in action." He snatched the snake up and pulled a small knife from his pocket. With a sickening slice, he slit the snake from its head down and let blood pour into the cup waiting for it.

He did the three cuts to look like the letter Y and then tossed it aside. He demanded we keep singing, while he added things to the blood. Then, he dipped his hands in it and reached for me.

I flinched away, but then I returned despite everything in me screaming for him not to let him touch me. We allowed him to paint our faces with blood, and then, without warning, he snatched Constantine's hand and ran the knife along his entire palm. We screamed, and Constantine cried from the pain. All the while, the Minister continued to pray loudly.

"Put your hand in the cup, son!"

Hesitantly, he did it. The Minister reached for a bottle of water and poured it all over Constantine's hand. Slowly, the once deep wound closed. There was no scar either.

It was real.

Rule 57- Eisley

Everyone has a mask.

I'd spent the day mourning for the loss of Spencer, Soleil, Emi, and oddly enough, my teapots. I stared at all the newly empty shelves and fought back tears each time. Who had been so cruel?

A knock on my door brought me from my grief, and I opened it to find Kansas holding a box of Coronas and a large brown bag that smelled delicious.

"Thought you could use some company."

"I do." My mood lifted instantly as I let him inside.

"You cleared half the flowers?" He sat the food on my coffee table. "Probably a good thing since you've got another one on your porch."

"What?" I hurried outside and to my dismay, there was another bouquet. It had no card, but I knew why I'd received them. They were Emi's flowers.

"Whoever is sending them needs to fuck right off," I said, slamming the door and leaving them on the porch.

"I mean, they're pretty flowers." He shrugged and joined me on the couch.

"Too much of a good thing." I sighed and reached for a beer in the box.

"To us," Kansas said.

I took a large gulp and sighed. "Constantine knows."

He chuckled and reached for a tinfoil tray, opening it, and reaching for forks. "Yeah? Good for him."

"He's..."

"Jealous?"

"I don't know?" I sat back, brushing my hair behind my ear. "Maybe? And you can't talk, mister. You've been jealous of him for years."

"Yeah, because you were waiting for a dead guy. How could anyone compete with that?"

"It's not a competition. You guys mean the same to me."

He took a bite of his food, staring at me with his bright, expressive green eyes.

"Can we talk about something else?"

"Of course," I agreed and reached for my tin of food. We ate and I tried to chat about regular things, but considering the events from the last few weeks, it felt awkward. We sat facing each other, sipping our drinks and dancing around several topics. He pushed his glasses up and wiggled his septum piercing.

"All right, what do you want to ask about?"

"Emi." My voice came out so small. Tears flooded my vision. "Was it hard?"

"Yes. I was scared that someone would come in at any time. I had to move quickly. I felt terrible, but then I found all that shit on her computer and I had to turn it in."

"What stuff?"

"She planned it all. With the documentary crew. They were paying her every step of the way for a good story. Eisley, I think, she was going to kill all of you guys."

"No. That can't be." Kansas set his beer down and pulled me into his embrace.

"It is. I saw her emails. It was all there. Down to how much she was getting for each event."

"She admitted to killing them?"

"That's the only thing she didn't say. But all the pieces are there. I'm sorry, Eisley. She wasn't your friend. She only started talking to you because they asked her to."

Was that true? Was Emi luring me to my death this whole time? I was silent for a long time before deciding I wanted to move on.

"Therese told me they are doing a combined funeral for Emi and Soleil, since they were roommates and all."

He pressed his lips tenderly to the top of my head, and I kissed his chest. He stiffened, and I looked up at him. His hand came up and his thumb brushed away my tears.

"You're beautiful when you cry. I hate it, and yet, long to be the one you run to."

I sat back and we stared at each other before leaning in and pressing our lips to each others. One kiss turned to another, and Kansas was shifting closer, pressing me into the couch. I tasted beer on his tongue and inhaled his cologne. It was so familiar, so safe, so sexy.

He slid me down the couch and moved on top of me. The strength of his desire pressed against my thigh, and my body responded in kind.

"Last time was too quick. I want to take my time with you."

He lifted me bridal-style, and I wrapped my arms around his neck and pulled his face to me. Passion filled the kiss, and when he pulled away, his green eyes were full of determination. He started toward the stairs. "You're not going to be able to think about anything but how good I make you feel tonight."

Rule 58 - Eisley

Begging can work, sometimes.

Kansas peppered kisses on my neck and shoulders as he took me up the stairs. "God, you make me so incredibly hard," he murmured. "I can't stop thinking about you."

"Yeah?" I giggled. The stubble on his jaw tickled my neck. "You're not mad that I made you wait?" He paused at the top of the stairs. A low growl came from his throat.

"Virginity is just a concept. I don't give a shit who's been inside you. I only care about the cock going in relatively soon." My tummy fluttered as he shoved his tongue down my throat and continued to my room. He laid me on the bed. "Two of us taking turns isn't enough for you?"

"What?" I looked at him in confusion and then followed his eyes to the vibrator resting out in the open on the nightstand. I covered my face in embarrassment. "That's not mine."

"It's not?" He smirked.

"I mean, it is, but it was a gift." I swallowed. "Constantine..."

"He likes his toys, doesn't he?" he said and then dismissed it with a shake of his head. He slid over me and began kissing me again. "I don't need toys to have a good time with you."

Kansas lifted my dress just under my breasts and ran his tongue down my belly, swirling around my navel. He cupped my panties, his tongue running over the lace fabric, up my folds, to where my clit hid. I moaned as an ache grew inside me.

"You teased me for years." He licked my panties again. "Only letting me get close, but no further. I'm not mad you waited for Constantine to have his little cherry-popping moment, but fuck, I wish I could have been the first to make you come." His fingers ran up and down my slit above my panties. "I worried for a while that you'd stay a virgin forever."

"I'm sorry," I gasped as he teased the edge of my fabric. "But I'm not anymore. I wanted to. I wanted you just as much as you wanted me. I just—"

"I know." He urged my hips up and slid my panties down to my knees. Gently, he pushed my thighs apart. "The Minister said a lot of fucked up shit, but making you think you had to save yourself was probably one of the more sinister things he did."

Kansas spread my folds, and I looked up to see him grinning. "You've got a beautiful pussy, Eisley. I'm going to taste it now, and I'm not stopping until your legs are shaking." My heart hammered as Kansas moved closer and his tongue came into contact with my wetness.

I fell back onto my pillows and reached for his hair, fisting it in my grip, pushing him deeper into me. He chuckled and kissed me, taking more of my body into his mouth.

"Holy shit," I gasped as he continued his beautiful assault on my pussy.

"Having fun, princess?" He paused, coming up for air. "Or do you want me to stop?"

I shook my head.

“No, don’t stop,” I panted. “Keep going.”

He shifted, and a finger slid into my entrance. I couldn’t help my response to his touch. I bucked my hips, and with his empty hand, he squeezed my thigh.

"Calm down, princess. We’ve got a long night ahead of us.”

“I’m ready,” I gasped. “I’m close.” I reached for his hair again, and he took that as a cue to focus on my clit, sucking it deep into his mouth. I cried out as my body erupted. I stiffened, and Kansas continued sucking and fucking me with his finger. I reveled in the waves of hot pleasure, and when I started to come down, I tried to push him away, but he refused.

“What did I tell you?” He chuckled. “Legs shaking.” He dove in again, slower, coaxing another softer, but powerful orgasm from me. When I begged him to let me go, he whispered, “I never thought I’d hear you begging for me to stop like that.”

He unbuckled his pants and stood, quickly undressing. I sat up on the bed and did the same. I wanted to feel him bare against me.

I stared at his body, ignoring the Y shaped scars. I’d seen most of it before, thick arms, covered in patchwork tattoos. Broad shoulders and large muscles lining his stomach. My eyes trailed down, and my heart sped up at the sight of his cock. Thick, rigid, and long, my mouth began to water at the knowledge of what he was about to do with it, with me.

I took a moment to look, and when I did, I saw something that made my mouth fall open. Kansas had a relatively new tattoo. It was a death’s head moth, like Constantine’s. Only on the other side of his chest.

Suddenly, I could feel the weight of the tattoo I’d gotten

for Constantine and raised my hand to cover it. Kansas didn't notice it.

"I'm not using a condom," he said, climbing back onto the bed. "I got a taste without it. It's already done."

"Okay," I whispered. His tone told me this was not up for debate. Much like Constantine, when he decided something, that was that.

"I've waited so long for this, princess," he said as he kissed my neck and lowered me onto the pillows. He reached for my legs, pulling them up. Kansas took his cock, stroked it some, and then his eyes returned to mine. Maintaining complete eye contact, he pushed his cock between my folds and then inside me. I lost my breath at the sensation. Would I ever get used to it? It felt so good. Kansas hoisted my legs higher and began to thrust.

I was rolling in my pleasure as he pushed down on my mound and began massaging it as he thrust.

"You're perfect," he told me. "You're the perfect little princess for us."

Us?

"Your breathing is quickening. Your pussy is tightening around my cock. Are you trying not to come?" he asked.

"I want to make it last," I gasped. He thrust into me and lifted, touching something deep inside I didn't understand.

"Don't worry about lasting. I want you to come again, princess." Keeping one hand on my mound, he moved the other to my clit and began to rotate his thumb in small circles.

A sensation took ahold of me, almost like glass shattering in my ears as I became way more wet down there and my body relaxed. Kansas stopped moving and lifted his head to meet my gaze. We stared at each other in wonder.

"Did I just—" Fear rose in my belly with mortification close behind.

"Squirt all over my cock?" His eyebrows rose, and he laughed. He thrust deep into me again and moved over me to let my legs relax into the missionary position to continue fucking. "Yeah, you did, princess. And we're gonna do it again."

Rule 59 - Kansas

Let them hang themselves.

Eisley kept her black curtains drawn in her black room, causing me to wake up hours later and not know exactly what time it was. Climbing out of her bed, still naked from the long night of sex, I walked to the bathroom and saw through one of her hallway windows it was light out.

I struggled to take a piss, as my cock was still hard, and wanted to go again. I'd never felt this voracious, this hungry, for a woman before, even after my first time. But with Eisley, I couldn't get enough.

I returned to bed and she turned over, still asleep, still nude, like me. I pulled her into my arms and pressed my cock into her ass. She didn't stir, and despite wanting to fuck her, I closed my eyes and fell back asleep. I'd get my chance again soon. When we both eventually woke up, Eisley was suddenly modest, trying to cover her beautiful tits with her blanket. I tugged it down playfully.

"I love seeing your tits," I said with a grin. "I like licking them more." I rolled over her, taking one into my mouth. I nipped at it and swirled my tongue, helping it rise to a point. She gasped, then giggled, shoving me away.

"Stop! At this rate, we'll never get out of bed."

"I don't see an issue," I muttered, kissing her breasts more. Keeping my mouth on one, I pinched the other.

"I do!" She laughed, and I let her go. Stealing the blanket, she stomped to the bathroom and declared she was showering and to let her do it in peace. Rolling my eyes, I reached for my glasses on the nightstand and slid them onto my nose.

"Anything you want, princess." She scowled but shut the door. Sliding my boxers on and nothing else, I went downstairs. I hoped by not putting all my clothes back on I could push for another round before I had to take off. Fuck, I was an animal in heat around her. I couldn't think about anything but shoving my cock as far as I could inside her.

I walked into the living room and began cleaning up the food and beer abandoned last night. I tossed the glass bottles in the kitchen sink and the food in the trash. I looked around and admired how well she'd picked up the mess I'd made the other night while she was upstairs sleeping soundly.

It was absurd, as I knew exactly what I was looking for and how to get in, but I had to make it look like it was a stranger snooping, not me.

The doorbell rang, and I opened to find a kid in a baseball cap sprinting down the porch steps and across the yard to his bike.

"Hey!" I stepped out onto the porch and yelled. The kid turned and reached for his bike, hopping onto it. He shot me the middle finger and sped off. I stared after him for a long moment, processing what had happened. I turned to go inside and saw white envelope taped to the door with my name on it.

How did anyone know I was here? I snatched the letter off the door and walked inside, tearing it open. Inside was a printed note, that after a quick scan, I determined was from that stupid documentary director. I thought I'd taken care of his ass the other day. Had the police dropped their investigation?

> *Kansas,*
>
> *You sure can tell a story. I'm surprised you're going to school for computers and not a literary major. The story you weaved for the police is just that, a story. We know the truth, as I think you do. Why don't we discuss what the truth would mean if it was told to the proper authorities?*
>
> *Stop by the set today. We've moved.*

On the backside were directions to the new location. They were on the backside of the woods that lead to the Church. How did they get approved for that? The police in this town were shit, but they couldn't be that bad at their jobs. They probably hadn't gotten permission and were simply sneaking around.

"I hate to dine and dash, but I have a meeting for school. I just got an email. It's online, but all my stuff is at the hotel," I said to Eisley as I entered her bedroom.

"Thank you for coming all this way. I know it was a pain with school and all."

"I'm making it work." Taking one last look at her beautiful frame in a towel, I stalked to the bathroom to shower and take my leave. When I came down the stairs, she was sweeping her kitchen.

"Someone broke in the other night and tossed all my tea everywhere." She sighed. "I keep sweeping, but I think I'll need to mop. The floor is sticky."

"Someone broke in? And you didn't mention it?"

"Well, no. Everything seemed fine," she said sheepishly.

"Fine?" I reached for her chin. "Eisley, someone broke into

your house. Three of your friends are dead. You think that's fine?"

"You said it was Emi that killed them. Do you not think so anymore?" Her eyes filled with dread, and I saw an opportunity.

"I do, but she's obviously not the one that broke in and trashed your kitchen. Don't you have cameras?"

She looked up to the one in the corner. "I totally forgot."

Having already deleted the video of me coming in after Therese, I had no problem pulling up her cameras and letting her take the lead.

"Oh my god. It was Therese." Eisley handed me her tablet and I stared down at the video playing of her friend trashing her kitchen looking... giddy.

"Why would she do it, you think?" I handed it back to her.

"I have no idea. I thought we were on good terms. How did she get in?"

Having just dropped a grenade, I was more than happy to take off and leave her with a million questions. Constantine will be pissed, but it made me feel slightly better. Let the trash take itself out. She'd be less sad when I killed her.

"I have to go, Eisley."

She followed me to the door, asking when she'd see me again.

"I'm not sure. I'll call when I can. I have to catch up on school and make some calls to see how long I can stay."

"Are you going to get kicked out?" she whispered, as if scared for the fallout. "I don't want to ruin your life, just because I was stupid and scared."

"I'm glad you called me. Don't ever hesitate to call me when you're scared." I pulled her into my arms and inhaled the smell of her perfume. So uniquely hers. The smell invaded my dreams at night and my musings during the day.

"What if you're back at school?"

"Then call Constantine."

Rule 60 - Kansas

If someone starts to monologue, get out now.

I glared at every person along the way on the set. I had the letter in my hand and tossed it in the stupid fuck's face the moment he stood up.

"Well, hello Kansas. It's nice to see you again." Dave, the director, extended his hand, but I didn't take it. "Our fine film has had some twists, but we're still going strong."

"Film?" I scoffed. "This is all bullshit. All your actors are dead. What kind of movie is that?"

"A fabulous one!" His eyes widened, and he grinned wide. "What a story, don't you think? A small crew comes to make a documentary, only to get caught up in a string of murders. I couldn't write it better if I tried." He laughed. "And I have you to thank for all of it." I pushed my glasses up my nose.

"What are you talking about?" Dave rested his soggy ass on the small table and shrugged.

"I know Emi didn't kill those people. You know it too. That's why you framed her."

"I didn't do shit. Her computer was filled with shit between you two."

"Yeah, but all of it is circumstantial at best. Why do you

think the police in this piddly-ass town let us go? They've got nothing. And neither do you, except a need to cover up what you did." He clicked his tongue.

"You think I killed those people? I was halfway across the country." I pointed to my chest.

"Yes." He nodded thoughtfully. "I'm still trying to work that one out. If you were unable to do it, then someone did it in your place. Someone you care about enough to create a coverup for. Maybe..." He raised an eyebrow and snickered. "Someone you've bonded with through trauma? Someone who's close to all the people who hurt you?"

Trauma bonded? Fuck him.

"Stop going to Eisley's house," I snarled. "You're not welcome there, or here, or the rest of the town. Haven't we made that clear?"

"Shelley Vale wants our money. The restaurants we eat from every day, the hotels we stay in each night. The amount of superstore trips we make for fake blood and new clothes. They're begging us to stay!" He stood and put his hand on my shoulder. "Sorry kid, but we're here for a while. And we have Eisley to thank."

"She has nothing to do with this." I shoved his arm off of me.

"Doesn't she though? Her biggest client's throat is slit the same week someone claiming to be her husband comes back to town. Then, at the funeral, she gets into a rather embarrassing scuffle with the girlfriend, who is then murdered too. Any decent detective would put two and two together."

"You're grasping at straws, trying to get a story," I smirked. "Good luck. I want no part of it."

"Oh, we'll get a story; and I think in the end, you'll be quite involved. You may even get a credit in the film."

"Fuck off," I spat and started back toward the stairs, and

then I paused. There, resting on the couch, as if it were nothing important, was a mask. A Ghostface mask.

"Ah, you like it?" Dave strode across the trailer, picking it up and sliding it over his head. "12.99, same day shipping."

"I don't know what you're talking about." Keeping the mask on, Dave stalked slowly toward me.

"Oh, I think you do. We bought these for our entire cast. We're gonna make it an entire plotline. Who is Shelley Vale's Ghostface?" A chill went through me as Dave reached behind his back.

"I'm really glad you came to see me today, Kansas. As one of the Sinister Minister's last living victims, I thought it was important for you to know that we've switched gears. We're no longer filming a documentary."

"Good. Leave." I stepped backward, reaching my hand back to feel for the door.

"You don't understand." His eyes peered out of the Ghostface mask, gleeful, yet soulless. "We're making a horror movie."

"No, I got that." I gulped, and right as he pulled the knife from his back, I found the door handle and tumbled backward down the stairs. He swung and I turned, but not in time, and the knife went through my stomach and back out in an instant. I collapsed, holding onto the deep wound. I blinked rapidly, seeing spots. The blade had felt cold and tight and heavy, all at the same time.

"You gonna run?" Dave loomed over me and shoved the door open. "A quick kill is never any fun for the audience."

What. The. Fuck.

I fell back, rolling out of the trailer and onto the damp dirt of the cleared forest. Blood was rising in my throat as I lay doubled over, holding onto my bleeding belly. It hurt so bad!

"Come on, Kansas. Don't puss out on us now." He climbed down the steps and kicked my back. My mouth fell open and blood spilled from it. I rolled onto my back and then, I saw shadows. Figures surrounded me, all wearing the same mask. I rolled back and closed my eyes. I braced myself for more excruciating pain, but no one else stabbed me.

"Do you need help getting up?" a female's voice called, seeming genuinely concerned. I forced myself to my feet and stumbled forward, my eyes on the woods. It was a long trek, but I could get there.

"We'll give you a head start, Kansas, but it won't do much good. I have a vision for your death. With you going to school halfway across the country, people will be none the wiser."

"What did you put on the knife?" I gasped through the pain. Dave held the knife up to the sun.

"You like it? It's my own concoction. Something the Reanimator can't heal."

I inhaled deeply. Fuck. I took a heavy step forward through the circle and then another. And one more. I could do this. The pain was tolerable. I was lying to myself, as I held onto my side. If I let go, if I stopped putting pressure on the wound, I would bleed out. This was unbelievable.

"Run!" a shriek came from behind me and I bolted into the woods.

Grimacing through the pain, I stumbled over rocks and roots, falling every few steps. I could hear their laughter and screaming as they taunted me. But they were blindly confident.

I was grabbed a few times. My shirt was ripped off, a knife scraped down my back. Enough to cut but not to kill. I was kicked and shoved, too.

Finally, I saw the decrepit building in sight. All I had to do was get inside and tumble down the stairs. Constantine would save me.

"Ah, perfect," Dave called as I pushed through the doors. "Actually, it's really good. Are you filming this?" he asked one of his minions. "It's like a homecoming. He spent his childhood here, and now, he returns to die."

I stumbled to the stairs, and having no strength left, collapsed, and rolled down them, feeling every single one.

"What the—" Constantine came from another room and found me at the foot of the stairs. He stepped over me and looked up, seeing all the film crew in their masks, staring down at us.

Constantine laughed dryly, pulling his knife from his boot. "Well, this is convenient."

Rule 61 - Eisley

Get to know who you're dealing with.

"Hi, does Boogie have time for walk-ins today?"

"If you get here in an hour."

I took a deep breath and took in my reflection in the bathroom mirror. "I'll be there." I gave her my details over the phone. I grabbed my car keys and flew out of the house.

I'd spent all morning fuming and rewatching the video of Therese coming into my house and destroying my most prized possessions. I wanted to go over and kick her ass, but I knew it'd do no good. She was just like all the others. Her family had connections, and despite it being her that had committed the crime, I would be the one who ended up in jail.

So, I needed a distraction.

When I reached the parlor, a pretty woman with a pixie cut and a chain hanging from her ears to her nose came from the back and smiled kindly. "Eisley?"

"That's me."

She went behind the glass counter and reached for her book. "Right on time. I'll go grab Boogie and see what he's up to." She marked something on her book and then turned to go back.

I went to the counter and looked at all the jewelry underneath. Lots of hoops and studs, along with plugs. I'd always wondered what I'd look like with stretched earlobes. I raised my hand to my ear and rubbed it.

"Are you wanting your ears pierced today?" The woman returned with Boogie behind her.

"They already are. I was looking at all the plugs."

"We can help start the stretching process." She extended her hand to me with a wide grin. "I'm Laurel, the piercer."

"She's really good," Boogie said. I scrunched up my mouth.

"Maybe."

She cocked her head. "Well, think about it, and after your tattoo, if you're still up for it, we can do it. It's pretty painless the first few sizes."

I thanked her and then explained what I wanted to Boogie.

"I can do that."

I was sitting in his chair within the hour, pulling my shirt down, and closing my eyes to let him work his magic.

"Boogie says you're married to Constantine. They're good friends," Laurel commented, coming to sit with me. I nodded tightly. I was still not comfortable with the sharp pain of the tattoo machine digging into my skin.

"Are you friends with him?" I asked.

"I think Boogie is the only one who can claim friends." She snickered. "I know Constantine. We went to high school together. We've hung out when he was with Boogie. He's not really social." She chuckled. "I mean, you know."

I didn't. I barely knew the man Constantine had grown up to be. All I knew before jumping into bed with him was that he was hot and wanted me.

"What was he like as a teenager?" I asked her.

"Broody. He got in a lot of fights. The teachers hated him. I think he had a shit home life too. Right, Boogie?" He nodded.

"I had a tiny crush on him in school." She pinched her fingers together and laughed. "But honestly, which emo girl didn't?"

"I mean, his aesthetic does scream bad boy." My cheeks flooded as I recalled his blue, brooding eyes. "Leather jacket and all."

"He used to wear eyeliner too." She cocked a brow. "What about you? What were you like in high school?"

"Kind of boring. I was shy. I didn't have a whole lot of friends."

Just Kansas.

A bell rang and she stood to go attend to whoever had walked in. With every line he carved into my skin, I felt more and more sure of my decision. Confidence rose with the endorphins, and an hour later, Boogie pulled away and told me he was done.

He pulled his gloves off and offered me a hand mirror. I admired the ink and thanked him. Cautiously, I pulled my top back up over it and went to the front to check out.

Laurel was there, leaning against the counter as I paid Boogie.

"You, uh, think about those ears again?" She wiggled her eyebrows. "I happen to know on good authority that Constantine thinks they're hot." I gave her a questionable look.

"He does? Wait..." I leaned forward on the counter. "Have you met some of his exes?"

"I wouldn't say that. He never really dated." She backed away. "I shouldn't have said anything. I'm sorry."

"No, it's fine," I assured her. I took a large breath and nodded. "Let's do it." She took me into another room and sat me up on her large chair. She tried to backpedal as she washed, gloved, and prepared everything. "I'm not trying to cause problems. What's in the past is in the past and all that."

"It's fine," I laughed. "Really. I don't focus on stuff like that. It's just interesting to hear about what he was like before."

"Well, he was depressing, mostly." She smirked. "Hopefully finding you will change that. Bring out a little sunshine on his gloomy attitude. Get him to open up and relax some." She came toward me with a small cone-shaped needle and a small hoop. "Stay still," she said as she slid it through my ear and followed it with the hoop. There was a tightness in my earlobes but otherwise, nothing.

"There ya go!" she said brightly. "Come back in two weeks and I'll put the next ones in. We can go up to zero, but from there, you're on your own." I reached for my now itchy lobe and tugged on it.

"Thanks." We walked out together.

"Did Constantine know you were coming today?"

I shook my head.

"Ooh, what a fun surprise. I think he'll like it. I mean, who wouldn't like a hot girl with tattoos and stretched ears?"

Just then, my phone started to ring, and his name appeared on my screen. I looked from her to the phone and thanked her again before stepping out. I took the call as I was walking to my car.

"Hello?"

A deep growl came from the other side. "Where the fuck are you?"

Rule 62 - Eisley

Fall themed attractions? Dangerous.

I was nervous the entire drive home. Constantine was so angry he couldn't find me.

"I've been pounding on your fucking door, driving around town looking for your car. Why didn't you say you were taking off somewhere?" he shouted into the phone.

"I didn't realize I needed your permission to do things. What, just because you're back and claiming our little ceremony was real, you think you can boss me around?"

"This has nothing to do with you being my wife. There's a murderer on the loose, and it's not smart to be running around and not telling people where the fuck you are."

I swallowed the lump in my throat. "I'll be home in an hour."

He swore and hung up without saying goodbye. I drove in silence, taking in what he said. A murderer was on the loose. Did that mean that Emi's name had been cleared?

When I returned home, the sun was starting to fall. Constantine sat hunched over on the steps of my porch. Strands of his inky black hair hung over an eye when he looked up. A scowl seemed permanently planted on his face.

"What are you doing here?" I asked, cautiously walking toward him. He stood and bounced down them. He was wearing all black, including his leather jacket and boots. I recalled Laurel's comment about him being emo in high school. He never got over it.

"I was looking for you. Where were you?"

"I—" I cleared my throat and crossed my arms. "I was just out. You said there was a murderer on the loose? Is someone else dead?" My heart rate sped up, considering all the people it could be. If Micah was right, and they were taking out people from important families in town, then it could have been him, Rem, or Therese.

He shrugged and looked at the ground. "I was just pissed. I know they say it was your friend, but I'm not buying it. I shouldn't have said that." A surge of relief and disappointment flew threw me so fast I was a little dizzy. I should be happy someone wasn't dead. But that only made the case for Emi being the killer more solid.

"I actually came to try to take you out." He ran his hand along the back of his neck.

"Out?" I smiled.

"Yeah, like a date. You know that thing couples do. I know it's a little backward, but I thought maybe we should try it."

"Sure, do you have a place you want to go?"

"Well, it is October. I saw a flyer for this fall attraction. Hayrides, cider, hay bales. We can pick pumpkins. Spooky shit at night. You up for it?" He offered his hand, and I took it.

"Spooky shit? Always. Let's go." I'd never been on an official date before, and Constantine was right, we had done things backward. I was calling him my husband, and bringing him into my bed, but I didn't really know him as an adult. I only knew the eleven-year-old boy I'd spent with in captivity.

The farm in which the event was going on was a familiar one.

"I buy seeds from here all the time. They have a whole store." I pointed to the building off to the side as we walked past it with all the other people going in. We bought our tickets and were given pamphlets on all the things we could do tonight.

"What looks good to you? Corn maze, pumpkin painting, apple picking, hayride?" Constantine listed off a few and looked at me.

"I'm kind of thirsty. You want to go watch them make cider and donuts?" Putting his arm around my waist, he pulled me into his arms and we walked to the correct building. The smell of apple cinnamon and crisp fall leaves filled the air and I sighed contentedly.

"I wish I lived in a place where it was fall every day of the year," I mused as we stepped inside the warm barn.

"You mean like Halloweentown?"

Blink 182's song came to mind, and I grinned as the lines about Jack and Sally played through.

"I don't think it'd be that bad." I grinned and joined the clump of people watching donuts being made from scratch.

"Frosting or not?" I asked Constantine.

"Not."

"Sprinkles?" I asked.

"I'd rather die." He grinned.

"So edgy," I teased and leaned up on my tiptoes to plant a quick kiss on his beautiful lips. "I love it."

"I love you," he said in response. I blinked and stepped away, suddenly aware of everyone else in the room. We got our delicious fresh donuts and cider and then opted to take the walking trail through the corn. It wasn't a maze or anything with a time limit. It was perfect for adults with no curfews.

"So, should we talk about what I said?" Constantine asked once we were far enough inside to be alone.

"When?" My stomach knotted.

"In the barn." He squeezed my hand. "When I said I love you."

"You did." I nodded.

"I meant it. And not in the 'we've been through hell and are forever linked' way."

"We barely know each other," I protested. "How could you love me?" I looked up at him in wonder. Constantine flashed me his crooked smile that made my heart do crazy things.

"How could I not? You're independent, you're successful. You love people more than you should and want to believe the good in them. You're smart as fuck about plants, and you're a stone-cold fox who's fun in bed." Blood rushed to my face.

"Don't say that so loud!" A giggle escaped my lips.

"What, that I enjoy having sex with my wife?" he bellowed. I pushed him playfully and he laughed. "I'm sorry. I know it's not great timing, but I've been thinking about it all day and I needed to just get it out there. Eisley, I'm in love with you."

"Constantine..." My hand ran to my shirt, where the fresh ink lay under it. "I'm in love with you too. But..."

If he knew my secret, would he still feel that way? Could he love someone... crazy?

I winced. The word had been etched into my brain since I'd left the Church. That's what they called me, the school kids. Crazy.

"It's because of Kansas." Constantine pulled me from my dark place.

"I love him too." I agreed. "You asked where I was today. I was getting this." I tugged on my top and pulled it down just enough to show him the second Death's Head Moth on the other side of my collarbone. One moth to represent both men I loved. He stared hard at it for a long time.

"Are you mad?"

He ran his tongue along his teeth and sighed. "No. I've always known you loved him too. That's why I did what I did."

"Did what?"

"I stayed behind."

Rule 63 - Eisley

Don't hesitate, just run.

Ten years ago.

I pulled up my dress. It was heavy and itchy. White lace that smelled like mildew and dragged on the ground. I was allowed to see my reflection for the first time since I'd arrived at the Church. I was so... different.

I was thin, my eyes so tired, my hair so long and fragile. How had I lasted this long in that room? I was skin and bones.

"This dress was handed down to you by a Mother who is a seamstress." The Mother who had pulled me from our room said. She had ripped my clothing off and thrown me in the bath. She scrubbed my skin so hard it was red and screaming. She washed my hair too, and brushed it for a long time, getting all the tangles out. Finally, she made me put on this dress and added a headband with a long piece of fabric on it.

"What's a seamstress?" I asked.

"She makes dresses. Specifically, wedding dresses."

I blinked. Wedding dress?

"Why do I need one?" I asked, uneasiness creeping down

me. The Mother chose not to answer. Instead, she asked if I was hungry. I almost laughed. I'd been hungry since the day I came here. What was being full? She brought me oatmeal and toast, still warm.

"Don't get it on your dress!" she barked at me. "The Minister will be very upset if you don't look perfect for the ceremony."

"What ceremony?" I asked, and again, I was ignored. "I don't want to do a ceremony." I pushed my bowl away. Something about the way she was treating me made me want to vomit. I stood up from the small table I'd been eating at.

"Eisley, you were explained that you are a woman now, weren't you?" I froze. My eyes blinked rapidly at the horrific memory of my body bleeding from my private area. That's what they'd told me. That the bleeding meant I was a woman. She saw my reaction and nodded. "Well now that you are a woman, it's time to become a wife. To join the Family."

"I don't want to become a wife." I backed away from her.

"This isn't about what you do or do not want." She said with such authority it shook me. "You will be married, and tonight, you'll fulfill your duties to your husband and the Family."

"I don't understand."

"You will. The Minister will be there to teach you. For now, keep your dress clean and your hair nice. I will return once we are ready for you." She stormed out of the room, leaving me to soak in her words and grow more and more terrified with each minute.

I stared at the wall, wondering where Kansas and Constantine were. They'd been taken, too, by a Father. We had reached for each other but were pulled away and dragged to different rooms. Were they together? I hoped so.

I stood and paced in my too-long dress. They were so much smarter than me. I heard them talking at night. All the time, they spoke in hushed whispers about how to get us out. I was sure today that if they were trapped somewhere together, they were planning a way out of here.

And they'd never leave me behind.

When the Mother from before came for me, I was dragged out and brought down the hall. It felt almost like a death march. I trusted nothing here in the Church. Too many times I'd been tricked into thinking I was safe, only to be attacked moments later.

We entered a small room. It was darker than the others. Hundreds of candles were lit all around, and a mattress was placed against the wall. There was a table, along with a tripod with a camera attached. Were they making a movie?

The only people in the room were the Minister and Kansas and Constantine. Relief washed over me and I broke free of the Mother's grasp to launch myself at them. I rested between them, trying to put my arms around them both. Any other time, they'd hug me back, but today, neither made any attempt to touch me.

"You're here!" I gasped and stood back. I looked at them both. They wore the same all-black suit.

The Minister cleared his throat and reached for me, pulling me back by my dress.

"Yes. Both of your potential husbands are here. Now, Eisley, do you understand why you are here today?" He reached for a large book from the table. "And what will happen tonight?"

"No. Why am I here?"

"Today is a wonderful day," he bellowed and waved. "One that has been long coming. For five years, we have planned and waited for this blessed day when Eisley would take one of these young men to be her husband, and for those two to enter into the Family. The other shall bless us with his sacrifice."

What was he talking about? I looked over to Kansas and

Constantine, whose heads hung down, almost as if they'd given up. No. They couldn't. They couldn't give up.

"Eisley, I have prepared the rings that you and your husband will present each other as a symbol of your faithfulness to each other. Once you give your ring to either Kansas or Constantine, you will be wed, you will be bed."

And the other will be dead.

I was beginning to understand things. I'd heard Kansas and Constantine talking. Offering, sacrifices, blood.

He handed me two chains. Each necklace held a gold ring on them.

"Once you are older, they will fit and you can wear them properly," he explained. "Now, which young man shall be given to the Reanimator, and which shall serve the Family in other ways?"

I turned to both Kansas and Constantine. Both of my friends, my constant companions, my... *hearts.* They shared a look of utter desperation, pleading for me to pick them.

I looked at Kansas first. With his bent glasses far too small for his head. He was so smart. He'd kept me going so many times, reassuring me I could survive with just the bare minimum. He made sure I kept walking, talking, and without him, my spirit would have died years ago.

Then, Constantine. He was tough. He brought us news and items when it got rough. When they were starving us out, he provided for us. He was the one who insisted every night I sleep between them, right in the middle, so that I stayed warm. Each night, I fell asleep to the rhythm of both their hearts. I couldn't pick which one to stop forever.

"No."

"No?" the Minister asked. "No?" His voice grew louder. "Eisley, no is not an option. If you will not choose, then I shall." He stormed over and snatched Constantine up.

"You will serve the Family as Eisley's husband." He glared at me with cold, evil eyes. "Give him the necklaces."

The iciness in his voice made me do just that. I handed both to Constantine. He took one and handed me the other. Looking up to the Minister for guidance, he nodded for me to put it over my head and down to my neck. He then returned to his book.

"A man and wife shall lay together in the carnal way for all to see. The Family cannot succeed unless the newly coupled touch, flesh to flesh. With the rings, Eisley, you promise to not allow another man to enter you, nor give you the ultimate pleasure a body can experience. You will wait for your husband to bestow his seed and his gifts to you. Do you understand?"

I did not.

His words, however, would be ingrained into my memory forever.

I would wait for my husband.

We were forced to sign a marriage contract, Constantine and I. I stared at it, absorbing it all before it was violently ripped away from me.

"And now..." The Minister smiled gleefully. "We shall take the offering and finish the ritual. You two shall do your part shortly after. We need his blood first." He left, leaving the door wide open. Our eyes shot to Kansas, who was crying and shaking in the corner. I flew to him.

"I didn't choose!" I explained. "I don't want this! I love you both!" Kansas looked up, his eyes red and terrified.

"I love you too. I don't want to die."

"You won't." Constantine was beside us. He cocked his head toward the door left open. "Go. Take her with you."

What? I blinked my tears away.

"You're not coming?"

"I can't. Not right away." We stood, and he put his hands on my shoulders. “Eisley, you need to go. I'll be okay.”

"But you won't! Constantine, I can't leave without you!" Tears streamed down my face as Kansas's hand reached for mine and began to tug.

"You see this?" Constantine raised his necklace and grabbed the matching one around my neck. "It's going to keep me going. Don't talk to anyone. Don't look back. Just run. Run, and I'll catch up. I love you, Eisley."

"I love you too Constantine."

He shoved me into Kansas, and we bolted out. We ran as fast as we could, not looking back until we were out of the Church and deep into the forest. With each step came a sense of freedom, fear of being caught, and utter grief, knowing we would never truly ever leave the Church. We would never leave because he didn't.

Rule 64 - Constantine

Slashers don't get days off.

"You waited for me." I squeezed her hand, bringing her back.

"I did. I'm glad." Her hands went to her neck, and her smile fell. Her ring was still missing.

"I don't have the necklace right now," she confessed. I knew this already. I'd asked Kansas about it and he'd smirked; the stupid grin on his face enough to tell me it was safe with him.

"I'll get it back." I looked off into the now pitch-dark cornfield. We were still at least a mile out.

"You're not mad at him?" Her expressive eyes grew large with worry.

"For being in love with you too? That doesn't seem fair to be mad at him."

She considered my words. I was careful in what I chose to say regarding Kansas. I wanted to see how she, as an adult now, handled what we were to each other.

She shuddered from a cold gust of wind. We'd left right when she got home from the tattoo shop, and she was still wearing a shorter dress. I wasn't sure she even owned pants. I slid my jacket off and set it over her shoulders. She inhaled deeply and melted. I could almost hear her pussy crying. She pushed her arms through and snuggled into my warmth.

Just as things were starting to feel good between us, a piercing scream rang out from somewhere in the corn. We froze and suddenly Someone was sprinting out of the corn. Reflexively, I pulled her into my arms protectively.

She screamed as a gangly teen launched at us. He was wearing a Ghostface mask and had what I realized quickly was a large, plastic butcher's knife. Eisley was so startled, she slipped from my arms and stumbled back, falling to the dirt. I launched at the guy, ripping his mask off and shoving him to the ground.

Two more people leapt out, donning the same mask and fake weapons. When I kept punching the teen, they pulled their masks off and stepped up to me.

"Hey, it was just a joke man. Let him go!" One of them reached for my shirt and tried to tug me off of him. "Don't hurt him!"

"Just a joke?" I waved the mask I'd taken from the first one and waved it at them threateningly. "Isn't this the mask the killer's been wearing? That's what the police said." I stood and glared at them. It was so over the top, trying to fake genuine concern that a serial killer was running around.

Oh wait, that was me.

They shrunk away, looking ashamed and scared of me.

"It's just a prank, man, we aren't going to hurt anyone."

"A prank is funny." I stalked slowly toward them, pushing them into the other side of the corn. The knife in my boot burned hot against my leg. If Eisley wasn't here, they'd be dead already. "This isn't funny. Someone could get hurt."

Another blood-curdling scream rang out somewhere deep in the field, diverting our attention behind us.

Jesus fucking Christ, could I get a break?

Flashlights began lighting up the sky and a moment later police were running down the path. "How many of you kids are in here?" One demanded of the teenagers who were this close to getting away. I snatched one by the shirt and dragged him back so he couldn't run.

"Uh, officer it's just a prank. Don't tell my mom."

I dropped the kid and stepped back with Eisley. She put her arm around me and snuggled into my chest.

"How many of your friends are here today with those masks, kid?" The officer asked again.

"Seven," he admitted, hanging his head. The officers muttered to themselves and reached for their radios.

"Come on, we're taking you back to the entrance." As the three teens were being dragged back toward the entrance, a couple passed them. I swore inwardly, and my mood fell, as I recognized the pair. They were Eisley's pretend friends. Therese and Rem both perked up and came over to us. She ran to hug Eisley.

"Hey! I didn't know you guys were here!"

Eisley didn't hug her back. I could see it in her eyes. Kansas told her about her friend's break-in.

"It was a spur-of-the-moment date night," I said curtly, hoping she'd catch the hint.

"Ooh, same here. Let's double."

Eisley was standing silent, her face blank, as if unsure how to handle the situation. Did she take her on now, or wait until they were alone?

"Yeah, that could be fun. We're doing the hayride after this. Join us." Rem, who didn't seem to have a clue as to what was happening, invited us.

"I've never done a double date." Eisley said finally and reached for my hand. The four of us started walking again. I'd never dated at all. Sure, I'd taken women to bed. I said all the right things to get them there, but did I take one out to ensure my cock got wet? Never. Much like Eisley had waited for me, I was waiting for her.

"So, how did you two meet?" Therese leaned out and smiled at us. "I never heard the story."

"Childhood sweethearts," I replied coolly. "We even had this little ceremony when we were kids." I raised the ring around my neck and showed her. Therese's eyes lit up with the information.

"Oh! And your necklace?" She motioned to Eisley. "That's adorable!" She laughed and looked up at her boyfriend. "My middle school boyfriend was Callum White. Can you imagine me being married to him?"

As we walked, Therese gave us the fourth degree, asking us all sorts of things I wasn't interested in sharing. Most questions I simply had to lie about, but she didn't seem to care, she just needed to hear her own voice.

All the while, Eisley hadn't said a word.

"I'm so glad we found you guys in here," Therese sighed in relief. "It's been so crazy since you know, everything." We popped out of the trail and got more cider and donuts, per Rem's insistence.

"You're so quiet, Eis. Are you okay?" Therese asked.

My eyes lit up as I waited for Eisley to respond. I wanted to see her lunge at the bitch. Scratch her face, rip her hair, kick her in the shin. I wanted her to be angry. She deserved to be angry.

But she didn't.

"I'm fine. I've just had a long day. A long week, really."

"Same, girl, same." Therese looped her arms through hers and dragged her away. "Did you guys get your pumpkins yet? We did ours first, so we could put them in the car and not have to search for a good one in the dark."

"I like creeping in the dark." I said, and gave Eisley a smirk.

She rolled her eyes.

"Yes, you do."

The rusty tractor pulled up and people began climbing out and down. We took their place, sitting on the scratchy hay bales. The cold wind was picking up, and Eisley moved closer trying to warm up. I put my hand on her knees and she looked up at me with a forced smile and then rested her head on my shoulder.

"You guys are adorable," Therese sighed from across from us. She and her boyfriend looked stiff, almost as if they weren't dating at all. She was scrolling through her phone, and he was looking everywhere but at her. I was fascinated by the turn of this entire evening. Therese acted as if she had done nothing at all, and Eisley was letting her get away with it.

I wondered if this had something to do with Kansas's and I's spell. They hadn't frozen her out like we'd wanted, but something was amiss.

The tractor jerked and roared to life. A moment later we were rolling forward and bouncing slightly with the ride.

"So, I told you things have been weird, right?" Therese set her phone on the stack beside her and sat up, focusing on Eisley. "My dad has been going off his rocker."

"What do you mean?" Eisley furrowed her brow. I fought back the urge to roll my eyes. Eisley, my beautiful wife, always so caring toward everyone. Even the ones who deserved it the least.

"He can't remember shit. Like, I know he's old but damn. I was telling him about some of the documentary stuff and he had no idea what I was talking about. I spent an hour trying to break down everything that's happened. Spencer, Soleil, Emi, and he couldn't grasp it. It's so stressful." She sighed deeply and relaxed her back against the railing and reached for her phone. Rem glanced at her and then opted to turn his attention to us. Everything about this night had been blown. My first attempt at genuine romance and it was fucked by these two stupid fucks.

I couldn't wait to kill them next. I might even take the mask off and let them know, right before I plunged the knife into their chests, that they brought this on themselves for interrupting my first date. Or maybe I could offer Therese up to Eisley. Would she want revenge for her teapots?

"I don't think he's forgetting stuff," Rem said quietly, causing us both to lean in to hear him. He licked his lips and looked around nervously. "I think he's starting to sweat. I mean, look who the killer is targeting."

"I thought they said it was Emi," Eisley shook her head. Rem laughed dryly.

"I think it's a cover-up. See, Therese and I have been over on the set, helping out, trying to organize a lot of their files and shit. They've got information on the entire town. Shit that's been covered up for ten years. Shit people don't want known. Spencer's family, Soleil's family..." he gulped and looked from me to Eisley miserably, and pointed between him and his girlfriend. "Our families."

"Yeah, but that's not fair," Therese sat up. "Why were Spencer and Soleil punished for what their dads did?" It took every ounce of facial muscle not to reply with, *'because they would just do it to some other unsuspecting victims in time'*. That's how rich people operated. I'd never give a fuck about a billionaire hurting, because of all the people they'd hurt to get where they were.

"He's got this theory that they are coming after us, but I don't know," Therese said. She paused, and her face changed from one of confidence to one of fear. Her lip trembled as she continued. "It's not fair."

"I guess I don't understand why they are acting out revenge for a group that's dead," I said.

"Not everyone," Rem stared pointedly at me. "You two made it out, did you not?"

Therese's eyes grew big as she recalled that little factoid. So, the spell was slowly working. She hadn't recalled that.

"Is that— the little marriage thing?" She looked from me to Eisley and back at me. "You are certifiably psycho." Silence followed, moved forward by raucous laughter from Therese. "Just kidding. No, I think trauma bonding is legit and you guys are so cute together." She nodded to Rem, who stared at her. "But seriously, I'm glad we caught you, because if Rem's theory is right, then we're all in danger." She made a large circle with her finger. "All because our parents were royal assholes."

Rule 65 - Eisley

Warn the others.

I watched her all night pretend like we were best friends. As if she hadn't broken into my house and destroyed my most prized items. As if I didn't fucking know.

Dozens of scenarios of how I'd confront her ran through my head all evening, until finally Constantine took me to pick my pumpkin and part ways. I left him on the porch with a chaste kiss and a promise to call him.

I awoke the next morning to the doorbell going wild. I reached for my phone and tried the app with all my security cameras, but they weren't showing anybody at my door. Was it broken? Already irritated, I got out of bed and went downstairs to get the door. I threw it open and a glass vase was thrust into my hand.

Oh no.

"We've actually got a few bouquets for you, Miss," the delivery man said. "Hold on." He ran down my steps, and I leaned out the door. Two men in uniform hopped out of the van and began carrying up the same bouquet I'd been receiving for weeks.

Every time someone died.

I couldn't comprehend what was going on, but I let the men through to set all nine bouquets in my living room.

Nine?

They tipped their hats at me and quickly disappeared, leaving me with what felt like nine dead bodies in my living room. I stared at them until my vision grew blurry. Then, I reached for one and lifted it above my head slowly. I wasn't sure what I was doing, but I couldn't have these here. Not taunting me, as if the deaths were my fault. I hadn't killed anyone.

Blinking rapidly, I went to my front door and ripped it open. With a scream of pure anguish, I flung the beautiful arrangement over my head and let it crash into my yard with a shattering scream as the glass collided with the cold hard ground.

I ran back inside and grabbed another and another. The more flowers I threw out, the better I felt. I didn't know who was doing this to me, taunting me, threatening me, but I was done! Once all nine vases were out of my house, I slammed the door and pulled out my phone. If nine people were dead, in this town, everyone would know about it.

I pulled up my apps and went to our town's page and the blood drained from my face. I clicked on the article our local newspaper put out and after I read through it, my phone slipped out of my hands and landed on the hard floor.

The documentary crew.

Nine of them. All lined up like they were found ten years ago.

My hands shook as I bent down and retrieved my phone. I went upstairs and got dressed, putting on my only pair of sweats and a hoodie. I put my hood over my hair and stormed out of the house, walking past the mess in my yard, and got in my car. I had to talk to someone about this. Maybe Rem was right. The flowers were a sign.

On the way, I tried to call my friends, even Therese, but no one was answering. Micah's rental was closest to my house so I stopped there first, knocking quickly. He answered, but when he looked down at me, his face furrowed in confusion.

"Yeah?" he snapped.

"Micah, did you see what happened? The documentary crew is dead."

He stepped out into the yard and shut the door, which was odd for him. Micah was always so friendly. He normally would have welcomed me in.

"Yeah and so is my girlfriend. And my best friend and his girlfriend." He shook his head. "What's your point? Why are you here? Eisley, right?"

"What?" I blinked. Did he... not remember me? "Micah, it's me. I'm Emi's best friend." I pointed to my chest.

"Emi's best friend is dead." He waved his finger at me and snapped them. "I know you. You're that crazy goth chick from high school who's a cam girl now. I don't know what you want, but I'm not interested in being one of your clients or whatever. I've got bigger problems right now." He turned to go, and despite my tearful protests, he shut the door in my face.

I sat in my car for a long moment before steeling myself to try Therese. It was now or never. I had to confront her about what she did so that we could help each other. If someone was killing us one by one, we couldn't be fighting amongst ourselves.

I took off toward Therese's place. I knocked and tried to explain to her that Micah was being weird and the recent murders, but she simply stared at me. She let me cry and go through my entire speech before shaking her head and laughing.

"Who the hell are you?"

"What?" I paused. "Therese, it's me. I saw you just last night."

"I was with my boyfriend all night. I don't know what you're talking about." Her eyes then lit up. "Wait, I do know you. You were the girl Spencer was obsessed with! Is that why you're here? Is Rem one of your Onlypics clients?"

"No. Therese, we're best friends."

"I remember you in school. You were a freak then too. I'm not your fucking friend."

I took a deep breath. If that's how she wanted to play this fine, but I couldn't walk off her porch without warning her.

"Rem thinks you're being targeted. I think he's right."

"Why would people be after me?" She gave me a once-over and smirked. "Maybe you're in trouble. When you're letting creeps watch you naked, eventually one is bound to come try to find you. Might want to take some of Spencer Foxworth's money and get some professional help." She reached for her door knob and before she went inside, she turned one last time. "Get the fuck off my porch, whore, before I call the cops for harassment."

I didn't bother trying Rem's door. Micah and Therese had probably already talked to him, and I couldn't bear to see another person act like they didn't know me. Did they all think so little of me? I sat in my car in my driveway, sobbing, and sometime later a familiar silver Chevy Nova pulled in beside me. I lifted my head as Constantine rounded his car. I rolled my window down and sniffled. He leaned over to meet my gaze.

"Why are you crying?" he demanded. "Those documentary guys were assholes."

"No, it's just... My friends. I went to see them today and they pretended they didn't know me. Therese and Micah said some really shitty things."

"About what? You?" His face contorted from concern to rage. I shrugged and sniffled.

"About my job. Micah told me to go whore around somewhere else." He raised his eyebrows.

"This is why you're crying? Because some guy called you a whore?" he snapped back and went to his car. I stiffened and opened my door.

"Constantine, no!" He wasn't listening. He leapt into his car and peeled back out of my drive before I could stop him.

Oh no.

Rule 66 - Eisley

Don't trust anyone.

I pulled my phone out and tried to call Constantine, but he wasn't answering. I called again and again, but still, he ignored me.

Desperate, I called Kansas, and like always, he was the only one who showed up when I needed it.

"Hey, everything okay?" he asked.

"No. I don't know. Constantine just lost his shit and I'm worried he's going to get arrested or something." He didn't say anything. "I'm just freaking out right now!" I screeched.

"Woah, alright. I'll be over in a bit. Stay calm. Everything's going to be fine." He hung up and I broke down on the couch. This was all so fucked up! Nine people were dead, and the killer was letting me know each time he killed someone else. My friends were blocking me out of their lives, and Constantine had run off to defend my honor. Everything seemed to be falling apart around me and there was nothing I could do about it.

A knock on the door came during my deep sobbing and I went to it, throwing my arms around Kansas when I found him on the other side.

"Shh." He patted my back. "It's going to be okay. What's with the mess on your lawn?"

For the first time today, I relaxed and let out a dry laugh. "It's been such a fucked up day."

Kansas bent down and lifted me into his arms. Cradling me, he took me to the couch and set me down. "Okay, tell me everything."

"I think someone is fucking with me," I confessed. Through tears, I told Kansas everything. How each bouquet had come after someone died, how the newspapers were reporting the documentary crew deaths, and how my friends were acting.

"So-called friends. Eisley, none of them were your real friends. Emi's emails told me that. And as far as the doc crew..." He swallowed deeply and shifted in his seat. "I don't know."

"It's like going back in fucking time. Something's not right, Kansas. Someone is trying to take out everyone who might reveal the truth." Kansas shook his head.

"Why would they kill the kids of those people and not the people themselves?"

"To send a message?" I didn't know the answer. All I knew is that it felt like the walls were closing in on me, and I was a sitting duck.

"My cameras are broken. The ones Spencer set up," I said. "They were working just fine yesterday, when you showed me the video of Therese destroying my kitchen. She stole—" I stopped short.

"She stole something?"

I looked away quickly. "My sense of security. I don't feel safe here. It's like I'm always being watched."

"Why are you lying to me?" He narrowed his gaze. His glasses slid down his nose and he didn't move to raise them back up.

"What?" I couldn't meet his gaze.

"Why are you protecting her?" His voice deepened and it took on a threatening growl. "Tell me what she took."

"Some of my plants from my garden," I admitted.

"The poison plants?"

I nodded.

"Well, be careful who you drink from." He sat back, his lips curling into a smirk.

"That's not funny."

"No. But I don't appreciate being lied to."

I stood up and stormed into the kitchen. Out of reflex, I picked up the tea kettle off the stove and filled it. I set it back to heat, and while I waited, I stared blankly out the window. My backyard was just as it always had been. Since before any of this crazy stuff started happening. It was odd to think that just three weeks ago, things had been so different. I was just a content creator, my bat flowers had just bloomed, and twelve people were still alive. In another month, would I still be? Footsteps came from behind me and I turned to offer Kansas an exhausted smile.

"I'm sorry. This all really fucking sucks. I thought eventually it would stop, you know?"

"What would?" He came toward me, pulling me into his chest and wrapping his thick arms around me.

"The terror. I spent half of my childhood locked away, not sure if I'd die one day over the next. Then, we got out, muddled through, tried to be normal, and now, ten years later, it feels like I'm one step away from being trapped again."

"The problem is you stayed in Shelley Vale. You were expecting gold to come from shit. When everything is said and done, we should leave. Sell this place and never look back." I blinked. Constantine had said the same thing. Could I leave this place? I wasn't sure I had much of a choice anymore.

"Maybe. Although I doubt anyone is looking to buy in Shelley Vale these days."

"Then just leave. Who cares?" His breath was warm on my neck and it sent shivers down my back. His hands began to roam under my hoodie, but then the whistle on my kettle went off and I pulled away.

I hurried to take it off the heat and turned toward my cabinets to grab teacups and balls to steep leaves in. I picked a jar of my harvest blend that hadn't been destroyed and scooped it into the steepers, placing them in the ceramic pot.

"It'll cool some in here and we can take it to the living room," I explained as I started to travel the kitchen. I stumbled and the pretty plum-colored round teapot went flying out of my hands, crashing to the ground. I gasped at the sharp explosion of sound as it instantly became a hundred pieces.

"No!" I cried out. I loved that teapot. I had so little of them left! Tears exploded, like my teapot had, and ran down my face in large hot drops. Kansas hurried over and crouched down.

"Are you okay?"

I sat up and cried again. This was the icing on a horrible cake.

"I'm fine. I just want today to be over with." I brought my knees up and shoved my head down to cry without him staring.

"It's going to be fine. Look, I'll get it cleaned up." The tinkle of him lifting some of the pieces brought me strength enough to lift my head and suck it up to help. I began picking up larger pieces with him and then one slipped out of his hand and he winced.

"Ah," he gasped and let the piece drop. My eyes went to his hand, where a deep gash was exploding blood from his palm. In a flash, I was up trying to find a towel. *He'd have to get stitches.* I spun back around with a towel in my hand and froze. Right in front of my eyes, Kansas's wound sealed itself back up. Slowly, his head lifted and we made eye contact. His eyes went wide, his mouth fell open, and I stepped away from him.

What the fuck?

Rule 67 - Constantine

Don't get caught.

I stared at my phone, eyeing all the missed calls. She should have known better than to tell me what those rich fucks called her. A quick text from Kansas told me he was keeping her company, which worked well, as I'd be busy for a while.

I knew where the fucker lived and drove right over. I was on his block when I saw him sitting on his porch, smoking a joint with Rem. They were laughing and relaxing as if they didn't just break Eisley's spirit an hour ago.

The freezing spell worked after all, but that only meant her friends were showing their true colors. For their entire friendship, they'd been lying to her. Now, she knew how they felt.

And they'd fucking pay for it.

I drove right past Micah's place and waited. I parked a block away where I could clearly see his house.

As I sat and watched the stoner's house, I grew more and more angry. He was the selfish prick who had me taken in because of his mushrooms. He had no intention of admitting they were his to get me out, and when he finally did, they slapped him on the wrist and sent him home.

Every one of Eisley's friends had a similar situation happen at least once in their past. They were all born into families with money and connections. They could do whatever they wanted in Shelley Vale and no one would bat an eye.

But no more.

Toward evening, Micah stepped off his porch and got in his car alone. I waited for him to drive the other way to start my car and slowly follow him. We drove about twenty minutes, toward the outskirts of town, and ended up at a two-story brick building. The parking lot was full, so I parked as he got out, slipped on a white button shirt over his tee, and plopped a... security hat? On his head and walked inside.

He worked here. Then I saw the name on the building. It was his dad's place. I snickered and drove around the back. Some people were smoking and sitting on boxes but didn't even turn to look my way.

The sun went down shortly after and I watched from the back of the parking lot as patrons left and within a half hour, the daytime employees did as well. The lights all went out, and the cars disappeared, and I joined them, parking a half mile away.

Sliding my backpack over my shoulder, I walked back to the building and circled it, looking for cameras. They were only at the front entrance. Was that why they hired security? It seemed like cameras would save money in the long run, but who was I to tell rich fucks how to spend their money? Feeling cocky, I went right to the back door and was shocked to find it ajar. A thin cardboard box propped it open. Had Micah been taking a smoke break and simply forgotten to shut the door? Or maybe he'd had no reason to feel scared, so he kept it open always. Either way, I strode right in, letting my eyes adjust to the utter darkness.

With the darkness came confidence. I unzipped my bag and removed my knife and mask, sliding one over my face, while the other rested in my fist. Listening closely, I heard something off in the distance. A TV maybe. I began walking slowly toward the light and sound. Then, I heard his obnoxious laughter and relaxed. I shook my head as I inhaled deeply, smelling the familiar scent of decent weed. The stupid fuck was high. That would make for an interesting chase.

I turned into the room he was in. His feet were propped up on a large table, and his back was toward me. In front of him were a dozen screens I assumed were meant to be security footage, but instead were all connected and playing one large version of the Adam Sandler movie, *Little Nicky*. I recognized the film almost instantly. What was this guy, twelve?

Another joke was said and Micah threw up his hands in laughter, as if he were in the theater watching it for the first time. I stepped forward, confident he couldn't hear me, and gripped the knife tighter. This would be an easy slash.

"Aw fuck. I need a drink." He spun around in his chair and stood. I froze, and for a long moment, we were eye-to-eye with each other. Both of us confused and shocked at seeing the other. He ducked and ran under me, crashing into something in the darkness. I rolled my eyes and followed him out slowly, not feeling the need to push my lungs.

"There's no point in running, Micah." I raised my voice to disguise it.

"Who the fuck are you?"

"Why? Do you have enemies, Micah?"

More crashing of metal on metal came as he ran.

"No! I didn't do anything. I'm not the problem here." I caught him in the lobby and I hurried over, swinging my knife into the thick rack of women's dresses. I made contact with something, but it was a quick swipe.

"Fuck!" he hissed and darted out of the rack holding his

arm. Blood pooled down his skin, staining his white security shirt.

"Micah, this is pointless," I teased. "I'm going to get you regardless of if you run or not."

I followed the loud sounds he was causing. I dodged the racks and shelves he pushed in my way. I stepped over everything calmly, knowing that eventually he'd slow down or fall, and I'd go in for the kill.

He turned a corner and I followed behind. We both jumped when I turned and bumped into him. Reflex made me thrust my arm out and right into his thigh, sinking my pig sticker deep into the muscle. He screamed and pulled away. The knife stayed in my grasp. He fell against the wall and began to wail. God, he was worse than Soleil.

"Why are you doing this?" he cried out, trying to stumble away.

I kicked his ribs, rolling him over, and I straddled him. I wanted to look into his glazed eyes as they went out when I stabbed his heart. I raised the knife and then froze.

"Micah? Bro, are you in here? I'm out!" a man called. Micah and I stared at each other for a minute before he started to scream.

"I'm in here! Help! I've been stabbed!" I jumped off of him and rolled, darting out of the room and to the closest exit, which was the front. I paused, remembering the cameras, and then turned back around. I found the back door exit in complete darkness and sprinted outside. Police sirens were blaring and becoming louder at an alarming rate. I looked around and with a deep sigh, I stretched and took off toward the thick tangle of trees down the hill.

Rule 68 - Constantine

Don't let them take you alive.

The sirens were intense, ringing loudly in my ears as I fled the scene, swearing to myself over and over. I didn't kill him. Fuck!

The woods I'd rushed into were hilly and I was struggling to stay upright. My boots slid with every step upward, and my legs buckled on the way back down. This wasn't a popular track, made clear but how heavy the branches and leaves were. It was a tangled mess, a dream for someone like me normally. The chaser, but now, trying to get away, this was intense on my body and mind.

Dogs barking from a distance, along with large flashlights pulled me forward. I continued to swear as I ran, trying to make it through the trees. I didn't even know where this led out. Would I put so much energy into finding an exit only to find police on the other side waiting for me?

Flashlights, dogs, and voices grew louder, and my steps grew faster, until as I was running down a steep hill, I slipped and tumbled down, impaling a thick branch right through my thigh muscle. An involuntary scream came out of my mouth and I quickly slammed my jaw shut.

"What was that?"

"Where did that come from?" Hissing, I stared down at the branch, firmly planted in my leg, and swallowed. I grit my teeth and reached for it, gripping it with both hands. I began to pull, but the hot flash of pain was too intense and I had to stop almost instantly. My forehead grew slick with sweat as I assessed my situation. I only had moments to make a decision.

Taking a deep breath, I moved my hands up about seven inches and snapped the branch, leaving it inside my leg. I struggled to my feet and started forward. The limp was involuntary. I could feel the branch inside me with every stretch of my leg, but it was be captured or get away, and I was choosing the latter.

Despite my best efforts. I struggled to keep quiet. My grunts of pain, paired with the blood I was leaving everywhere, would lead the dogs to me soon. I needed to get the fuck out of here. Hiding in a tree or underbrush was no longer an option.

My entire body was soaked through with sweat from the pain and effort it was taking me to move. My vision was tunneling, but I continued to drag myself forward, finally reaching the paved road. Relief washed over me, but only for a moment, as I saw nothing but the road. Which way was my fucking car? I turned left and decided that it was better than just standing by the trees. If I got somewhere with buildings or cars and passed out, I could claim that I'd been attacked too, but only if I was far enough away from the original crime. It was too obvious if I was still by the woods.

I collapsed twice. The pain was excruciating. Blood gushed from the wound with each step. I was lightheaded, and still, I mustered on until finally, I saw the parking lot in which Micah's dad's store was and knew that my car wasn't far away..

I lay on the seat of my car, unsure if my body would let me move past this. I closed my eyes and opened them sometime later, still sore, still very much impaled, but no longer sweating. I pulled myself up and reached into my pockets for my keys. I winced as they were on the right side, where the branch was firmly lodged only a few inches away. I attempted to press the pedal with my right foot but a quick test told me that wasn't going to fucking happen so I rested it back and adjusted myself to drive with my left foot. I closed my eyes, took a deep breath, and turned the car on.

I focused hard on the road. I didn't need to be pulled over as a potential DUI. Although once I got somewhere safe I'd be dousing my insides with liquor. I drove carefully, gliding right through town and past the police station, which had an empty parking lot. I let out a chortle, which was the best I could do. One fucking pothead rich boy gets stabbed and the whole police force comes running. Fifty-plus kids stolen from poor families and forced to do unspeakable things in horrible conditions in the middle of the woods and no one bats an eye.

I hoped he fucking bled out.

I drove past Eisley's house. A single light upstairs was on, but it wasn't her bedroom. I slowed down, even stopped at her driveway entrance, but then continued. I wasn't up for explaining how I got this wound. She wasn't stupid. If Micah survived, which, most likely he would, she'd see my wound and put two and two together.

I got to the woods and forced myself to get out and start the much smoother, but still long trek through the woods and to the Church. Knowing I was safer here, I paused against trees when I needed to and eventually made it through the doors and tumbled down the stairs.

I let out a scream as my fall caused the branch to dig deeper into my body. Kansas flew out from wherever he'd been hiding.

"Get this fucking thing out of me," I said through gritted teeth. I darted my hands to my leg and closed my eyes. I felt the pressure when Kansas grabbed it and began to pull. Finally able to let it out, I screamed as he tugged it out at an agonizingly slow pace. The moment it was gone, relief and an explosion of blood poured from my body. I steadied my breathing and looked down. I couldn't see anything through the gush of blood, so I reached into my pocket and pulled out my small pocket knife to rip my jeans further to assess things.

Kansas stood off to the side and watched right along with me as the blood stopped flowing and my skin and muscles began building themselves back up and fusing together until there was no wound, and I was simply sore.

I was too tired to stand, so I fell back against the walls and sighed. I let my head roll in Kansas' direction, and his expression darkened. I was just about to tell him that Micah had most likely survived my attack and we'd have to figure some shit out when he opened his mouth instead and blurted.

"We've got a problem."

Rule 69 - Eisley

Use the internet.

How did Kansas do that?

He fled the scene, and I let him, too confused and scared to do anything else. I finished picking up the broken teapot alone and cleaned up everything else. I poured the boiling water out, no longer wanting to eat or drink.

I wanted to tell Constantine. I stared at his number on my phone but put it away. It wasn't fair to involve him in whatever fucked up shit Kansas was involved in. For years, I'd worked my own flavor of witchcraft, but just simple things that fed on energy. Candle magick to manifest financial success, tarot cards to help me work through stressful situations, and reading tea leaves to make me think about things from a different angle. Nothing like healing a deep gash in your hand. That was... I didn't know.

Staring blankly at the wall, eventually, my eyes dried up and exhaustion led me to lock all of my doors, check the windows, and trudge upstairs, shutting and locking the door behind me. I thought I'd sleep, but I tossed and turned all night. Kansas, the boy I'd known since I was five. How could I not know something was up? Did it have anything to do with that girl he talked about?

Harper.

I tried to recall if he had told me a last name, and I concluded that he hadn't. I was sure that she had something to do with this. Why else would he tell me about her? Had she gotten him into dark magick and he had been trying to ask for my help? The theory took shape in my head. It was the only thing that made sense. Kansas was a sweet soul. He'd been hurt, and she must have seduced him and forced him to do something... weird.

I got up and went for my tablet. I didn't like to snoop on people. It always felt gross to stalk complete strangers on the internet, but I needed to know who this Harper woman was, and what she was involved in.

Kansas didn't post much himself. Just some shares about stuff going on at his campus. My heart sighed when I stumbled upon a random selfie. Up close, he was even more handsome.

I didn't see any relationship status or posts where people tagged him. Nothing. I clicked on his friends list, wondering if they'd remained cordial after they broke up. I clicked on her profile, and my heart dropped.

Her page was littered with articles shared by others about her death.

Campus missing person case closed.
Harper Blackery, promising student, taken too soon.

I clicked on each link, reading the gory details about how the pretty brunette had gone missing in September, and they found her body a month later. Just weeks ago. Her throat had been slit along with her stomach. Her insides were missing when they found her. Because she'd been in the water for so long, investigators weren't sure if animals had taken her organs or if the killer did. The case was still open.

Cold fear slid down my body slowly, as I took in what the articles were saying. It was such a huge case, Kansas had to know about it. He knew and didn't tell me. Instead, he told me they'd dated. Not that she'd gone missing and was murdered. Why would he leave that bit out?

Something wasn't right.

Did Kansas have something to do with Harper's death? The Kansas I knew and loved and allowed to touch my body in the most intimate of ways? This was far more serious than the ability to heal. What had he gotten himself into?

Exhaustion begged me to sleep, but fear kept me up. I rested my head on my pillows and stared up at the ceiling. What was I supposed to do? I closed my eyes, and suddenly, a shrill alarm burst from my phone. I bolted up and reached for it, pressing the buttons on my screen to unlock it to find what the noise was, and then, my heart stopped.

> ALERT: SHELLEY VALE POLICE HAS ISSUED A WARNING AND CURFEW OF 8 PM. A SERIAL KILLER IS ON THE LOOSE AND UNTIL THEY CAN FIND THE SUSPECT, PEOPLE ARE ADVISED TO BE ALERT AND SAFE.

Below the warning was a list of suggestions such as, go nowhere alone, don't go out in the dark, trust no one. All stuff that one would say to give themselves an excuse if another person died. They broke a rule.

I clicked off the alert and went right to the town's social media group. There was no doubt the alert had been sent to everyone. Naturally, people were in a panic. I read through hundreds of comments that kept coming as fast as I read them, and then, an article came through from Shelley Vale's newspaper team. I clicked on it and a large photo of Micah appeared on my screen. I let out a large gasp and dropped my phone. No!

Shaking, I raised the phone to my eyes again and read the article. My heart rate slowed as he hadn't been killed, but only stabbed. He was in the hospital now but would be okay. But, the biggest part of the article was that he identified his attacker, and they'd brought in a sketch artist to draw what he saw. I had to scroll all the way down the page, but then, I saw it.

A Ghostface mask, a 'Y' shaped scar along his chest, and a Death's Head Moth tattoo on his right shoulder.

Constantine was the killer.

Rule 70 - Eisley

Triple check the locks.

It was a dreary blue morning with a threat of rain when I finally exhausted all comments and articles about Harper and my friends' murders. The crew's deaths were changed from murder to suicide. The coroner and detectives concluded that they had been so immersed in researching the Sinister Minister and the Family that they did what they had done ten years ago and sacrificed themselves as a gift to a god no one understood. That didn't make their deaths any lighter. If they hadn't come here in the first place, they'd still be alive.

My mood, after reading every gruesome detail, reflected the outside world. I, too, wanted to cry quietly. My body continued to cry for sleep, but my mind was too overwhelmed to do so. Eventually, I gave in and took a sleeping pill, allowing myself the break I desperately needed. It was starting to rain when I drifted off to sleep.

Thunder clapped, and my windows lit up with lightning strikes in the distance. Stirring, I climbed out of bed, my body still groggy but lighter. I reached for my phone and saw it was after eight p.m. As I walked downstairs and waded through my house, I laughed. None of those stupid rules the police gave out pertained to me, as the killer was someone I knew and loved. One misstep and I was as good as gone, regardless of if I obeyed curfew.

Despite having done it last night, I went through the house again, making sure every door and window was locked. Even the basement's windows.

I had pulled out some Rice Krispie cereal and milk simply to put something in my stomach when a loud clap of thunder roared through the house and my lights flickered once, twice, and then went out. This old house never did well in storms. I put the milk away and ate my cereal in thick silence. I could now hear every creak inside the house and every branch snapping outside. The wind whistled through the old floorboards and the windows rattled with every thunderclap.

I was better off going back to bed and trying to figure things out in the morning when the power would be back on. I unlocked my phone to use the flashlight and it lit up, only to die a moment later. I'd forgotten to charge it while I slept.

Carefully, I made my way to the bedroom, barefoot and cautious. I paused at my mirror and stared at the hauntingly beautiful tattoos on my shoulders in the mirror, my mind drifted off.

Storms in the Church were awful. You could hear them going on outside, and water flowed through any crack it could. Many times, we'd have to raise our mattress and try to set it on something to keep it from getting wet and moldy. It would take all three of us sometimes, our collective eight-year-old strengths, to keep it upright.

The Family never cared about our crying. They'd either offer us a mop and demand we clean it up, as if we had flooded the room on purpose, or gave us a bucket to pour into the sink that was taken the moment we were done with it. On the lucky times our room didn't flood, it was cold and we'd be forced to huddle together, even more than usual, to stay alive. Back then, there was no jealousy. We were working together to survive. One didn't go hungry alone, nor did they suffer alone. I missed that.

I returned to my bedroom and sat on the edge of the bed. I ran my hand over my right tattoo, for Constantine, and then the left, for Kansas. Both men I couldn't bear to part with. Both men who I discovered were monsters. My thoughts went to Harper and then all of my friends. What were the odds that the men I loved, the only men I'd ever loved, were psychos? They had to be horrible, awful coincidences.

Why would Kansas brutally murder that girl? I'd pissed him off plenty of times and never once did he touch me in any aggressive manner. What could she have done to set him off? I didn't think that was even possible.

And Constantine. Sure, he was broody. He looked like the poster boy for bad boys in every sense of the word, but he'd seen what his father, the Minister, had done to so many people. He wouldn't want to become the very thing he was tormented by for years. I couldn't believe it. I didn't want to believe it. Constantine had a good heart. The boy I had abandoned ten years ago had a good heart. There was nothing that could change his soul so drastically. Not anything I wanted to experience myself.

If Kansas or Constantine had stumbled upon something so evil that would cause their entire being to shift and morph into monsters, I needed to run before it found me.

Panic shot through me and despite having no electricity, I began packing a to-go bag. I couldn't see much, so I opened my black curtains and prayed for a bout of lightning to brighten the room. I stuffed my duffel bag with underclothes and some of my thinner skirts and tops. I grabbed my wallet and some important documents from my closet and tossed them in as well. I looked toward the bathroom, debating grabbing my pills. I hated taking them.

Something on my bedside table caught my eye. I frowned, recalling what it was, and reached for it. I unfolded the thick worn certificate and read each word again in the dim light.

While we both knew there was nothing legal about this marriage certificate, for ten years, we took it as so. We wore our rings around our necks as a remembrance, and I had saved my virginity, my first full sexual experience, to share with him. Although we had been only eleven, so young, still children, we were bonded to each other. He was my husband, and I was his—

"Wife." I spun around and fear prickled my skin as Constantine stalked into the room, dripping head to toe.

"Get out," I demanded.

He shook his head. His blue eyes blazed, boring into mine. "Why are you afraid of me?" he asked, stepping closer.

"I'm not."

"You saw the article, didn't you?" Slowly, he revealed the Ghostface mask from behind his back. He slid it over his head and cocked his head.

"And you recall that night in the Church when you were high on your ass, don't you?" His voice, muffled from inside the mask, crawled over my skin in such a way I knew if I didn't get out now, I would be his next victim. I reached the wall and began to sidle it, hoping to get to my open door. He caught me, putting his hand on my hip.

"What are you going to do with that information, Eisley?" I could smell his woodsy cologne and the hairs on my neck and arm prickled. Even now, scared shitless, my body betrayed me. I still wanted him.

"Nothing."

He leaned in closer, his breath hot on my cold skin.

"You know what you should do?" he asked. A flash of lightning lit up the room and I saw his eyes dilate through the black fabric of the mask. It was absolutely terrifying. He stared down at me, his prey, his next victim. I shook my head, and he laughed. "Run."

Rule 71 - Constantine

Prepare for rain.

She screamed and shoved me back. Caught off guard, I stumbled back, falling onto her bed. Eisley rushed past me and flew down the stairs. Loud thumps on the hardwood floor came as she ran through the house, taking off out the front door. I sighed, slid the knife back into my boot, and started after her.

"Eisley!" As I stalked through her house, I noticed she hadn't taken her shoes or a coat, but her keys were gone. Jesus, there was no way she was going to attempt to drive in the fucking rain. I glanced out the front window and watched as she climbed into her car.

I stormed down the porch. She'd turned the car on but hadn't moved. She knew as well as I did that it was far too dangerous to drive in these conditions. I crept over to my car that was parked beside hers. She was looking blankly ahead as if trying to figure out a plan.

She didn't have one. Running out into the middle of a fucking thunderstorm with no shoes and a flimsy sheer night-gown told me that. I slammed my hands against her window, and she screamed. She threw her car into reverse and whipped out of her driveway.

Fuck.

I ran to my car and pulled out as fast, trailing behind her. What the fuck was she thinking? The rain was so heavy, it dropped like bullets onto the roof of my car, making it hard for me to think. Where was she going? The police?

I sped around her and cut her off. She dodged me by turning sharply down another road, and I realized then that I could easily get her where I wanted her if I paid attention to the road signs. I followed her, cutting her off again and again, until finally, we were near the woods that led to the Church. *Bingo.* It was perfect timing as the rain was getting even harder. I drifted directly in front of her. She slammed on the brakes, and finally, turned her car off. We jumped out of our cars.

"I spent five years trapped, but I got out. I survived. I'm free and I'm going to go out that way." She clenched her fists and glared at me through the freezing rain. I raised my eyebrows as she sneakily shoved her keys through her fingers, creating brass-knuckles. I'd love to see her try. I stepped forward, ignoring the cold shiver passing through my bones.

"Eisley, little Eisley, you can't run from me."

She turned away, putting her hand over her forehead to see better. Bad mistake. I caught her throat, pulling her back toward my chest.

She gasped but didn't struggle. She was breathing heavily, but not from fear. Her ass pushed against my raging erection, her hands shoving me away, but only hard enough to say she fought.

I ran my hand over her body, tugging the soaked nightgown up and then abandoning it in favor of her breast. I squeezed until she cried out in pain.

"You are mine," I growled into her neck. "You're not going anywhere."

"I wasn't!"

"What was the bag for then?" Where would she go without telling me? Without telling Kansas? When I saw the bag, I went into panic mode and pulled out my knife. I'd only intended to scare her, but the gleam in her eyes, the excitement I saw underneath the fear as I slid the mask on and pushed her to the wall, it turned me on too.

"Drop the keys." My hand cupping her breast slid down, running along the fabric covering her cunt. I followed the line teasing her as I pressed against her clit. "Now," I growled.

"Why? Are you afraid I'll hurt you?" she asked.

"Oh no, it's not you I'm afraid of." I brought my hand to her throat and squeezed. "Drop them." Her fist opened, and they clunked to the ground.

"I know what you did," she said when I let go of her throat. She stumbled forward, her bare feet scraping the pavement. Her entire body shook from the cold, and I fought the urge to cover her. "To Spencer and Soleil."

I blinked and cocked my head. Oh really? I don't think she did. A slow smile curled my lips upward. Despite the darkness engulfing us, I could see her eyes, shining bright and hard. They were challenging me.

That was a bad idea.

Keeping eye contact, I bent down and pulled up my drenched jeans, sliding the knife out of its sheath. Her eyes widened. Did she not expect me to react to the harsh accusations?

"What are you going to do then?" I grinned. "Turn me in? Let them lock me away?" I stepped forward, and she stepped back. "You know all too well what it's like being trapped Eisley, and you want to do that to me?"

My eyes flicked to the woods behind her. The more I

moved forward, the more she fell into the trees. Her feet touched dirt, and she jumped.

"It's better than being killed myself."

"Who said I was going to kill you?" I reached for her chin, but she pulled back in time. I raised the knife to the sky and waved it vicariously as I laughed. "Oh, because of this?"

She turned and sprinted into the woods.

I turned back and grabbed her keys off the ground. I got both our cars parked to avoid any accidents. Then I stretched my neck, took out my knife, and started into the woods after her. That was a good enough head start.

With every step I took, I was looking around, expecting to find her collapsed on the ground or against a tree. I spotted her within a few minutes but continued my slow trek toward the Church.

A large crack of thunder elicited a scream from her. I paused as the lightning came down and struck a tree. It splintered and fell at her feet. I jerked forward to run to her, but I stopped myself. She was unfazed by the smoking tree and kept moving. Slowly, I was catching up to her, and for my own amusement, I ducked behind a thick tree. She searched for me, then sighing, she fell back against her own tree a few feet ahead of me.

What a fucking tease.

Using the heavy rain to cover the sound of my feet, I walked right up to her tree and yanked her into my arms. She tried to scream, but I quickly shoved two fingers into her mouth.

"You've been a bad girl, Eisley," I whispered in her ear as I pushed her to her knees. I moved with her, keeping my fingers buried in her throat. "You know what happens to bad girls?" My other hand, still grasping the knife, went to her thigh, tugging up her battered gown. The blade slid up her skin, sending cold shivers through her body and, with it pressed against mine, through me as well.

She began to choke on my fingers, which only made me dig further in. Her tongue darted around them, sending my cock into delirious excitement. As I traced the knife around to her backside, I pushed her forward, letting her hands catch her, and reached for her panties.

"I don't like being the bad guy, Eisley." I slid her panties to the ground and pulled my fingers from her mouth, bringing them right to her exposed folds. "But I will if I need to get my point across." My fingers probed her little pussy, spreading her lips and slipping between the wetness that had pooled there.

She cried and gagged, trying to hold things together.

"Tell me, wife." I pulled my fingers from her body and replaced it with the hilt of my knife. She froze and then realizing what it was, she tried to bolt. I snatched her by the hair and pulled her back. I pressed the hilt into her wet and wanting pussy. "Were you running because you were really scared I'd kill you? Or were you running because you like it when I chase you?"

Her breathing hitched as I slowly pulled back the knife and then thrust it back into her. She cried out but didn't plead for me to stop. Small moans escaped her lips, accompanied by tiny movements in her hips.

I reached around, wrapping my hand around her neck, and tugged her up, keeping the knife firmly inside her. I brought my lips down onto her needy ones. Our tongues danced, and she lifted herself and slid back down, fucking herself with the knife. My hand slid back to her neck and tightened again. A low chuckle escaped my lips as I kissed her shoulder and whispered, "If this is what gets you off, Eisley, then we're in trouble."

Rule 72 - Constantine

The reveal is the best part.

I waited until she was right on the edge of coming before removing the knife and my hands from her body. I pushed her away, and she fell into the wet mud with a cry of anguish. I pulled her up by her arm and she spun around, glaring daggers at me.

Keeping my grin and eyes locked on her beautifully frustrated face, I raised the knife to my lips and slid the hilt into my mouth, tasting her. Her eyes went wide, and she shivered. I removed the knife and flicked it around so I could grip it. I pointed forward with it.

"Come on," I growled. Gripping her forearm tightly, I dragged her forward.

"Slow down!" she yelled, stumbling. "I'm barefoot!"

When the Church came into view, she let out a small gasp and started fighting my grip. "No. Please don't take me there. Not again."

"You've already been there," I argued, not stopping.

"Yes, and I don't need to go again." She dug her heels into the ground and finally tore herself from me. "No."

I took a deep breath and then snatched her around the

waist, tossing her over my shoulder. Eisley pounded her fists on my back, but I ignored it, striding right through the main floor and down the stairs of the Church. As we started down, she calmed down.

"You cleaned it up."

"I did. Some of it. I wanted it to be livable while I do what I have to do here."

I had picked up all the forest debris and garbage from the shitty teens over the last ten years. I'd also swept up the glass and boarded up windows. It wasn't great, and after we left Shelley Vale, I hoped to never see this fucking place again. My father's legacy would die here.

I set her down and waited for her to bolt, but she didn't. She looked up at the stairs, but her expression was so transparent, I could almost hear her thoughts. If she left now, she'd have to battle the storm again. It would do her no good. I had her car keys.

"Do you want a towel?" I asked, stepping deeper into the room. I shed my jacket and peeled the shirt off. I unbuckled my belt and tugged it out of the loops of my pants.

"Yes, please." Her voice came out so soft, I almost didn't hear it. "Constantine, what is that?" I turned curiously and followed her gaze to the table in the center of the room.

Cautiously, she looked toward the stairs. She was considering risking it by taking slow steps back. I didn't blame her. The first time I'd seen the altar, I'd been terrified. And I hadn't even been on it then.

"Eisley, I suggest you stay right where you fucking are." I lowered my gaze. "If you run, I will catch you, and you will not like what I do after." Her panicked brown eyes flicked to my unbuttoned pants and then back to my face.

"You—Is this what you did with them?"

I cocked my head and chuckled.

"This? Nah, I just slashed 'em up. They aren't worthy of all that trouble. They were in the way." Her body trembled, but it wasn't the cold that had her chilled to the bone. Now, it was me. I pinched her jaw.

"But I am?" she asked. "Worthy?"

"Absolutely. Now, why don't we get started." I forced her to her knees, and she dropped quickly, her hands resting on her thighs. She looked so innocent, so... submissive. Her dress might as well be non-existent. I could see every curve of her body. Her nipples were tight and peeking out, begging to be played with.

My cock responded to her pose. Eisley was a brat, who needed to be tamed. Bringing my hand back to her jaw, I squeezed until her lips parted and her tongue rolled out lazily.

Yes.

I tilted my head and spit. She caught it, swallowed, and looked up at me again as if asking for more. *Oh, Eisley, how much more I could give you?*

"When did you figure it out?" I asked.

"The mask." She stood, and as I began to walk to my room, she followed. I handed her a towel from a small stack I'd stolen from the hotel. "I remember you bringing me here while you wore the mask."

"What else do you remember?" The mask was too generic for that to be the thing that tipped her off. That night had been a wild ride. For everyone involved. I turned, and she handed me my towel back. She was still soaked, but the mud was mostly cleared away, creating a hauntingly beautiful creature.

"Why are you killing them?" she asked instead of answering me. "They had nothing to do with what happened to us." She motioned around the room. The one we'd been trapped in for so long. I thought that I'd have trouble returning, but now, I felt nothing. It was merely something that had to be done to finish things.

"They had everything to do with us, Eisley. Your friends were never really your friends. They used you, and eventually, they would have turned into their parents, who directly did this." She shook her head.

"No, Spencer wouldn't have. Soleil either."

"Really?" I snapped. "Because they didn't seem to give a fuck about you before they realized they needed you for the documentary. You heard what they said to you the other day. Their true feelings. Those rich assholes were born and bred to fuck the lower class over. Them being dead saves the world a lot of fucking hurt."

Tears dripped down her dirty cheeks. I reached around and pressed her chest to mine. My hand ran down her curves, squeezing her ass.

"You know it's true. They never would have let you be a part of them. You were just a pawn in their games."

"And what am I to you?" She pushed against my chest but I didn't let her go.

"My wife," I said. She clasped the ring around my neck and looked up at me, so beautiful, perfect, so fucking hot. My cock throbbed against her thigh. "My princess." I touched her soft cheek and pinched her mouth open again. Grinning, I leaned in and instead of kissing her, I spit and she took it again with a soft moan. "My good girl."

A shadow appeared in the doorway. Finally. Eisley turned herself, finding Kansas wearing his Ghostface mask, shirtless, and smiling at us while leaning against the doorframe.

"And our plaything."

Rule 73 - Eisley

Relax your breathing.

"What's going on?" My heart beat like a hummingbird trapped in my chest.

"You said you knew I was the one killing everyone because of the mask." Constantine spun me around and wrapped his hands around my chest and stomach, binding me to him. "That mask?"

Kansas sauntered into the room, confident and amused. "They are relatively easy to get. We bought ours for 12.99 same day shipping."

"Ours? You guys have been talking? Since when?" I couldn't believe it. My mind raced, trying to put the pieces together. Kansas stepped up to me, sandwiching me between them. He cupped my sex. My breathing stopped. I had lost my underwear in the woods. Heat flamed my face as I recalled why they'd been discarded.

"You look like hell." He smirked, gazing down at me through the Ghostface mask. His fingers probed my body, spreading my pussy and diving in. "But it seems like you like it there."

"Could this be hell?" Constantine asked. "Being here with us?"

Kansas's finger swirled around my clit, and despite wanting to feel ashamed, embarrassed, and push him away, I couldn't. I closed my eyes and rested my head back against Constantine's chest.

"Speak up, princess," Kansas demanded.

And there it was. A clue. Flashes came to my mind every time they called me princess while in the throes of passion. I should have known. It was too specific to be a coincidence. Why hadn't I realized?

"What are you doing?" I gasped as Constantine pushed his leg between mine, spreading my thighs open. Kansas took that opportunity to move deeper into me, sliding a finger inside me. "We can't—"

"Who is we?" Constantine peppered kisses across my neck, making me shiver. His hand went to my breast, teasing my hard nipple. "Because we can do whatever we want together."

"Together?" I gasped, trying to understand what they were saying. One man had his hand inside me; the other's cock was pressed against my ass.

Constantine hummed. "It's fitting that we started here together, and now, we'll finish together." The double entendre in his words sent my heart fluttering again. My gaze fell to the bed on the floor. For a moment, I was thrown back in time to when the mattress we had all shared was filthy, littered with mildew, and had no blankets. But this was different. We were reclaiming this room on our terms.

Kansas pulled away, and Constantine dropped his arms.

"What do you want, Eisley?" Constantine asked.

"You, both of you." I nodded. "I can't give one of you up for the other."

"We're not asking you to," Kansas said. "If you want us both, then you'll get us both. Lead the way."

Did I really want this? Two men at once? My eyes went from one to the other, and my stomach stopped twisting and relaxed. It was the easiest answer ever. With these two, yes.

I dropped my knees onto the bed and crawled forward, sitting up. I rested my hands on my thighs and waited for them to join me.

They stood side by side for a moment, and I took their glorious bodies in. For a moment, I was alarmed at how similar their Y-shaped scars were, but their beauty made me forget just as quickly. Both rigid, toned arms and stomach, both scarred, tattooed and dangerous. Both perfection.

"What do I do?" I asked, shrinking into myself. It was embarrassing, not knowing where to start. Constantine reached for his already unbuttoned pants and shoved them down his thighs, taking his boxers with him. His cock sprang out as if it had been waiting for a lifetime for this very moment.

Kansas removed the mask and pulled his glasses out from his back pocket, sliding them back onto his face. Then, he dropped the rest of his clothing too. The men stood nude, hard, and staring at me as if I were their dinner and they'd been starved for far too long.

Kansas moved first, stepping onto the bed behind me and pulling me to his chest. Constantine followed but crawled in front of me.

Kansas slid his hands down my body, still damp and dirty from the storm. He reached the edge of my dress and began to pull it up, slowly, unveiling my body. I raised my arms and allowed him to free me from the ruined nightgown. With his knees, he nudged me to sit on my ass and began peppering my neck and shoulders with his kisses.

Constantine, with little prompting, took my thighs and spread them, diving his body between them. I gasped as his tongue began lapping at my arousal, while Kansas massaged my breasts, pinching my nipples.

The pleasure was everywhere as both men ravaged me with their mouths. There was so much sensation, I couldn't focus on just one, and they began to blend in one beautiful mess of pleasure.

Kansas shifted so he could kiss my breasts, licking a nipple and then taking it into his mouth. Constantine ran his teeth along my clit, and I screamed out in ecstasy as my orgasm came swiftly, rippling through my body. Constantine sat up with a grin and leaned over to kiss me, shoving his tongue in my mouth so I could taste myself.

"More," I gasped. I wasn't done. I couldn't be. My core ached with the need to be filled.

"More? I think we can do that," Constantine said.

Kansas stood and exited the room without an explanation.

"He'll be back. Come." He patted the bed. His cock, sticking straight up in the air, looked massive and intimidating. "I want you to sit on my lap, facing me."

I stared at it for a moment, but Kansas returned, and I relaxed. I saddled Constantine and nervously reached for him.

"It's okay, princess." Constantine smirked. "We're going to do all the work, you just need to get up on top." He lifted my hips and helped situate his cock at my entrance, and then slowly, I began to slide down, taking in every inch of him.

I shuddered at the new sensation. It felt so different from this position. He was deeper, more snug, and the pleasure was so much more intense. Kansas rejoined us and reached for my hips.

"Come on, princess, fuck him for me."

Constantine began to thrust his hips upward, and I cried out as the pleasure intensified. I couldn't handle it. It was too much. I was being stretched so deliciously, I screamed with every thrust of his tortured hips.

Kansas held me firmly to Constantine as I rode wave after

wave of unbridled passion. As we moved, Kansas's cock slid against my backside with us.

"Are you ready?" Constantine demanded.

"For what?" I gasped.

"I wasn't talking to you, princess," he growled and slowed his pace. Kansas slid his fingers down my backside, searching for the most private hole on my body.

"No!" I cried out in surprise as his thumb pressed against it.

"Sssh." Constantine pulled me down by my shoulders and hugged me to him, causing my ass to be thrust into the air. "Go ahead," he said to Kansas.

I whimpered as I felt liquid pour onto my ass and touch my puckered hole. I tried to shift my hips, but Constantine kept my body firmly locked in place.

"You're going to like it," he assured me. "We're using plenty of lubrication."

"Remember that plug you had, it's just like that, but bigger, better. You took it so well," Constantine continued to purr words of encouragement into my ear as Kansas pushed one finger past the tight ring of muscle.

I cried out as he wiggled his finger around and then slid it in and out. The pain was so sharp. How could this feel good?

Constantine murmured, "Be a good girl and let Kansas stretch your little asshole, okay? You're going to feel so full; you won't be able to stop coming."

I felt the head of Kansas's rigid cock press against my hole and slowly push itself inside. Tears slid down my face as he kept pushing. I could feel them both inside me, with a thin layer between them. My body screamed for them to stop, but they both continued to push against my openings until I took them to their bases.

"You look so beautiful," Constantine gushed, reaching up and tangling his mouth with mine. He relaxed his hold on me and slowly began to work his hips. "You're always the most beautiful when you're crying."

More liquid was dumped around my ass, and Kansas began to move too. His thrusts were slower, but eventually the pain began to lessen, just like they'd said.

"Yes, let yourself go, princess," Constantine coaxed.

Kansas reached forward and took my breasts in his hands as he fucked my ass at a more rapid pace.

I gasped as my orgasm began to build. I couldn't understand where the pleasure was more focused, as both men were touching something inside me so deep, so intimate, so carnal.

Soon, I arched my back, encouraging Kansas to go deeper. I needed more of him. I needed more of Constantine. I needed them both all at once forever. Kansas shoved himself hard against me, and I cried out as my orgasm rumbled through me with such force I grew dizzy and my eyes rolled into the back of my head.

"Such a good girl coming for us." Constantine kissed me tenderly as I collapsed against his chest. They continued their delicious assault on my body, and a third orgasm came, bringing me to sobs. I cried so hard, that Kansas came, and a moment later, Constantine went stiff and I felt the pulse of his seed spilling into me.

As we pulled apart, I lay between them, the evidence of all of our orgasms a sea between my legs. I closed my eyes and rested my head against Kansas's chest, and Constantine pressed my back to his.

I didn't need to choose which one to save, because they saved me.

Rule 74 - Eisley

Pay attention when you're being taught something new.

"Why do you call me princess?" I asked, and both men chuckled. "What?"

"Princess is your shortened nickname," Kansas confessed. "Constantine came up with it after the first few days of us hanging out and catching up."

"Okay, so what's the long nickname then?" I asked.

"Pillow Princess." Kansas rolled his eyes and snickered. "You know what that means?"

I shook my head.

"It means," Constantine's hands crept up my shoulders and trailed down, sliding between my arm and body and cupping my breast "you let your partners do all the work."

"I do not!" I protested as his fingers rolled my nipple until it hardened.

"Oh, really?" Kansas reached between my thighs. "Out of all the times, you let me finger you when we were teens, how many times did you reach for my cock?"

I blinked.

None.

"And have you touched either of ours yet?"

No.

I sat up and crossed my arms. "Well, that's not fair. I just haven't been given the opportunity."

"The opportunity?" Kansas laughed and rolled out of bed. "We'll see about that."

Constantine left the room, still naked and beautiful. I tugged the blanket over my bare body and clenched. My entire body ached. I was already missing their touches. I wanted more. I wanted them again. I could feel arousal pooling between my legs again recalling the night before.

They returned in dry jeans. Looking dangerous and sexy.

"We cleaned up some. You want to prove you're not a pillow princess? Show us." Kansas raised an eyebrow. Constantine walked in, holding his knife. He saw my eyes grow wide, and he shrugged. He handed it off to Kansas.

"You never know when you might need it." He winked, and I blushed furiously. Steeling myself, I sat up on my knees on the mattress.

"Fine. Come here."

"Who?" Constantine asked.

"Both of you." My nerves fluttered like butterflies in my belly. "I want—"

"Tell us," Kansas said, stepping toward me, knife in hand. "Tell us what you want to do." With shaky hands, I reached out and tugged on the loops in his jeans.

"I want to suck you off."

"Then do it," he ordered, pointing the tip of the knife toward his zipper. Constantine sat beside me, pulling my hair out of the way.

"You're such a good girl, Eisley."

"I don't know how." My voice trembled as hard as my fingers did, trying to unbutton his pants.

"Why don't you show her," Kansas said to Constantine while continuing to brandish the knife.

My raven-haired husband smirked and moved closer so our faces were inches from Kansas's groin.

"Pull him out and we'll do it together," he said.

I finally got the zipper down, and Kansas's cock sprang out, hanging between our faces.

Constantine ran his tongue along Kansas's length, all the while eyeing me.

Kansas let out a low groan and reached for his head, pushing him deeper. It was insanely arousing, and as Constantine continued blowing Kansas, he maintained eye contact and his hand went between my thighs. He pushed apart my folds, sweeping his thumb across my clit. I moaned, and Constantine pulled back from Kansas. He swatted the hand with the knife away.

"You don't need a knife to my throat for me to suck your cock; I'll do it anytime." Constantine chuckled at Kansas. He then nodded at me. "It's your turn, princess. Suck him off and show us what you've learned."

Nervously, I reached for Kansas's hardness and brought my body forward to the edge of the bed. My heart beat loudly as I took him into my mouth and tasted him for the first time. It was soft, but rigid. I began to follow what I'd watched Constantine do, and soon, Kansas was moaning my name and urging me to take him deeper.

"That's right. Yes, good girl, Eisley," he moaned.

I closed my eyes and focused on the feeling of Kansas in my mouth. I was enjoying every time he pulsed, and the taste of his cum as he dripped every so often.

Constantine sat beside me for only a moment, and once I had a rhythm, he shifted, moving behind me. His hands wandered, pinching my nipples and kissing my shoulders. He pulled my hips back so I was on all fours and then began to stroke my sore but aching flesh. Then he slid a finger inside me.

"Don't stop," he warned. The sound of a zipper being undone and pants being shifted stirred my attention, but a low growl from behind me kept me from checking to see what was going on.

The head of Constantine's cock pressed against my swollen lips, and he pushed inside of me slowly, as if testing the waters. I arched my hips and pushed my backside into him, encouraging him to thrust.

"Good girl," he purred and rocked his hips. Kansas shifted my hair and pushed my head deeper.

"I want you to choke, princess."

I continued rolling my tongue and sucking Kansas's cock, all while Constantine began coaxing my orgasm to life, thrust by thrust. I began to moan with them, as I closed in on total ecstasy.

Something metal-like touched my neck. I brought my hand to the necklace and found my ring had been returned.

"I thought you'd want it back." Kansas pushed my head forward to take him to the base.

"And I thought it fitting to give you one." Constantine dug into his pants pocket and leaned over me. I struggled to see but saw pieces of the exchange. When Kansas pulled back, he had his own necklace with a ring the same as Constantine's.

"Now, it's official, princess." Constantine bent down, his chest pressing against my back. "You're ours 'til death and then after."

A large groan came from Kansas as he shot hot spurts into the back of my throat.

"Swallow it." He held my head, giving me no choice, although I had every intention of taking every last drop of him I could.

"Good girl, Eisley. Now it's your turn." Constantine pulled out long enough to sit me on his lap and tug me onto his cock in a sitting position. He reached for my legs and pulled them up. Kansas quickly got down and began to lap at my clit as if he'd been dying of thirst and I was his only source for survival.

Constantine thrust his hips and Kansas sucked my clit and reached upward, pressing on my mound. A flush of liquid rushed out of me.

Mortified that I'd squirted again but still reeling in pleasure, I tossed my head back and enjoyed my men treating me like the princess I was. And as I came again, right with Constantine, my body collapsed completely and the words echoed in my ears.

I was a good girl.

Rule 75 - Kansas

Plan ahead.

The taste of her was still on my tongue as Constantine turned his head on the mattress we shared and our heads leaned in over her to connect. The day we'd both been waiting for had finally come. Eisley was here and loved us both.

"Do you like it?" Constantine smirked, and his blue eyes drifted to my bare chest, settling on my necklace. His voice was low, barely a whisper, to not wake the goddess between us sleeping deeply. I raised the ring and assessed it.

"I do. It's a nice surprise."

"Once we get out of this fucking place, we'll get new rings that actually fit." He turned on his side so he could run his hands along Eisley's perfect, naked body. After another round of making her come so much she begged us to stop, she pleaded for sleep, and I gave her a pill to help.

"I don't want to get up." I sighed. My cock stirred, watching my partner in crime's hands roam over her.

"Do you think she'd wake up if we went for another round?" His hands dipped between her thighs, pushing them open. I gulped, my mouth becoming dry. Now that I'd had a taste of Eisley's glorious honey between her legs, I couldn't get enough. Constantine looked up at me with a wicked grin as he rolled her onto her back, exposing her tits to the cold air.

I took a nipple into my mouth, just as Constantine spread her pussy open and started finger-fucking her.

Eisley let out a small moan. Her eyes fluttered, but sheer exhaustion from running through the storm, the abundance of sex, and sleeping pill had sapped her completely.

I licked around her nipple and reached for the other one to play with. Her back arched slightly and a small smile crept over her lips.

Constantine settled himself between her thighs and trailed his tongue over her slit.

Eisley's breathing hitched, but she still didn't rouse as Constantine licked and sucked her pussy and I teased her breasts. My empty hand slid down to my cock and began to stroke. Masturbation was nothing compared to being inside her, but watching her writhe in pleasure as we took her in her sleep was enough to keep me hard and leaking cum.

Her mouth fell open in a large groan, and I stopped sucking on her nipple to lean up and take her mouth against mine. Even in her sleep, her tongue darted out and found mine.

The idea struck me then, and I pulled away and sat up. Constantine paused, but only for a moment to see what I was doing. I moved closer to her head and positioned my stiff cock right at her lips and gently pushed against them.

Her jaw slid open, and I pushed my cock inside. As if by pure instinct, she began sucking. I lost my breath for a moment with how strong she sucked the moment I was all the way in. Her tongue swirled slow and lazy around me while I helped her head began move back and forth, taking my length in and out of her gorgeous, swollen lips.

"Holy shit," I gasped, looking down at Constantine. His eyebrows rose, and he nodded approvingly.

"She'd been starved for so long she can't help it now. Fill her fucking throat."

I grinned and fisted her hair, pushing my cock further down her throat. She gagged but didn't stop. Her eyes began to shift under her lids but still slowly as if dreaming.

"Dude, she's getting wetter." Constantine laughed. "I think this is turning her on." He raised her ass and slid inside her. Her eyes fluttered open. We waited for her to react, but her eyes rolled into the back of her head and she shut them again. She stopped sucking, so I reached down and massaged her cheeks and she began again.

"God, she's so fucking beautiful," I muttered. I looked over at Constantine, who was holding her steady and slowly fucking her. He hadn't been kidding when he told her she would be our plaything. We'd both held out so long for this very moment when we could finally all be together. Now that it was here, we weren't letting her go.

Her sleepy moans grew longer, more whiny. She bucked against Constantine and sucked me harder. I burst, shooting my come right down her throat. She fell back, and I returned to her breasts, my hand reaching down to finger her clit while Constantine pounded her G-spot inside her.

She continued to whimper and moan until finally her back arched and her orgasm overtook her. She shuddered and then went slightly limp, long enough for Constantine to blow his load and set her back down. She cuddled against us again afterward with a sleepy smile.

"A few more hours," Constantine said. "And then we gotta figure shit out. There's three left."

I nodded. Therese, Remington, and Micah. Constantine had almost killed Micah, but according to him, there'd been a hiccup. Thankfully, it was the stoner of the group and he was too high to remember who exactly it was.

"We don't really need them to do the ritual," I reminded him. "We took everything from the documentary crew."

"Yeah, but at this point I'd say let's just slash 'em all." He cackled. "I'm not leaving things up to chance. One loose lip and we're fucked."

Fair enough.

"Do you think she'll try to save them?" I pushed her hair away from her face.

"It doesn't matter. I'm not going to give her the option. We're going to slaughter them, then do the ritual. Same thing they did for me; same thing we did for you."

"I don't want to cut her." I sighed, looking at the Y on Constantine's chest.

"It's a necessary part of the ritual unfortunately." He frowned, eyeing my scar given by him. "I don't want to maim her either, but she's going to be beautiful, reanimated."

She would be like us.

Rule 76 - Kansas

Be prepared to die.

Two months Prior

Hundreds of candles, 237, to be exact, sat around Constantine's high-rise apartment, flickering ominously as we finished setting up the rest of the altar. If anyone walked in they'd call the cops on us. Satanic panic and all.

"We're almost done," Constantine muttered from the short table he was leaning over. He'd just set out the bowls with Harper's insides in it. Thankfully, he'd kept them frozen, so they didn't smell.

I'd thrown up three times, trying to gather all of her organs.

"You all right over there? You look like you've seen a ghost." Constantine smirked when he saw my gaze lingering on her heart. It was moist from the thawing and made my stomach revolt again.

I shook my head and watched him in awe. He was so confident in his movements. If he was nervous about doing his first reanimation ritual, he didn't show it. When I walked in earlier today and announced I was ready, he simply patted me on the back, stripped down to his boxers, and started setting everything up.

"How long did it take for you to gather everything?" I asked, bending down to straighten the red silk sheet resting on the floor. I eyed all the plants and dried herbs scattered around the altar.

"I didn't. My dad had an extra kit in the coffin he buried all those gold bricks in."

"What? Then why did I have to ki—" I shook my head as anger flooded through me. "You made me kill Harper for nothing?"

"Not for nothing." He scoffed. "Someone had to die. It was just convenient that she was annoying as fuck."

"Fuck you," I spat.

"Hey!" He flashed the knife at me, pointing it right at my chest. "I'm doing you a fucking favor, ain't I?"

"A favor? I'm still not sold on the entire idea. I'm only doing this because..."

His expression darkened. When he first confessed what the Minister had done to him, murdering him, only to bring him right back to life, cursing him to immortality and the forever lingering need to murder others, I didn't believe him. How could you believe that? He'd been 'reanimated', his words not mine, ten years ago, and yet he continued to grow, to age. It was a bullshit story to spook me. But then, when I laughed in his face, he reached into a kitchen drawer and whipped out a steak knife. Without missing a beat, he stabbed his hand all the way through and removed the knife so quickly I didn't have time to react past screaming.

Grinning wickedly, Constantine raised his hand to the light as the wound poured blood for only a moment before it slowly began to seal until the wound was gone. He flipped his hand around to show that there wasn't even a scar.

"See."

"If you're immortal, then how did you still age?"

"237. That's how many candles are used in the ritual. You know why that is, Kansas?"

I shook my head.

He held up two fingers. "Two lives, three times seven. Twenty-one."

"What?"

He laughed dryly and shrugged. "I don't know, man. It was written down in my dad's lunatic ramblings he called his bible. Either way, it was true. I aged and was able to be hurt until my 21st birthday. Ever since then, nothing." He stabbed the knife into his thigh and removed it, only for us to watch it heal.

He tossed the knife in the sink. "I'm still trying to figure out that part. Not entirely sure why. I'm grateful, though. Who the fuck would want to stay eleven for eternity?" He snickered.

"Are you sure you can't die?" I stared at his hand.

"I'm not really testing it, but everything else my dad wrote has been true. I mean, other than the pedo porn shit. We're not going there."

"If you were reanimated and the Minister was reanimated, how did he die?"

"My dad was not reanimated. He didn't have the scars." He motioned to his chest. "In his journals, he wrote that he didn't want to do it, risk actually fucking dying, and leaving the Family with no leader. He was a fucking coward is what he was. That's why he was constantly having to sacrifice members of the family. For little spurts of healing, rather than true immortality, like he gave to me."

So he had no problem killing his own son, but wouldn't risk it himself? That sounded about right.

"So once this is all over, I should be good to go? I won't be able to die?" I asked.

"When you're twenty-one, if the books are correct. We'll both be immortal."

"And what's the catch?" I asked, tugging on my septum piercing. There was always a catch.

"Okay, so one thing. One small thing..." He put one finger up. "You'll have this little... urge."

"Urge?" I scoffed. "To what?"

"Kill."

"What?"

"It's nothing, really." He quickly moved on to explain things in more detail.

Constantine ran me through all the texts and books he'd collected over the last decade, refreshing me on the things I'd learned while still in the Church and teaching me new things he'd learned after.

"I could feel the changes happening in my body when my birthday hit. Things just felt different. My stamina was higher, I was stronger, and that desire I'd felt when they did the ritual returned, and I couldn't get it out of my head. I had to do something about it, and when I did, it all stopped. I mean, for the most part." He shrugged.

"What do you mean?"

"That urge we talked about in the kitchen? Every few weeks, the idea pops back into my head and starts to drive me mad until I take care of it."

Like a period?"

"I mean, kind of. Once a month, I have to deal with a little blood. It's inconvenient, messes up my clothes, I'm moody as hell. Yeah, sure. It's like a period. Hopefully, we can do that thing where ours sync up." He wiggled his eyebrows and laughed.

"Bro, this isn't funny." But yet, I laughed too.

That night, I agreed to go through with it. I had to find someone to harvest their blood and organs, and my ex, Harper, was calling me for the twentieth time that week. I'd only fucked her for a few weeks to try to get Eisley out of my system. It'd been months since we broke up and she was still in my DMs. It was easy enough to lure her out, let her blow me, and then do what needed to be done.

I'd tossed her in the river, and now, it was time for me to be reanimated.

I lay naked on the satin sheet while creepy music of people singing poured from his TV. I closed my eyes as he began reading from the book. I thought of Eisley and how beautiful she was and the last time we'd kissed. She'd let me touch her down between her legs, and she was so wet. My cock rose, and I began to stroke it, per Constantine's instructions. The Reanimator required blood, semen, and tears from the person set to receive his gift. I'd asked him about that when he did his ritual, and he refused to comment on it. Considering he was a child when his had taken place, I respected that.

I continued to focus on Eisley, and how soon I'd be going to visit and we'd get to spend some time together. She had been telling me all about a flower she'd been growing. Once we were all reanimated and gone from that forsaken fucking town, she'd have her greenhouse filled with beautiful gothic flowers. My cock exploded and spilled onto my abdomen. I waited until I came down to look for Constantine. He wasn't paying any attention. He'd set fire to all of Harper's organs.

The smell of burnt flesh filled my nostrils, but I knew I couldn't move. I had to simply let him work. Constantine continued to chant while tossing other items into the fire. Then, grabbing the blood, he turned and offered it to me.

This was the part I'd dreaded the most. My hands shook as I dipped them into the large bucket and bathed myself from head to toe in the blood. It was cold and thick and smelled so richly of iron. My semen mixed with the blood, and as I reached my face, I realized that I had the tears as well. I spread it everywhere, Constantine helping on my backside, and then I rolled back and closed my eyes.

He stood above me, holding a dagger and staring directly at my chest. I braced myself, knowing this was it. He'd either been lying this entire time and I would die, or something inside of me would change forever.

The swish came down and I gasped as the coldness hit my heart. I didn't feel the pain I thought I would. Instead, it was a heavy, freezing weight. I couldn't breathe, and I closed my eyes, accepting my fate.

And then, I awoke. I winced as my fingers ran along the new Y-shaped cut I had.

I was sticky and smelled horrid, but I was alive. No, I was *reanimated*. I could feel it in my bones. Something was different.

"Welcome back, Kansas." Constantine sat on the couch, most of his body covered in blood from working on me, arms spread, looking smug.

"It worked," I gasped. "Now what?"

Constantine leaned forward and gave me that wicked grin. "Now, we go get our girl."

Rule 77 - Eisley

Trust your gut.

"So, you did kill her. Harper, your ex."

Kansas nodded.

"I did. I didn't date her for that purpose, but it worked out the way it needed to."

I had slept for so long. When I finally roused, I wanted explanations.

"Were you in love with her?" Despite knowing she was dead and it had been brutal, jealousy flared inside me.

Kansas reached out and cupped my cheek. "Princess, no. Never. I've never loved anyone but you."

"You promise?" I don't know where this desperation came from, but now that we were all lovers, I let myself speak openly and raw with them. His hand slid down, picking up the ring now returned to its rightful place around my neck.

"Absolutely. Constantine wasn't the only one who made a vow that night."

I smiled, feeling reassured. The ring around his own neck told me he wanted this too.

"Uh, guys?" I said as they started to dress up. "I don't have any clothes."

"Oh, right, hold on." Constantine sauntered out of the room and returned with a black backpack, tossing it onto the bed. "There you go."

"What's this?" I bent down and picked it up, eyeing it curiously.

"One of the times I snuck into your house, I packed a few things. Clothes, mostly." He snickered and went for his own bags to dig out clothes. I dressed quickly and joined them.

"Okay, now, show me what exactly that creepy altar is out there."

We went out into the main room and they gave me the rundown of why the altar was set up, and what ritual would take place once they'd collected all their items needed. I'd been right. They were dabbling in dark magick. And they wanted me to join them.

"Yours won't be bad. Kansas's was nothing." Constantine grinned. "Mine was brutal. Surrounded by the Family, flaying me alive." He shuddered as his hands went to his chest, where it looked like someone had performed an autopsy on him. "But we won't have to do that with you."

I winced at the image being brought to my head. Constantine, so young, so frightened, being held down and cut open, dying right on the table, only to be brought back and able to not get hurt or die?

"You underwent this ritual too?" I asked Kansas, who nodded and stepped closer. I rested my hands on his chest and traced the scars I knew were there.

"I did. But it was far less brutal for me." He tilted his head to Constantine. "He stabbed me through the heart just once." He shrugged. "I closed my eyes and then woke up and was changed. Everything was already done and sewed up."

"I woke up to my dad still pulling the needle and thread through my abdomen." Constantine snickered. "Fucking psycho."

"Like Frankenstein," I whispered.

Constantine grinned. "Exactly. That's why my username to watch you online is—"

"*Ministersmonster*!" I gasped, recalling the name. "That was you?"

He nodded.

"What about the Minister?" I shook my head. "Why did he have to keep killing to heal himself, but you guys can do it on command?"

They shared a look and then told me about how the Minister had refused to do it on himself.

“He tried my mom, and she died. So he spent the next ten years preparing to do it again with me. He got it right the second time.”

I ran my hand along the silk sheets prepared on the table. "And you want me to do it too? How can I trust that you aren't just going to murder me?"

Kanas cleared his throat and toyed with his septum ring.

"Eisley, do you think either of us would come back to this place willingly just for shits and giggles? We're back because we want to make sure we are finally bonded together forever. When Constantine approached me about it, I was skeptical too, but then he continued to show me that not only was he telling the truth, but it wasn't all that bad." He threw up his hands. "Now's the time. We're all finally twenty-one. We go through with this and we'll live forever with each other."

"Promise?"

"Promise?" Constantine laughed and cupped my face in his hands. "Princess, we don't have to promise. This is guaranteed. We are going to go out there, slash your little fake friends up, get what we need, and then we're going to fuck you on this altar until you die from dehydration, then bring you back to do it all over again for the rest of our miserable fucking eternities. Got it?"

His eyes blazed with passion. He believed every word of it and so did I. Okay. I was in.

I swallowed and nodded. He let me go and smiled.

"Now, let's get you home so you can work on an alibi, and we can get this shit done."

"Alibi?" I stumbled over my feet, and Constantine sighed. I looked back and saw Kansas still in the same place as he was before. Was he not coming?

"You go." He waved us on. "I have to do some planning."

"If you insist." Constantine then crouched and pulled me into his arms. I let out a small squeal of delight as he carried me up the stairs and back to our cars. "I'll be back in an hour," he tossed back to Kansas.

"Planning?" I asked Constantine, wrapping my arms around his neck.

"Yeah, we're trying to figure out what to do after we've performed your ritual."

"What do you mean?"

"Well, wife, we just killed like fifteen people. We're gonna need to get the fuck out of Shelley Vale ASAP."

Rule 78 - Eisley

Always have an alibi.

"I don't think I can do this." I stood in my kitchen with Constantine later that afternoon. When we got back to my house, I went straight up to shower and put some makeup on.

"You have to. We need you to have a tight alibi. You can't have murdered someone if you've got ten thousand people saying they were watching you bake brownies in your kitchen."

I rolled my eyes. "Not the literal work. I don't feel right about it. The Minister only killed one person. You've done that."

"Yes, well, princess." He walked around my kitchen, opening and shutting drawers. He found my knife drawer and pulled out a particularly large one and waved it at me. "Consider this extra credit."

"Constantine, you can't... you said yourself there's been too many deaths already. You need to stop."

He put the knife back in the drawer and shrugged.

"I understand what you're trying to say, but those families

deserve to feel the pain they inflicted on all those kids. So, sorry, but yes, your friends all gotta die."

"Why them though?" I walked around the island to him, resting my hands on his chest. "They did nothing wrong."

His phone vibrated in his pocket, and he stepped back to answer it. "Kansas," he muttered and brought the phone to his ear. I could hear his voice, but he turned away from me.

I hadn't filmed a video or done a live in over a week. I hadn't even looked at any of my creator socials. Could I really do this now? Constantine ended the call and turned back.

"I've got to go. We have a small issue."

"Issue?" I furrowed my brow and twisted my fingers.

"We did a spell to freeze your friend's interactions with you. Remember when they seemed to forget you? That was us." He pointed to his chest. "We thought it would be easier for you that way. With the power going out, our spell unfroze. Our timeline just sped up quite a bit." He put his hands on my shoulders and squeezed. "Go live and chat for a few hours. Show some tits if you need to, bounce, giggle, whatever, but make sure your face is on that screen until I come back for you. Got it?"

"What if you don't come back?"

He looked up at the clock on the wall.

"If you don't see me by midnight, shut it off. But I'll be back before then." He headed toward the door, planting a kiss on my forehead.

"Where are you going first?" I called to him. He spun around and smiled at me so coldly, I shivered.

"Don't ask about stuff you really don't want to know."

"Be safe."

How could I be okay with this? I wasn't. I had to do something. I didn't want to live forever if that meant my friends had to die. Steeling myself, I went live.

I took the idea from Constantine and decided on brownies. With everything in front of me on the island, I pushed the little red button on my phone, and a moment later, names and hearts were popping up wildly.

Eisley!!!!

So glad you're back!

Are you okay?

You're hot.

I smiled at the comments and then looked directly into the camera. "Hey, witches! I know, it's been far too long. I've been dealing with some stuff. I can't disclose at this time to protect identities, but I wanted to let you guys know I'm okay. Today I'm going to show you how I make my famous pumpkin cheesecake brownies and chat along. Now, what kind of tea blends have you tried lately?"

I spent the next hour talking with people about various tea recipes, then I shifted to brownies.

"You know who loves my brownies? My friends. I should text them and see if they want to come over. You guys liked Constantine so much, why not show you my friend group?" I let out a fake giggle. Despite the permanent smile on my face, I was dreading this. I grabbed my tablet and messaged Therese, Micah, and Rem, inviting them over for brownies.

"Ooh, I have a recipe for spooky pizza too. Should we make that?" I asked my viewers. I got no response from Micah or Rem, but Therese texted back about ten minutes later.

Sure, babe! I'll be over soon. Sounds fun!

It felt entirely too enthusiastic, considering what she'd done to me, and how our last interaction went, but Constantine had said her spell was broken. I could save her. The doorbell rang sometime later, and I waved to the camera, promising to return. Like she always had, Therese barged into my house, bursting with energy.

"It's been so crazy! You know Micah was attacked, right? Ugh, and Rem is on this whole 'everyone's out to get us' bullshit."

I led her to the kitchen, relieved to have my friend back.

"So, this is your setup? Are you live right now?" she asked, looking at my phone attached to the ring light. I nodded and waved.

"I am. Say hello!"

She frowned and then waved. "Hello."

I laughed and reached for her wrist, tugging her forward.

"It's fine! They'll love you. Come closer." We got right up in the camera and responded to the comments for a while, and slowly, Therese started to relax.

"You said something about homemade pizza?"

"Yes!" I turned to my cupboards, gathering the dry items for the dough. I spun around, my arms full of flower and corn-meal, and froze. "What are you doing?" Therese held a large knife, while glaring daggers at me.

"I know the truth."

"What truth?" My eyes flicked to my phone, which was going crazy with pings. The screen was facing her, not me. Everyone watching my live could see her brandishing the knife.

"That you were one of them. Those dirty kids from that church in the woods. My dad told me. I came here to confront you the other day, but I saw all the flowers and presents you had unopened everywhere and lost it. I destroyed all your teapots, like you destroyed my friends. You can kill them, Eisley, but I'm not going down that easily."

"Therese, you're scaring me. I didn't hurt anyone."

"Ha!" She threw her head back and howled. Still gripping the knife, she lunged for me. I screamed and dropped my arms. I ducked out of the way in time, and then she tried again, coming for me. I was trapped against the fridge and the wall.

"You're trying to make me look like the crazy one, but it's you that's crazy!" She screamed.

I jerked my arm up and caught her wrist. I began to shake it violently, and the knife flew across the room.

"Don't use that word."

I shoved her back and she hit her head on the island countertop, dropping instantly. Realizing my live was still going, I ran to it. My viewers were frantically telling me to call authorities, and some said they already had.

I wasn't sure how to respond, but I didn't have any time because a booming knock came from my front door. I could see flashing blue and red lights from the window. Then, I turned back to the kitchen, where Therese was still unconscious and there was a knife on the floor between us.

Fuck.

Rule 79 - Constantine

Have confidence in your partner's abilities.

I pulled into Eisley's drive after finally catching Micah alone and finishing the job. A swift jab in the chest was all he needed. I didn't have time for his running games. Or the patience. It'd taken some time to catch the fucker, as he'd spent most of his time on his porch getting high, but eventually, he went inside alone, only to be greeted by me in my mask with my knife.

As soon as I saw the sirens, I knew something had gone wrong. Naturally. There was never a time when police meant good things were going on. But still, I had to remain calm. I pulled into her drive and walked up the steps of her porch, finding the door open.

"Is everything alright?" I called loudly.

"It's fine!" Eisley sniffled loudly from the kitchen. I went in that direction and found her sitting on a stool, with two officers standing like a wall in front of her.

"What happened?"

"Just a simple spat between friends. We sent the other girl home," one of the officers turned and answered me. "We're just reminding this young lady that recording someone can be illegal in some places and that it's best not to mess with certain families in this town."

"Certain families?" I raised an eyebrow. Who had been here?

"Therese," Eisley answered, reading my face. "Thank you, officers, I won't do it again."

"Thank you. Come on, Nate," the officer said to his partner, and I followed them to the door, making sure it was locked behind them. I returned to the kitchen to find Eisley shaking and crying softly, covering her face in her hands.

"Care to explain?" I crossed my arms and looked around the room. There had been some sort of fight. Flour and some other dry goods were exploded all over the floor.

"I thought I could save her by keeping her on the live with me. But then she attacked me."

"On the live?"

"Yeah, my followers called the police, not me. I shut it off before they came inside. And of course," she threw her hands up. "they took her story over mine."

"Which was?"

"Therese told them that I'd pulled the knife on her and chased her around the kitchen. She did that, not me."

"Naturally, they saw her point of view. Where did she take off to then?"

"No idea. She hit her head pretty hard. I think she might have a concussion."

"Fucking great," I muttered. "We need to find her."

"Do we though?" She stood and strode over to me with a hardened expression. "I don't want to do this if this means all my friends die. I think this is just some sick and twisted game you're playing with me. Magick isn't real. The Reanimator isn't real, and you just wanted revenge for what their families did to us."

"You can say it all you want, we all know that's not true." I looked around. "Let's get this place cleaned up and then you can pack a bag. This isn't a safe place anymore."

"What do you mean? This is my house."

"Yeah, and she's broken in once already, destroyed your stuff, and now she almost murdered you in it. Let's just go back to the Church, where Kansas is, and figure out a plan for the last two." I reached for her to take her up the stairs.

"Last two?" She flinched.

"Remember what I said about not asking questions?" I raised an eyebrow. Her shoulders slouched, and a swarm of guilt ran through me. I softened and reached for her, pulling her into my embrace. I kissed the top of her head. "It's fine. No one is going to hurt you ever again. You want to stay here tonight? Let's just go get Kansas so we can be together, okay?"

She sniffled and nodded.

We left and drove to the back of the woods, and on the way, we passed the front entrance, which was still lined with caution tape from the teenager's deaths, and now even more from the documentary crews deaths.

"They didn't really commit suicide, did they?" she asked me.

"No. They did however try to kill Kansas for their movie, so it was deserved."

"I guess eventually someone will have a good story to make about this whole thing. When we're long gone."

"If they can make money off of it, you know they will. Hopefully, they'll skip the doc route and go for a Hollywood blockbuster." I grinned. "Get some real actors to come to Shelley Vale and film."

She smiled, genuinely smiled, for the first time in days. "Who would you want to play you?"

"Hmm, maybe one of the kids that played in the newer *It* movies. They'll be old enough by then. Unless they cast men in their forties to play a twenty-year-old, then you gotta go Patrick Wilson, always."

"I think he'd make a good Kansas, with the lighter hair. Maybe Ian Somerhalder for you," she teased.

"And you?" I loved watching her face light up. I hoped once this was all over and we ditched this fucking town, I'd see it a lot more.

"Well, Mia Goth has been knocking it out of the park with shit lately, but you gotta have that BIPOC rep, so I think they'd be smart to get a Latina actress completely new to the industry for me. My name and how they over exaggerate my tits and brains will be her burst onto the scene." She sighed, imagining it. "I'd love to be a final girl."

That's right. The final girls always survived.

I drove to the woods, and when we got out, I insisted on carrying her through the trees again. I liked having her in my arms.

"Did you call Kansas and let him know we were coming to pick him up?" she asked as we made it to the Church and I set her down.

"I didn't feel the need. He'll be ready in minutes," I said and stopped dead in my tracks right at the head of the stairs. The thick smell of blood was wafting up from down below.

"What?" Eisley said and tried to step down, but I put my arm out to block her.

"Kansas?" I called. Footsteps echoed from down below, but no answer. "Eisley, go to the entrance." I kept my voice low.

"Everything's good!" Kansas's voice drifted upward, and relief flooded through me. He came to the bottom of the steps and gave us a thumbs-up. "Well, not for Therese. I've got her blood draining into a bucket and her insides placed in a bowl. Had to since all the other stuff was thawed out from the storm. Bitch surprised me, got a few strikes in before I was able to catch her and stop her crazy ramblings. Little Miss Know-it-all. You guys can come on down. I'll need help carrying her back up in a few. Probably just bury her."

"Therese is dead?" Eisley asked. Her face contorted in confusion, as if she wasn't sure whether to be upset, or at peace.

I inhaled deeply and put my arm around her middle.

"Come on, let's go put you in bed and give you something to rest. It's been a long day."

"How can I rest? Therese's dead body is down there."

When she wouldn't go, I bent my knees and picked her back up, bringing her down, past Kansas, the altar, and back to my room. I laid her down on the mattress as gently as I could.

"Wait here," I warned her. She stood anyways, and I reached for the door handle and froze. If I locked her in here, I was no better than my father or the rest of the Family. I removed my hand and shook my head, my eyes drifting back to the woman I would give anything for. My wife. "Eisley, please."

Kansas came by holding a bottle of wine he'd taken from her house, which I knew from before that it had something in it to relax her. "Here, drink this, and we'll come back in a bit." He offered it to her, but she refused so he set it beside the mattress.

"And then what?" she asked, curling her legs under her.

He stood beside me and grinned. "And then we start the ritual."

Rule 80 - Eisley

There's always two killers.

They'd laced my drink. I knew, about twenty minutes in, after I'd had a few sips to calm my nerves and stop the sobbing that something wasn't right. I was seeing double, and everything was fuzzy.

Those fucking bastards. My body grew heavy and I fell onto the bed, staring at the ceiling and seeing gold swirls drift along the stone ceiling.

Time meant nothing now, as my mind was too rattled to think straight. What had they put in there? And then things made sense. Not all herbs and plants I had saved were poisonous. No, they'd taken some of the salvia too. If that was what was in my system, I'd come out of this high in a short time and then I'd run.

I closed my eyes and relaxed, letting the hallucinogenic drug take over my mind and body. I'd had salvia before. I'd tried a lot of drugs meant to give you visions and make you dig deeper into your body and soul.

I thought about the ritual they were planning somewhere far away from me. Therese was dead. I had to accept that. My husbands were the ones killing people to serve a higher being.

God? No, but something powerful and gracious to his followers. Was I ready to become one? I'd spent so long running from the Church, this place, only to return willingly ten years later. What was going on?

"Eisley, can you hear me?" a voice I vaguely recognized called, and I laughed. Could I hear him? I could! Did I care what he had to say? Not even a little. "She's fucking blown, man. I knew we shouldn't have given her that whole bottle."

"She'll be fine. Come on, let's get her up." Hands went under my arms, but I was made of noodles, and I couldn't help him. Whoever was trying to get me to stand gave up and laid me back down, picking me up like I was his bride and he was taking me over the threshold of our new beginnings.

I blinked rapidly when we stepped out of the bedroom and into the main room, where thousands of candles had been lit.

"Woah," I said.

"We're not going to be able to do this," one of them said.

"She'll be fine. I'll just hold her. Actually, I think this will work great."

I was laid down on the hard table with the red silk cloth, surrounded by oodles of candles, all flickering menacingly at me. They were chanting loudly like tiny little monks. A giggle escaped my lips.

"What if she moves?"

"She won't."

"I won't," I repeated.

"See, she's coming to, already. Now hold still, princess."

Something cold licked my skin right between my breasts, and I yelped from the prick of it. A pinch, almost. Then, one of them yanked my blouse up and began sliding the cold thing down it, hacking at my top. A loud tearing sound came as he cut into my clothes, shredding them completely. Once my shirt was in pieces, he roughly yanked down my skirt and underwear and tore my bra in half, exposing my body completely to the room and the elements.

The sound of metal screeching sounded so far away; I barely heard it above the songs the candles were singing. I couldn't make out any words, but the deep timbres of their voices sent my body into goosebumps.

"She's so beautiful." Constantine, I recognized, leaned down, past the candles, to whisper into my ear. "You're so beautiful, Eisley. And once you've been reanimated, it'll be even more so. Are you ready?"

"I don't want to go alone." The words came out in a whimper. "Please don't make me do this alone." Constantine looked up at his partner, then back at me.

"Okay." A shift in the energy occurred, and I could hear a rustling. A moment later, I was being pulled up and urged to my feet. The stone floor was cold, and I flinched as my sensitive toes touched the ground, but I was caught by Kansas, my other husband, who was now as naked as I was. I was led a few steps forward and then brought right back and urged back onto the table, but now, I found a warm lap, instead of a cold, hard table.

Constantine had also shed his clothing and was helping me to sit on top of him. His erection rested under me, letting me know the full strength of his desire. He wrapped his arms around my middle and rested his chin on my shoulder. The gruffness of his stubble sent delicious chills through me.

"We're not going to let you go alone." My heart stuttered, and I relaxed against him, so sure of everything in my life.

"Are you ready, princess?"

"For what?"

His thick cock throbbed under me again, and Kansas came forward, lifting me. Constantine reached for something and turned it over on his lap. He set it back down and I could see him stroking himself. Kansas then brought me back to his lap, but this time, it was slow, calculated, and I stiffened.

"Ah!" I cried out as oily fingers explored my tight hole on my backside.

"Relax, Eisley. Remember how good it felt just last night?"

I did, but that didn't help me. I wanted to scream, but Constantine pulled me to him, continuing to add more lubrication to my ass in preparation for his cock. He began peppering my shoulders with kisses, in an attempt to distract me. I let out a moan as his finger probed me, and they took it as their signal that I was ready for more.

Kansas held me still and slowly I began to sink, taking every inch of Constantine's thickness deep into my small hole, stretching so wide. His hands explored my breast, tugging at my nipples, sending good thrills through me, relaxing me enough to not cry painful tears.

"Now, for Kansas," he whispered and slid his hands under my thighs and raised my legs to the sky. Kansas stepped between my legs, holding his cock in his hand. He found my opening and began to push into it.

"It's too much!" I cried out at the fullness I felt with both cocks inside me, separated only by a thin layer of membrane.

"No, it's perfect, princess. We're going to make you feel so good." Kansas dipped his head to take a breast into his mouth, running his tongue in slow, torturous circles over my nipple. I groaned loudly, and my arms went forward, falling over his shoulders, clinging for dear life.

I was dizzy with pleasure as one of them pulled on my nipples, while the other focused on my clit. Tongues licked my hot skin, biting, sucking, and tasting me. Four hands and two mouths were determined to give me as much pleasure as the two thick lengths inside me. Pressure began to build, intense, glorious pressure. I felt so tight, and with every thrust, I could feel myself stretching to better take them. It felt so good, to have one in my ass and the other buried inside my desperate pussy.

"Yes, you greedy girl. Take our cocks. Come all over them. Show us how much you want us." Constantine's words were growled into my ear, sending me reeling closer and closer to the edge.

"It's time," Kansas said and leaned over, taking a candle and lighting a bowl I hadn't noticed before on fire. It ignited in a flash and began to crackle. He thrust more, diverting my attention. Then, he leaned over to the other side, where another bowl sat, again, unnoticed until now. He dipped his hands in and ran them along my breasts, spreading something wet and cold onto my sweat-damped skin. I looked down dizzily and found it to be a deep red. Kansas continued to paint me, all while maintaining a relaxed rhythm inside me.

While Kansas painted me with blood, Constantine took candles and dripped hot wax onto my skin. I gasped, but the sharp sting was the perfect contrast to the pleasure being dealt with each thrust of their hips. The entire scene was so intense and arousing, I wanted to remain in this position for eternity, just the three of us.

I let out a scream of surprise as the bowl was dumped onto me from above, splattering both men on either side of me. No one moved and then we exploded into a frenzy of carnal lust. As if the blood stirred something in us, creating monsters of our desires and not the humans we once were.

I begged for Constantine to go deeper, harder, and for Kansas to go faster and not stop. I was too close to the biggest orgasm of my life. The music grew louder and drums beat in time with our thrusts and pants. Kansas began muttering things under his breath I couldn't understand, and Constantine continued to say hot things into my ear, keeping me so close I was almost weeping, pleading for release.

"Now, Eisley!" Constantine shouted, and as if I'd been

waiting for permission, I screamed as my body erupted. My vision grew hazy as wave after wave of pleasure poured warmness through my body, spreading it from my core into every part of me. It was so powerful, so hot, so tingly, I couldn't breathe. I closed my eyes and rode out the rest of my orgasm, continuing to roll my hips against Constantine and into Kansas.

Kansas pushed me back into Constantine's chest, and I blinked my eyes open. Constantine revealed the knife and pointed it directly at me. Swiftly, he plunged it into my chest, ending my life as I'd known it.

Rule 81 - Constantine

Keep a steady hand.

In the most intense sexual experience I'd ever had, I came as she did, all while keeping eye contact with Kansas, spilling his seed inside her at the exact same time. I'd almost feel poetic if it wasn't so scary.

In the ten years since I'd let her go, telling her to run and not look back, I'd never been scared like this.

As we pulled our cocks out of her limp, quickly dying body, Kansas helped me lay her flat on the table. I'd removed the knife, so that she'd bleed out quicker, her blood mixing with that of her friend's. The Reanimator would love this sacrifice. Her orgasm had been powerful. He would feed on that.

"I hate this. I don't want to watch."

"You think I want to?" I leaned down and pressed my ear to her chest still spilling blood. Her heart had stopped. She was officially gone. "Look away if you need to, but I need to get this done." Bracing myself, I gripped the knife and ran it along her chest, being careful to miss her fresh tattoos. I made the Y and then peeled back her skin.

Kansas had long since turned away.

"Count," I commanded, and closed my eyes. I couldn't look at her insides any longer as I began shouting the prayers I'd memorized so long ago. Repeatedly, I said them until Kansas called it.

"Done."

Two minutes and thirty-seven seconds.

Everything was 237.

I pushed her skin back in place and reached for the sutures. I had less than eight minutes before she woke up, if she was the same as Kansas. I'd done his in that time; I could do hers too. I worked quickly but carefully, sewing her skin back together. The scar was inevitable, but that was the curse given to us by the Reanimator. She'd look beautiful with it.

While I sewed her together, my life began to play before my eyes. What had I done? For so long, my entire life's goal was to bring us all back together. I knew even as I was a teenager, just a few towns over from her, that eventually I would do everything I had to do to get her back, even kill, and I did.

I killed before returning to Shelley Vale. Men, mostly. Rich men. I'd apply to their businesses. They would ask for a second meeting, where we'd have dinner, and then afterward, I'd cut them in the alley and watch them bleed out.

And then I read that Kansas was going across the country for college. That pissed me off. I told him to watch over her, and he left her. I hopped on a plane and rented a high-rise apartment, intending to get to know the man I'd spent so much time with as kids. What had he become?

It was a nice surprise to find he hadn't changed much. He was still the same old Kansas, with the same goal I had. We wanted Eisley, and we knew she wouldn't choose between us, so we wouldn't make her.

I finished and stepped back. Kansas and I shared a look. Had we widowed ourselves? Was she not coming back? And then, she let out a sharp breath and bolted straight up. She began to cough and furiously claw at her chest, looking for the wound that was no longer there, but feeling the crudely done stitches that were. Kansas and I settled on either side of the table.

"How do you feel?" he asked.

"Are you okay?" I asked.

"I feel... alive."

Kansas and I shared a knowing smile.

We did it.

She turned to me. "You stabbed me."

"I did."

"But I'm alive."

"Reanimated, but yes." I rested my hand on her thigh and squeezed.

"And now I'll heal fast, and I'm immortal?"

"That's how it works, yeah," Kansas added.

There was a long pause, where we all stared at each other, trying to contain our excitement.

"Now what?" Eisley asked.

"Well, I, for one, would like a shower." Kansas raised his hand and stepped back. Looking at him, covered in blood and nothing else, I remembered what we'd been through. I nodded.

"Right. Did you want to get out of here? For good?" I asked them both.

"You're just gonna leave all this here?" Eisley hopped off the table.

"Kansas actually is taking care of all of this, but yeah." I shrugged. "Now that the ritual is done, we never need to come back. Let's go back to your place. We can shower, rest, and then see about packing you up to leave for good."

"For good?" She followed me to my makeshift room, where I tossed her a t-shirt and boxers.

"Well, yeah. You honestly thought we'd stay here after we murdered half the town?" I chuckled.

"I don't know. My house, though."

"Princess." I rolled my eyes and tugged on a pair of pants and a shirt. "Wife, love of my entire existence. Money means nothing to me. Do you want to know just how much money I have?" I pinched her chin. "Millions. The Minister buried forty gold bricks in the coffin he claimed held my mother in it."

I dropped her chin and looked around the room, gathering all belongings that would lead to me directly. I knew the police in this town wouldn't look for tiny scraps of DNA on the mattresses or anything else. Especially after Kansas did his part.

"How did you find that out?" she asked, following behind me.

"My dad wrote a lot of shit down. Before I came out of the woods and told the authorities, I looked through his office. You know how much a twenty-pound gold brick is worth now? Almost half a million dollars."

She gasped, and I grinned. I'd been holding onto that little bit and it was great to finally tell her.

"So, we'll go to your home tonight. Clean and rest and start packing. You can use the excuse about feeling unsafe and that your husband has returned to move. No one will think twice."

Kansas joined us a moment later with his belongings and clothes in tow. Still covered in blood, although now dry, the three of us looked scary. We needed to get clean as fast as possible.

"Might wanna step back." We did as told and waited, watching the Church. A moment later, smoke rose from the windows and broken doors.

"Kansas, did you—" Eisley gasped.

“I thought it fitting. Frankenstein, fire, you get it.” He grinned wickedly.

The fire grew until flames exploded from everywhere.

"Let's just leave as quietly as we can, shall we?" Kansas said as we exited the forest.

Eisley snickered. We’d started a massive fire. Quiet was out the window.

The night was starting to fall. We couldn't be seen driving around, all three of us covered in the blood of the girl who would be called in missing in a few days.

"You got a cigarette?" Kansas asked me.

I reached into my pants pocket and pulled out a pack, offering him a stick and taking one for myself.

"You two smoke?"

We climbed into my car and headed back to her place.

"Only after sex." Kansas grinned. We reached her place with no disruption and quickly went inside. Eisley insisted on a solo shower and to be the first one in, so we waited downstairs, partaking in treats she had in her fridge while we waited.

“Put some tea on will you?” she asked as she ran up the stairs.

I put the kettle on, and looked for a pot to pour it in afterward. The only one I could find was the green one with the bats, the assassin’s pot. She didn’t have many options left after Therese had destroyed so many. I set it on the counter and started to look for jars in her cabinet.

"We'll need to get an actual house to keep all of her teapots and tea in," Kansas remarked.

"Absolutely. She'll have everything she ever dreamed of once we leave this shitty-ass town. She can have her wing if she wants. She'll truly be a princess then." I smirked.

Kansas laughed and leaned against the island.

"And what about her job? Are we okay with that?"

I gave him a pointed look. "I'm more concerned about the

job part. We've got the money, so why let her work? She should be able to spend her days gardening to her heart's desire, not putting out content to get a decent wage."

"Fair enough. What do you think? A week to pack everything up and take off?" he asked.

Before I could answer, there was a loud click from the doorway. We both turned and froze. Rem, the only survivor in our terror run, was holding a gun in one hand and a phone in the other. The phone was far more terrifying.

Rule 82 - Eisley

In a slasher, still be afraid of guns.

It took forever for me to get the blood smell out of my hair, but I scrubbed my body while I tried to wash and condition it out. By the time I turned the water off and stepped out, I felt wonderful.

My entire body felt tingly. It had since the moment I'd woken up from the ritual. I assumed it would fade eventually, but for now, it felt incredible. I couldn't wait for the guys to get showered so we could go back to bed. I was horny. It was like my body had been shot up with aphrodisiacs or something. I needed them inside me, now.

Humming the theme song from The Addams Family, I went to my bedroom and found a nightgown to wear. Now I actually had a reason to wear these sexy things. I had people to admire them, *forever*.

As I tossed my towel in the hamper and prepared to go downstairs, I looked around the room, sadness befalling me. They wanted me to move. I wanted that too, but this was my first real home. I'd miss it. Turning back, I headed down the stairs, and I heard a loud rustling in the kitchen.

"Everything all right?" I asked as I came into the room and then froze. Rem was here, pointing a gun at Constantine.

My husband looked at me with a hardened expression.

"Eisley, do you remember what I told you? Before?" I started to shake my head, but then Kansas spoke.

"Think."

Don't talk to anyone.

Don't look back.

Just run.

They wanted me to leave them behind. I couldn't do that.

"No."

Both Kansas and Constantine's expressions fell. They kept their hands up and continued to try to talk Rem down.

"I'm not going down without a fight. I know you're behind this crazy shit!" Rem shouted at Constantine. My husband shook his head.

"I don't know what you're talking about man."

"Why are you covered in blood?" Tears began to slide down Rem's dark cheeks. His eyes were wild with desperation. "Both of you. What did you do to everyone?"

"We didn't do anything," Kansas said. Rem spun the gun to him.

"Bullshit. I'm done. I'm not letting you guys get away. I heard you. You guys want to leave, but I'm not going to let that happen." He reached into his pocket and pulled out two sets of handcuffs. Keeping the gun swinging from one to another, he crept toward them. Both Kansas and Constantine let him put one hand each in the cuffs. Rem's head darted around, looking for a place to clip them to. He settled on an old pipe attached to the wall.

"What are you going to do?" I asked Rem. I didn't quite understand why my men were acting so oddly. If we all were immortal, then why did a gun matter? Rem pulled out his phone.

"I'm calling the police, and you're gonna be taken in. They won't let you just walk away from this."

My blood chilled instantly. Oh. Immortals sitting in a jail cell? Not good. "Can we talk about this?" I pleaded with Rem. "The cops were already here this afternoon. I don't need to deal with them again."

"You're sleeping with the murderers! What else is there to talk about?"

I steeled myself and looked around the room. What could I do to stall him? A loud whistle rang through the room and all of us turned to the stove.

Tea.

My head swung back to the counter, where my assassin's teapot sat, along with jars someone had pulled from my cabinet.

The hemlock.

"Okay, but I'm going to make some tea. It calms me down," I said to the room. I stared at my men, hoping they'd see my plan.

"Tea? Eisley, is it appropriate right now?" Kansas asked.

"Yes. Tea is always the appropriate response," I muttered. "I'm sorry. I'm so sorry," I told Rem as I hurried to turn the stove off and pour the hot water into the pot. "I'll make a blend."

"Did you know about them? The whole time?" He swung the gun in my direction and I threw my hands up.

"No!" I shook my head furiously. "I'm learning about all of this as you are," I lied. "I don't know what's going on."

"How long have you been off your medication?"

"What? Why does that matter?" I glanced at my men, who were both watching in a mix of horror and confusion. Cautiously, I stepped forward and reached for the teapot.

I poured water into the first hole, then the second, watching Rem to see if he noticed. My hands shook as I took a spoon and put tea leaves in one chamber, and hemlock in the other.

"Because we all know what happens when you're off them, Eisley." Rem cocked the gun and my insides twisted. Could I survive a gunshot?

"Eisley, what is he talking about?" Constantine asked.

Rem and I both turned to the men handcuffed on the other side of the room.

"Nothing. I don't need them." My voice came out shrill.

"No, you're lying." Rem was swinging the gun back and forth from them to me. "She does need them. She goes crazy when she's not on them."

I put my hands over my ears and closed my eyes. I didn't know what to do.

"Tell them the truth!" Rem boomed. "Tell them you're fucking crazy!"

"I don't like that word!" I screamed.

Rem swung the gun to me. Now he was the one who looked scared.

"I'm not crazy." I pressed my lips together tightly and turned to my husbands. "I have bi-polar disorder." I confessed. The two of them shared a look. "and I've been off my medication since October first."

Rem shook his head. "That's when this all started Eisley. I'm starting to think it was you who did all this. Not them." He stepped toward me and pressed the gun into my chest. "Are you Ghostface?"

"No!" My men screamed out and began fighting against their restraints.

Rem released me and turned on them again. "Shut the fuck up." He reached for his phone and dialed 911 again, getting the busy tone.

"Micah's dead. They found him an hour ago. That leaves Therese and me, but she's not answering her phone. She never not answers her phone. She told me she was coming here, that's why I came. Did you kill her?" he asked me.

"No." I answered honestly.

"What am I supposed to do? All of my friends are dead, and just because some kids got molested ten years ago, I'm next? It's not fair. There's nothing we can do about it. We need to move on."

"You can do that by leaving." I tried to point out.

"And let you three get off scot-free? No one's going anywhere."

"I don't know what you want from me." I wondered if Rem had any experience with a gun at all. Would he set it off by accident? He was swinging it so erratically.

Rem looked around the kitchen.

"I'm staying here until I can get the police on the phone."

"Fine." I snapped. Steeling my nerves. I went back to my original plan, and went to the cupboard, pulling out two teacups. "Do what you want, I'm having tea."

"You and your damned tea." Rem shook his head. "Four cups."

"What?"

"I said four cups. We're all drinking."

Swallowing, I took two more cups from my cupboard. I worked slowly, allowing the tea to steep. Putting my finger over a hole, I poured Rem's. Then, as I switched to the next cup, I put my finger over the other hole and poured the other three.

Rem put the gun in his pocket and took his cup. He waited for me to hand both Constantine and Kansas theirs as well.

"All right, now we all drink at the same time, and then you and I will go to the living room. We can discuss what's going on and figure out a plan."

"You're not leaving the room with her," Constantine snarled and tugged on his restraint.

Rem laughed. "I don't think you have a say in what I do. I could take this gun and shoot her right now and all you can do is watch. Drink your tea."

Both Kansas and Constantine tugged on their handcuffs to no avail and finally relented. They gulped down their drinks. I took them quickly from them, and drank my own.

The air was thick as we all waited for one of us to keel over, but no one did. Relief washed over Rem's face, and he then drank his.

"Come on, I'm going to see if there's something we can file online to get the police here." He pulled out the gun again and waved me forward.

"Are you holding her hostage?" Kansas asked.

"Yeah," Rem nodded. "If you manage to get out of those cuffs and try to attack me, I'll shoot."

I stood frozen, and Rem finally grabbed me and shoved me out of the room. The gun pressed against my back the entire trek to the living room, where he pushed me onto the couch.

"Stay there. I'm still not entirely sure it wasn't you who did all this. A crazy person off their meds? It makes more sense than two strangers."

"Stop using that word."

"What? Does the murderer not like that?" he mocked. "Tell me, did you crawl out of the Sinister Minister's church like that, or did you go nuts after?"

"Stop it!" I stood and screamed.

A loud rattling came from the kitchen and then a huge ting!

Rem and I both turned as both men ran into the living room.

"No!" I screamed in horror, expecting to hear a gunshot, but... I didn't.

I turned my head back to Rem and saw him frozen in place, choking. His eyes bulged as his throat closed. The hemlock I'd put in his tea was finally making its way through his system. He dropped the gun and then fell forward, dead.

The three of us stared silently at the last member of my friend group. It wasn't until I heard a beeping coming from his body that I broke out of my trance and bent down, fishing into his pockets.

I found his cell phone, and to my horror, he had it on some program to continue to dial the police every two minutes. He'd been calling them this entire time.

"We've got to go," I said and flew up the stairs. They followed quickly, and I explained what Rem had done. I threw on some clothes and my only pair of tennis shoes. "This is it."

I hurried to my safe, grabbing everything inside. I pulled the bag I'd packed the night before out from under my bed and stuffed everything inside. Constantine handed me a folded piece of paper, and I realized it was our wedding license. I kissed him and then turned to Kansas. "Let's go."

"Wait," Kansas paused at the bathroom. My heart sunk as he hurried in and ruffled through my cabinet, returning with handfuls of pill bottles. "Which ones do you need?"

"There's no time," I huffed and opened my bag. "Put them all in here. I'll explain later. I'm not..." I looked from one to the other, pleading for them to believe me. "I'm not crazy."

"We know, princess. We know, now come on." Constantine urged me forward.

Sirens greeted us as we reached the downstairs floor. Leaving everything but the bag in my hands, we hurried to Constantine's car and sped off.

I looked back and saw blue and red lights, but they didn't follow us. I felt only a smidge of relief as I decided that they must have stopped at the house and were finding Rem's body now.

"You're not mad that I didn't tell you?" I looked down at my lap in shame. My entire life after I'd escaped the Church I'd struggled to figure out why I was the way that I was. It wasn't until after high school that I'd seen the right doctor, who helped me realize what exactly my mind was battling. "You don't think I'm..."

"We will never use that word, Eisley." Kansas swore. "You don't ever have to hide anything from us ever again. We'll navigate all of this together."

I sank into the seat, relief washing over me. I knew I could trust them both. I loved them both.

"While we're confessing things..." Constantine glanced over. "Those flowers..."

I gasped. "No! You two?" I looked back and forth between them.

"I think we may have taken the joke a little too far," Kansas cringed.

"A bit!" I swatted them both, and felt a little less uneasy. I had nothing to worry about. No stalkers, no killers, no cult leaders, just these two who'd protect me with their life.

"What now, princess?" Constantine smirked as we sped off into the night.

"You're not afraid they'll catch us?" I asked. I was sitting in the middle seat and neither of them felt tense in the slightest.

"Nah. Sure, they'll assume we did it all. Or you, whatever." Kansas laughed dryly. "But they aren't going to look past Shelley Vale. If they do, they'll have to ask themselves why they were targeted, and their parents aren't going to let their dirty secrets be exposed."

"We're just gonna get away with it?"

Constantine snickered.

"As long as you listen to what I say. Do you remember the exact words I told you ten years ago?"

I nodded, and he continued, "Don't talk to anyone."

He took one hand off the wheel and reached for mine.

"Don't look back." Kansas took my other hand.

"Just run." I squeezed both of theirs.

And we did.

All three of us, right out of Shelley Vale and into eternity, reanimated, rich, and in love.

The End.

"Come play with us, Delaney"

Laney is my everything. Her smile became my obsession and when someone else threatened to take her from me, take her innocence, I took him out of the picture.

They separated us, in hopes that our desires would fade, but the longer we stayed apart, the stronger my obsession grew. I have one chance to show her what we could be, and if I have to slaughter everyone in my path to do so... so be it.

Stopping home for a night, Delaney sees Priest, her step-brother, for the first time since a suspicious and horrific murder occurred five years ago. He's sinfully handsome, and ink covers his tight muscles, tempting Delaney to touch something she's always been told was wrong; and yet, she invites him to join her at the Vincent hotel, where they soon find themselves trapped by the weather, their own forbidden feelings, and a murderer on the loose.

Memories are resurfaced, ghosts are everywhere, and deaths are aplenty when your psycho, hot, inked, stepbrother is afoot.

Slay Less is a forbidden stepbrother M/F horror erotic romance. If you liked Slash or Pass and want to continue the Final Girls horror romance series, click here:

Slay Less

One last thing before you leave the theater

Thank you for reading Slash or Pass. If you enjoyed it, please consider leaving a rating or review. Reviews are extremely important to authors and helps us continue to create books.

Did you figure out the easter egg for what movie(s) book 2 will be inspired by? My formula is (Slasher villain) meets (another horror story/movie) and in Slash or Pass, I teased the horror story/movie. If you did, totally post about it and tag me. I want to see who gets it.

(Book 2 is NOT Nightmare on Elm Street)

About the Author

After watching *Heathers* and listening to My Chemical Romance one too many times in her teens, Chicana author, Tylor Paige, was drawn to the darkness where the villains were still villains, but deserved love stories too.

Shifting her focus to Horror Romance, Tylor writes snarky, psycho vampires, troubled but beautiful Goblin Kings, and slashers so sexy you'll be begging your partner to buy a mask.

When she's not writing about women railing the villains, she enjoys watching horror films, sewing, comic books, and spending time with her writer tribe, Michigan Romance Writers. At the time of this update Tylor has now written and published eleven full length novels.

Oh, and feel free to call her Ty. She prefers it.

Acknowledgments

Oh, I hate this. Does anyone ever really read them? Maybe. It always just feels like a long list of people no one knows. But, I suppose, it should be done, so here goes. First off, thank you to the Scream Franchise, as well as all the actors who made all us whorror babies melt in our panties for decades over a guy in a mask. This book absolutely wouldn't have happened without Billy and Stu in that kitchen confronting Sydney.

Next are my author friends. Aiden Pierce, who I wrote alongside with during this book, her working on Circus Creeps, and me on Slash or Pass. She also read through my plot notes and offered comments where needed and my book is better for it. Thank you boo. Leesa Mason and Maude Winters are my other author besties. I love you, I miss you, I'll see you soon. Thank you Leesa for being my critique partner on and off when needed, and thanks Maude for all the RAD slash or pass stickers and swag.

My support team. Zainab, my editor, my best bitch. Thank you so much for working to the bone to get this book done in time. I know, I'm a wordy bitch, but please love me anyways? Victoria, my cover artist and graphic designer. Bitch you blew this shit out of the fucking water, you know that right? Holy fucking shit man. We did it. WE. Did it. I really feel like you were just as much a part of this books creation as I was. I applaud your talent, and can't wait to see the rest of the final girl books.

My alpha readers! Chelsea, Lee-Anna, Connie, Victoria, and Sadie. Pals, you guys rock. Thank you for letting me share my book before it was ready for the public, and hyping me up the entire way. I can't wait to see what you think of book 2.

Lastly, but not least, but certainly the hardest, my IRL friends.

Christina Hilyard was one of my closest best friends. She dedicated her life to helping everyone she could, whether that be as a nurse for terminal children, or at home, taking care of everyone as if they were her own.

In August, she was found not breathing in her bed. By the time they got her to the hospital she was brain dead. Even in death, she continued to give, as Christina was an organ donor. She was given her honor walk, and it was one of the hardest things I've ever had to do, say goodbye but not really, to her one final time. In donating, she is giving life to many more people, and I know she would be happy to know that. I am so honored to have known her and been her friend.

This is just for Christy, who will never read this.

I remember that first time I text you. I can't remember the meme, but I was so excited, waiting for your reply. You didn't know who the heck was sending you weird, definitely inappropriate memes, but over time, you would start messaging me back with your own, and if I missed a day, you'd check in, until finally, you asked if it was me. Sounds like a total romcom move lol. But that was the start of our friendship.

We turned it into a group chat with me, you, and Cassy, and the bitches were born. Not a day went by since 2015 that we didn't talk, even if it was just to share a dumb meme. For the last 8 years, we've partied together, and it's gonna be real fucking hard not seeing you storm in, painting dicks all over your canvas, and showing your tits once you've had a few shots. Never thought I'd want those moments again, but, here we are.

You were always there, and I took that for granted. Never in a million years would I have imagined you'd be the first to go out of our (now expanded) friend group. Someone who gave so much, only to be fucked over man. I'm sorry.

This world is cruel sometimes. The wrong people stay and the wrong people go. But I just wanted to say thank you. From our first party, where we told Cassy it was going to be a costume party and actually planned a sex toy party, to the last time I spoke to you privately, about your kids and how hard you were trying to make sure they were okay, I'll treasure it all, and wish forever that you were still here. I love you bitch, it is an honor to have been your friend.

Also by Tylor Paige

Final Girl Series:

Slash or Pass

Book 2

Book 3

Book 4

Little Deaths: a Vampire Mafia series

Seven Little Deaths

Lay Your Body Down

Bury Me in Blood

Little Taste of Death (FREE VALENTINES SHORT!)

Standalones:

Surrender to Forever- a Goblin King reimagining

Want more?

Are you interested in seeing Constantine and Kansas meeting for the first time as adults, before the events of Slash or Pass? Sign up for my mailing list and you'll get that chapter sent to you.

https://BookHip.com/KMFJWGH

Find me all over

Www.Tylorpaige.com
https://linktr.ee/Tylorpaige
Facebook.com/Tylorpaigeauthor
Instagram: @Tylorpaige
TikTok: @authortylorpaige
Join the Coven of Bitchcraft group on Facebook!
https://www.facebook.com/groups/376190999768893/?ref=share